EVIL OUT THERE

Claire anticipated the unnatural chill that always accompanied her small, spectral friend. She waited for it to materialize, to raise the gooseflesh on her arms and on her neck, but she arrived at The Willows without so much as hearing a ghostly whisper, and with only the air-conditioning to cool the teeming heat of the night. As Claire got out of the car and climbed the steps to the gallery, she struggled with a strange sense of disappointment.

Eulanie met her in the foyer. She grasped Claire's hands, and for a few seconds, seemed to struggle to find words. "We heard what happened. Thank the Lord you're all right."

Jane had stayed late and came from the kitchen, wiping her hands on her apron. Her face clouded with worry, she hugged Claire, sniffing back tears. "Child, you frightened us near to death." She released Claire, then moved to turn the lock on the front door. "This town, it's under siege. Some kinda evil out there. An' nobody seems to know where it'll strike next."

<u>BOOK YOUR PLACE ON OUR WEBSITE</u> AND MAKE THE <u>READING CONNECTION!</u>

We've created a customized website just for our very special readers, where you can get the inside scoop on everything that's going on with Zebra, Pinnacle and Kensington books.

When you come online, you'll have the exciting opportunity to:

- View covers of upcoming books
- Read sample chapters
- Learn about our future publishing schedule (listed by publication month *and author*)
- Find out when your favorite authors will be visiting a city near you
- Search for and order backlist books from our online catalog
- Check out author bios and background information
- Send e-mail to your favorite authors
- Meet the Kensington staff online
- Join us in weekly chats with authors, readers and other guests
- Get writing guidelines
- AND MUCH MORE!

Visit our website at
http://www.kensingtonbooks.com

DON'T TELL A SOUL

S. K. McCLAFFERTY

ZEBRA BOOKS

KENSINGTON PUBLISHING CORP.

http://www.kensingtonbooks.com

ZEBRA BOOKS are published by

Kensington Publishing Corp.
850 Third Avenue
New York, NY 10022

All Kensington titles, imprints and distributed lines are available at special quantity discounts for bulk purchases for sales promotion, premiums, fund-raising, educational or institutional use.

Special book excerpts or customized printings can also be created to fit specific needs. For details, write or phone the office of the Kensington Special Sales Manager: Kensington Publishing Corp., 850 Third Avenue, New York, NY 10022. Attn. Special Sales Department. Phone: 1-800-221-2647.

Zebra and the Z logo Reg. U.S. Pat. & TM Off.

First Printing: January 2003
10 9 8 7 6 5 4 3 2 1

Printed in the United States of America

The ad read:

*"Unpublished writer wishes to form support group.
If you are interested, please contact . . ."*

Among the replies the writer received was a letter
with promise. The friendship that followed
enriched the writer's life.

*Twila P. Hanna, this one is strictly for you. It is a small
and perhaps insignificant way to thank you for twelve years'
worth of twice-a-month meetings, for listening, and sharing,
and offering praise, encouragement, and advice. Thank you
for being there during the dark times, and celebrating with me
during the good. Your friendship in writing has meant more
to me than I can possibly convey.*

With love and friendship, through laughter and tears,

S. K.

Glossary of Cajun Terms

C'est alright	It's all right
Il est trop entiché	He is too hardheaded
Je t'aime	I love you
J'm'en fout pas mal	I don't give a damn
Mémère	Grandmother
Noncle	Uncle
Pépère	Grandpa
Peut-être que oui, peut-être que non	Maybe yes, maybe no
T'es paré	Are you ready?

PROLOGUE

Acadia Parish, Louisiana

Every event in Evangeline King's short life seemed to lead to this moment. The physical and emotional battering she had suffered for as long as she could remember, and which had turned her bitter and cynical at age thirteen, now seemed like a primer, lessons in survival. If not for the fact that she had regularly endured the heavy fall of her daddy's fist, she might not have survived the past forty-eight horror-filled hours. If not for an inborn mule-headedness, she surely wouldn't have been able to summon the strength to get free of the house in the pines and find her way deep into the cane fields bordered by the swamp.

Her father's cruelty had tempered her to punishment, just as a dishwasher's hands tempered and grew accustomed to scalding water. A quick-tempered little man with a short fuse and hard fists, he'd gotten his kicks out of terrorizing anyone and anything weaker or more vulnerable than himself. Her mom, Betty Lou, had cringed at the sound of his foot falling on the stoop. Molokai, the oldest, had gradually bent before his warped mind and become just like him—a raging bully, always in trouble at school, sullen and dangerous at home. Little Melissa coped by retreating, speaking in whispers with her thumb near her mouth, when she dared speak at all.

Evangeline, he couldn't seem to conquer, and her toughness had become a real challenge for him. She'd suffered through countless beatings over the years, endured cracked ribs and a dislocated jaw before she turned ten, but she hadn't begged him to stop like her mother, hadn't pleaded or cried or cringed in his presence, and, in a way, she knew, deep down inside, that she was every bit as hard as he was.

She'd hit the highways at thirteen, looking more like twenty, with a ripe body and eyes that looked at the world as if it wanted something from her, thinking that she could survive just about anything. The freedom of being on her own had been heady, and the knowledge that she could go anywhere, do anything, be whatever, whoever she wanted to be, gave her a feeling of power over her own destiny for the first time in her life. Then she'd accepted a ride from a good-looking stranger and it had all gone up in a cloud of vapor, like gasoline carelessly dribbled on the pavement in the blinding heat of an August afternoon.

Two months after running away from home, she crouched at the edge of the swamp, the memory of her daddy's mean streak fading to nothingness as the bay of the hounds rang eerily through the distant pines and over the stubbled field she'd stumbled across.

She wasn't sure how far she'd run, or which way to

go next. She only knew that the stitch in her side wouldn't let her go on without pausing to catch a breath. She didn't know how many times she'd stumbled and fallen, but her knees were raw, and a deep gouge from a cane stalk on her right shin seeped warm, sticky liquid into her shoe. The blood worried her more than anything.

The dogs would smell it.

The thought terrified her, and she spun, squinting into the dark, straining for any sign of her companion. She vaguely remembered hearing the quarrel of the hounds, all but drowned out by the panicked thunder of her heart. Where was she? When had she fallen behind? Evangeline thought of going back, but the pinpoint of light shining dully through the trees murdered the impulse. The light wavered, then came back—the beam of his flashlight, and out ahead two ghostly gray forms broke from the underbrush, streaking across the open field.

A bolt of electricity seemed to shoot out of nowhere, striking her in the chest, dead center. For a moment, it rooted her to the spot as the hounds raced toward her; then, fighting her way past it, she spun and fled into the heart of the swamp.

CHAPTER ONE

Louisiana State Penitentiary
Angola, Louisiana
Mid-July

Claire Sumner sat in the prison's small reception area, staring at the black-and-white composite sketch on the front page of the *Times-Picayune*. She hadn't taken the time to examine the impulse that had driven her to stuff the folded paper into her cognac leather bag. The fact that she had been to the prison countless times over the last ten years and by now was familiar with the routine of "hurry up and wait" that seemed to penetrate all levels of government, coupled with her acute aversion to lost time, was sufficient excuse, though the real reason was a great deal more disturbing.

Squeezed onto the edge of a hard, wooden bench by a rather large woman and three grubby-faced children, clutching the paper with more ferocity than was necessary, Claire could finally admit that it was the image of the lost child that had made her reluctant to leave it behind in her Lafayette apartment, and not some desperate, driving need to keep up with current events.

The artist who'd done the sketch was skilled, and had managed to breathe life into the dead teenage girl. The end result was stunning for two reasons: first, the mixture of innocence and world-weariness had grabbed Claire and refused to let go. It was a look that Claire, a lawyer and a children's advocate, had seen too many times on the small faces of far too many children, and one that never failed to cut her to the quick. And secondly, except for the hair that was cut short and blond instead of dark, the girl could have been Jean Louise Broussard's double. Below the sketch, the caption read:

MURDER REVISITS ACADIA PARISH

For the second time in less than a decade, the body of a young girl has been discovered in the dark waters of Bayou des Cannes. In an ironic twist, the girl, as yet unidentified, was discovered by the same eighty-two-year-old resident of Acadia Parish to discover the body of murdered teen Jean Louise Broussard ten years ago. The Broussard girl, who disappeared from Acadiana Middle School following a junior varsity football game and was killed by asphyxiation, was Mr. Prideau's only granddaughter. Forty-seven-year-old James Buford Sumner, convicted of the Broussard killing, is housed at Louisiana State Penitentiary at Angola's death row, awaiting his scheduled execution in early August.

The words "Louisiana State Penitentiary at Angola's death row," and her father, James Buford Sumner, had become synonymous over the past decade, so much so that she could not think of one without the other leaping to mind. Angola was hell in six low cinder block complexes called "camps." Situated on eighteen thousand acres and surrounded on three sides by the Mississippi River, "The Farm" was home to over five thousand inmates, a multimillion-dollar enterprise and the largest maximum security prison in the country. It was also one of the oldest. Claire knew more about its history than she wanted to know.

How many sweltering afternoons had she spent sitting in the reception area waiting for Jimmy to be brought from his cell to the visitors' room, hoping for some miracle that would put a happy ending to this nightmare? And when that miracle came it was like a bolt from a cloudless sky, totally unanticipated, more frightening in its implications than she ever could have imagined.

"Ms. Sumner?" When the corrections officer called her name, Claire started, coming back to the present with a jolt. She was gripping the paper so hard that her knuckles turned pale and bloodless. Collecting her frazzled thoughts, she forced herself to fold the paper and replace it in her bag. The officer was waiting, a five-foot-two-inch blonde in a black, short-sleeved uniform and billed cap.

Claire stood.

"Step this way, please."

By now, she was familiar with the routine search of her person and belongings. Her compact and keys were removed and put in a drawer for safekeeping. She was allowed to keep a carton of cigarettes, a gift for Jimmy from his sister Eulanie, and the newspaper. Then, without ceremony, the young officer led her to the visitors' room.

Claire held her breath. Tension gripped her as tightly

as she had gripped the newspaper a few minutes before.
She hadn't seen Jimmy in six months, but it hadn't been
for lack of trying. She'd been to the prison several times
on visiting day, and each time he'd refused to leave his
cell, proof of how stubborn he could be once his mind
was set on something . . . and Jimmy had decided to cut
all ties with the outside world, including Claire and
Eulanie.

The inmates on death row were locked down twenty-
three hours a day. Permitted an hour of exercise in a
cage, a small, enclosed area in the prison yard, they
had no contact with inmates not on the row, and few
privileges. In the past six months, Claire had speculated
about her father's decision to cut himself off from his
family, and wondered if perhaps the stark gray-and-
white of his environment, where hopelessness and
despair thrived and men clung to their sanity through
sheer tenaciousness, had seeped into his soul, hardening him beyond anything she would even recognize.

Even when she had seen him, he'd been sullen and
uncommunicative, doing everything in his power to discourage her from coming back. Finally, Claire had had
no choice but to respect his wishes. For nearly six
months, she stayed away. Then, two days ago, everything
had changed. The drawing had appeared in the morning paper, and suddenly nothing could have prevented
her from trying to see him.

He was seated when she walked in, his cuffed hands
clasped on the table in front of him. He glanced up at
the metallic scrape of chair legs on linoleum, but he
didn't say a word when Claire sat down.

Some men beefed up in prison, spending every free
moment building their muscles, bulking up as a means
of protection. Others, like Jimmy, went to wire, their
musculature stringy and spare.

At five feet, eight inches, he'd never qualified as a big man, but during his time on the row he'd lost flesh and melted away to sinew, a hard-faced man in his late forties who looked a good ten years older. His hair, brown a few years ago, was softened with a light sprinkling of gray, the lines in his face deeper, his expression more guarded, more closed, his gaze warier, more watchful than ever before.

Claire struggled with a confusing mix of emotions: anger that his execution was just four weeks away and he continued to distance himself from his only daughter; resentment that he'd been taken away from her to begin with; and, God help her, the smallest, most pathetic spark of hope, provided by the newspaper in her bag. "You're looking well," she lied, hating that her voice wavered slightly on the last syllable. She slid the cigarettes to the middle of the table. "I shouldn't be giving you these—they're bad for you—but Aunt Eulanie insisted."

"You worried about my health," he said softly, harshly. "That's rich." He waited a moment. "Thank Eule for me, will you? She's a fine woman, and a good sister."

Claire fought back a wave of anger and hurt so acute that it made her eyelids sting. She was his daughter, his only child! Why couldn't he give her what she so desperately needed? *You're a good daughter, Clairée, and I'm glad you came.* Confused and embarrassed at her highly emotional state, she faltered, then rushed on. "Aunt Eulanie loves you, Dad. She always has. We both do."

Jimmy snorted. "Love's wasted on a man like me. In a month I won't be drawin' breath. Hell, I've been dead to the world since I walked through those doors, and if you had a damn bit of sense, you wouldn't wait till they strap me on that gurney to forget about me. It's the only reason I agreed to see you. To keep you from coming back. Get on with your life.''

"Why are you doing this?" Claire demanded, but he cut her off with a harsh look.

"Charlotte Clairée, why do you have to be so hard-headed? Didn't I say I didn't want you here? I thought we agreed—"

"We didn't agree," Claire shot back bitterly. "You ordered, and I ignored you, just like always."

A sharp look. "Don't you be smart-mouthed with me. You might be some fancy lawyer on the outside, but in here I'm still your daddy, and I won't have you givin' me lip."

"All right. I'm sorry I got cross with you. But don't ask me to be sorry for ignoring your wishes. I had to come. I had to see you, and you need to see this." She took the paper from her designer bag and laid it on the table with the sketch where he could see it. "Look at her, Dad. Take a good, long look."

"A girl with blond hair," Jimmy said. "So what?"

"Not just a girl," Claire insisted. "A dead girl found in the bayou. There's been another murder in the parish." She could feel her excitement rising. If it meant what she feared it meant . . .

He went very still, and she had the strange impression that he was waiting. "That's news? Hell, Clairée, there's always a murder in the parish. Husbands killin' wives, drug deals gone bad. It's nothin' new, and it sure as hell doesn't have nothin' to do with me."

"Not a domestic killing, not a drug deal. A young girl. Look at her, Dad. Take a good long look. She looks enough like Jean Louise to be her twin sister."

He glanced from her to the paper, reading the article slowly, methodically, then waved it away. "This is why you came all the way out here? To show me a sketch of some kid they found facedown in the water?''

"Dad, please. *Look* at her.''

"I don't have to look at her. I *know what* you're thinkin', and if you're smart, you'll let this ride. It don't change nothin'!''

But Claire knew that he was lying. Something had changed. She could see it, sense it, though he tried with everything he had to hide it. The pulse at his throat had kick-started. It was leaping so hard she could see it from where she sat. This news had affected him. The girl's resemblance to Jean Louise had affected him.

More than that, he was frightened by it.

The realization stunned her. She'd grown up believing he was strong, nearly invincible; she'd never known him to be afraid of anything, not even the prospect of death by lethal injection. "Dad, what is it?'' she found herself asking. "Something has you rattled. What are you afraid of?''

At first he wouldn't look at her, perhaps fearful of what she might see in his face, his eyes. When he finally met her gaze, his dark stare was intense and burning. "I appreciate you comin', Charlotte. I know you mean well. But I don't want to see your face 'round this place again. I mean that. Mind, you drop this. There are things that can't be undone, things better left alone.''

"But if there's a chance,'' she persisted. "A real chance. If nothing else, we might be able to convince the governor to grant you a stay while the sheriff investigates.''

"Old Stick-it-to-'em Vance?'' He snorted. "You lived most of your life in Acadia Parish. You know how things work there.''

"It doesn't have to be like that—''

"No.'' He pointed a finger at her. "No. I don't want

to prolong this. You leave it be, Charlotte. You let me die. Walk away from here and don't you ever look back. I did my time alone. I'll do this alone, too."

Claire was beyond frustration. She could help him. She knew it could work. He could walk out of here a free man, if only he would let her help him. "Daddy, please," she said, shocked by how plaintive the pair of words sounded.

"Charlotte, you hear me, and you hear me good!" he ground out. He quivered with anger, and something else, some emotion she couldn't guess at and he wouldn't name. Only his voice betrayed him, turning hoarse. "I don't want to look out through that window when they put the needle in my arm and see my baby girl's face lookin' back at me. Don't you do that to me. Don't you make me suffer any more than I already have."

Nothing he could have said would have hurt her more deeply. He was sending her away, without a word of kindness or love between them. "I can't believe you're giving up," Claire said in a small, ragged voice. "On life." Silently, *On me.*

"My life was over the day I was sentenced to die. The rest is just a delayed reaction." Jimmy nodded to the officer standing silently on his side of the table a few paces away. The man came to his side. One last look, and he was done with her. "Good-bye, Charlotte."

Claire put her hand out, palm reaching. On the inside she felt as fragile as spun glass, and it was all she could do to keep from shattering. *Daddy! Oh, Daddy, please don't leave me!* It was the echo of a sixteen-year-old girl watching her father being led away in shackles and handcuffs after being sentenced to die for the cruel rape and murder of the best friend she'd ever had. The only friend. And the same sense of quiet panic set in. "Why are you doing this?" she whispered aloud. "I can help you. Why won't you let me help you?"

There were no answers. Just the murmur of the mothers, wives, girlfriends, children, surrounding her, crying, talking, laughing.

Down the long corridor, Jimmy did his utmost to concentrate on his hobbled gait. The rattle of the chains attached to the leg irons made an obscenely pleasant chink-chink sound. It was stifling hot inside Angola, but a chilly sweat soaked his pale blue chambray shirt between his shoulder blades and slowly inched its way down his ribs. He'd walked away from Charlotte Clairée physically, but he couldn't ever cut her from his thoughts.

She was his blood.

His baby girl.

All that he lived for.

And she had no inkling of the kind of evil she was messing with. The face of that child in the newspaper had said it all. There were forces in this world that fed off of innocence, that got off on destruction, that had no conscience. He'd thought if he just did what he was told, if he didn't fight it, that it would end with his death.

Naively, stupidly, he'd thought the nightmare that came to Angelique a decade ago was over. But he couldn't have been more wrong.

Another innocent.

Another victim.

Another child fallen prey to that black-hearted monster. It was starting again, and just like the last time, his baby was in danger. Only now, there was nothing Jimmy could do to stop it. He had sacrificed everything, and he would die with the sickening realization that it wasn't enough.

* * *

"You're a low-down, egg-suckin' dog, you know that? He's an old man, for Christ's sake! Where's he supposed to come up with seven hundred and fifty dollars?"

Fegan Broussard's verbal abuse didn't seem to faze the man in the crisp, brown uniform. He just stood there in the glaring mid-July sun, his mirrored sunglasses reflecting Fegan's displeasure. "This could've been prevented, Fegan. This ain't the old days, and your granddad can't do like he did way back when. It's illegal to catch turtles and sell 'em. If you want the truth, Amos Lee's gettin' off easy."

"Easy? That's a crock o' shit if I ever heard one! That bayou, it used to be free, Jack! Now, a man's got to have a permit just to put his pirogue in the water." He shook his dark head. "You're just pissed because of last week, is all, and hellbent on bustin' my balls for it any way you can."

Dave Matthews took the check Fegan signed, the sudden tightening of his mouth betraying the truth of Fegan's assessment. "Hell, yes, I'm pissed. And don't call me 'Jack'. One stupid mistake and she's got herself a lawyer so fast—" He broke off, no longer bothering to conceal his disgust. "I'm sleepin' in my car, thanks to you and that damn telephoto lens of yours."

"Be glad you got yourself a stationwagon. A lot of room to roll around in. And hey, the next time you decide to cheat, find yourself a girlfriend who lives farther away than the next block over. That's just plain stupid, Jack."

"Fuck you, coon-ass," Matthews said, uncapping his soda as he crawled behind the wheel of his Jeep Cherokee.

"My regards to the girlfriend!" Fegan called after

him. "Tell her if she ever needs anything to give me a call."

As if the day hadn't sucked badly enough, when Fegan got home, Frank's dark blue Lexus was nosed in against the rear bumper of Amos Lee's pickup truck. Amos Lee was in the rocker on the screened porch, an empty creel at his feet and nylon line curling over his knees onto the cypress planks of the floor. Beside him, Frank crouched with a fistful of glossy, full-color brochures. "They call it Golden Meadows, and it's the nicest full-care facility in the parish. They even got bingo and music, can you imagine? How 'bout we drive up there tomorrow and have a look-see. I just know you're gonna like it."

Frank shoved the brochures at Amos Lee, and Amos Lee shoved them back, the line tangled between his arthritic fingers. There was no telling whether or not Frank's comments had registered. The old man wore the same look he always wore these days, the same look he'd worn since he'd gone into the swamp a decade before, and stumbled upon Jean Louise.

"There are folks your age there," Frank persisted. "And a full-time nursing staff, in case you're ailin'. There's no need for you to be workin' at your age. You've earned a few good years, and they even have a dance on Saturday nights. How about that?"

Fegan took the steps two at a time, stopping in front of his brother. *"Occupe toi de tes affaires.* Mind your own business, Frank, and leave Amos Lee alone."

"Who asked you?" Frank demanded, his expression sullen. He was thirty-six years old, with a wife and two kids, and when his younger brother walked into the room he reverted to a petulant, argumentative eight-year-old.

"It's my house, Frank. I make the mortgage payments,

and if you want to hang around, then you'd better be nice."

"This is gonna happen, Fegan, whether you want it to or not." His round face shone with the heat. "He can't live alone no more."

"Amos Lee does just fine. Ain't that right, *Pépère?*" The old man said nothing. "What makes you think he'd want to live like that, anyhow, huh, Frank? Dances, bingo. When did you ever know him to care 'bout stuff like that? He's used to doin' what he's always done, and there ain't nothin' wrong with that." He handed the bait box full of chicken gizzards to Amos Lee, then turned to Frank. "What the hell's gotten into you, anyhow?"

"What should have gotten into me long ago! This latest episode is proof that he needs supervision. I'm trying to save him from himself, that's all. Is that so hard to understand? Somebody's got to take responsibility, Fegan, and we both know it won't be you!"

"Did it ever occur to you that he might not need savin'? No, I don't suppose so. And just what the hell do you mean by 'episode'? That old man didn't hurt nobody, and you can't blame him for what's goin' on in Angelique. If he hadn't found that kid, somebody else would have."

"But he did find her!" Frank shot back harshly. "And that isn't any better for him than it is for this family!"

"What about this family?" Fegan said, then laughed shortly. "Oh, I get it. It ain't Amos Lee you're worried about. It's Frank Broussard, and his exalted place in the community. What's the matter, Frank? You afraid this is gonna hurt your insurance business?"

Frank's face turned a dull shade of red. Veins popped in his neck, and for a few seconds, Fegan thought that he might explode right there on the screened porch.

"Officer Matthews said he fined him this morning for catching turtles with intent to sell. Seven hundred and fifty dollars, and I'm not gonna pay it, Fegan!"

"Nobody asked you to pay it," Fegan said, flinging open the screen door and entering the house. Frank followed. As the oldest Broussard sibling, he seemed to feel that it was his duty to chew his younger brother's ass out at every opportunity, a circumstance that had gotten a lot worse since Fegan resigned from his position at the *Chicago Tribune* and returned home ten months ago. Mostly, he tried to ignore it, because Frank was Frank, stiff-necked and too damned concerned about what everybody thought of him, and if his wife Christine was any indication, perpetually sexually frustrated. Christine was so anal, it made Fegan wonder how she'd ever managed to squeeze out their two kids. There were times when he almost felt sorry for him, but this afternoon wasn't one of them.

"Somebody's got to be responsible," Frank insisted. "Somebody's got to make the hard decisions, and think about what's best for Amos Lee!"

The kitchen was hot as an oven. The air conditioner was broken again. Fegan opened the fridge and grabbed a cold beer, allowing the cool air to bathe his hot skin for a few delicious seconds before he closed it again. "What would you know about what's best for him? You ain't around to know nothin'."

"What *about* that girl? His involvement didn't exactly go unnoticed."

"Involvement?" Fegan said, taking a quick swallow of the icy liquid. "What the hell do you mean, involvement? You make it sound like he had somethin' to do with it."

"The news anchors have been all over this. An old

man who can't talk! Who's detached and disoriented. Unsupervised. Do you know how this looks?"

Fegan took a long swallow, then fixed Frank with a look before wandering back outside. *'Dieu,* Frank! You'd try the patience of a fuckin' saint! Go home! And while you're at it, you can stuff those damn brochures. Long as I'm here, Amos Lee don' go nowhere he don' wanna go."

"Did it ever occur to you that you might not be the best person to make this decision?" Frank demanded, his hands at his spreading waist. He had a fancy watch on his left wrist, and a big gold ring on the pinky finger of his right hand. He liked expensive cars and prestige, and what he couldn't claim, he'd try to fake. They were nothing alike. Fegan didn't put any importance on looking like the big man, and his comfort with who and what he was had always bothered Frank. "You carouse all night and drink all day, and you haven't held a steady job since Chicago. You can't take care of a helpless old man, Fegan. You're not doin' such a great job of takin' care of yourself!"

"You don't know shit," Fegan said, slamming back through the screen door in search of another beer. The last thing he needed today was buttoned-down, zipped-up Frank telling him what a mess he'd made of things. As if he didn't already know. As if he needed to be reminded at every opportunity.

He opened the fridge, and swore. He was out of beer, and even worse, Frank had followed him into the kitchen, again.

Fegan turned to face Frank, and at the same time, a red BMW pulled up in front of the house.

Sliding her dark glasses down on her nose, Claire surveyed the bungalow with the screened porch shaded by the huge live oak in the front yard. She and Jean

Louise used to climb that tree. In fact, she'd been stuck in the high branches a time or two, too terrified to climb down. Jean Louise's older brother Fegan had rescued her. He'd always been doing things like that. Jean Louise had had a severe case of hero worship where Fegan was concerned, and if she was perfectly honest, Claire had been rather fond of him, too, only in a slightly different capacity. His dark good looks and lazy smile had made her pulse flutter. Strange that she should remember that now, when she hadn't thought of Fegan Broussard in years.

The house itself hadn't changed much in the years she'd been away. White paint and neat green storm shutters, crushed shell drive, and a mailbox that stated simply, "Broussard." A place out of time. It looked just as it always had.

Her heart was a little hesitant, but she opened the car door and stepped out, smoothing the wrinkles from the skirt of her taupe-colored silk suit. She couldn't be certain of the reception she would receive from Jean Louise's family, and it made her nervous. It hardly mattered that she had spent as much time under Amos Lee's roof as her own, back in the day.

She was Jimmy Sumner's daughter, and she hadn't seen Amos Lee, or the rest of Jean Louise's family, since the trial. There was no telling how the old gentleman would react to her suddenly materializing on his doorstep.

She was halfway to the porch when the subject of her thoughts emerged from the backyard, a tacklebox in one hand, a wicker creel in the other. Dressed in faded dungarees and a blue, short-sleeved chambray shirt, a ball cap on his head, he sat down on the steps, seemingly preoccupied with the contents of the tacklebox.

Like the shotgun-style house, Amos Lee seemed well-kept and little changed. He'd been old when his daughter Rae got divorced and moved back home with her three kids. A few years later, Rae, like that handsome but worthless man she'd married, had drifted away, leaving Amos Lee, then in his sixties, to raise Frank, Fegan, and Jean Louise to the best of his abilities. No one was quite sure what had become of Rae. Rumor had it that she'd taken up with a musician and ended up in the New Orleans red-light district, but no one seemed to know for sure, least of all her kids or her aging parent.

Claire's shadow fell across the rheumatic fingers fixing the turtle hooks onto lead wires, and the wires onto thin nylon rope with empty plastic milk jugs for buoys. The old man didn't bother to look up. "Mr. Prideau? Mr. Prideau, it's Claire Sumner."

Amos Lee didn't respond.

"Mr. Prideau," Claire persisted, forced to a near-shout by the argument being carried on inside the house, "I was wondering if I might have a word with you? I've driven down from Lafayette, and I'm staying with my Aunt Eulanie Sumner. She lives out on Brighton Road."

The voices, now too loud to ignore, overrode Claire's attempt to engage the octogenarian in conversation. "Do what you always do, Fegan. Ignore it. Dump it onto someone else. Tell the world to kiss your backside!"

"I'll tell you, that's for sure," an angry voice shot back. "You don't run me, Frank! Now, back off, or get out of my house!"

The screen door opened, and the argument boiled out onto the porch, the older man backing away from the younger, who had his head lowered and cocked belligerently. The muscles in his arms looked taut, as if he might grab for Frank at any moment, and barely held back. Frank must have noticed his tension, too, because he backed down immediately. "You haven't heard the last of this, Fegan!" he promised, brushing past Claire and all but sprinting across the grass to his Lexus. He spun out of the crushed shell drive, narrowly missing Claire's bumper, then tore up the street in a gasoline-fueled fury.

Unruffled by the exchange, Amos Lee took his creel and his tacklebox and, ignoring both his visitor and his remaining grandson, walked off toward the backyard and the bayou beyond. With opportunity slipping away, Claire sprang off the step and started down the sidewalk. "Mr. Prideau! Please! It's imperative that I speak with you!"

"Amos Lee don't speak to strangers, him," Fegan drawled, "and me, I ain't feelin' much like company at the moment."

"It appears that he doesn't speak to family, either," Claire said, turning to face him. He was leaning against the porch post, his faded jean shirt with the sleeves torn out open down the front, and the waistband of his jeans unbuttoned. His cross-trainers were scuffed and old, his skin smooth and tanned, and his eyes the same vibrant deep blue Claire remembered.

She took an involuntary breath, bracing herself against the potent force of his flagrant sexuality. Fegan Broussard had always been a heart-stopper, and it was obvious that much hadn't changed. His hair, thick and dark, and just wavy enough to be difficult, curled rebelliously around his frayed collar and a pair of gold hoop earrings. As Claire watched, his hard mouth curved in a generous and somewhat smart-ass smile.

"Well, I'll be damned," he said softly. "If it ain't little Char Clairée, Blackwater Princess . . . only she's not so little anymore, is she?" He pushed away from the post where he'd been leaning and came down the steps,

circling slowly around her for a good, long look while
Claire's face reddened and her temper soared. *"Mais,*
yeah. Girl's all grown up, and lookin' good. You say
you're visitin' Miz Eulanie? I ain't seen her in a while."

"I didn't say anything of the kind—at least, not to
you." Claire jerked her chin up, hoping for a more
dignified response, but finding nothing cutting enough
to faze him. He was the only one, besides her father, who
had ever dared to call her Charlotte, and his derivative of
the name, which he'd hung on her when he was sixteen
and she was twelve and embarrassingly knock-kneed,
still had the power to make her shiver.

"No need to be all stuck up, Char. It's not like you
weren't half in love with old Fegan, once upon a time."

"I was a child," Claire said. "And it was a crush,
nothing more. Unlike some people I could name, I've
matured. At the time, I didn't know any better—besides,
you're a pig for bringing it up."

"You ain't twelve any longer," he said with a grin.
"How long did you say you'll be in town?"

"I didn't say. And it's really none of your business."

"Amos Lee's my business," he countered. "What you
want with an old man, anyhow?"

Claire gave him a long, assessing look. Fegan was a
pain in the ass—uncooperative, unorthodox, earthy and
wild, and always had been—but if there was even a slim
chance that he could help her get information from his
grandfather, then she was going to jump at it. "What
do you know about this?" she asked, digging the newspaper out of her bag and holding it out to him.

He glanced at it, but he didn't take it. "A popular
topic of conversation these days. Ever'body 'round
Angelique's wonderin' what became of that kid. As for
what I know personally, that pretty much sums it up.
Why?"

Claire's frustration boiled up. "The resemblance is striking. Surely even you can see that."

"I see a kid, that's all," he insisted. "Is that what brought you here, Char? That why you so hot to talk to Amos Lee? Well, darlin', you're wastin' your time. Thanks to your daddy, Amos Lee ain't talked to nobody in ten years."

"Is that why Frank wants to put him in a full-care facility?"

"Full care, my ass. He wants to warehouse him, like some old broke-down pair of boots."

"But if he can't relate enough to communicate—"

"Never said he can't. I said, he don't." He took a Houston Astros ball cap out of his hip pocket and settled it on his dark head, fixing Claire with a look. "Now, unless you're of a mind to come on in and get reacquainted, you'll have to say good-bye. I've got places to go, baby."

Claire glanced off in the direction of the bayou, where Amos Lee had disappeared, and pretended not to notice Fegan. The attraction was still there, damn it. She could feel it: a jolt of electricity every time their eyes met, delicious, yet forbidden. He was Jean Louise's brother. They'd practically grown up together. So, why was she feeling as if she suddenly found herself in the middle of a mine field? Because he was dangerous, she thought. He always had been. "I'll go," she promised, turning toward her car, "but I'll be back."

Bracing a forearm against the porch post, Fegan watched her go. The last time he'd seen Clairée, she was sixteen and heartbroken, tears blotching her face a mottled red as she watched them lead her daddy away from the courthouse.

"Lot o' years gone by since then." Clairée wasn't sixteen any longer. She was a woman now, a lot stunning, a little unsettling. Beautiful, and incredibly poised in a way he would never have anticipated. He hadn't expected to see her again, and all of a sudden, there she was, rounded right where she should be, lithe and tall, and looking for trouble.

Though she hadn't said so directly, her inference to the dead girl from the bayou stated clearly enough that she was here to dig up information surrounding the girl's murder in the hopes of helping her father gain a last-minute appeal. He hadn't given her anything. Nor would he. He hated Jimmy Sumner, and he sure as hell wouldn't feel any regret when that murderous bastard was gone.

Not that any of that would matter. Clairée was stubborn. And it was a sure bet he would see her again very soon.

Now, why did he find that thought so disconcerting?

CHAPTER
TWO

"Serena, darlin', it's Cash. We still on for tonight?"
Sheriff's Deputy Cash Edmunds pulled into the parking
lot of Folley's Funeral Home and shut down the cruiser's
engine. It was four-thirty in the afternoon, and Serena
Dunne sounded as if she had just tumbled her luscious
ass out of bed. But then, she probably had. Strippers
tended to keep odd hours.

"You've got balls callin' me after last night. I've got
a shiner bloomin' on my left cheek because of you, you
crazy son of a bitch."

Even angry, her voice had a smoky quality that got
him hot, and if it hadn't been for the fact that the sheriff
was waiting for the coroner's reports on their Jane Doe,
he would have headed right on over to her house for
a daylight double-header. "Hell, Serena, what'd you
expect me to do? I love you, darlin', and you know it
makes me crazy to see another man put his hands on
you."

"It was a lap dance, Cash, and in case you've forgotten, it's my job! Deal with it, or leave me the hell alone!"

"Serena, honey, it won't happen again, I promise. C'mon, let me make it up to you. Friend of mine has a little shindig planned for next week. I thought maybe you'd like to go with me."

"Shindig?" Serena repeated. "Cash, you know I don't get off on sawdust-covered floors."

"This is first-class all the way. If you want, we can skip the garden party and put in an appearance at the after-dark festivities. It's black tie, and exclusive," Cash told her, enjoying dropping that little bombshell almost as much as he enjoyed the mental picture of the curvy redhead clinging to his arm as he entered the mansion. "I got a couple of C-notes. You can go shopping up in Baton Rouge, get some slinky, sequined number—unless, of course, you'd rather stay in and read." Serena was like a greedy crow. She liked glittery things, and the price of her forgiveness was the prospect of a shopping trip.

"When is it again?" she asked, and he could almost hear her lick her lips. "I'll have to ask for the evening off."

Cash smiled to himself. "Why don't I drop by and we can talk about it? Say—seven-thirty." He turned off the cell phone and hung it back on his hip, beside his beeper. Then, he opened the door and stepped out onto the parking lot.

Remy Broussard was sweeping the graceful arc of the concrete walkway. Remy did odd jobs for a few of the businesses around town to supplement his income until his cash crop came in. Remy was a grower, dealer, and small-time loan shark, none of which was anything the boy could brag about, except in certain circles, and in front of Cash, who, for a cut of the profit, looked the other way, allowing Remy to stay on the streets and conduct business as usual.

Cash headed directly for the man with the broom. Remy pretended not to notice. "Broussard, I ought to shove that broom right up your ass."

"You kiss your mama wid dat trash-talkin' mouth?" Remy asked, but Cash could see he was nervous. "What business you got bustin' my chops at work, Cash-Man? You gonna get me fired, dat's what!" He glanced around, then reached in the pocket of his coveralls and put a hundred-dollar bill in Cash's palm. "What can I say? Business been slow."

"You better not be holdin' out on me, Remy. If there's anything I hate, it's a small-time piece of shit like you who thinks he can hold out on me. You want to keep doin' business, you'll pay up."

Cash turned his back on the Cajun, heading for the low stucco building. He passed Folley's boy-toy, William Keyes, in the hall. William, six feet tall and slender, with sandy hair and a sharp, fox-like face, gave Cash a sidelong glance and knowing smile. "Homer's in the cold room," he said. "Is this business or pleasure?"

Cash threw him a black look. "Sheriff's department business." He didn't like dealing with William. The man gave him the creeps. It wasn't the idea that he was gay that bothered him. It was knowing that he was gay *and* up to his sleepy-lidded eyeballs in certain activities that Cash would rather forget about. He didn't want to be any more involved in Ashton's business than he already was. He just stayed on the fringes and did what he was told. And with William Keyes's gaze boring a hole into his back just above his shoulder blades, he couldn't get down the hall fast enough.

Homer Folley, funeral director, doubled as parish coroner. A small room in the back of the building served as a morgue. Jane Doe was lying on a stainless steel slab, her skin a translucent pale blue-gray. Folley was adjusting a toe-tag, but looked up over his reading glasses as Cash walked in. "Afternoon, Deputy Edmunds. Nice day, isn't it?"

"It was until I walked in," Cash complained, taking out his handkerchief and covering his nose and mouth. "Christ, Folley. It smells like a meat locker that's lost its refrigeration in here. How do you stand it?"

Folley shrugged. "You get used to it after a while. Desensitization. Besides, we all come to it sooner or later, now don't we? Makes a man respect death." He clucked his dismay as he pulled the sheet up over a lifeless face mottled with dark bruises. "It's a cryin' shame, a girl so young. Got a niece nearly her age. Sure would hate to think of her comin' to such a violent end." He clucked again, a sympathetic sound, quite possibly the only sympathy the girl had ever gotten. "You got children, Deputy?"

"No family to speak of. Mama's all that's left. You got those reports?"

Folley crossed to a desk illuminated by a banker's lamp. On the blotter was a stack of manila folders. Homer riffled the stack. "Now, where is it? Oh, yes." Reaching out, he pushed a button on the intercom. "William, are you finished with Jane Doe's report?" He turned off the intercom, massaging his knuckles, then got up to push in the drawer, sighing. "Have a good sleep, child," he said, then slowly slid the drawer into place.

In a moment, William appeared, entering the room with a catlike grace that made Cash's skin crawl. He placed a folder identical to the others on the top of the stack, shot Cash a dark look, then left the room as silently as he'd entered.

Homer glanced at Cash over his glasses. "You two know one another?"

"I've seen him around a time or two."

"Hmm," Homer said. "Could have sworn something passed between you just now. Oh, well. Not that it matters. William's a free spirit, and he comes and goes as he pleases. There you are, deputy." Homer handed over the folder. "Is there anything else I can do for you today?"

"Nothing that I can think of, Homer. You'll understand if I say that I hope I don't see you 'round."

"Most of my clients don't—see me, that is. You have a good day, now."

The years following Jimmy's incarceration had been difficult. Melba Weldon Sumner had never been a particularly strong woman. Always plagued by health concerns, the tragedy that befell her family had broken her, and within a year of Jimmy's imprisonment, Melba was dead. After her death, the care and custody of sixteen-year-old Claire had fallen onto Eulanie Sumner's slim shoulders. Alan Harris, Aunt Eule's husband of five years, had been long gone by then, run off with another woman.

Eulanie hadn't shed a tear over his departure, much to the scandalous whisperings of the neighborhood. Instead, she'd resumed the use of her maiden name, while throwing all of her energies into making a success of the family farm. As far as Claire knew, Aunt Eule had never entertained a selfish thought in her entire life. "Work hard," was her ethic, "pray often, and never turn your back on your own," a philosophy that she had put into practice when she assimilated her parentless niece into her life.

Claire credited Eulanie with the fact that she'd stayed in school, and gone on to further her education, first at Louisiana State University at Baton Rouge, then at Harvard Law School. And though her career had taken her away from Acadia Parish, she'd never broken ties with Eulanie.

The parish that had been home to her through her adolescent years was another matter. Coming back to Angelique, the place of Jimmy's downfall, wasn't easy. Driving past the courthouse on the way to The Willows brought back unwelcome memories, memories of a young girl whose innocence had been torn away in the blink of an eye, cruelly and irrevocably. On the day Jimmy stood accused of killing Jean Louise, Claire's sense of security, of well-being, had shattered . . . but the bitterness left behind by the wreckage her young life had become, seemed everlasting.

The lane leading to the two-story house was long, unpaved, and dusty, and it passed the outbuildings long before it reached the residence. The weathered Case tractor was parked half in, half out of the tractor shed, the hood off; a slight figure in grease-stained overalls perched on a stool plied a wrench that looked too large for her gloved hand. Nearby, Ned Avery, the hired man, stood with his straw hat in hand, looking disgusted and ineffectual. "Miss Eule, I don't know what you pay me for if you insist on doin' ever'thing yourself."

"Oh, Ned, quit your complaining and hand me that seven-sixteenth-inch socket. My hands are a lot smaller than yours are, and they don't allow for much room to maneuver in these things." Eulanie pulled her head up to reach for the wrench, noticed they were no longer alone, and banged her dark head on the block and tackle hanging overhead. "Ow. That smarts. Claire, for heaven's sake! You should have warned me you were coming." She frowned as she climbed down, taking off her work gloves and wiping at a smudge on her cheek. "I'm afraid you'll have to forego a hug until after I've freshened up."

Claire kissed Eulanie's cheek, smiling. "Aunt Eulanie, it's ninety-three degrees in the shade. You should be resting instead of out here, meddling in Mr. Avery's business."

"You tell her, Miss Clairée," Ned agreed. "She don't listen to me, nor to Doc Trelawney, nor no one, for that matter. Most stubborn lady I ever seen."

"Dr. Trelawney?" Claire repeated, looking from one to the other. "Is something wrong?"

"It's nothing much, dear."

"'Nothin' much,' she say," Ned grumbled. "She fainted dead away on the floor a couple of times. Doc says he thinks it's her heart, and wants to run some tests, but will she go? No, ma'am. She too blockheaded, her."

"I beg your pardon?" Eulanie said irritably. "I will not be talked about as though I'm not even here. Besides, I am not blockheaded, Ned Avery! I'm busy. And I don't like being told what to do by someone half my age. I'll go when I'm damn good and ready." She threw down the grease rag and gave Ned a look. "Claire and I are going to the house for some refreshments. I suppose it's futile to ask if you care to join us?"

"You two go on," Ned replied. "I'll just stay and finish this up—then I can drop the starter off at Jonesey's repair shop on the way home."

Eulanie shook her head, grumbling. "Well, don't act like you're doin' me any favor, Ned. You've been dyin' to get your hands on that tractor all mornin'. Man's got serious control issues." Eulanie didn't argue as Claire led the way to the BMW, but climbed in and cranked up the air. "I swear," she said, "every July seems to be hotter than the last. I can't decide if it's global warming that's at fault, or all that space junk NASA has floatin' around up there." She dabbed her forehead with a folded white handkerchief. "What are you doing here, Claire? I thought you had a case to prepare for this weekend."

"I did have, but I've asked a colleague to take over. I'm taking some time off, and I was hoping that I could impose on my favorite aunt."

"Favorite aunt, indeed," Eulanie said with a snort. "I'm your *only* aunt . . . but I'm very glad to have you, whatever the reason. Come on in, darlin'. I'll send Hugh out for your bags directly."

The Willows was one hundred and forty-three years old and still impressive by any standards. Built by some enterprising Sumner ancestor during the years immediately preceding the War Between the States, it was a fine example of the Greek Revival style of architecture, and had been left largely untouched by that raging conflict. But what the Yankees had spared narrowly missed being consumed by fire a few years later when night riders from the neighborhood, bitter over their own devastating losses and resentful at what they considered the Sumners' appalling lack of patriotism, attempted to torch the place.

Adele Sumner, daughter of the house, and Jubie, freewoman of color who had a small house on the grounds, had beaten back the flames with sopping rag rugs; then, dressed only in her nightgown, a shawl around her shoulders and her hair wild, Adele denounced the culprits for the cowards they were from the steps of the church next morning, calling each by name and casting shame upon their households. Years later, the more notable families in the parish had crossed the street rather than face down Adele's caustic tongue and judgmental stare.

The Sumners, it seemed, had always been on the edge of parish society, always something of a scandal, but they'd managed to hang on to The Willows through it all. It was the foundation, home base, the place where stability began and family survived, though for Claire, the large, red-brick sprawl with its double galleries and graceful columns, lush green lawn, and huge live oaks had nothing of Jimmy left in it. It was true that he'd grown up here, but the restlessness that had taken him away from the parish to work the oil rigs in the Gulf, and to other places, had driven him away from the quiet sameness of farm life at the age of sixteen.

Most of the rooms on the second floor of the mansion, with the exception of Claire's old room and Eulanie's master suite, were no longer in use. Jane Avery, Ned's sister, had free rein over the old mansion during the day, with her son Hugh to help with the heavy chores, but after six most evenings, Eulanie was on her own. Jane was a pleasant woman, close to her employer's age, with a round face and large, dark eyes. "Good to have you home, Miss Clairée," Jane said softly. "There's a slice of Key lime in that tea, just like you like it."

Claire smiled, slowly regaining her focus. "Jane, you'll spoil me."

"Good," she said, nodding once. "Maybe then you won't want to leave." She moved around the table to pour a tall glass for Eulanie. "Shame about that child they found," Jane said, positioning the pitcher on the wicker table. A stiff breeze swept in off the river, hot and moist and carrying on it a strange sense of disquiet. "Heard that old Mr. Prideau found her. Strange it is. But then, Amos Lee's strange, too. Little up 'round the bend, they say, and this here latest sure don' help."

"What is that smell?" Eulanie broke in. She wrinkled her nose as a thin wisp of dark smoke crept through the French windows onto the long gallery.

"Damn me," Jane said, making tracks to the house, "there goes the gumbo!"

Eulanie's attention shifted immediately back to her niece. She'd seen the look that flitted over Claire's face when Jane mentioned the dead girl, despite her attempt to conceal it. There wasn't much that slipped past Eulanie's notice. She was fifty-four years old, but she was a long damn way from senility. She watched Claire for a while, then turned and looked out over the balustrade at the long tatters of gray-green moss swaying gently in the breeze. "I know what this is about, Claire," she said softly.

"I don't know what you mean."

"Your father called this morning, and he's not pleased. I don't suppose there's anything I can say to dissuade you?"

Claire looked up from stirring sugar into her glass, but she didn't give an inch. "Oh, don't bother with that look," Eulanie told her. "It didn't work when you were sixteen and sneaking out to meet that Robillard boy, and it won't work now."

Claire resembled the Sumners; her eyes were dark, like Jimmy's, and Eulanie couldn't look into them without seeing her brother looking back at her. Right now, they were direct, challenging, and vastly unsettling. "Was that all he said?"

"He indicated that you mentioned the trouble in Angelique with a look in your eye that didn't bode well for his peace of mind. I have to assume it's the same look you're giving me now. I'd ask what's gotten into you, but I suspect that I already know."

"It's like he *wants* to die, Aunt Eule. More than that—it's like he's afraid to live."

Eulanie snorted, a somewhat uncharacteristic, very unladylike sound that did not go well with her blue-and-white-striped seersucker shirt and pleated tan pants. "Jimmy has never been afraid of anything in his entire life."

Inside the house, the phone rang, followed by a brief pause, and then Jane pushing open the door. "Miss Eule. It's for you. Somethin' 'bout a farm contract."

"I'll be right there," Eulanie promised, then turned back to Claire. "Darlin', please. Do not torment yourself over this. Some things in life just don't work out, no matter how much we wish otherwise. I resigned myself to this eventuality a long while back, and so has Jimmy. And I don't want to see him spendin' his last days on this earth worryin' about his daughter. If you can't do it for him, then do it for me. And just let this lie."

Claire lifted her gaze again, and the intensity in her dark eyes made Eulanie flinch. "You really believe that he killed Jean Louise, don't you?"

Eulanie sighed. "I don't know. Men do some strange things when they drink—at times, uncharacteristic things. I would like to think Jimmy didn't have it in him to be so heartless, yet I can't dispute the fact that he confessed. All I can say for sure is that he's my brother, and I love him." She got up and, reaching out, patted her niece's hand. "Settle in, and get some rest. Perhaps in the morning, things will look a little clearer."

As her aunt slipped quietly into the house, Claire settled back in her chair and sipped her tea, restless beneath the hot kiss of the wind off the river. "You might believe it," she said softly. "But I can't. Not ever."

* * *

On the outside, Jimmy had never been much of a
reader, but the magazines Eule sent him now were well-
thumbed before he passed them on to Trick Adesco.
Adesco had the cell next to Jimmy's, and for the most
part, he was an okay sort, despite the fact that he'd
been condemned to death for the double murder of
his former girlfriend and her lover. It was late on the
evening of the day after Clairée's visit, and the cold
dread brought on by their conversation continued to
linger. Ten o'clock. The head count would begin in
half an hour. Jimmy struggled with the harder words in
the article in *National Geographic* magazine, while a few
feet away Adesco murmured something to himself, then
cursed in quiet disgust.

"Hey, Sumner."

Jimmy took his time answering, sounding the syllables
out in his head. Hy-dro-grap-hica-lly. Hydro-graph—"

"Sumner!"

"Jesus, Adesco. What the hell do you want?"

"Hey, man, ain't no need to take my head off. I was
just wonderin'—what's a nine-letter word meanin' a
hard and compact aragonite?"

Jimmy snorted. "Aragonite? Now, if I knew that, what
the fuck would I be doin' in here?"

"Hey, man, what's the matter wit'ch you? You got a
bug up yo' ass, an' it's been dere for two days."

Jimmy remained stubbornly silent. Talking about family and family problems wasn't something he ever
resorted to, no matter how much he wanted to. He had
kept to himself for nine years, hoarding his secrets like
a miser hoarded his gold or a doper his stash. Somehow,
he had convinced himself that if he just played it their
way, they would leave his loved ones alone. But after

the visit yesterday, and the news of the kid found in the bayou, he was no longer sure that was true.

Nervous. God, he was nervous. And he didn't know how the hell he would ever come down enough to actually sleep. Adesco had gone quiet, and Jimmy felt the sting of remorse. The man was just doing his best to pass the time. "Alabaster," he said, relenting. "Adesco . . . aragonite. It's alabaster."

Adesco didn't reply. In fact, he had gone dead silent. Not a noise, not a whisper of sound, not a breath came from his cell just a few feet away.

"Adesco?"

Jimmy went to the bars and was struck by the changing play of the light on the opposite wall. A shadow, the elongated shape of a man, turned slowly, as if doing some weird pirouette, head cocked at a strange and unnatural angle. Jimmy's blood went cold. "Jesus. Adesco? Guard!" he shouted. "Guard!"

The sound of footsteps approached Jimmy's cell, but they were unhurried; the man wore an expensive dark suit, not a uniform. "Hey, Jimmy. It's been a long while, now hasn't it?"

It was hard to speak. Jimmy's mouth was suddenly dry as dust, his throat felt paralyzed. "What the *hell* are you doin' here? You said you'd leave us alone. *You said this would end it.*"

"And I've kept my word, all these years," he said with a smile. It was a fine smile. His teeth were even and white. Perfect. But a man only had to look into his eyes to know how deceptive it was. "You've been alone, now haven't you, Jimmy? All alone? No friends. No family, to speak of. Eulanie hasn't paid you a visit in what, three years? And Clairée . . ." He paused, as if considering. But it was done for effect. Everything the bastard did, every move he made, every word he uttered was staged, calculated. "Now, what's this I hear about Clairée?"

"You leave my little girl outta this," Jimmy said, low and feverishly.

"Or you'll what?"

The implication was clear. He was powerless. "She don't know nothin', and she won't know nothin'. Not so long as I live and breathe."

"And there's our difficulty," he said, wrapping a manicured hand around one of the bars, leaning close. "You barely exist now, Jimmy. Why, you're just one step away from where your friend is, over there. And I'm countin' the days." He laughed, the sound smooth and rich. "About Clairée . . . well, I sincerely hope she's a good girl, and disappears on her own. It just doesn't pay to be too curious, and your family has seen enough tragedy. It would be a cryin' shame if anything happened to someone so young and vibrant."

He straightened, letting go of the bars, giving Jimmy a final frosty glance before slowly walking away. Jimmy could barely breathe. He felt the bed sheet wrapped around his own throat, just like it was wrapped around Adesco's and knotted; he fought against it. "Guard! Guard!"

"Hey, Sumner," Adesco complained, "what the hell's wrong wid you, man? You gone crazy from readin' too much over there, or what?"

Jimmy came erect on his bunk and sat with his knees pulled up and his head in his hands. He was breathing more normally now, but the dream just wouldn't leave him. It felt real, and he couldn't seem to shake off the cold chains of dread that it left in its aftermath. "Sorry," he managed to squeeze out. "Bad dream, that's all. I didn't mean to wake you."

"Bad dream," Adesco's disembodied grumble floated

through the bars. "Dat's what you get for readin' those trash magazines. Last time I borrowed one of dem things from you, I dreamed that Britney Spears was puttin' the moves on me, and when she turned around, it was some blond African chick with a face like Libby Dole and tits down to her navel. Man, dat ain't no place I ever want to go again."

Me either, Jimmy silently agreed. Aloud, he said, "It's over. Just shut up and go back to sleep."

"All right, man," Adesco said. "All right. But first I just gotta ask—who was the dude in the dark threads?"

"What the hell are you talkin' about?"

"You know. The suit. Mr. Grim Reaper his ownself, come to watch you sleep. Walked in here like he owned the place. And maybe he does, for all dat. That was Armani he was wearin'. Had me an Armani once. Sleek and black, with a vent in back. Cool, man. Really cool. I bet Peterson got himself a nice wad o' cash for making hisself scarce." He snorted, then was silent. "Hey, Sumner? Ain't you gonna say somethin'? Sumner? You still breathin' over there?"

Just barely, Jimmy thought. Just barely.

Fegan's work kept him out late, up till all hours, and when a client didn't like the information he provided and decided to stiff him for his fee, it didn't always pay well. It was either so damned boring that he had to resort to a thermos full of coffee to keep from falling asleep, or so insane that he seriously considered an early retirement and a nice cozy spot on a beach somewhere. In the ten months since he'd handed in his resignation at the *Chicago Tribune* and headed back to the parish, he'd been shot at, sued for libel, and arrested for trespassing twice. Yet, when he weighed his current means of employment against the everyday bullshit of dealing with a press room full of overly educated, overly competitive, cutthroat assholes who would have gladly sold out Grandma's homegrown for a lead, he couldn't help but see the up side of things.

Like the fact that he set his own hours, fished the tree-shaded waters of the bayou when he felt like it, and, since no one expected him to be articulate, he could work when hellishly hung over. It also didn't hurt that his choice of lifestyles rode Button-down Frank like a rented two-dollar mule. And anything he could do these days to annoy Frank was a definite plus.

Just for kicks, he tried to imagine his brother slouched in the driver's seat of an aging, black Pontiac TransAm parked in the back of the lot of the Pink Cadillac Bar, watching the entrance while he pretended to nap. The image wouldn't come, and, after a while he gave up on it and returned to watching the tavern's entrance.

He'd been looking for Manny Poutou for several days. He'd made some discreet inquiries, talked to some of Manny's friends, but they were all close-mouthed to the point of paranoia. Everybody in the parish knew that Manny was big-time trouble with a capital "T" and his wife Terri wasn't too far behind.

If he hadn't needed the cash to compensate for the money he'd used to pay Amos Lee's fine and to make the mortgage, he would have let Terri Lynn find her own trouble. As it was, he'd checked at Manny's job and found he'd been canned for bustin' a guy's head with a soda bottle on the assembly line. It had taken a good ten minutes of fast talk, and a few slight alterations on the truth, to get the foreman to open up, and then Fegan kind of wished he hadn't asked.

Manny Poutou's altercation had followed close upon the heels of finding out that his fellow worker had been a little too friendly with Terri Lynn, Manny's wife. The foreman couldn't give him anything more concrete than that, but it was Friday night, and Fegan knew enough about parish nightlife and guys like Manny to take it from there. He'd checked with Cash Edmunds, Sheriff's Deputy for Acadia Parish, and there was an outstanding warrant on Manny for simple battery.

And that was where it got complicated.

Acadia Parish Sheriff's Department was a low-budget operation, and Cash had informed Fegan that, much to his regret, he couldn't waste his valuable time chasing down a low-life like Manny when they had serious drug problems to contend with and were in the midst of a murder investigation. Sooner or later, Manny would surface and they'd arrest him. "It's as simple as that."

"Ain't nothin' simple about it, man," Fegan had argued. "Manny Poutou's some mean-ass shit. When he does come back, he's gonna take this out on his old lady—you know he will."

"Then she needs to get a Protection From Abuse Order going. Tell her to go to the courthouse—"

"Protection From Abuse ain't gonna keep him from puttin' her in the hospital, or worse. It's a piece of paper. And if she's in the hospital, how the hell am I gonna get paid?"

"Not my problem, Fegan," Cash had said. "But just to show you I'm not totally unfeeling to Mrs. Poutou's plight, if you locate the suspect, give me a call. I'll come down and pick him up."

"That's good of you, Cash. That's a lot of help. To serve and protect, my ass!"

It was half-past eleven, and he'd seen a lot of action, but no Manny. He was beginning to wonder how he would get through the next two hours when headlights glared on his windshield, shining in his eyes. He glanced up as a familiar, late-model red BMW pulled into the parking lot. The small knot of men hanging around the bed of a bright yellow pickup stopped mid-conversation to stare at the attractive brunette behind the wheel. "Damn it, Char," Fegan murmured. "You been away too long. Might as well put a neon sign on the roof that screams *I don't belong here.*"

Fegan watched her park the car and get out. She was wearing a short red skirt, high heels, and a sleeveless white blouse that clung to her curves in all the right places. With her shiny, dark hair hanging loose and an air of studied purpose, she was an attention-getter, all right. And she got attention . . . Fegan's, and his cousin Remy's, who separated from the small group congregating by the truck. Remy trotted across the crushed shell parking lot, catching up to Clairée in time to swing the door wide and hold it for her as the yellow truck across the way began to rock slightly on its wheels and the crowd began to hoot noisily.

Seeming not to notice, Clairée smiled her thanks, said something Fegan couldn't catch, and disappeared into the dim and smoky interior. Remy turned back to give his friends the high sign and, laughing as he settled his hat farther back on his head, followed.

Fegan resisted the urge to go in and drag her out of there.

Charlotte Clairée Sumner's life really was none of his business, despite the fact that she'd once been an almost, sort of, surrogate little sister. She'd been at their house almost as much as he had, and he'd thought of her as their resident pest. It was all very confusing, trying to meld the Clairée from his wild youth with the red-skirted, high-heeled fox who had just swept through the parking lot, followed by his salivating cousin. And Fegan had to admit, the images she evoked in him these days were far from brotherly.

It bugged him that she was anywhere in Remy's vicinity, but he'd given up putting his nose into anyone's business for altruistic reasons the day he gave up his byline and his desk in the newsroom. He wasn't into saving anyone's ass but his own, unless he was being compensated monetarily for his efforts. And Clairée didn't qualify as a client. "So Remy's a bad-ass, womanizin' dog," he said, determined to shrug it off. "So he's about to hit on Char? What the hell difference does it make? Besides, you're better off mindin' your own damn business. Either she'll learn, or she won't."

It sounded good, but he couldn't quite stop himself from obsessing about her. The Pink Cadillac wasn't exactly the sort of place where nice girls hung out. In fact, it was his kind of place, full of good-timing, hard-drinking good old boys looking to chase away the boredom and maybe hook up with some pretty little piece for a few hours, or a few days. A carefree good time, lots of laughs, and no worryin' about the morning after. Clairée sure had no business being there, and she sure as hell had no business being there with low-down, no-good-for-nothin' Remy.

He reached for the keys, fighting the impulse to put his nose in their business. The less he knew about Remy, the better he liked it. Manny wasn't gonna show tonight. He'd just go home and check on his granddad, maybe have a beer and watch the stars from the back porch. Fegan started to turn the key in the ignition just as the action in the yellow truck ceased, the door swung open, and Terri Lynn Poutou slid out, followed closely by Angel Lavin.

Fegan leaned out the open car window. "That Angel

Lavin, he's lookin' for trouble, him. Terri Lynn, where's your kids?''

"My mama has 'em over in Lafayette—not that it's any of your business. What are you doin' out here, Fegan Broussard? You lookin' for that asshole I married?''

"Just protectin' my interests. You get yourself killed, I'll never see that money you owe me.''

"I'm scared," she said with a drunken laugh. "And you're fired. Manny Poutou can go get screwed. I don't want to see his big, ugly face no more.''

"You put a check in the mail, Terri Lynn.'' Fegan hit the ignition and the Pontiac engine roared to life. At the same time, a darker shadow separated from the underbrush at the edge of the parking lot and moved into the light. "Shit," Fegan said under his breath, jamming the gearshift into Park. Manny Poutou had a double-barreled shotgun cradled in the crook of one arm, murder in his dark eyes, and he was headed for the entrance to the Pink Cadillac.

CHAPTER THREE

Jimmy had been born restless, or so Aunt Eulanie had told Claire countless times over the years. It had been explanation enough for the fact that he'd never stayed with one job for more than twelve months, and had moved his wife and daughter from Louisiana to Texas, to California, and all over the Southwest before returning to the parish where he'd been born.

Claire had often speculated that life might have turned out differently for them all if they had just kept on moving, and had never returned to Louisiana. Perhaps if they'd been in another place, Jean Louise would have lived, and she herself wouldn't have been assaulted by a wave of bittersweet memories as she entered the Pink Cadillac Bar.

She had the oddest feeling that she'd fallen through the looking glass as she stepped onto the cypress plank porch, and for a split second, she imagined that she saw a childish hand reach out and touch the screen door. Strangely, she knew that hand was her own.

For the time it takes to draw a hurried breath, it was a hot summer evening, with the sun falling fast on the bayou, and her mother waiting impatiently in the Ford stationwagon in the parking lot.

Jean Louise fidgeted at Claire's side. "He in there?" she hissed.

"Don't know," Claire said. "I think so." Alberta Malloy, a resident of the small town of Angelique who tended bar on weekends, caught sight of Claire and laughed.

"Hey, Jimmy, looks like you got company."

Jimmy stubbed out his cigarette in the plastic ashtray and turned in time to catch Claire's eye. "Charlotte Clairée, what are you doin' down here?"

"Mama wants to know if you'll come home to supper."

He tossed back a whiskey and got up, slowly making his way to the door. "Now, why would I want to do that?"

" 'Cause Mama wants you to. She misses you, Dad. We both do."

"Get yourself back to the car, and tell your mam that I'll be on home in a little while. I'm waitin' to talk to a man about a job. Now, git! You, too, Jean Louise! Your grandpa would scalp you if he knew you were down here."

Claire reached for the door handle, the recollection as slow to fade as a trail of exhaust on a hot summer's day. It was eerie, how much the old place *hadn't* changed. The Pink Cadillac had the same plank floor, liberally coated with fragrant sawdust, the same old tunes on the antique jukebox, mixed with the new, and Alberta Malloy, a little grayer and slightly more stooped, still doling out hard liquor, the occasional soda, and ice cold beer on tap behind the monstrous mahogany bar. Cigarette smoke floated in a thick, blue haze near the ceiling, and the noise of the conversation, the music, and the laughter was only slightly below a decibel level that would risk permanent nerve damage.

The odd residue left by the flashback gave Claire second thoughts; she was just about to turn and go when someone slipped an arm around her waist. Startled, she glanced up, but it was only Remy Broussard grinning down at her, his brown eyes alight with the red glare from the neon beer sign hanging above the bar.

"Hey, sugar. You new in town?" His voice was warm and liquid, almost as warm and liquid as his cousin's. Claire immediately checked the thought. She wasn't about to let thoughts of Fegan Broussard ruin this opportunity. Smiling, she disengaged from his grasp, heading to the bar and sliding onto a stool.

Undaunted, Remy followed, taking the seat next to hers, signaling Alberta. "I'll have whatever the lady's havin'," he said. "And put it on my tab."

Alberta socked a fist on her hip and glared at him. "Until I get some cash for what you already owe, Remy, you ain't got no tab."

Claire took a ten out of her handbag and laid it on the bar. "Two beers, please."

"Not only is de lady fine, she knows how to treat a man. Unlike *some* folks I know." His hand closed around the bottle. "Hey, don't I know you? Dat face, it sure looks familiar." She started to speak, and he stopped her. "Jes' you wait, now. Gimme a minute." Narrowing his dark eyes, he pointed at her. "Sumner—used to hang wid my little cousin, Jean Louise. Clairée—*mais oui*, dat's it. Clairée Sumner. Ain't seen you for a long damn time, and all of a sudden here you are, hangin' in the Pink Cadillac. Alberta better watch out. Customers like you gonna bring some class to this low-down dive. Ain't that right, Alberta?"

"You gonna drink that beer?" Alberta said. "If not,

get yourself gone and give that stool to a payin' customer.''

"Dat Berta, she's jealous, her! She got a thing for Remy.'' Remy blew the barmaid a kiss, then winked at Claire as the older woman turned three shades of purple. "So . . . what'ch you doin' back in the parish—more importantly, what'ch you doin' here? Only three things bring anybody to de Pink Cadillac.''

"Oh, really?'' Claire said.

"Yeah, dat's right. De trinity—crawfish, ice cold beer, and a little action. You don't look hungry to me, sugar, and so far you ain't touched that beer.'' Remy finished his drink and Claire nodded to the bartender, indicating that she should set him up again.

A couple entered the bar, the woman in her late twenties with dark curly hair, a tank top that was too tight, and shorts that barely covered the cheeks of her behind. The young woman squealed as her companion, tall and wearing a straw western hat, slid into a chair and pulled her onto his lap.

"So how 'bout it, Clairée?'' Remy crooned. "Why you here?''

"I'm looking for someone.''

"Anybody I know?''

Claire shrugged. "Maybe. Someone who's well-connected.''

"Shit,'' Remy said. "Remy was born well-connected. What are we talkin'? You lookin' for some Ecstasy? Or is a little nose candy more your thing?''

Claire shook her head. "I don't want drugs. I want information.''

"Information?'' Remy swore. "What kind of information?''

"The accurate kind, if I can get it. And I'm willing to pay.''

Remy's expression closed as he picked up his beer and faced the mirror above the bar. "You some kinda undercover narcotics agent? 'Cause if you are, then I was lyin', and I don't know shit about nothin'."

"It doesn't matter to me what you do for fun or profit," Claire said. "What does matter is that someone in the parish gets his kicks out of killing young girls."

His look turned sly. "Dis about dat girl *Noncle* Amos Lee found last week, or Jean Louise?"

"Both," Claire admitted. "I have reason to believe the two deaths are connected."

"Or maybe you want dem to be," he suggested.

"If you can't help me, then I'll find someone who can," Claire said, sliding off the stool.

Remy's fingers closed over her arm. "Did I say dat? My work takes me lots of places, and sometimes I hear things."

Claire went still. "What kinds of things?"

"Dat depends. What kind of cash are we talkin'?"

"Fifty dollars," Claire said.

Remy snorted. "Ain't enough, dat."

"One hundred, then."

Remy shook his dark head. "Two-fifty, up front."

Claire hedged. "I don't have that kind of money on me, and even if I did, I'm not that gullible. I need to know that what I'm getting is worth it."

"Is straight from the coroner's report good enough for you?"

Claire counted out five twenties, and laid them on the bar. "It's all I have with me, but I can give you the rest first thing tomorrow morning."

Remy folded the bills and shoved them into his pocket. "I trust you, *chère,*" he said, back to being his old charming self now that he was certain he'd made a score. "Like I said, I do some odd jobs around, woodwork, yard work, sweepin' up, most recently over to Homer Folley's funeral parlor. You know Homer's the parish coroner, too, right? Dis week, Homer, he wanted the drawers on his desk fixed, and some of dem notes he wrote 'bout the autopsy of dat kid, they fell right out on de floor. Imagine dat.''

"Somehow I'm not having to work hard to picture it." Claire frowned at him. "There had better be more," she warned, "or I'm going to demand a refund in a very loud voice."

"Take it easy. I'm gettin' to it." He glanced up, and something in the mirror caught his eye. "Sorry, sugar, but dis is gonna have to wait. I gotta see a man about a dog. You stay here—I'll be right back."

Claire frowned as he slid off the stool and started to weave his way through the crowd toward the back, where the restrooms were located. She had a strange feeling of anticipation in the pit of her stomach, and she wondered if he planned to skip out on her. Then, she noticed his beer still sitting on the bar, beaded with condensation that coalesced, then trickled down to form a puddle. From there, her gaze drifted up, to the mirror behind the bar, following the same path that Remy's had taken before he excused himself, and Claire froze. A big man with a closely shaved head and a face like a boxer came to a stop a few yards away. As Claire watched with a mixture of horror and fascination, he leveled the shotgun he carried at the table just behind her, where the young couple groping one another sat.

The woman with the dark, curly hair looked up and screamed. Almost simultaneously, her partner stood up, dumping her onto her ass on the floor. "Hey, Manny," he said nervously, stepping back, holding his hands out, palms toward the man with the gun. "Look, man, I don't want no trouble."

"Looks like you got it anyway, don't it, Angel? Looks like you gonna get a chance to live up to your name, too. I hope you enjoyed that slut. Man, I hope she was worth it." He took one long step forward, smashing the butt end of the shotgun into the smaller man's chin. Angel dropped like a hot rock.

This is a really, really dumb thing to do, Claire told herself, cringing a little at the thought of getting involved. Remy was smart. He'd seen trouble coming and made himself scarce. *But she wasn't Remy,* she thought as she slid off her bar stool, carefully edging nearer to the woman crouched on the floor, and this wasn't the first time she'd done the wrong thing for the right reasons.

Claire moved, and the muzzle of the double barrel followed, the man's black eyes squinted above it. "What the fuck do you think you're doin'? Get away from there, or you goin' to hell wid her."

Claire held up a hand. She'd had some experience with difficult situations. She had gone out on a ledge once to try and persuade a mother of three forced to put her kids in foster care that there was a better way of coping with the ups and downs of life than to become a messy splat on the sidewalk. Stepping onto the ledge hadn't been the wisest thing to do—but it had worked, and that young mother now worked as a receptionist in Claire's office.

Sometimes, when parents were threatened with losing their kids, they went a little crazy. Usually, it was just a matter of getting them to calm down, to think rationally, of getting them to open up. This situation really wasn't all that different. At least, she hoped it wasn't. "Manny? That's your name, right? Manny, my name is Claire. I'm an attorney, and I can help you, if you'll let me."

"I don't need no lawyer *yet.*"

"Manny, put the gun down, please. We can talk about this, calmly. We can work something out."

"You crazy, lady? The time for talk's way past. It's time for me to put that crazy bitch where she belongs. Where she should'a been when she threw me out." He swung the barrel of the weapon down, training it on the woman crouching on the floor.

Not taking her eyes off him, Claire edged closer, then slowly dropped to a crouch beside Manny's estranged wife. "Dumb, Claire," she grumbled under her breath. "This is really, incredibly dumb."

"What you whisperin' to her?" Manny demanded.

"I'm not whispering anything to her," Claire assured him. "I was talking to myself. I do that when I'm nervous, and this isn't exactly the smartest thing I've ever done, putting my own life on the line for a whore like—what's your name, honey?"

The woman raised streaming eyes to Claire, ringed around with black mascara, and Claire thought that she looked like a confused raccoon. "Terri."

"A whore like Terri," Claire said, smiling a little to soften the harsh assessment. "You said she was a whore, right, Manny? And you'd know, of all people, isn't that right?"

"Not even a whore. Whores at least make a livin' off it. Dis here slut, she gives it away."

"A slut, then, and hardly worth your notice. Not really worth going to prison over, when you think about it. I'd be willing to bet she'd like that thought, wouldn't she? You behind bars at Angola? Even if they take pity on you, and you escape a death sentence, you won't ever see the light of day again." Claire tipped up Terri's chin, looking down into her raccoon eyes. "Gee, Manny, I don't know about you, but I don't think she's worth it."

"Who you callin' a slut?" Terri demanded.

"She's tryin' to help you, you dumb bitch."

"Who you callin' dumb, Manny?" Terri screeched. "I got my GED. You're the one with half a brain. Not enough wit to know I was gittin' it on wid your best friend last Christmas!"

Manny's face was taut and his eyes seemed lit from within. "Get back! I'm gonna finish dis now!"

Claire groaned. She was taking a real chance, but Manny's fury had a righteous quality to it, and something inside her whispered that he wouldn't willingly kill a stranger in cold blood. Like being on the ledge with the distraught twenty-three-year-old who'd just lost her job and was out on the street, she had to step carefully, and try not to push too hard. "She didn't mean that," Claire insisted. "She's scared, that's all. And sometimes we do and say things we shouldn't when we're scared, or angry . . . like you and the gun. You wouldn't normally bring a loaded shotgun into a bar and threaten anyone, would you?"

Terri sobbed, on the verge of hysteria. Screaming and cursing, tears ran in dirty rivulets over her cheeks. "You crazy dog, Manny! The kids'll hate you for this!"

Claire saw Manny tense. The veins stood out on his temples, and his dark eyes glittered with hatred. "Might as well hate me for somethin' I done, as for some shit you tol' dem!" he said. "Least you won't be around to fill 'em full of your poison no more!"

Rearing up on her knees, Terri suddenly lurched at Manny. Claire dragged her back, sitting her down hard on her rump on the floor, leaning into her face. "Sit down and shut up, before you get us both killed, or I'm going to step back and let him have at you." She turned to Manny. He was still angry, but it wasn't the same blind fury that had goaded him into the bar with the gun. "That's what this is about, isn't it? Your kids. Did she threaten to take them away from you?"

"She said she'd make it so my boys hate me," Manny admitted. "I tracked them down at her mama's, and the youngest, he wouldn't even look at me. Dat's when I decided she needed to die. I stood out there in de parkin' lot and bided my time while she did Angel. Now I'm gonna do her."

"You'll pay for this, Manny, you no-good son of a bitch!" the woman on the floor screeched, breaking free of Claire's grasp.

"Closed casket, honey," the big man promised, leveling the scatter gun at his wife's face. "There ain't gonna be enough of you left for Homer and his boys to putty back together!"

Claire sucked in a breath and thought about Jimmy and Aunt Eulanie. Jimmy wouldn't be happy to hear that his daughter had been fool enough to put herself in such an impossible situation, but Aunt Eule . . . Aunt Eule was going to be seriously pissed.

Manny was just beginning to test the tautness of the trigger when he suddenly went very still. Behind him was Fegan Broussard, looking like a man who could easily pull the trigger on the weapon he was holding, every bit as dangerous, every bit as lethal in intent as Manny Poutou.

As aware of Claire as she was of him, Fegan pressed the nose of his .38 hard against Manny's spine an inch below the big man's nape. Manny tried to look back, to see who was behind him and to gauge the threat, but when Fegan cocked the weapon Manny went stiff as a two-day-old corpse. "That you, Fegan Broussard?"

"That's right, Manny. How'd you know?"

"Those damn cross-trainers. Ain't seen nobody else

with shoes so disreputable. When you gonna buy yourself a new pair?"

"Why would I want to do that? These shoes are just
barely broke in. Been lookin' for you for a while now.
Where the hell you been?"

"I been around. Not that it's any of your business.
How 'bout you step back on outta here and lemme
finish what I come here to do?"

"Can't do that," Fegan said. "If I put down this gun,
you'll kill Terri Lynn, and if you kill Terri Lynn, my
bank account'll suffer some serious symptoms of with-
drawal, and I don't happen to like dead-end cases—or
dead clients, for that matter."

"She needs to die, Fegan. Shit, she's been beggin'
for some buckshot for weeks—and when you come right
down to it, ain't much you can do to stop me, now is
dere? You'll just save me some prison time, dat's all. I
kill her, you kill me . . ."

"You got it all worked out, *mon ami,*" Fegan said.
"Mais yeah, except for one little detail. I got no intention
of killin' you. But I'll sure enough make you wish you
were dead." Down on the floor, Terri Lynn moved, and
the crowd, which had scattered to the fringes of the
room, seemed to flinch. From the corner of his eye,
Fegan saw Clairée drag at Terri Lynn to keep her still.

Fegan swallowed hard. *Damn.* He wished he were dealing with anything but a domestic situation. Domestic
disputes were unpredictable, and so was Manny. Anything could happen, and like the fool that she was,
Clairée had put herself directly in the line of fire. He
could see her, just beyond Manny's big shoulder, sitting
on her pretty behind in the middle of the sawdust-
covered dance floor, holding on to a wild-eyed Terri.
There was no way Manny could carry out his threats
against his estranged wife without hurting Clairée, too.

"You really think I care what happens to me, Broussard?" Manny demanded, but he didn't move, and he didn't pull the trigger.

"Now, maybe not so much," Fegan admitted. "But that alcohol buzz you got goin' is gonna pass, and you'll care plenty when you're stone cold sober and breathin' with the help of a respirator. You ever piss through a plastic tube, Manny? That kind of paralysis don't go away, and that's a fact." He dug the pistol's muzzle a little more forcefully into Manny's back to press home his point, and hoped to Christ he didn't have to carry out his threat. "How 'bout it, Manny? You really want to be as limp as a mess of boiled collard greens for the rest of your life?"

A second's indecision, and Manny raised the barrel of the shotgun to the ceiling, holding it out at his side. Fegan took it from his grasp. At almost the same moment, the door opened and Cash Edmunds walked in. " 'Bout goddamned time you got here," Fegan said.

The deputy's blond hair was neatly combed, not a hair out of place, and he smelled faintly of after-shave. "Stop your complainin', Broussard. I'm here, ain't I? That's all that matters. Though your timing could've been better. I happened to be in the middle of some personal business when the call came in from dispatch." He jerked Manny's hands behind his back and cuffed him, then turned the larger man toward the door.

"Deputy, wait." To Fegan's amazement, Clairée was up off the floor in an instant, heedless of the sawdust clinging to her red, thigh-hugging skirt. "It should be noted in your report that while Mr. Poutou had ample opportunity to harm his wife, he failed to carry out his threats."

"Clairée Sumner," Cash said. "What the hell you doing back here?"

His question seemed to annoy her. "Does that really matter?"

"That depends on whether you're serious," Cash said with a laugh. "You really want to vouch for this piece of shit?"

"I'm an attorney, and Mr. Poutou has a right to counsel."

Fegan groaned inwardly. "Damn it, Char! Will you stay out of this?"

She flicked him a glance, then dismissed him. Her straight dark brows lowered, and a vertical frown line appeared between them. "Mr. Poutou has rights, and one of those rights is to a fair and just hearing. I want it noted on his arrest report that extenuating circumstances led up to this unfortunate incident, and that he acted with some amount of restraint during the confrontation."

Cash frowned. "If you intend to represent him, then you haul your pretty behind down to the station. Otherwise, get the hell out of my way."

"She was just leavin'," Fegan assured the deputy, taking Clairée by the arm and steering her through the door and into the night.

When they reached the parking lot, she pulled her arm from Fegan's grasp. "Just what the hell do you think you're doing?" she demanded.

"I guess I'm the one who ought to be askin' that question," Fegan replied. "What? You ain't got enough trouble over in Lafayette? You got to come back home to Angelique to get yourself killed?"

"You're blowing it all out of proportion, Fegan," Claire insisted, incensed that he would take it upon himself to slip into the big-brother act. He wasn't her brother. In fact, he was nothing to her but an ongoing source of problems, an obstacle standing between her

and whatever information Amos Lee might have, net-
tling her about matters that were none of his concern.
"I had the situation completely under control, at least
until you came in with the *Dirty Harry* routine."

"Under control?" he said, his voice rising with his
irritation. "You sound like you were the one holdin'
that scattergun. Do you know the kind of damage a
weapon like that does at close range? If I hadn't come
along when I did, they'd have been scraping you up
with a stick and a spoon by now."

So that was it, Claire thought. He wanted to play the
hero to helpless little Clairée, the wise and benevolent
protector. Well, there was one tiny flaw in his plan. She
wasn't the least bit interested, and she didn't need a
protector. Most importantly of all, she didn't need him.
"I know about guns, Fegan. In fact, I happen to own
one, along with a permit to carry it. So, I don't need
you to educate me."

"And where was your license to carry in there?" he
shot back. "The only firepower I saw was the one bein'
used in a hostage situation. And that ain't all. What the
hell business do you have with Remy?"

"You know, Manny was right about one thing—you
really should learn to mind your own damn business."
Claire stared at him, wanting to hate him, yet unsure
why. Maybe it had something to do with the fact that
she found him so incredibly attractive. She really should
make it a point to stay away from him, but that would
only work if he cooperated. And Fegan Broussard was
notoriously uncooperative. He always had been.

"Remy's bad business, Char. You remember that.
Where he goes, trouble ain't too far behind." He leaned
his weight into one hip, cocking the opposite knee,

looking easy and smooth, as if he didn't give a damn about anything, especially her. "Seems like the least you could do is thank me for savin' your pretty little ass back there."

Claire shook her head. "My 'ass' was never at risk. Manny Poutou wasn't going to kill anyone, least of all me. In fact, he was probably in more danger of killing himself than that faithless bitch he married." But she didn't really know that, could never really be certain what results desperation like Manny's would produce, and she did owe him something, whether she wanted to admit it or not, for bringing a non-tragic end to the situation. "But I will thank you for not resorting to violence when you easily could have. For not carrying out your threat."

He snorted. "Like I want to spend the best part of my evenin' down at the sheriff's office, answering questions. "Shit! C'mon. I'll walk you to your car." He reached for her hand, and amazingly, Claire didn't even try to pull away, but she did feel a strange thrill as his strong fingers folded around hers. He was warm, hard, and vital, and he'd just had a birthday on July the fourth. Fegan was thirty, four years older than she to the day. But at that moment, she felt fourteen, with all of the accompanying insecurities and nervous jitters, and she couldn't quite figure out what it was about him that transformed her from a competent professional into a silly teenager.

At the car, she fumbled with the keys, managing somehow to trigger the security alarm. The lights flashed, the horn blew, and Fegan laughed as he took the keys and turned the mechanism off. "Classy car," he said softly, switching gears with amazing alacrity. "Classy lady. But I remember when the lady refused to wear shoes. Used to drive your mama crazy."

Claire smiled. "She hated the fact that I was so wild. It was 'all that Sumner blood', she said. Aunt Eulanie running the farm, and Dad—" She broke off, acutely aware of the awkwardness of the moment. Jimmy was a sore subject with him, and had been since the tragedy of Jean Louise.

Strangely, he didn't seem to notice. He'd braced a forearm on the roof ledge of the BMW, staring intently down into her face. "Sometimes wild's a good thing, Char," he replied. "Sometimes it's a fine thing."

They were standing quite close, so close that Claire could smell the sweet tang of tobacco on him, and see her own reflection mirrored in his deep blue eyes. Staring up at him, unable to tear her gaze away, acutely aware of her own breath, Claire murmured, "I'm afraid that Mama didn't see it that way."

"Your mama was doin' what mamas do," he said softly. "At least, most times. Protectin' her little girl from the big, bad world. But you don't need protectin' anymore. You know what you're about . . . leapin' tall buildings in a single bound, stepping in front of twelve-gauge shotguns, keepin' good old girls from gettin' their brains blown out, drivin' every man with a pulse outta his head with the way you look, the way you talk, the way you move." He brushed her hair back with his fingertips, settling it behind her ear, then delicately traced its outer edge and around the sensitive lobe. "Kinda admirable, when you think about it. Is that who you are these days? Charlotte Clairée Sumner . . . champion of the poor and the drunk, and the criminally stupid?"

"Is that supposed to be flattering? Because if it is, then you definitely need more practice—and there's just one more thing. These days, nobody calls me Charlotte."

"I do," he said with a lopsided grin. "And you let me. Why is that, I wonder?"

She wasn't going to tell him that it was different somehow when he said it. That the way it rolled off his tongue had always sounded unbearably sexy, like he was thinking of something scandalous as he said it, something wicked. It made her think of hot, sweaty nights and a heated embrace . . . most assuredly, she would never let him guess that when she pictured herself in that situation, she was always with him. "I suppose it's because I can't stop you. You always were hardheaded, a royal pain in the ass. You did what you wanted, when you wanted."

"Life's too short not to, sugar," he told her. "You ought to know that. Do you know what I want right now?"

"A cigarette?" Claire said, hoping to lighten the mood. It didn't work.

He just stared down at her, his smile fading, and her heart did a crazy little two-step in her chest. "Not a smoke, darlin'. I want you."

Claire could have easily moved away. She could have discouraged him in at least a hundred ways. Instead, she made the situation worse by meeting the kiss halfway, by leaning into the long, hard length of his muscular frame as his arms closed around her. "I wanted to do this back at the house," he admitted. "It's all I been thinkin' about."

"Me, too," she whispered, almost against her will. He had that effect on her, like a dangerous dare that she couldn't ignore, and couldn't resist. His presence, his magnetism, that pure animal something that set him apart from other men and made every woman's head turn when he entered a room, made her do things she knew were unwise, downright foolhardy. In keeping with the spell he put her under, she parted her lips as he claimed them, welcoming him into her mouth. It was a deep kiss, the kind of kiss that made her want to curl her toes. A kiss that was intentionally beguiling.

Sexy Fegan, always the tease.

There was something about him that promised fulfillment, a damn rousing good time. He made Claire want even more than he was offering, so that she never even flinched when she felt his fingers working down the buttons of her blouse, his own shirt already half open to the sultry Louisiana night. She slipped her hands inside the worn, soft cotton fabric, urging the gap wider, running her fingertips over his smooth, dark skin as she savored the feel of naked male under her hands. Then, she felt the warm metal chain and the oval-shaped medallion lying in the shallow valley over his heart and pulled away from his mouth.

Feeling a strange pang, like a tiny stab to the subconscious, she lifted it, studying it even as he worked small, excruciatingly provocative nibbles down her throat. A Saint Christopher medal, patron saint of travelers. Jean Louise had given him one just like it just before he left home at the age of eighteen. Holding the warm medal in her hand, she felt how worn and smooth its edges were, and knew it had to be the same one.

"Why don't you come on back to my place," he murmured against the hollow at the base of her throat; then, finally noticing how quiet, how still she had gotten, he pulled back just far enough to look down at her.

Fegan saw the medal lying in the heart of her palm, the medal his sister had given him so long ago . . . a sister in her grave because of Clairée's old man. Of course she would recognize it. She'd been at the house the day Jean Louise gave it to him. "You never took it off," she said. "You've worn it all these years."

"It was the last thing she ever gave me," he said simply, failing to add that he had never seen Jean Louise alive again. He didn't need to say it aloud. Clairée knew it, just like he did, and for a split second he had the strange impression that it was as raw a knowledge for her as it was for him. "She was my baby sister, Char. She didn't cry to Frank when Mama left. She came to me."

"And she was my friend," she said, the reply squeezed out, tight-sounding. "The best friend I have ever had in this world. But I didn't just lose her, Fegan. I lost my dad and my mom, too."

"You're not comin' with me, are you?" he said, already certain of the answer.

"I can't."

"You can. You want what I want. I can feel it, Char. Ain't nothin' wrong with that."

"Want you?" She smiled, settling the medallion carefully between his pecs, then laying her hand against his cheek. "Oh, yeah. I've wanted you forever—or, at least, that's how it seems. You always were a major turn-on." A weary sigh. "Unfortunately, there's no room for someone like you in my plans." She sniffed once, and started to put her blouse back together. "I really should be going. Aunt Eulanie will worry if I don't get home soon." Then, without looking back, she got in the BMW and drove from the parking lot.

Fegan watched her go with a mixture of anger and regret. She was right about one thing. There was no room in her life for someone like him, and he had no business even thinking that way about the daughter of Jimmy Sumner. But none of that did a damn thing to ease the unsatisfied ache in his midsection, or the

certainty that he was going to live with the regret for
letting her walk out on him for a long, long time. When
her taillights were just a red dot in the tangle of vine
at the edge of the parking lot, he turned and went back
inside the bar.

CHAPTER FOUR

In the place between sleep and full consciousness, Claire found Jean Louise. It happened each morning, and had for almost a week. She'd dreamt of her before, infrequently, dreams about childhood: the pranks they'd played; the long, lazy summer days spent poling Amos Lee's pirogue along the edge of the bayou; going still when an alligator basking in the afternoon sun slipped silently into the silt-rich water and glided away; and giggling at Fegan's stern warning that if they weren't careful, they'd get eaten. Those dreams, half sepia-toned memory, half nostalgia, were welcome. But this . . . this was different.

The Jean Louise who came to Claire was a budding adolescent. Small and dark, with Fegan's sapphire eyes and a figure with a great deal of unrealized promise. As gawky as a long-legged colt, she perched on the end of Claire's bed. *Dieu, Clairée, I never thought you'd be comin'*

*back here. You said so when you left. Said you hated the bayou,
hated the town.*

"I can't believe you're here," Claire said.

Not here? the girl demanded. *'Course I'm here! Where else
would I be?* Her blue eyes turned sly, mischievous. *Saw
you last night, kissin' Fegan. Thought you said you didn't like
him.*

"I didn't kiss him," Claire insisted. "He kissed me."

Go on, pick nits. She stretched out a hand to examine
her nails, and Claire noticed how bloodless she looked.
Her skin seemed waxy, transparent. *Is that why you came
home, to see Fegan?*

"Not for Fegan. For you, silly . . . I came because of
you. I need to know what happened."

The light left Jean Louise's eyes, and they gradually
glazed over. Her lips took on a slight tinge of blue. *Don't
stay here, Clairée. You can't stop him. No one can . . .*

Claire came fully awake with a start, pushing back the
damp, tangled sheet and sitting up. She glanced at the
foot of the bed, but it was empty, and the covers were
smooth. She could find no evidence that anyone had
been sitting there, but the room was unusually cold.
Sliding off the high bed, she went to the thermostat
and adjusted the air; then, hugging her arms against
the unnatural chill, she opened the French doors and
stepped onto the second-floor gallery.

The air outside was balmy and a fitful breeze played
through the tattered gray Spanish moss in the live oak
that shaded the gallery and the front portion of the
house. A menacing gray-blue showed at the horizon,
just above the trees and the red tin roof of the tractor
barn in the distance. A storm gathering, Claire thought,
perhaps in more ways than one.

A half-hour later, she sipped juice on the lower gallery
and watched Eulanie pick up her fork, then put it down

again. Eulanie was a firm believer in a hearty breakfast, and she'd barely eaten more than a few forkfuls of her buttered grits, bacon, and toast. "You ain't hungry, Miss Eule?" Jane asked, frowning.

"It's no reflection on your culinary skills, Jane. No one has a way with a mess of grits like you do. The plain truth is, it's just too hot to eat. It's old age creeping up, I guess, but the heat wears me out."

Claire exchanged looks with the housekeeper. Eulanie, seeing it, growled, "Oh, for pity's sake. Don't look that way, either of you."

"What way's that, Miss Eule?" Jane asked.

"Like you're afraid I'll fall dead on the floor at any moment. I'm fine."

"I believe you," Claire said. "But I'm also worried about you, and it would ease my mind considerably if you would see a doctor. It's just a check-up. Where's the harm?"

"The harm is that I've got contracts to fill. Life on a farm just keeps going, and I've got a tractor down. I don't have time to waste on tests just to have some young overachiever with a medical degree tell me what I already know. *I am fine.*"

Claire sighed. "Aunt Eule, except for Daddy, you're the only family I've got left. I can't afford to lose you, too."

Eulanie's expression clouded. She leaned forward, laying a hand over Claire's. "I'm not going anywhere—except to that shed out there to get that old Case off its blocks and workin' again. But if it makes you happy, I'll call Trelawney and make an appointment for sometime next week."

"Promise?" Claire said. A rangy-looking bluetick hound trotted around the gallery and loped up the steps, plopping down beside Eulanie's chair.

"Promise," Eulanie replied, reaching down to pat the hound's broad head, but looking at Claire. "You came in rather late last night." Her gaze was sharp, and Claire wondered if there was anything Eulanie missed.

"I hope I didn't wake you."

Eulanie snorted. "These days if I sleep from twelve till three, I consider it a full night. Jeb's in the same sad shape, isn't that right, boy?" The dog let out a single, bone-chilling bay, thumping his long tail on the gallery floor. It was as close to a grin as he could manage. "It's no fun getting old, Claire."

"You're not old," Claire insisted. "But you do need to take better care of yourself."

"There she goes again," she said, leaning down to offer Jeb a strip of bacon, then extricating herself from the linen tablecloth.

She whistled once and the hound followed, trotting along beside her. Claire watched her progress with a critical eye. She certainly didn't look like someone with a heart condition. Maybe she worried for nothing. Maybe everything really *was* all right, just as Eulanie insisted, but she remained concerned and skeptical, and made a silent vow to hold Eulanie to her promise.

Homer Folley's funeral home was in the larger neighboring town of Point Breeze, eight miles from Angelique. A low brick building painted white, it had a large sign on the small patch of green that passed as a lawn, proclaiming that it had been established in 1953. Three generations of Folleys had been in the mortuary business, a circumstance that would eventually change, since Homer was the last of his line. At fifty-three, he was unlikely to beget a fourth generation to carry on, given the fact that William, Homer's housemate, was a young man nearly half his age.

Claire stepped out of the BMW, adjusting her cream

linen suit. She'd chosen the sleeveless vest and skirt for the coolness factor, but the weather had turned so oppressive that even naked would have been seriously overdressed.

Head down and walking fast, her main objective to find Remy and get out of the heat, she nearly fell over the man trimming sod away from the edge of the sidewalk. "Hey, *chère*, you wanna watch where you're walkin', or you'll end up on your ass on de grass." He turned his ball cap around, the bill jutting out at his nape. "Fine lookin' ass you got dere, too. You busy tonight, sugar? Maybe you want to trot on down to de Royale? Dey got a hot band playin', and I got a few bills burnin' a hole."

"Courtesy of yours truly," Claire said. "You're a jerk, Remy. And I don't date jerks. You promised me information, and then you skipped out on me."

"What, me? I din' skip nowhere, *chère*. I got a page on my beeper when I was walkin' my dog, and with Remy, business always comes first, 'cept when it comes to pleasure. Besides, dat was just a down payment. You said two-fifty. All I got was a C-note. I thought we had us a deal."

"You're such a blatant, unrepentant con artist."

"Guess you changed your mind 'bout dat information."

Claire's gaze narrowed. "Will you take a check?"

"Local bank?"

"Lafayette."

"That'll do." He glanced at the amount. "You got an ID?"

Claire raised her brows and gave him her best, most penetrating female-lawyer-dealing-with-male-stupidity look, and he backed down. "Shit, man, the lady can't take no joke."

"Give me the rundown, and I want details."

Another glance at the building. "You ain't gonna leak dis, are you? 'Cause I don' want to lose dis here job." Then, when she threatened to tug the check from his hand, "All right, all right. Easy does it, sugar. Easy does it. Dere was some pretty weird shit in Jane Doe's file. Took me a while just to figure out Homer's handwriting. Looks a lot like chicken-scratchin's."

"What weird shit, Remy?" Claire persisted in an attempt to keep him focused.

Remy shrugged. "Cause of death was asphyxiation, but she had some kind of burn marks. Not from a cigarette, or fire. Electrical burns."

"As in electrocution?"

"As in apparatus . . . like a stun gun."

"She was tortured? Oh, my God."

Peut-être que oui, peut-être que non. Maybe yes, maybe no. Old Homer seems to think so."

"There's more, isn't there?" Claire said, sensing he was holding back.

Remy shrugged. "Her heart weighed in at nine point two ounces. Can you imagine dat?"

Claire had the mad urge to put her hands over her ears. She didn't want to hear the grim details, not really. She worked defending and protecting, and watch-dogging the best interests of children, and unfortu-nately, she empathized only too well. The inability to set aside the more troubling cases had cost her sleep, and shaken her faith in humanity. Admittedly, letting go didn't come easily. "Yes, damn it, I can imagine it."

"You too impatient, sugar. You need to learn to lay back and go with the flow."

Claire glared at him. "Damn it, Remy. I don't have the time, or the patience, or the freaking luxury of going with the flow. Either tell me what you know, or cough up the cash."

"Dat kid was found facedown in the bayou, but there wasn't no water in de lungs, and dere was clay under her fingernails." He paused, as if waiting for her reaction.

"So?"

"No clay in the bayou, sugar. Dirt's black down there from all de rotted vegetation. Bruise marks on her wrists, too, 'long wid traces of adhesive. Dat kid was restrained with duct tape, then a plastic bag was put over her head . . . but it din' happen in Angelique."

"So she was killed elsewhere, and dumped in the swamp."

"Probably dey was hoping de evidence wouldn't last long, if you catch my drift."

Oh, she caught it all right. Feeling a little nauseous, she muttered her thanks and turned toward the parking lot and the BMW, Remy's voice trailing out behind her. "Hey, Clairée! Dis mean you ain' goin' out wid me?"

"You got it, Slick" Claire said, sliding into the driver's seat and cranking up the air.

The dinner hour had come and gone, but Claire didn't appear at table. Eulanie's queries were all met with the same vague answer: "Sorry, Aunt Eule, but I don't seem to have much of an appetite this evening."

"You're not takin' ill, are you?" Eulanie looked concerned.

Claire tried to smile, but had no doubt she'd failed miserably. "No, nothing like that. I'm just tired." It hadn't been a total fabrication. She was tired, sick at heart, her spirit worn raw by the certain knowledge that she lived in a world where a thirteen-year-old could be tortured and killed. She found herself staring at the artist's sketch, and wondering if somewhere a family watched and waited. Or was there no one who cared? Too often, the life a runaway fled fully matched the uncertain future they ran to, horror for horror.

Unable to stop her mind from churning up scenarios, feeling she would go mad and fling herself from the second-floor gallery if she didn't escape the house, she went for a walk. The Willows consisted of one hundred and fifty acres of soil that was perfectly suited for the cultivation of sugar cane. The property's eastern boundary bordered on Bayou des Cannes ... the same dark stream that channeled its winding way past the town of Angelique ... the same dark waters in which the dead girl had been found.

It was past seven in the evening, and the sun would soon be going down. That same dark channel dappled gold in the distance looked strangely serene, and even though she knew the impression was deceptive, it proved an irresistible lure. Before she had time to reconsider, Claire found herself at the small, wooden dock and adjoining boathouse at the water's edge.

The earthy fragrance of water and mud, a variety of plant life living and dying in an unending cycle of decay and regrowth, and an abundance of wild creatures were the stuff of Claire's childhood and they brought back memories. Jimmy had taught her to fish from this dock, and he'd insisted that she bait her own hooks. Jean Louise had no qualms about handling the nightcrawlers, but Claire, who had always had an aversion to insects, struggled with her fears while Jimmy's soft, patient voice talked her through the process.

With the rough boards of the dock underfoot, Claire closed her eyes and breathed deeply, as if the soft evening air would somehow help to preserve the memory, make it linger. But it faded, and as it did, the feeling of quiet despair returned.

Had she ever been so frightened? she wondered. So unsure of herself? So aware of her own glaring inadequacies?

What if she couldn't pull it off? Finding evidence linking two crimes a decade apart seemed a monumental task—Mt. Everest, figuratively speaking, and she was on the ground in Nepal looking up. She was an attorney, not an investigator. She dealt in legal briefs, loopholes, and continuances, not leads and information. Yet, what choice did she have? And how would she live with herself if she failed and her father lost his life?

Unfortunately, there weren't any answers. Just the deepening blue of the storm that had been gathering throughout the day and the low hum of an outboard motor in the distance. In a moment, the small green aluminum boat belonging to Amos Lee Prideau came into view. Claire strained to see the identity of the man at the controls. From the breadth of his shoulders and the ease with which he brought the craft into shore, she guessed it wasn't Amos Lee. The bright wink of the sunlight on a pair of small gold hoop earrings confirmed her suspicions.

"Evenin', mamzelle," he drawled as he nosed the bow in and cut the engine. "Care for some fresh crawfish? Got some nice, big ones." He tipped up the wicker creel to reveal the mud-colored shellfish crawling over one another. "Got some big cats, too, if fish is more your fancy."

"Crawfish, catfish. Have you given up surveillance completely, or is this just your day job?"

He shrugged, grinning. "Man's got to do something for relaxation. What do you do when you're not busy bein' a lawyer-lady? Or'd you forget how to relax?"

Claire bristled. The question hit too close to home. She couldn't remember the last time she'd been out on a date. She'd been through all of that. In fact, she'd done it to death, and nothing constructive ever seemed to come of it. Finally, she'd stopped putting pressure on herself to find that perfect relationship, the man who could slide on into her life as if born to it . . . the one she belonged with. She was twenty-six. She had plenty of time. "Is that why you stopped here, to give me a hard time about my social life? If it is, then you can take your crustaceans and get on out of here."

"I stopped by because I saw a pretty lady standin' on the dock, and I wanted a better look. Nice to see you in somethin' sweet and feminine, instead of those business suits you usually wear. Specially since you ain't wearin' no slip."

Claire glanced down at her pale peach sundress. With the setting sun at her back, her figure was clearly silhouetted—her long legs, the space between. "You're an unprincipled letch, Fegan Broussard."

The grin widened, and deep dimples flashed in his sun-bronzed cheeks. "I know, but you like it." His smile faded just a little. "Wanna go for a boat ride?"

"With you? I don't think that's such a good idea."

"There was a time when you begged me for a boat ride into the bayou."

"I was a child, and I didn't know any better."

"And now you know better," he said, taking off his long-sleeved white shirt. "But you can't resist. Come on, Char. It'll be fun." His T-shirt advertised Wooley's Naked Bait and Tackle, and stretched taut over his shoulders and chest. Claire couldn't quite stop herself from wishing that he'd take it off, too. "Oh, yeah, that's right. You're all grown up now, a lawyer-lady, and lawyer-ladies don't like to have fun. Ain't that right?"

It was a dare, and they both knew it. Claire watched as his soot-colored lashes drifted down slightly, masking the challenging light in his blue eyes, giving him a lazy, careless look. He was offering her an escape, and though getting into a small aluminum boat with Fegan wasn't wise, she found that she was strangely grateful. In fact, on a deep, nearly unconscious, almost primal level, the thought excited her, though she would have jumped fully clothed into the bayou before admitting it to him. "All right. I'll go with you, but there's one condition."

"And what's that, darlin'?"

"I won't share a boat with catfish." She pointed at the bucket and creel, watching as Fegan lifted both onto the dock, then reached up and offered his hand.

"No catfish in this boat," he replied. "C'mon back here and sit beside me, Sugar, and if you're extra nice, I might even let you drive."

Their pace was slow, leisurely. Wherever Fegan was taking her, he was in no particular hurry. Claire perched on the narrow aft seat, a wooden board that showed her bottom no mercy. They hadn't been gone for ten minutes, and she was already numb and wanting to squirm. Only the knowledge that if she moved, she would come into contact with the muscular arm a mere inch from the modest spread of her flowered chintz skirt kept her still, and watchful.

The dark water parted for the bow of the boat, fanning out on either side in continuous twin waves that multiplied as they swept by, becoming many, slapping the muddy shore with a far greater force than that which they had used in passing. Houses stacked on thick pilings nosed right up to the edge of the bayou, their screened porches overhanging the stream. High-pitched squeals and childish laughter drifted out over the water, shadowed figures darting back and forth in the dim recesses of the porch. In a moment, they were left behind, and the silence so indicative of the time before twilight fell enveloped them again.

Another quarter-mile, and a houseboat came into view. Tethered to a dock, it was a gay mix of yellow, red, and green. Fegan cut the motor, drifting toward the dock. "Friends of yours live here?"

"Guess you could say that I know just about everybody on this bayou." He tied the craft off and stepped onto the dock, reaching down to pull her up beside him. "A cold one sure would taste good about now. Think these folks got some beer?"

The place appeared deserted. No footsteps sounded inside. The curtains were still, and the only sound was the lap of the water against the wooden hull and the bothersome buzz of the mosquitoes. He stopped to glance back at her, one foot on the deck, the other on the dock. "You comin'?"

"Trespassing on private property?" She shook her head. "Not on your life. And you shouldn't, either."

"Why? These folks ain't gonna care."

"Fegan, no one's home! Aside from not having respect for the property of others, it's a good way to get your head blown off."

"Me? Nah! I can handle myself just fine—better than those city boys you been hangin' out with." He boarded the houseboat and headed to the galley doors. "Not even locked," he said over one broad shoulder. "What kind of fool leaves a fine boat like this one open to intruders?"

Claire watched in disbelief as the door swung open. He was going in. "C'mon, Fegan, this isn't funny. Fegan?"

"Won't take but a minute," he said, disappearing into the shadows of the galley. "We'll be outta here before you know it." For a moment there was quiet, then his voice filtered through the half-closed doors. "Hey, man. The lady and I, we just wanted a beer. No harm meant, honest. What the—hey look, ain't no need for that. Put down the gun. Put down the—" Pop!

Rooted to the dock by the unexpected exchange, Claire teetered on the edge of panic. "Fegan? Oh, God, Fegan! I'm coming in!" Holding her hands in the air, she crept onto the deck, each step feeling as though it was her last. "Fegan, are you—?"

Claire pushed open the doors and saw him standing in the galley, a smoking bottle of champagne in one hand, two crystal flutes in the other. He quirked a brow. "Hey, sugar, you thirsty?"

Claire lingered in the open doorway, one hand on the jamb, one over her heart, which thumped under her ribs like a terrified bird. Her gaze moved from his handsome face to the photographs on the wall of the galley: three kids, two boys and a much smaller girl, posed in front of Amos Lee's old Cadillac; a young, dark-haired boy hugging a redtick coon hound, his wide grin as infectious then as it was at this moment; two young girls perched in the lower limbs of a live oak tree, one tall, one short, both smiling coquettishly for the camera . . . "Damn you, Fegan, did you have a good laugh?"

"*Mais* yeah, I did," he admitted, taking the champagne out on the deck to the modest table and chairs. "You should've seen the look on your face when you came flyin' in there."

"I thought you'd been shot," she said, giving him a shove as she passed by him. "That was a dirty trick, the worst thing anyone has done to me in a long, long time."

"Ah, c'mon, Char," he said softly, cajolingly. "It was just a joke."

"You could have told me you owned the place." Claire crossed her arms in front of her breasts, pretending to be angrier than she really was. In a lot of ways, he was still that boy in the photo, clutching the goofy-looking, pale-eyed dog, and grinning for all he was worth—and maybe he always would be. It was part of his charm, one of the things that made him so attractive to the opposite sex . . . and in that respect, she was no exception.

"Be honest. If I'd told you we were comin' here, to my houseboat, would you have come with me?" His gaze was soft on hers, his blue eyes startlingly vivid against his sun-tanned skin. She said nothing, giving him the argument he wanted. "No, you wouldn't have. You would have made some lame excuse 'bout havin' to wash your hair, or somethin', and we wouldn't be here right now, enjoyin' what's left of this beautiful evenin'."

Claire shot a glance at the threatening sky. The thin strip of horizon showing beneath the deep blue clouds had gone a sickening greenish yellow. "It's going to rain," she replied, simply for the sake of contrariness.

"You don't like rain, then you don't belong in Lou'si-ana." He splashed champagne into the flutes and offered her one.

Claire accepted it. She took a sip, then another, and some of the tension slowly slipped away. "I thought you were living at Amos Lee's in Angelique."

He didn't sit, instead choosing to lean against the starboard railing, lithe and dark-skinned; wonderfully, enticingly male. Claire stood with her back against the same rail, a few feet away. "Most of the time. I bought this place a couple of years back, so I'd have somewhere to stay when I came back to visit. The house damn near went for back taxes last summer. Guess you could say I rescued it. I was hopin' Pépère would come around, take interest, but he seems to prefer livin' in the cottage out back. Maybe the old place has too many memories for him to handle bein' there—I don' know."

"But you kept the houseboat," Claire said. It was the first time he had opened up, the first time he'd been anything but flip with her, and the feeling it gave her, being allowed into his world, his life, was unbelievably heady. She didn't stop to question why that was. She was strangely afraid of destroying the moment.

He sipped his champagne, smiling. "It's the only way I can get away from Frank. Sometimes, I just wanna pop him one, you know? So, I come out here, with the fish, and the birds, and the quiet, and he leaves me alone. What about you, Char? Where do you go when it all gets to be too much?"

"There isn't any escaping it, Fegan, and I don't have the luxury of time that you have. I can't let Dad down— I can't let myself down—" Claire broke off, sighing. "I don't expect you to understand. I know what you think." Her voice softened. "I know what you feel."

He toyed with the stem of the flute. It looked fragile in his strong fingers. "Jimmy ask you to come?"

Claire shook her head. "He doesn't want me here."

He digested this piece of information in silence. "I ran into Remy earlier today. He was down at the Cadillac, flashin' a wad of bills big enough to choke a two-year-old filly. Now, where do you s'pose he came by that kind of cash?"

She shrugged, unwilling to give him what he wanted. "Why don't you ask Remy?"

"I did," he replied, raising his gaze to hers. His expression was questioning, frankly curious, and for a moment, it flashed in Claire's brain that this was what he'd been like in Chicago, only to the nth power. "He told me a lady gave it to him for services rendered. A very generous lady. How 'bout it, Char? You buyin' information from Remy?"

"What if I am?" she asked, tilting her chin up, wondering why it was always like that between them: challenging, competitive, intense. He possessed the power to walk into a room and put her senses on high alert. It wasn't a matter of him pissing her off. It wasn't anger, exactly, or hostility—in fact, she wasn't quite sure what it was between them, except that she didn't react precisely that way with anyone else.

He tossed back the last swallow of champagne and put his flute on the table. "Remy's bad business. You get mixed up with Remy, you're askin' for big-time trouble."

"I can look out for myself," she assured him.

Her gaze was so direct, so filled with determination, that Fegan was almost convinced. Remy was blood, but Fegan had a way of finding out things, and there was a lot about Remy that Clairée didn't know. Fegan didn't want Clairée within five hundred yards of him. Trouble didn't just find Remy; he went looking for it. "I wish I believed that," he said. Reaching out, he touched her. He had to. He needed the feel of her, warm, willing . . . needed the taste of her, honeyed and wild, wanted to drink in the temptation that was her perfume until she filled up his senses, until there was nothing but her in his world. "Wish I could get you outta my head."

She gazed deeply into his eyes, that unflinching, straightforward glance that had always annoyed and perplexed him. Her lips parted, revealing the glistening pink tip of her tongue poised behind her strong, white teeth. "Why do you want to?"

" 'Cause you're as bad for me as I am for you."

The champagne flute dangling from her fingers, she leaned closer, never taking her eyes from his. "Am I?" Fegan's heart pounded heavily in his chest, sledge-like, pushing the hot blood through his veins.

The fingers of the hand not holding her champagne played along his cheek, his jaw, down his throat, and he needed no further encouragement. He kissed her. A kiss that shot through him like lightning, searing, a kiss that left no room for doubt about where this encounter was leading.

His intent communicated itself clearly to Claire. She understood what he was feeling, she knew the flashing bright-white sense of need that cried out for something hot and fast and purely physical, something that would only bring regret in a minimal sense of the word, and only after the heat had incinerated the intense sensual craving gripping them both. "Let's go someplace more private," she whispered against the corner of his mouth. "Someplace we can be alone."

In the past, Claire had had a short but notable list of lovers. Rudy, the professional soccer player, who'd had a silk stocking fetish and whose apartment had smelled like old sweat socks. She'd gotten as far as the living room, but she hadn't lingered. Julio, a district attorney from San Antonio, whom she'd met on a blind date and dated for six months. He'd wanted a backyard full of kids, had been on a fast track toward marriage and commitment, but Claire hadn't been ready for anything quite that permanent. And John Milan Westford, you've-got-your-own-private-jet? sort of wealthy. She'd progressed to the meet-the-parents stage when suddenly she'd realized he was so boring that she almost fell asleep during sex. There had been one or two others somewhere between, but no one truly memorable. No one she had ever wanted as much as she wanted Fegan.

She pulled his T-shirt up and over his head, dropping it onto the deck, then proceeded to dribble champagne in the hollow between his shoulder and his collarbone. He sucked in a startled breath, then watched lazily as she kissed him there, tonguing all traces of the liquid from his smooth, bronze skin.

"Now, where'd you learn somethin' like that?" he questioned softly.

Claire smiled. "You'd be surprised what I know," she said, mere inches away from his mouth. "Now, if you don't mind, I'd like to go home."

Long after Claire had left a bemused Fegan at the dock, long after the lights in her bedroom at The Willows winked out, the beam of a flashlight fell upon a patch of woods not too many miles away. He didn't come here during the daylight hours. He couldn't risk being seen out here, couldn't afford to have anyone get curious. The neglected house in the pines—indeed, his life, his somewhat unusual habits—would never bear up under an intense scrutiny. It wasn't something that kept him awake nights. He slept like a baby, secure in the knowledge that he'd been born under a fortunate star. The world would continue to smile upon him. He was the perfect example of a favorite son.

Stepping carefully, he followed the narrow path that skirted the house, stopping in the weed-choked cemetery beyond. Surrounded by a hedgerow of honeysuckle that he'd personally ordered planted, it had an air of quiet peace about it, a solemnity that seeped into his bones. It wasn't often that he felt anything, but coming here in the dead of night, he knew a sense of purpose, of being what the universe had made him. A taker of life. The deliverer of death. Every parent's worst nightmare.

Shining the light on the bone-white crypt, he ran his fingertips lovingly over the notches he'd carved into the stone. The angel kneeling atop the crypt had its eyes closed. Somehow, it seemed appropriate. No one saw. No one would ever know.

Then, his morbid need for the moment satisfied, he made his way back to his home, his other persona, his other life.

CHAPTER FIVE

"Yeah, uh-huh. When and where did this occur?" Cash Edmunds jotted down notes while cradling the phone in the curve of his shoulder. "You're sure about that? All right, then. Someone will be stoppin' by to talk to you this morning. Bye, bye, now." He hung up the phone, got out of his chair, and walked to his superior's office, rapping lightly on the wooden door.

A muffled "What is it?" came through the panel. Cash opened the door, but not fully, just far enough to put his head and one shoulder into the room. Sheriff Vance Pershing had a reputation for not being a morning person, and since the floater had been found in the swamp, he'd been in a particularly vile mood. A slight man with narrow shoulders, a flat-top hair style that was still more blond than silver, and wiry build, he reminded Cash of an older Gary Busey, only sadly lacking Busey's legendary affable charm, he thought with a heavy helping of sarcasm. Pershing didn't bother to look up from the paperwork he was initialing. "I assume you intruded on my morning for a reason, Deputy. Are you going to tell me what that is? Or have you developed a fondness for the feel of that doorknob?"

Cash reddened slightly. Pershing didn't like him, and didn't like the fact that power and influence had helped to get him this position. Not that Cash gave a particular damn. This job was the only thing his connection with Ashton Morlay had gotten him, and it was little enough by way of compensation. That Pershing didn't bother to hide his disdain still rankled. "Sorry to interrupt you, Sheriff, but that was Mrs. Reed on the phone, and she says there's something odd going on at Miz Felix's place out on Bayou Road."

"Did she, indeed?" He scribbled a line in that cramped and miserly scrawl, paused to push his wire-rimmed glasses up on his sharp nose, then scribbled again while Cash fantasized about ripping the Bic pen from his grasp and forcing him to use a pencil with a dull point. Always a Bic pen, the cheap kind, blue ink only, not black or red or green, the rigid, anal old bastard . . . and Christ help anyone who had the balls to borrow it. That damned pen was some sort of weird and symbolic fixation with him.

Cash ground his teeth behind an affable smile. "Yes, sir. She says she saw a rather large black man hanging around out there."

"I am sure she did. But the man she saw is Miz Felix's nephew, John. He comes by once a week to make sure that his aunt has everything she needs, and to make any minor repairs that might be necessary." Pershing picked up his pen once more, shifting his attention from Cash to the papers in front of him. "How long have you been here, Edmunds?"

"Six years last April, sir."

"And how often have you taken similar calls from Mrs. Reed during that time?"

"At least once a month, I reckon."

"Now, there's a conservative estimate," Pershing said. "In case you haven't noticed, Mrs. Reed has a little trouble with paranoia. Last week it was drug dealers. This week, it's a phantom black man. Next week, she'll be headed back to the hospital for a 'rest'. But for all that, we can't just dismiss her complaint on the infinitesimal chance that there's some validity to it, now can we?"

"You want me to drive over there and check it out?" Pershing's penetrating gaze drifted up to Cash's again, and it was all he could do not to flinch.

"Why don't you do that, Deputy?" Pershing said. "It would do my heart good to know that you're busy keeping the fine citizens of our parish safe from the phantom bad elements of society." Hatred dripped from every syllable. Cash felt it, and returned it, though in a far more covert fashion. "And be sure to close the door on your way out."

Cash did as requested, closing the door, resisting the urge to slam it, and settled instead for a one-fingered salute given to the drawn blinds of Pershing's office. "Incompetent old prick." Snagging his hat from his desk, he headed for the door, unable to get clear of the stuffy office fast enough.

Settling into the driver's seat of the patrol car, he put Pain-in-the-ass Pershing out of his mind and his blood pressure dropped a little. Pershing might be a major threat, but he was also clueless, so married to detail that he couldn't see the big picture. And it was a damn good thing he was so shortsighted.

Cash didn't have that particular handicap. He prided himself on his foresight, the ability to turn any situation to his own advantage. For every scenario, he had an angle.

He got to the stoplight on Rodeo Street and took a left, heading south on Montego past a string of bars and businesses. Two men stood conversing on the corner. The taller of the two took a plastic packet out of his jeans pocket, exchanging it for a bill, which he shoved deep into his pocket. Cash jammed the gearshift into Park and flung himself out of the car. The customer saw him coming and flattened himself against the brick wall at the mouth of the alley, but Cash ran right past him, grabbing the dealer and shoving him back. "Where the fuck you been? I've been lookin' all over for you."

Remy threw Cash a nervous grin. "Hey, Cash-Man. I been around. How's the girlfriend?"

"You tryin' to make friends with me, Remy?" Cash demanded, shoving the Cajun's face into the brick, holding it there. " 'Cause I don't make friends with no drug dealers."

"Who, me? Make friends wid a cop? No way."

"You got the cash?"

Remy grimaced. "I got the cash, man. I just don' got it on me. It ain't safe to carry a lot of cash; you know? Dere's some bad-ass shit out dere. And de cops . . . dey don't do nuthin' about it. Imagine dat."

Cash shoved him again, so hard that his cheek bounced off the brick. Then, he put the muzzle of his .38 behind Remy's ear. "You wouldn't be tryin' to stiff me, now would you?"

"Naw, man," Remy insisted. "I got it. I got."

Reaching into Remy's pocket, Cash pulled out a small wad of bills. "This'll do for now. I'll get the rest from you later." He gave the man a final shove, then walked back to the car. Five twenties, three tens, two ones. Not bad for ten minutes' work. Then, with Remy's wad

warming in his trouser pocket, he drove toward Bayou
Road.

"May I help you?" Pretty, petite, and blond, Mary
Pershing resembled her father, only without the razor-
sharp edges. Two years older than Claire, Mary had
been cordial right up to the day of Jimmy's arrest. Then,
suddenly, everything changed. Mary stopped speaking
to her in the hallways of the high school, and started
crossing the street to avoid her.

It was odd, Claire thought, how something like that
stuck in one's mind, like a burr in a silk stocking, jagging
and uncomfortable years later. Uncomfortable? Maybe.
But she wasn't intimidated anymore. She didn't give a
damn what Mary Pershing thought—or her father, for
that matter—as long as she got what she came here for.
"I'm here to see Sheriff Pershing."

"The sheriff's unavailable at the moment," Mary said
sweetly. "But Deputy Edmunds will be back shortly, if
you'd care to wait."

"Actually, no, I wouldn't," Claire said, glancing at
the sheriff's inner sanctum. It was a cubicle, really,
masquerading as an office. The blinds were partially
drawn, but she could see Vance Pershing through the
slats, head bent in concentration, his small, square reading glasses perched on the end of his sharp nose. Claire
turned toward the closed door.

Seeming to sense her intent, Mary came out of her
chair. "Hey! Hey, wait a minute! What do you think
you're doing? You can't go in there!"

"Can't I? Watch me." Pershing glanced up as Claire
opened the door. He was clearly annoyed at the inter-
ruption. But she stood her ground, determined to get
the information she'd come here for. Mary hovered

behind her left shoulder. "I tried to tell her you were unavailable, Daddy. But she wouldn't take no for an answer. Should I radio Cash for backup?"

"That won't be necessary, sweetheart. I think I can handle Ms. Sumner without help from Deputy Edmunds." He sat back in his chair, his expression unchanging. Claire searched her memory, but she couldn't recall ever seeing Vance Pershing smile. "Well, Ms. Sumner, since you're in, you might as well have a seat."

Claire ignored the chair he gestured toward. "I'll stand, thank you."

"Very well, then," he said. "What brings you to my office?"

Claire suspected that he already knew the reason for her being here; all the same, he didn't let on. Instead, he sat with his old wooden secretary's chair tilted back, his arms folded over his narrow chest. A tattoo of a bantam cock with spurs on its feet etched in shades of blue, red, and green showed plainly on one stringy forearm. *Appropriate,* Claire thought. *Telling, too.* He wasn't going to make this easy for her. Aloud, she said, "I need to talk to you about the young girl found in Bayou des Cannes."

He uncrossed his arms and sat up. "You have information pertaining to the case?"

"Not exactly, but I do have this." She took the newspaper out of her bag, placing it squarely on the blotter in front of him.

He glanced at the drawing, then at her. "That's old news. Tell me something new."

"Have you noticed the resemblance to Jean Louise Broussard?" Claire plunged on. "You're an observant man, Sheriff. You must have made note of the fact that the two were similar . . . height, weight, age."

"Lots of little girls have similar builds, Ms. Sumner. Now, if this is your only reason for being here, you're wasting my time."

"Two teenage girls, Sheriff, both asphyxiated, found in the same spot by the same man, and they looked enough alike to be sisters. Are you going to sit there and tell me that you really believe this is a coincidence?"

Pershing looked irritated. A ceiling fan made slow revolutions overhead, circulating the stale air of the tiny office. "Ms. Sumner, what is it you want from me?"

I want your help, she wanted to scream. *I want someone in this parish to wake up and see what's going on here!* But always in the back of her mind lurked the fact that Vance Pershing was responsible for Jimmy's arrest and conviction. Pershing had taken her father away from her, and the hope that he would help give him back was slim to none. "Sheriff, there's a very good chance that the same person responsible for the most recent killing is also guilty of killing Jean Louise. If you look at the facts—"

"I have looked at the facts, Ms. Sumner, and I assure you that one case has absolutely nothing to do with the other."

"The least you can do is to pull the case files and compare them. Maybe there's something that was overlooked."

"Are you suggesting that I don't know how to do my job, Ms. Sumner?"

"How many innocent men do you suppose are on Louisiana's death row right now, Sheriff? Cases of mistaken identity, victims of a failing and imperfect and sometimes downright unjust legal system?"

"James Buford Sumner confessed."

"But under what circumstances?"

"Exactly what are you saying, Ms. Sumner? Are you

trying to imply that my office is corrupt? Or that Judge Morlay is anything other than an honorable man? I would take care how I answer if I were you, because I don't take kindly to those who question my integrity, and Morlay is on his way to the State Capitol."

"And my father is on his way to the death chamber," Claire said coldly. "In a few weeks, he's going to be executed for a crime he didn't commit. I can't rest with that knowledge, and do nothing to try and prevent that from happening, Sheriff. Can you?"

Pershing never flinched. "I went to Angola to visit your daddy a few months back—did he tell you that? No? I was happy to see that Jimmy had made peace with his fate, and you should be, too." He picked up his pen and turned once again to the paperwork. Pointedly. "This interview is over. *Good day, Ms. Sumner.*"

Pershing continued his work until he heard the outer door close and the click of Clairée Sumner's heels faded. Then, he carefully placed his pen on the desk blotter and sat back in his chair with a troubled frown. The last thing he needed right now was Jimmy Sumner's daughter stirring up unpleasant memories, asking uncomfortable questions, calling up ghosts that should have stayed dead and buried.

He hadn't liked the conclusion of the Broussard case. In fact, he hadn't been one hundred percent certain that Jimmy Sumner had perpetrated the crime. It had nothing to do with evidence. There had been plenty of evidence, from an eyewitness testimony that placed the victim in his company on the evening in question, to pornographic material depicting young girls, and the victim's clothing found stuffed under the front seat of Sumner's car. It would have been enough to convict Jimmy Sumner without a confession. But Pershing had always had an unfailing sense of intuition, and there had been something in Sumner's face that night that had given him more than one sleepless night. It wasn't anything he could put a finger on. Just a feeling. A thread of reasonable doubt.

It had taken a decade, but he'd finally made peace with his part in Jimmy's conviction, and laid those doubts to rest. And then Clairée Sumner appeared to bring it all back.

Coming out of his chair abruptly, Pershing walked to the window looking out over the intersection of Euclid and Vine. The heat index was through the roof, and except for a few passing cars, the street was nearly empty. That July ten years ago had been a hot one, too, but he didn't like to think about that. He didn't like the feeling that there was something that had gotten by him, something he'd missed.

"Twenty-six months in Nam and twenty-nine years in public service," he murmured, staring out at the street, but seeing instead the black water of Bayou des Cannes, and the pale, outstretched arm of a young girl, dark hair floating out like a skein of wet silk. "I'm fifty-six years old, and ten months away from retirement, and all they're gonna remember me for is two little girls who just happened to be killed on my watch." It was a long time before Pershing moved away from the window, before he let go of his bitterness and returned to his work.

Cash parked the car in front of the wild rose hedges, and took a moment to survey the place before getting out. Bayou Road was not a bad neighborhood, but it was isolated, and a man couldn't be too careful. The yard at the side of the little white house appeared to be deserted. In fact, nothing stirred anywhere, including the brown and white rat terrier lying prone on the front porch. Cash opened the car door, and the dog didn't bark. In fact, it didn't even flinch. Not exactly an eyebrow-raiser. It was too damned hot to move. Even the gators had abandoned their sunbathing and sought the murky waters of the bayou.

A single fan turned in the front window of the house, but he detected no movement inside, and the place lay in shadow. He wondered how anyone survived the month of July in Louisiana without air conditioning—then he remembered his paternal grandmother, who not only didn't have air, she didn't have indoor plumbing, and she didn't seem to care all that much, either. But then, Granny Edmunds had always been a little crazy.

Not so amazingly, he broke a sweat before he reached the porch, and as he lifted his fist to knock, a warm thread of moisture trickled down the back of his neck and into the blue collar of his uniform shirt. "Miz Felix? Miz Felix, it's Deputy Edmunds from the sheriff's department . . . ma'am, I was hopin' to have a word with you."

The door creaked open and a broad, dark face showed through the crack. Most folks would have swung the door wider at the sight of a uniform, but Martha Felix held it ajar just enough for one suspicious eye to glare through. "I ain't done nothin' illegal," she said.

"No, ma'am," Cash agreed. "It's a courtesy call, that's all. One of your neighbors reported seein' someone 'round here, and I just wanted to make sure that everything is all right."

"No one 'round here—just my nephew, Johnny. He's a good man who keeps himself outta trouble. Ain't no law against a nephew helpin' his aunt, so far as I know."

"No, ma'am, there surely ain't. Is your nephew here today?"

"He fixed my fan, then went back home. What'ch you want Johnny for?"

"Just thought to have a word with him, is all. You sure that everything's okay? You want me to come in and have a look around?"

"I don't like strangers in my house," Miz Felix said. "Now, if you don't mind, I've got somethin' on the stove. It's almost dinnertime, and you're keepin' me from it." The door clicked shut, and Cash heard the deadbolt being slid into place. As he turned to walk back to the patrol car, he saw the living room curtain being pushed back, just enough for Miz Felix to peer out and watch his progress. "Must be somethin' about paranoia and this neighborhood," Cash muttered, sliding into the driver's seat and turning the key in the ignition. The entire exchange hadn't taken more than five minutes, and it must have been ninety degrees in the patrol car.

If he lived to be as old as Methuselah, Fegan would never forget the bone-biting chill of a Chicago winter. In his wildest nightmares, he could not have conjured up the feeling of numbness that seeped into fingers and toes, that made his eyes water and sting and reddened his cheeks and the end of his nose. He'd been told that it was the wind off the lake. Winter near water had its own brand of discomfort, and there wasn't anything a Louisiana boy could do except to buy the heaviest damned overcoat he could find and shiver his ass off until the spring thaw finally arrived in mid-March or early April.

March was two months away, and it might as well have been twelve. Back home, the azaleas were a blaze of bright pink and deep glossy green, but outside his apartment windows, the bleak, white blizzard howled like something caught in hideous unearthly torment. He'd handed his assignment in to his editor the previous morning, and he had no plans to venture far from the bedroom and the voluptuous warmth Diana provided. Sliding a lazy hand down over the soft curve of her breast, he closed his fingers over the hard, little tip of one nipple, and the phone rang.

"Let it ring," she whispered, pulling him down on top of her and kissing him, while the wind howled around the corners of the building, snatching at and rattling the old windows, seeping in around the edges of the glass.

It was seven-thirty-five in the morning. Nobody on God's green earth would call him at seven-thirty-five except Frank, and if it was Frank, then that meant something was wrong with Amos Lee. He fumbled with the receiver, damn near dropping it. "Broussard."

For five heavy thuds of his heart there was absolute silence, and then the voice, thin and raspy, began its nightmare walk into his world. "I saw the article in the paper, Mr. Broussard . . . the one about the girl who was found near the pier. Excellent write-up. Very thorough, though you missed a few small details. Shall I relate them for you?"

"Who the fuck is this?"

"A reader . . ." A raspy chuckle. "You might even say, a fan."

"How the hell did you get my number?"

"Does that really matter? You injected such empathy for the girl . . . I was wondering, what was it about her that reminded you of your sister? Her eyes? Or the fact that she was found in the water?"

Fegan slammed the receiver down so hard it bounced off the hook onto the carpet. But it only rang again. Even ripping the wires from the wall couldn't stop it from ringing, and ringing, and—

Sunlight, harsh and yellow-white, poured in through the slats in the louvers, falling on the cypress planks and playing across the rag rug by the side of the bed. Heart still flailing against his ribs, Fegan dug the heels of his hands into his sandy eye-sockets and listened to the insistent buzzing of the doorbell. "*Va t'en!*" he growled. "*Fout ton campe!* Go the hell away, will you?"

The doorbell rang again, and kept ringing. "I hope your fucking finger falls off!" Fegan said, rolling up to one elbow and squinting at the clock on the bedside table. Five to twelve, and he hadn't fallen into bed until almost nine-thirty. Too little sleep, and the cobwebs from the dream didn't do a great deal for his temper. As he threw on his jeans and zipped the fly, he thought about where he was going to shove Frank's damned brochures.

"Do you know what the hell time it is?" he demanded as he flung the door open.

Clairée, dressed in a pale green silk blouse and tan linen trousers, took a second to glance at her Rolex. "Five minutes to twelve," she said. "Do you always sleep late?"

Fegan braced a palm against the doorjamb. "It's not late for me. It's early."

She looked him up and down, and he could have sworn he felt the warmth of her gaze slide over the bare skin of his chest, down past the open waistband of his jeans, all the way to his bare feet, before it slowly returned. His bad mood evaporated like steam off a puddle, and he smiled in spite of himself. "Well?" she said. "Are you going to invite me in, Fegan Broussard? Or will you leave me to languish on your doorstep?"

He pushed the door wide, then closed it again as she entered on a whiff of Opium perfume. Fegan followed a few paces behind, picking up the pack of cigarettes from the old bureau and shoving one between his lips, striking a match as he watched her wander around the living room. "Somethin' in particular you're lookin' for, Char? Or is this a social call?"

She had been fingering a lace doily that graced the back of a faded blue armchair, but at the sound of his voice, she turned to face him. "Sorry. I'm not being terribly polite, am I? I just didn't expect the house to look the same."

Fegan took a deep drag off the cigarette and let the smoke escape as he spoke. "Yeah, well, I ain't much of a homebody, and I guess I still see it as Amos Lee's place, for all that I make the mortgage payments."

"And I see it as Jean Louise's," she said with a self-deriding laugh. "Perceptions are strange, aren't they?"

"That why you woke me, to talk about the way people perceive things?" Fegan wondered.

The question tripped her trigger. "Yes," she said. "No. I don't know. Call it impulse, call it a bad decision. Call it whatever you want—it's becoming more blatantly obvious by the minute that I shouldn't have come here. At least there's one thing I can change."

She started to brush past him, intending to rectify her mistake, but Fegan stopped her by blocking the exit with an outstretched arm. "This isn't funny, Fegan. And I'm not in the mood for games."

"Me, either. I'm like a grizzly bear with a sore ass before I've had my coffee. You drink coffee, don' you, Char?"

Claire glanced up at him. "Actually, no. I never developed a taste for it."

"You ain't never had mine. Old Fegan makes the best cup of coffee in all of South Lou'siana. He's a master of the art, him."

"I didn't know that pouring water into a coffeemaker

could be considered an art form." Inches away from him, she was bathed in the warmth radiating from his skin, her senses teased by the scent of sleep-warmed male. Claire's defense mechanism kicked off a silent warning only she could detect. She sensed the danger in being here like this, alone with Fegan. She had the wild urge to reach out and touch that place where the pulse jumped at the base of his throat, to press her lips to the pierced lobe of his ear. He was so sexy, so provocative without even trying to be, and she knew that he was more than willing. . . .

"What's the matter, Char?" he asked, reaching out, caressing the corner of her lips with the pad of his thumb. "Cat got your tongue?"

"I really should go," Claire said. She still couldn't quite fathom what insane impulse had brought her to his door, but she could feel the danger now that she stood in the warm, dim interior of the house, shadows playing over the broad, naked expanse of his bare torso, his half-smiling, half-serious, too-handsome face close enough to kiss. If he touched her again, she would fall apart. That's how fragile she felt. Like a china doll . . . ready to shatter, unequal to the task she'd undertaken. But why turn to him? It was a question that had no hard and fast answer.

"C'mon," he said softly, convincingly. "Don' go. Stay. Have some coffee. You owe me that much for draggin' my ass outta bed."

"Sorry," Claire murmured. "I never meant to—I should have known that you'd be out late."

"Oh, hell, don' apologize. Better you than Frank." Reaching out, he took her hand in his. "Come into my kitchen, said the spider to the fly," he said, leading the way to the kitchen.

Claire laughed. "It's supposed to be a parlor."

"Yeah, well, I ain't got no parlor. But I got a French press that'll knock your pretty self right back on your pretty behind. C'mon, darlin', you're about to get caffeinated."

The kitchen was light and airy, the walls a soft sage green, the sheer curtains the same soothing shade. A small, round table sat squarely in front of the louvers, an antique hurricane lamp placed on its center. The room was spare, but highly functional with a large, double-door refrigerator, a ceramic-top range, and a shelf filled with cookbooks. Somehow, Claire couldn't picture Amos Lee making the improvements. "You like to cook?" she said, taking a seat at the table.

"*Non*, baby, I like to eat." He put water on to boil and ground the coffee beans. "I make a mean crawfish bisque, blackened chicken, but shrimp jambalaya— now, that's my specialty." A few minutes later he was filling two cobalt blue mugs with black coffee, placing sugar and cream within easy reach and sinking into the seat opposite hers.

He added a little cream to his coffee, but ignored the sugar bowl, while Claire sweetened hers heavily, then creamed it until it was a rich caramel brown. She took a tentative sip while he watched her closely. "It's very good, actually. Surprisingly so."

"Arabica beans. That's the secret to a smooth cup of coffee. No second-rate junk beans in this house." He watched her for a while over the rim of his cup, saying nothing, his eyes nearly a match for the rich, vibrant blue ceramic. Gradually, Claire felt the tension leave her. There were times when just his presence had that effect upon her—a soothing, relaxing air of familiarity, a sense of true belonging, the feeling that if not for the problems looming on her life's horizon, she would have been exactly where she was meant to be.

But her problems were too big to be forgotten, dismissed, or ignored, and Fegan was unpredictable. A change of expression, a tilt of his raven head, a come-on line, and she was immediately wary, her senses on red alert while she waited to be seduced. Just now, he still wore a slight air of drowsiness, the creases from the pillow at the corner of his left eye hadn't eased away completely, and his dark curls were slightly tousled.

Watching him watching her, Claire had to admit that it looked good on him. Damn good. Even worse, it all seemed so natural, sharing a few quiet moments in a shaded kitchen with a half-naked Fegan.

"So, why you here, Char? You think up some new way to torture me?"

"Would I do that?" she asked sweetly.

He laughed. "Yeah, sugar, you would."

Claire sighed. "Truth is, I need your help."

"You? Need *my* help?"

"Don't look so skeptical. You have certain skills, don't you?"

He raised his mug, cocking his head ever so slightly. "Of course I have skills. I thought we already established that."

"I'm not talking about that."

"Then, just what exactly are you talkin' about?"

"I want to hire you."

"Oh, no," he said, putting his hands up, palms out, as if to ward off a really bad idea. "I've already got a heavy caseload—besides, we had this discussion, and I ain't about to help prolong your agony."

"I'll pay you," she said, and watched as he shook his head in disgust. "I have resources. Just name your price. I don't care what it is, I'll meet it."

"This ain't Remy you're talkin' to, sugar. And I ain't for sale."

"You'll take money from strangers to spy on their husbands and wives, to find their stray cats, to prove they're not hurt when they claim that they are. Why not me?"

"It ain't the same thing," he insisted, coming out of his chair, pacing the breadth of the kitchen.

Claire followed him, so that when he turned back, she was standing before him, looking him directly in the eye, determined to have his attention, to have her way with him. But Fegan had never been easy. He wouldn't be maneuvered. He was too sharp, too stubborn for that. "It *is* the same. They want information. I want the same thing."

Fegan lost it, and his sharp reply echoed through the dimly lit house. "Goddamn it, Clairée! Why can't you let this go?"

She paused, patiently waiting for his shout to die away, waiting for the moment when he would listen to reason. "Because this is important to me. More than that, it's everything. And because I'm afraid, Fegan. Do you remember when Jean Louise and I climbed the live oak out back? We went almost to the top, up where the branches swayed in the breeze. Jean Louise climbed back down, but I realized how far away the ground was and I froze."

He squeezed his eyes shut, a pained expression settling over his face as he fought the memory. "Christ, Char, don't. Don't do this to me."

"If it hadn't been for you, I would have fallen. But Jean Louise found you, and you climbed up and helped me down."

"You're not a kid anymore, Char. Neither am I . . . and Jean Louise . . . well, she ain't here, now is she?"

"Yes, *she is*," Claire replied. "She's here, in my thoughts, in my heart. She's all around me. Someone took her away from us, Fegan. But it wasn't my father. And if I don't uncover the truth soon, it will be too late."

"Believe what you have to believe. I can't help you with this," he said stubbornly. "I won't."

Claire had held out her heart in both hands and he'd spurned her for it, crushing her hopes, hardening her resolve. Her hair had fallen into her face. She brushed it back, collecting her composure bit by bit. "You don't care that he's innocent, do you? It doesn't matter to you who pays for your pain as long as somebody does. I'm disappointed in you, Fegan. More than that, I'm disgusted. I had no idea how bitter you'd become, but I can see it now. You're no better than Sheriff Pershing."

"You talked to Vance Pershing?"

"It was a decidedly one-sided conversation. Kind of strange, isn't it? Everywhere I turn there's another obstacle. Someone else to tell me to just let my father die. If I didn't know better, I'd say it was some sort of conspiracy. But things like that don't happen in Angelique, do they? It's a safe little town where people don't bother to lock their doors at night, and young girls with everything to live for don't lose their lives to senseless killings." Squaring her shoulders, she moved past him to the door of the kitchen. "Thanks for the coffee," she said. "Thanks for nothing."

Fegan listened to her soft footfalls until the front door closed, blocking out the sound. Then, when he could no longer contain the tension building inside him, he whirled and put his fist through the kitchen wall.

CHAPTER
SIX

"*Hey, Clairée*, let's go down to Timmy Tyson's garage and get us a soda," a childish voice whispered in Claire's ear.

Worn out from her confrontation with Fegan, the last thing she wanted was to succumb to the poignant memories rushing in around her. "It's *Claire*, damn it," she stubbornly insisted, knowing the impulse to resist the pull of the past was futile.

Her first act upon graduating from law school had been to legally change her name from Charlotte Clairée to Claire. It had been an act of symbolism and defiance. Clairée's life had been marred by tragedy, tainted by heartbreaking loss over which she had no control. The Claire Sumner who had stepped out of the courthouse with a fresh identity had taken control of her life and her future, determined that while the past had a hand in shaping who she was, it would haunt her no longer.

Then she came home to Angelique, and discovered

that there truly was no lasting escape, no way to divorce herself from the past, from who and what she had been . . . Jean Louise's best friend and surrogate sister . . . daughter of a convicted killer . . .

She fought against the rising tide of bitterness summoned up by her thoughts, but the memories were stronger, more insidious than her will to hold them at bay. *"Aw, c'mon, Clairée!"* Jean Louise whispered.

"Dear God, Jean Louise, not now," Claire pleaded, so softly that her voice was barely audible. She felt ragged and worn, like she'd suffered some huge defeat, and she wasn't quite sure what to do next, other than to seek quiet, regroup, and strategize about what to do, where to go next.

Fegan had been her best hope, or so she had thought—the closest thing she had to a friend in this town, the one person she trusted, the one person she could turn to, and she couldn't have been wrong about him.

"C'mon, Clairée," the childish voice persisted. "It's hot, and I'm thirsty," and it sounded so plaintive, so cajoling that Claire felt herself soften to the memory of a more innocent time, a better place. . . .

"Can't," she heard her own voice answer, a little sulkily. *Her daddy had started his new job as a mechanic a few days before, and money was tight. They were staying with Aunt Eule at The Willows, and though Clairée secretly wished that they could stay in the big house forever, she knew her daddy's pride wouldn't allow for such luxurious living. "I don't have any money,"* she finally confessed. *"Let's go find Fegan. Maybe if we ask real nice, he'll pole us out into the bayou, and we can hunt for that big alligator."*

Jean Louise pulled a face. "Fegan doesn't have time for us. He's too busy sniffin' 'round Marjory Girard."

"Sniffin'?" Clairée said, making snuff-snuffling sounds till

they both burst into giggles. "Why would Fegan want to sniff Margery?"

"Danged if I know," Jean Louise said, wiping tears from her dark blue eyes. "But that's what Frank says. I think Frank likes Marjory, but Marjory likes Fegan. Fegan says Frank needs to loosen up—his bumhole's too tight."

Clairée stared at her friend in adolescent awe. Jean Louise didn't have a mother or a father to see that she spoke well, or to make her attend Sunday services at the Baptist church like Clairée, or make her go to Mass. But she had two older brothers, and a granddad who spent his evenings in the bayou catching turtles and crawfish and frogs for parish dinner tables, a circumstance that no doubt contributed to her wild streak, her worldly wisdom. . . . Though she was younger, Jean Louise led, and Clairée, older but more sheltered, followed. Her eyes widened. "His butthole's too tight?"

Twenty-one-year-old Frank chose that moment to walk past. Clairée's gaze followed, and they both laughed again, but as Frank turned to give them a dark, disapproving look, the fun bled out of the activity.

"Let's go get a soda," Jean Louise said again. "We don't need money. Your daddy's workin', and that means Timmy's away. You hit the machine just right, the soda comes out, and you don' gotta pay. I saw Fegan do it. It's magic. Sorta."

They rode their bikes across town to the service station. Clairée stood lookout while Jean Louise extracted a soda from the machine. But as Clairée delivered a kick to the center bottom, a shadow crept over the machine. Charlotte Clairée! What the hell do you think you're doin'?"

The memory disintegrated as the pickup truck behind the BMW blew his horn. Claire blinked. The light at the corner of State and Elm was green, and as she made a left into Tyson's service station, she silently thanked Jean Louise.

"Be with you in a minute!" a voice called from the

dim interior of the cinder block building. Tim Tyson was draped over the hood of a '92 Oldsmobile. The only thing visible was the bottom half of his dark blue coveralls.

"Mr. Tyson?"

He smoothed his bald spot with a grease-stained hand. "Yes, ma'am. Is there something I can do for you?"

Timothy Tyson preached on Sundays at the Grace Baptist Church. He'd given Jimmy a job when they'd returned to Angelique in 1987, and was one of a small number of friends and neighbors who hadn't turned away from Claire and her mother after Jimmy's arrest. "You may not remember me, Mr. Tyson. I'm Claire Sumner, and I was wondering if I might have a few moments of your time."

"Why, of course I remember you," Tyson said, wiping his hands on a rag. "Jimmy's daughter, Clairée. It's been a lot of years. How are you?"

"I'm fine, thank you," Claire said.

"Would you care for a soda?" he said with a smile, delivering a kick to the bottom of the old vending machine. "My treat."

Claire laughed. "I would have thought you would have replaced it by now."

"I thought about it, but it's become a tradition in this part of the parish—a draw for the neighborhood kids, and that's not all bad. I've even managed to talk a few of them into attending Sunday evening youth services at the church. But that's not why you're here, is it?"

"Actually, I'm here on Jimmy's behalf. I need to know about that time," Claire said. "Dad was working here when Jean Louise Broussard was killed."

Tyson nodded, sinking onto the wooden bench outside the door of the garage under the shade of a faded green-and-white-striped awning. "Yes, ma'am, he surely was. Your daddy worked evenings four days a week as my mechanic, and pumped gas on Saturday till two in the afternoon. Always did say he missed his calling. I never saw anyone with a way around a carburetor like Jimmy Sumner. And he was an honest man, too. Couldn't say that about some I've employed over the years."

Claire frowned. "Mr. Tyson, I know that it's asking a great deal. It's been ten years, but is there anything about that time that stands out in your mind—anything unusual in connection with Jimmy?"

Tyson thought for a moment, then shook his head. "Memory's never been a problem for me. I could tell you what kind of sandwich your daddy had in his lunch that day if you're interested—but anything unusual? No, I can't say so. Jimmy worked late the night before the Broussard girl was murdered. He was trying to finish up Mr. Morlay's car, as I recall. Morlay's driver had brought it in the previous day with a hole in the manifold, and there was a mixup with the part. That driver was fit to be tied. He insisted Mr. Morlay couldn't wait. Guess he had some big party in Baton Rouge that next day, so Jimmy drove to Lafayette to pick up the replacement, then drove back here and worked all night to finish it on time. Jimmy was conscientious, all right, and he took a lot of grief from that Keyes fella. Lot of men would've popped him one. But Jimmy was cool-headed. That's part of the reason I never could believe he killed that little girl. Don't care what he said. I just don't believe he had it in him to do something like that."

"Ashton Morlay?" Claire's frown intensified. It was the second time that day that Ashton Morlay's name had come up, and it was getting damned hard to stifle her instinctive reaction to it. Morlay had joined the prosecutor's office the month before Jean Louise's death, and he'd pushed hard to get the death penalty in the case; in fact, he'd insisted that he would accept nothing less. "Jimmy was working on Morlay's car the day before Jean Louise's murder?"

"Yes, ma'am. In fact, he finished it up in the wee hours of that mornin'. That's why he didn't work his regular shift the day of the murder." Tyson sighed, shook his head. "You know, I've thought about it a lot since, and wondered if maybe I hadn't sent him home early, none of this would've happened. He would have been here the evenin' that poor child died, and he would'a had an alibi. Is there anything else I can do for you?"

Claire thanked him for his time and his kindness, and drove the five miles from Angelique to The Willows.

Eulanie was in her small, first-floor office hashing out the details of a contract with a local sugar mill. Claire riffled through the mail, then, upon discovering there was nothing from Jimmy, she replaced it on the round, marble-topped Queen Anne table in the foyer, next to the vase of red-flecked white lilies, then headed for the stairs. As she passed the open door to Eulanie's office, the older woman motioned her into the room. "The second crop should be ready to harvest in three weeks. That's right, you provide the equipment and the labor, and the transportation to the refinery. That's why I sell to you for a fraction of what it's actually worth." Eulanie's thin brows drew down in an ominous frown. "No, I most certainly will not hold! Mr. Perry has my number. He can call me when he's ready to cut a deal. Good day to you, too!" She dropped the receiver on its cradle, then squeezed the bridge of her nose between thumb and forefinger. A moment of quiet, and she fixed Claire with a look. "Claire, where on earth have you been?

I've been worried sick about you. We waited breakfast for you."

"I'm sorry," Claire said. "I suppose I should have left a note. I had some errands to run, and wanted to finish early." They both recognized that the excuse rang flat, but Eulanie was too polite to call her on it. Two p.m. wasn't exactly early. Not wishing to go into the details of her frustrating morning, Claire inclined her head to indicate the phone. "I couldn't help overhearing. Is there a problem with the contracts? If so, I'd be glad to help if I can."

Eulanie sat back with a sigh. "John Perry and I worked hand in glove for fifteen years. I gave him a fair price on the cane, and he provided the machinery and the trucks and the manpower to harvest and transport to the refinery. Then last spring, John had a stroke, and his son Roy assumed control of the business. Within weeks, he had sold a portion of the business to a new partner. That's when everything started to go south on us. Suddenly, Roy isn't anxious to work with a middlin' concern like The Willows. I've reminded him several times that his daddy and I had a handshake agreement. Roy just reminds me that business isn't done on a handshake these days, but I suspect this new partner of his has more to do with the situation than he's willing to allow."

"Would you like me to speak with him? In a legal capacity?"

Eulanie shook her head. "I am most certainly *not* going to embroil you in my business concerns. It'll all work out in the end, and if it doesn't—well, I'll just find another refinery." She massaged her shoulder, grimacing.

Her left shoulder, Claire noticed. "Aunt Eulanie, are you all right?"

"What? Oh, this? It's the dampness, is all. It affects my arthritis."

"Bothers mine, too," Jane said, coming into the room without knocking. "Especially bad today. I'm surprised the rain has held off so long, but it'll be here by nightfall." She held out a parchment envelope. "This just arrived, Miz Eule. Special messenger, too. Guess they wanted to make sure you got it."

Eulanie opened the envelope, scanning the invitation, then handed it to Claire. "Now, there's something unexpected. A Democratic fund-raiser for Ashton Morlay. Seems he's got his sights set on Baton Rouge."

"Good riddance," Claire said. "At least he'll be gone from here."

"Would that it was half so easy," Eulanie replied. "The judge may have decided to resign the bench in order to pursue other avenues, but he's not gone yet, and he'll never leave the parish—not completely. His roots are deep, and he's got too many holdings here, none more lucrative than the Perry Refinery."

Claire had been staring down at the gold-embossed "M" on the white parchment lying in her lap. But at the mention of Ashton Morlay in the same sentence as the current source of her aunt's business woes, she glanced up sharply. "I can see I forgot to mention that the judge bought heavily into the Perrys' business interests after John became ill. I found out last week that he's Roy's mysterious partner."

"Ashton Morlay is doing business with Roy Perry?"

Eulanie answered by plucking the invitation from Claire's lap and dropping it into the wastepaper basket. "That's sufficient reply, don't you think?" At the doorway, she turned. "I almost forgot. You had a visitor earlier. He said to tell you 'that the answer's still no'.

A rather intriguing young man, I must say—so much so that I invited him to dinner."

Claire stifled a groan. "Aunt Eulanie, please tell me you didn't."

"I certainly did," Eulanie said, a mischievous smile curving her mouth. "What's more, he accepted. I'm rather looking forward to having guests again, especially one so handsome. This old house has been too quiet for too damned long." Eulanie went out, pausing just long enough for one last addition. "Dress for dinner, will you, dear? And wear something nice."

He'd certainly dressed for the occasion, Claire thought. A charcoal-gray jacket, white silk shirt, and black trousers, his only concession to his unconventionality the absence of a tie. He'd toned down his street talk, too, in deference to Eulanie, who Claire could tell was favorably impressed. "How is the private investigation business, Mr. Broussard? A great deal of excitement, I would imagine? Fast cars and dangerous cases?"

"Actually, most of the time it's pretty boring. I spend a lot of my time on the phone chasing down leads. Not all that different from my former occupation, really. Only I don't have a deadline, and I don't have to answer to an editor about my abuse of the semi-colon . . . The reports I write these days are for my clients, and for my own records."

Eulanie arched a brow. "I think you're downplaying it just a bit. The papers said that you were instrumental in bringing about Manny Poutou's arrest a few days back, while he was holding his wife and another woman hostage. That must have been a real adrenaline rush."

"Actually, I had a little help with that," Fegan replied, his gaze meeting Claire's.

Eulanie followed his glance, while Claire did her level best to change the subject. "Alma really outdid herself this evening. This is the best *crème brûlée* I've ever eaten."

"Charlotte Clairée!"

Claire flinched. "She was in trouble, Aunt Eule. I couldn't very well just stand back and watch while he blew her head off. Besides, Mr. Poutou was just expressing his anger and frustration at what unarguably are difficult and stressful circumstances. I don't believe he really meant to kill her."

Eulanie held up her hands in surrender. "I believe I've heard enough. Tomorrow's a workday for me, so I think I'll say good night. Mr. Broussard, I would like to thank you for a very entertainin' evening. Claire, I promise you that we will talk about this tomorrow, once I've had a chance to calm down."

Fegan rose. "I really should be going."

Eulanie wouldn't hear of it. "Nonsense. The evening's still young, and you haven't even seen the bougainvillea. The courtyard's breathtaking at night. Isn't that right, Claire? Why don't you give our guest the grand tour?"

Eulanie left the room with a soft swish of silk, and as the sound receded into the background, Claire turned on Fegan. "Was that absolutely necessary? I went to considerable trouble to keep my name out of the newspaper. The least you could have done was keep quiet about it."

"Did I say anythin'?" he demanded, slipping back into the Fegan she was familiar with, the one she found so infuriating, so intriguing, so damned sexy. He hid a smile behind his coffee cup. "So, you gonna play hostess and show me the bougainvillea, or what?"

"I don't know that I should," Claire replied. "I'm still angry at you for wangling this invitation."

He shrugged. "Your aunt likes me, sweetheart, and so do you. You're just too stubborn to admit it." He glanced at the windows. "Would you look at that? Don't think I've ever seen a moon so big. What'dya say, Char? I'd sure like to see it up close."

Claire hesitated, but only for the time it took for her heart to execute a stuttering beat. He'd been intentionally, pointedly charming all evening, the perfect gentleman, and she wasn't quite sure what to make of it.

"C'mon, Char. It's me. Fegan. Cut me a break. I haven't had a chance to apologize for this mornin'."

"Does that mean you'll reconsider?" Claire said, still wary, but warming to the look in his dark blue eyes.

"It means I'm sorry if I upset you, and I'm runnin' out the white flag. I'm willin' to declare a truce if you will." He stood, coming around to her chair, sliding his warm hand over the cool, bare skin of her wrist, and with a gentle but insistent tug, brought her out of her chair.

The French doors in the dining room opened onto the courtyard. In fair weather, Eulanie opened the doors wide, to allow the outside in. In the summer months, the courtyard became a shady haven from the overwhelmingly strong sun and the oppressive heat. It was also one of Claire's favorite haunts. When she felt the need to reflect, to get away from the world, she sought out the tall, red-brick enclosure with its huge potted palms, flowering vines, and centrally located fountain.

Claire walked to the stone bench along the south wall, near the old wrought iron gate, conscious of the fact that the pale gold shantung silk she wore left her shoulders bare. She wasn't sure why she'd chosen it. She hadn't worn it in more than a year. But then, everything about tonight seemed outside the norm, unusual ... perhaps even a little exciting. "I hope you know what a privilege this is," she told him. "I don't think any man has set foot back here since Dad left."

Fegan stopped beside her, his hand braced against the brick of the archway. "Kinda strange, don't you think? Two beautiful women and no gentlemen friends to compliment their beauty, to make them laugh. Why is that, I wonder?"

"Aunt Eulanie got burned pretty badly by her ex-husband. She says he spoiled her for other men. After he left, she channeled all of her energies into making a success of the farm."

"And what about you?" he asked, his voice a whiskey-soft whisper in the darkness. "You don' bring your gentleman friends home to Angelique to meet your family?"

You're here, aren't you? Claire wanted to say, but she swallowed back the words. Somehow it didn't seem appropriate in light of the events of the day. "This isn't exactly a safe topic of conversation," she said instead. "And I don't know if I like where it's leading."

"What's not to like?" The moon overhead slipped behind a bank of clouds, plunging the courtyard into deep shadow. He'd claimed that he wanted to look at the moon, but he never took his eyes off her. "You look good with your hair up," he said, reaching out to trace a fingertip along the hollow behind Claire's ear. The teasing contact made her shiver. "Almost as good as you do when you wear it loose, and it floats around your shoulders like a dark cloud."

"Fegan?"

"Yeah?"

"What do you know about Ashton Morlay?" It was a lame attempt to focus her thoughts in a direction other than the one her mind wanted so desperately to explore. Where would this night lead if she allowed it to flow naturally? What would happen after?

"I know that I don't like him. Why? What's goin' on, Char?"

"His name keeps cropping up, and it's not because of his good works or philanthropic interests."

"This have anything to do with the fact that he prosecuted your daddy's case?"

"Jimmy was working on Morlay's limo when Jean Louise disappeared."

"Jimmy was a mechanic. He worked on cars. What's that got to do with anything?"

"I don't know. Maybe nothing at all. Maybe it's just a coincidence. It just seemed strange . . . then Aunt Eule happened to mention the problems she's having with the refinery. Problems that didn't exist until after Roy Perry took over and took on a partner."

"Morlay."

Claire nodded. "He's changed the terms of the contract, and I'm not convinced that there isn't some scheme to drive her out."

A strand of dark hair had escaped her French twist to curl at her nape. Fegan brushed it with a fingertip, then lifted it and watched as it slid through his fingers. "It's hard for small farmers these days, and gettin' harder all the time. Too much overhead, not enough profit, and one bad blow from the Gulf can wipe a man out—or a woman. You know that."

"You think I'm paranoid."

"I think you're in desperate need of a distraction," he said, moving closer. "And maybe you need to relax. Kick back a little . . . take your mind off certain things." He brushed one dangling earring so that it swayed gently, teasing the sensitive skin of her throat.

Claire's pulse leapt, and a subtle warmth followed in its wake, stealing through her torso and along her limbs, leaving her feeling a little languid, aware that she wanted, was hoping for more ... yet she hadn't quite forgiven him for that morning, for the fact that he could be so doggedly stubborn, and continued to refuse her. "Why did you come to dinner this evening?" she asked, keeping her gaze carefully averted, afraid he would detect the eagerness in her eyes and interpret it for what it was.

"To see you," he replied. He took her hand in his, fitting his palm to hers, then threading his fingers through hers and closing them in his warm, secure grip. Claire's response was slower, less deliberate. She hesitated, then folded her fingers onto the hard ridge of his knuckles. "And because I knew that if I asked you out, you'd refuse ... especially given what happened this mornin'. I like you, Char. I like how you turned out. More than that, I like what you do to me."

"I haven't done anything to you." *Yet.*

"Hell, you know what I mean."

She did know, because she felt it, too. Just being near him heightened her senses, triggering a physical reaction she couldn't ignore. Her heart seemed to beat faster, her blood pushed a little more forcefully through her veins, and her skin flushed all over. It was like her body was fine-tuned to respond to his every word, every look, every nuance, no matter how slight ... like she could feel his touch before he ever laid a hand on her. The sensation confused her, infuriated her. She didn't want to react to him so keenly. She didn't want to give him that kind of power over her, yet she couldn't seem to help it. The heightened state of awareness she struggled with in his presence made the reality unbearably heady, the anticipation almost more than she could withstand.

Claire moistened her lips with a flick of her tongue. She hated feeling nervous, uncertain, off-balance, but as his free hand settled at her waist, and gradually urged her against him, she was exactly that. "You said you wanted a chance to apologize, yet you haven't—apologized, that is."

"Sure I did," he murmured, grazing the curve of her cheek with his lips. "Don' you remember?"

"Say it again," Claire insisted, rising onto her toes, meeting and melding with his mouth, briefly, then again, and again, and—"This time with sincerity."

"Whatever you say, Char Clairée." Seizing her free hand, he backed her against the courtyard wall and kissed her with all the pent-up passion that had been simmering between them for days, until the last ounce of tension gripping her had bled completely away. Then, he kissed her again, and when she couldn't stand it anymore, Claire tore her hands from his grip and sought him, glorying in the taut smoothness of his cleanly shaven face, the dark silk of his hair. She slid her palms over his shoulders, her fingertips gliding over his small, hard nipples beneath the silk shirt, the hardness of his ribs and flat stomach. Then a noise from above the garden intruded. Claire glanced up in time to see Eulanie open her window, adjust the curtains. In a few seconds the bedroom light winked out. "Let's go somewhere quiet," he said, voice rough.

"It's quiet here." She was reluctant to leave, to give up the option of turning in her tracks and going back to the house.

"Not quiet enough for where this is headed. Unless, of course, you're plannin' to run out on me, like you did the other night."

"Would I do that?" Claire asked, smoothing away a smudge of her lipstick from the corner of his sensual mouth.

"*Mais*, yeah. You might, but I wouldn't suggest it. You kiss me like you mean it, Char, you touch me like you want to, and twice burned means that you might not get another chance.''

"No going back?"

"Somethin' like that. I don't mind a slow build-up," he said, sinking down onto the stone bench and pulling her down onto his lap. "But a cock tease is for sixteen-year-olds, and I'm long past that. Unless I'm readin' you all wrong, so are you."

"I like to weigh my options. What happens if I go for that slow build-up?"

"Then we stop right now and I go home frustrated, which seems to happen a lot since you came home. You go back in the house ... watch TV, read a book, or whatever it is you lawyer-types do in your off time. Maybe I'll call you in a week or two. We can take a boat ride, do a movie or somethin'. But your dreams, darlin', they ain't gonna be your own, I *guar-an-tee.*"

Claire stared down into his face. She could see the need in his eyes. God help her, it echoed her own desires, yet she couldn't give in easily, couldn't let her desire for him turn into a male conquest. "I happen to like boat rides, but I don't feel like watchin' TV, and my dreams ... they haven't been my own since I walked onto Amos Lee's porch." She got up and walked to the wrought iron gate, smiling back over her shoulder. *"Laissez les bon temps rouler,* Fegan. Let the good times roll."

The houseboat was dark when they arrived, a black hulk silhouetted against a blacker tangle of vine, Spanish moss, and bald cypress. Fegan took Claire by the hand, helping her aboard, then leading her into the galley. They got as far as the table before he pulled her into his arms again. "Really, Fegan," Claire laughed as he nuzzled her throat. "I'm not a buffet."

"No, but I'm hungry. And maybe I don't want to wait."

She felt his hands at her back, and he inched her zipper steadily toward the small of her back. Then, he peeled the soft, shimmery gold from her breasts, his mouth following in the fabric's wake. He nibbled the outer curve of one breast and Claire gasped; then, he gave his full attention to its stiff peak.

His mouth was hot against the coolness of her skin, at first a shock, but Claire quickly warmed to the pleasure it brought, sliding her arms around him, arching her back to bring him even closer. The gown began a slow slide, over her ribs to the gentle flare of her hips. Claire caught it at her waist, tugging the neckline up to cover her breasts, and with a chuckle, Fegan took her hand, leading her deeper into the lightless recesses of the boat.

The houseboat had all the comforts of home. A small living area, a bathroom, complete with an old-fashioned claw foot tub, and a bedroom with a double bed and a bow window overlooking the moonlit expanse of Bayou Road. They kissed on their way to the bedroom, Claire pausing just long enough to unbutton his shirt and pull its tail from his dark trousers. Slipping her hands into the shirt's gaping front, she eased it off his shoulders, sighing as it fluttered to the carpeted floor where it lay in a ghostly puddle. His skin was smooth and dark, as soft as the silk she'd just divested it of, and flawless except for the paler contrast of a scar that slashed diagonally over his collarbone. "Don't ask me to stay for coffee," Claire warned him as he backed her up against the edge of the mattress. "I can't spend the night."

"Whatever you want, darlin' " he said. "However, whenever, you want it."

"I don't like messy entanglements, Fegan, or unrealistic expectations."

"Neither do I, sugar. Neither do I."

"Just so you know," she explained, bracing one knee on the bed, then half-reclining. Fegan followed, one continuous fluid motion, planting a hand on either side of her shoulders, a knee between her knees, and slowly covering her body with his.

"You talk too much, Char. We got to do somethin' 'bout that." He closed the hand's breadth of distance between them and took her lips again, only this time the playfulness of their encounter was gone. Claire reveled in the feel of his weight bearing her down into the soft mattress, the insistence of his tongue as she opened to him. She wrapped him in her embrace, her hands sliding down past his belt to his slim hips, molding to the tight, muscular curve of his ass as she strained to get even closer.

Somewhere between the awakening of full arousal and the stage where they began to tear at what remained of their clothing, a shadow, dark and not overly large, passed through Claire's peripheral vision, through the bedroom door and moved toward the bow window.

Fegan felt Clairée stiffen beneath him. A heartbeat ago she'd been pliant—no, not just pliant, she'd been eager—and now she covered up her sweet body faster than he could unveil it.

"Char, baby. Tell me you haven't changed your mind."

"Fegan," she whispered. "I hate to break it to you, but we're no longer alone." She lifted a hand and pointed to the window at the foot of the bed where Amos Lee patiently sat, a carton of bait at his feet.

"Shit," Fegan said, shielding Clairée from view. *"Pépère,* is that you?"

* * *

"Jesus H. Christ." As if the evening hadn't ended badly enough, Frank's Lexus was blocking Fegan's drive at the bungalow. Behind it, with its nose to the Lexus's bumper, was the sheriff's cruiser, its driver's door open and the flickering blue-and-red strobe on its roof throwing splashes of bright color over the front of the house. "Wait here. I'll be back in a minute." As usual, she didn't listen to a thing he said. He got out of the car, and she followed, dogging his steps, persistent, even lovelier for the fact that their interlude had been aborted.

Cash Edmunds, one hand resting on the roof of the cruiser, alternately questioned Frank and spoke into the radio. He glanced up as Fegan approached with Claire, and Amos Lee, oblivious to the circus atmosphere, continued toward the back of the house and his cottage beyond. "Put that on hold, will you, Rally?" Cash said. "Looks like there's been a development. Subject has been located. Catch you in five." Edmunds put down the radio mike. "Hey, Fegan. I see you found him."

"I didn't find him," Fegan corrected. "He found me."

"You all right, Amos Lee?" Edmunds asked, but the old man ignored him. "Guess that's what passes for a yes in crazy Cajun."

Fegan's hackles went up. "Cash, you can leave."

"Can't do that till I get some information."

"We'll talk about it tomorrow," Fegan told him. "Right now, I'm not in the mood for any bullshit!" He circled back on Frank, who stood stiffly by the patrol car, that older-brother-knows-everything look on his face. "What the hell's goin' on here, Frank?"

"I might ask you the same question," Frank all but

spat. "I came by to see Amos Lee and his house was wide open. With the door ajar like that, and no one around, what was I supposed to think?"

A white Camaro stopped in front of the house, and Remy got out. "What's goin' down that's so all-fired important that you had to drag me away from my poker game? Where's *Noncle* Amos Lee? Hey, Angel Face," he said, looking Claire up and down. "You lookin' good enough to eat. What'ch you doin' later?"

"She's goin' home," Fegan said. "What next, Frank? You gonna call out the National Guard?"

They were almost nose to nose, and it was becoming clear that neither was going to back down. Claire tugged on Fegan's arm. "Step back, and calm down," she said, but she was completely overridden by Frank, who seized the advantage to get in his brother's face.

"Who the hell do you think you are, criticizing me for my concern? At least I give a damn about him! Where was he, anyhow? And where's the truck?"

"Out on Bayou Road, past Miz Felix's place," Remy put in. "Looks like he ran off de road. Up to its rear axle in mud. Me, I don' know how he got clear of it without gettin' hurt." At Fegan's glare, he shrugged. "Well, hell, don' thank me for rushin' on over. Look, y'all, I got things that require my attention, important things. Hey, sugar, you need a lift home?"

"I've got it covered," Fegan replied sharply. "Will you butt the fuck out!"

"Guess not. Frank, you need Remy again, do me a favor and don' call. In fact, ditch my number. I sure as hell don' need dis here crazy shit."

"He was out on Bayou Road?" Frank parroted. "Amos Lee was out on Bayou Road alone?"

"He's fine, Frank. Go see for yourself."

"You didn't happen to mention where you found

him," Frank persisted. He was like a hungry hound with a meat bone, hellbent on worrying it until the bone gave way, or his teeth did. But from the look on Fegan's dark face, Claire feared he was treading dangerous ground.

"He came to the houseboat," Claire told him. "And we brought him here."

"We?" Frank sneered. "And just what were you doing at the houseboat?"

"Back off, Frank," Fegan warned. "Wait for me in the car," he told Claire. "I'll be there in a minute."

"Only if you come with me."

"She's outspoken, for a tramp. But you like them that way, don't you, Fegan? Fast with a comeback, fast in bed."

Fegan reacted, pulling back his fist, smashing it into Frank's mouth. The blow knocked Frank sprawling. Dazed, he sat up, dabbing at the blood that smeared his lower lip and glaring his hatred for his younger brother.

"Come on, Char. I'll take you home." Then, to Frank, "When I get back, you'd damn well better not be here."

"I'll go, all right. But I'm warning you, Fegan. You haven't heard the last of this!"

CHAPTER
SEVEN

The storm that had threatened throughout the evening broke just after midnight with close lightning and high winds. Sheets of rain lashed the windows and pummeled the brick facade of The Willows, scattering leaves and twigs over the second-floor gallery, while inside the house Claire dreamt of the houseboat and the warm, sure feel of Fegan's hands on her flesh, the sheer excitement of his mouth dominating hers. While she moaned in response, caught in the throes of a nighttime fantasy, her dream lover lounged wakeful by the bedroom windows at the bungalow on Mayfly Street, a half-glass of whiskey cradled in one hand, attention focused on the lightning flashing blue-white through the slats in the louvers.

The lights of the cottage had winked out more than an hour ago. Amos Lee was asleep. Fegan had checked on him just before the storm broke, and it never ceased to amaze him how the old man could sleep the deep, untroubled sleep of a child, despite the havoc that had touched and changed their lives. On nights like this one, Fegan envied that ability to drown out the past. What he wouldn't give to slip away into some other dimension, to block out the crashing thunder and blinding light.

He didn't like storms, but it was aversion through association, not fear. The night their old man left, the wind had howled around the eaves of the apartment in New Orleans. He'd been eight years old, and he remembered like it was yesterday . . . the shrill sound of his mother's screams, the crash of a chair being hurled at the living room window. The splintering glass barely missed a sleeping Jean Louise, but the rain coming in through the gaping hole woke the toddler. Their mother was too drunk, and too hysterical, too caught up in her own misery to notice when Fegan crept in and took the child to his own bed while Frank, a few feet away, muttered and thrashed in his sleep. . . .

Storms brought memories, and the unwelcome memories brought a deep-seated uneasiness that sat on his soul like a hundred-pound weight. The trouble that had dogged him in Chicago had begun with a snowstorm, and abruptly ended on a summer night just like this, with the wind moaning down the alleys and the lightning and the thunder loud enough to block out the screams of a young victim . . . the final victim of the West Side Strangler.

Eight women in five months, each one killed with an item of their own clothing . . . a belt, a pair of pantyhose, a shoelace from a jogging shoe . . . and no obvious connection between them except that each one was taken from the Projects on the west side of Chicago, each was female, and a phone call had been made to a journalist at the *Tribune* announcing where to find the bodies of the final seven victims. . . .

The last victim, Chandra White, younger than the others, had still been alive when the call came in. Her life had depended on Fegan finding her, and he'd let her down.

You couldn't help your sister, Mr. Broussard, but unlike most men in your position, you have a second chance.

Who is she? Where is she? Why the hell don't you just let her go?

Releasing her would defeat my purpose, and I can't do that. If I let her go, you wouldn't have any reason to talk to me, would you? And I so enjoy our conversations . . . You're such an important man, and I'm a lowly worm . . . Do you run, Mr. Broussard? I think I caught a glimpse of you running along the Navy pier last week.

Fucking insane bastard!

Would you run for this little girl's life, Mr. Broussard?

Fegan was slow to shake off the effects of the memories. Most days, he managed not to think of it more than two dozen times, but nights like this brought it all crashing back, breathing life into his anger, reviving the crushing sensation of impotence that came from bowing to the knowledge that he was a mere mortal . . . hardly hero material, no matter how much he'd wished for the sake of Chandra White that it was otherwise. As he bolted the last of the whiskey and turned toward the liquor cabinet, Clairée stepped out of the shadows.

Raindrops glistened in her dark hair like diamonds, on the shoulders of her pale terra cotta trench coat. She didn't say a word, just stood there, looking like a dream, her dark eyes large and luminous from sleep. Fegan forgot about the liquor cabinet and the bottle of Jim Beam he'd just opened. He forgot about the glass that dangled from his fingers, too, until she slowly crossed the room and took it from his hand, placing it safely on the tabletop. Then, she slid her fingertips over the hollows of his cheeks, and brought his mouth to hers.

Nothing good had ever come from a storm before, Fegan thought, *but maybe this time things would be different.* "You were right about one thing," she said huskily, "my dreams weren't my own. They were all about you. About us." She broke off kissing him, pulling back far enough to meet his gaze. "I didn't ask for any of this, Fegan."

"I know that." Quiet acknowledgement. It was what she wanted, he sensed—for him to understand that she hadn't planned or anticipated the outcome of her homecoming. Not the problems in Angelique, or their mutual, uncontrollable attraction. "But not askin' for it don' always mean the problem'll go away. Some things ain't easily solved, Char."

"Is that what this is? A problem?"

"You tell me," he said, unsure exactly where he stood with her, unwilling to commit to anything just yet.

She didn't move closer, but she didn't move away, either. "I don't know what it is. I don't know what to expect, or where to turn."

Fegan reached out, wiping away the rain from her cheek. "You can always turn to me."

Her eyes were wide, luminous in the darkness of the room, filled with doubt. "I turned to you this morning, and it didn't work out as well as I'd hoped it would. I'm not so sure I can trust you."

"Trust me," he said softly, beguilingly.

Claire heard and moistened lips gone suddenly dry with a flick of her tongue. "That wouldn't be prudent, now would it?"

He chuckled at that, a deep, throaty laugh that sent ripples of desire through her. "Sugar, if you were into prudent, you would never have come back to Angelique. And prudent sure wouldn't be standin' here, lookin' like you do.''

"And how's that?'' Claire asked, stepping close.

"Like you just tumbled out of the sack, like you're ready to be put back to bed.''

"You're my weakness,'' she said, sliding her hands under his open shirt, peeling it down over his arms and away. "I can't seem to resist you, but that doesn't mean I have to like it.''

"Oh, you like it, darlin','' Fegan drawled. "And so do I. Ain't nothin' wrong with that.''

"I'm out of control.'' She kissed and nuzzled his collarbone, then settled her face in the curve of his throat, inhaling slowly, deliberately drinking in the scent of his cologne. "And the worst part about it is that it feels too good to stop.''

Fegan's pulse felt heavy and slow. His focus was gradually changing and with it his body. Clairée wanted one thing from him, and that realization pushed thoughts of Chicago into the background.

Straining onto her toes, she kissed him, forming and reforming the sensual contact, keeping him guessing, catching his full lower lip between her strong, white teeth. "Charlotte Clairée,'' he groaned against her, "you're gonna push me too far.''

She stepped back abruptly, catching his hand, walking a half-circle around him while he resisted following, gently tugging on his hand until their arms were outstretched. Claire's lips curved in a slow, seductive smile. "Am I?''

It was all he needed. She barely had time to suck in a startled breath before he swept her up and stalked the length of the hallway to the bedrooms at the back of the house. Like the kitchen, the bedroom showed subtle signs of change. Fegan had made it his own with drapes and bedspread of rich sapphire blue, and carpet that was deep and soft underfoot. It was pleasing to the eye, to the touch, to the senses, just like Fegan, who set her on her feet by the bed, then reached for the sash knotted at her waist. The knot proved no challenge at all. He opened it in a flash and parted the coat to reveal her sleek, black slip and long, bare limbs.

Claire felt his hot gaze move over her, touching, searing her body. It had taken every ounce of courage she possessed to get in her car and drive over here, to deliberately seek him out. It may not have been the wisest thing she had ever done. In fact, she was fairly certain that it ranked high among the most impulsive acts in the history of womankind, something she was bound to regret when the morning's blush touched the sky. Fegan was a difficult man, complex, unpredictable. Getting involved with him went so far beyond being unwise that it wasn't even remotely amusing.

He was thirty years old, and to her knowledge he still hadn't had a serious relationship. Claire glossed over the fact that the same could be said about her, and focused instead on what that said about him ... that he had commitment issues? That he took women lightly? That sex was a bodily function as far as he was concerned, and emotions or tenderness rarely entered in; she was being extremely judgmental, forming assumptions based on her insecurities, not on truth. From a legal standpoint, she had just crossed the line. From an emotional one, she'd crossed the point of no return the moment she got out of bed and took the car keys from the dresser.

"Can I take your coat?" he said, his voice soft and liquid. She could smell the faint taint of whiskey on him, mingling with the spicy scent of his cologne, wild mixing with civilized, intellect bowing before primal instincts. Reaching out, he turned her so that she stood with her back to him. Claire shivered and burned at the feel of his knuckles brushing the bare skin of her shoulders, sliding the fabric off with a striptease slowness, whisking it away. Lifting the ribbon-thin straps, he eased them down, then allowed the garment to slip to the floor as he kissed her nape. "You're beautiful, Char. You always were. Too beautiful for your own good, maybe. You got to watch out in this big, bad world. There are men out there who'd jump at the chance to take advantage of you."

Claire tilted her head back, leaning against him, reveling in the feel of his strong embrace enfolding her, his hands on her breasts. "Is that a warning, Fegan?"

"I don' know. What do you think?"

Claire turned to face him, looping her arms around his neck. "I think that if you were my first there would be some validity to that statement. You aren't, and I'm a big girl who knows what she wants, what she needs."

"And what is that?"

"You. Come to my rescue, like you always do."

"Who, me? I'm not your rescuer. Me, I ain't got hero potential." He couldn't be the man she wanted him to be. He didn't have it in him. He didn't save or protect— he let people down.

"Maybe not. But you can make me forget."

Something flickered in her eyes, something Fegan recognized, empathized with, felt echoed in his own dark depths. She'd taken on a task that would have staggered a team of trained professionals, setting out to prove a guilty man innocent, to save the worthless skin of a father who'd betrayed his family. Armed with nothing more than her own grim determination and the bright embers of a love that a daughter had for her father, she was taking on the system, taking on a town . . . but tonight, for whatever reason, the burden weighed too heavily on her. She was asking him to take it from her, just for a little while, begging him, really, with her big brown eyes. "You sure that's what you want?" he asked quietly, reaching out to tuck a strand of hair behind one ear.

She didn't say a word, just leaned in and kissed him, and there was so much tenderness, so much trust in the gesture that the last of Fegan's resistance shattered and fell away.

Her reasons for being here didn't really matter. They were together, alone, with only the storm as witness, and she needed him as badly as he wanted her. Without another word, he took her hands and brought her to the bed.

Naked, he laid her down, taking just enough time to take a condom from the drawer of the nightstand; then, as the stark blue-white slashing through the louvers played over them both, he made slow, passionate love to her.

Claire touched him as he covered her, running her hands over his shoulders, his biceps, his back, and his hips. She couldn't seem to get enough of him, the satiny texture of his skin, the soft curls at his nape, the rough scrape of his newly emerging beard on her face as he kissed her, then buried his face in the curve of her throat even as he buried himself deep inside her.

Attuned to his every nuance, each ragged breath and poignant sigh, she drank in the scent of his skin, marveling that each thrust could carry her deeper inside her own being, to the place where they met and melded, joined, and were one. Slowly, gradually, the pleasure unfurled, like the petals on a blossom of the night-flowering jasmine—fragile, yet precious; perfect, yet all too rare. Claire's previous lovers had been selfish, and often halfhearted when it came to pleasing a woman. Fegan was focused, and she had the very real and intense knowledge that he focused solely on her. His movements were measured, the strokes gentle, yet so deep that each time he left her, she gasped, and ached to have him fill her again. Beads of perspiration formed on her upper lip. She moved restlessly on the pillow until he took her face between his hands and, frowning down at her, deepened his thrusts even further . . . and Claire's world exploded in a burst of brilliant light and crashing pleasure.

Spent, Fegan rolled to his side, gathering her close, strangely touched at the way she fitted her body to his. Suddenly, the nightmare that was Chicago seemed a lifetime away. He drifted off with Clairée in his arms and for the first time in months, he slept without dreams.

When he woke, the storm had passed, sunlight poured through the louvers, and he was alone in the bed. Not a trace of her remained. Nothing but the small smear of coral lipstick on his pillow to prove she'd ever been there.

It took most of the morning, and the tow truck from Stemple's Garage, but Fegan finally managed to get Amos Lee's truck back to the house. Rick Stemple took the beer Fegan handed him and wiped the sweat from his brow with a wrinkled blue bandana handkerchief. "I dunno, Fegan. Looks like dat frame's in pretty bad shape. It's not a good idea for somebody your granddad's age to be out rattlin' 'round alone in a truck like this here one."

"Tell me somethin' I don' know," Fegan drawled. "Listen, *mon ami,* what do I owe you?"

"Shit, I got a *mémère* Amos Lee's age. Just give me a ten for gas, and we'll call it even." He drained the beer and crawled back in the truck. "If I were you, I'd put that heap up on blocks. That'll keep him from tryin' to take it out again by hisself."

Fegan waited for the tow truck to clear the drive, then walked to the back of the lot. Amos Lee was puttering in his garden, hoeing his tomatoes and peppers and turnips, picking out the weeds and casting them to one side.

"Pépère," Fegan said. "We got to talk." The old man went on with his weeding until Fegan reached out and gently took the hoe from his grasp. "Here, lemme do it. It's too hot for you to be workin' so hard. Can't have you gettin' heat stroke." He worked the ground with vigorous strokes, taking out his frustration on the rich, dark soil. "Wish the hell you'd talk to me. I know you could, if you wanted to. I need to know you understand."

Amos Lee bent down, plucking a pair of radishes out of the ground, wiping the dirt off onto his overalls, offering one to Fegan, just as he had when Fegan was a child. Fegan took it, shaking his head at Amos Lee's amused half-smile. Despite his age, his brown eyes still sparked with life, though most of the time the look in them was faraway. As Fegan leaned on the worn handle of the hoe, Amos Lee made a quick motion, fingers to mouth, his grin never wavering.

Fegan shook his head, but he took a bite of the radish, because it was what his granddad wanted, because it was something they had always done, and it brought the old man pleasure. The ritual had significance and Fegan understood. *Close to the earth, one with the bayou—respect both and they'll provide for you.* It had worked for Amos Lee's generation, but waste from the chemical companies had found their way into the water, and these days a kitchen garden couldn't help to pay the mortgage.

Times had changed.

"You can't take the truck no more, you understand? Frank damn near had a coronary over it, and though I'd stick my head in a gator's mouth before I admit it to him, he's right. You just can't keep doin' like you did before Jean Louise. Things have changed, *Pépère.* You've changed. Besides, you don't even have a valid driver's license, and if you get caught, you'll get fined. Damn good thing Cash didn't think to ask last night. You need to go somewhere—all you got to do is tell me, and I'll take you." Fegan clamped a hand down on Amos Lee's shoulder. His grip wasn't hard, but it got the old man's attention. "You got that?"

Amos Lee lifted a finger to his ear. He'd heard. Then, making the sign that Fegan was to wait, he ambled into the cottage. In a few minutes he was back, the curious half-smile fixed in place. He reached out and took Fegan's hand, turning it over, pouring a slim gold chain into his palm. At one end was a crucifix. "This was Mémère's. Jean Louise used to wear it," Fegan said.

Amos Lee nodded, pointing a finger directly at Fegan, then with a quick, curving motion of his gnarled hands, he made the sign for a woman, pointing at Fegan again.

"You want me to give this to Char?"

A jerky nod, and the conversation ended. Amos Lee gave a wave and turned toward the cottage. In a moment, the door closed behind him.

Fegan stared down at the crucifix in his hand. He'd been trying to put Clairée out of his thoughts all morning, and he hadn't exactly succeeded. The way she'd materialized from the midst of the storm had caught him off guard. He hadn't expected to see her again so soon after the fiasco at the houseboat. And he sure hadn't anticipated that she would initiate their first full-blown sexual encounter.

But she had.

And then she'd fled, like a wraith in the night, leaving a faint whiff of her perfume and the tantalizingly wild tang of sex in the air, on the sheets, and in Fegan's mind. He'd changed the sheets, the untamed taint in the air had been replaced with the aroma of smoked ham, eggs, and coffee, but he hadn't figured out how to put it out of his mind, and he suspected that it had to do with the fact that there hadn't been any closure. No parting kiss, no awkwardness, no telling her that he'd call, and then forgetting to. It didn't feel finished, somehow. But then, maybe it wasn't, he thought, staring down at the puddle of gold in his hand.

Twice, she'd asked for his help, and twice he'd turned her down. But his refusals didn't put an end to it, and the fact that they'd become physically involved only complicated matters. He didn't want Clairée to get hurt, but she was too damned stubborn to drop the inquiry into the murders, and he wasn't altogether sure she could ever accept a truth she didn't want to hear.

There was no doubt that her belief in Jimmy's innocence was unshakable. He saw it in her eyes every time he looked at her. It was the look of firm determination, absolute belief, and in her rare unguarded moments, the panicky look of someone racing against the clock. She never would have turned to him if she hadn't been desperate.

Somewhere in the depths of her inner self, she was still that panicked kid, clinging to a limb high in a tree and unable to climb back down. She truly believed that he could save her. But she couldn't be more wrong.

But he wasn't the man she thought he was. He was someone she didn't even know, and he couldn't help her. It was beyond his power to help anyone. He'd proven it many times over.

With Jean Louise.

With Chandra White, and God alone knew how many might have lost their lives since he turned his back and walked away.

He placed the hoe in the garden shed and entered the bungalow by the back door, but the cool shadows of the house weren't any kinder, any less unrelenting than the harsh, glaring sunlight of Amos Lee's truck patch. Clairée couldn't dispute the facts, no matter how badly she wanted a different ending. Jimmy had confessed to killing Jean Louise after the sheriff had found a plastic bag with her clothing and pornographic magazines depicting young girls under the front seat of his car. Years after, Fegan had read the confession and wished that he hadn't, because it filled him with an anger for which there could be no outlet.

Jimmy Sumner confessed to the killing. He admitted to the method, and to dumping Jean Louise in the bayou. And after that, he'd stopped talking.

As bad as it would have been to relive through his words her final hours, the torment she went through, it was worse having to speculate, and the senselessness of it all had been the thing that sent Amos Lee over the edge.

Yet, as difficult as it had been for Fegan, Amos Lee, and Frank, it had been worse for Clairée. His baby sister had lost her life, but when Clairée's father stood accused, he couldn't, or wouldn't, defend himself. Jimmy's obstinacy had frustrated his attorney and scandalized a community that wanted answers as much as they wanted justice.

In two weeks, they'd have that justice. But unless Jimmy had a change of heart, or Clairée succeeded, he'd take the answers with him to his grave.

CHAPTER EIGHT

"All I can say is that this had better be important. I was two strokes under par, and just about to beat the pants off Terry Bradshaw when your call came in." Bernie Freeman settled into the leather chair behind his desk, blessedly hiding his plaid pants from view. *No, Frank thought, they were more than plaid. They were tartan plaid, and they weren't just loud; they screamed.*

"You teed off with Terry Bradshaw in that god-awful outfit? God, Bernie. I've seen more stylish trousers on a trained monkey."

"You get your charm from your mother, Frank?" Freeman asked, tenting his fingers in front of his chest. "Because the notion that you called me off the ninth green and into the office on a Saturday to discuss my wardrobe doesn't set well on an empty stomach. What's this about, anyway? Don't tell me you've had a change of heart about the new purchase, because the owners are packing, and closing's already scheduled for week after next. Oh, and by the way, what in hell happened to you? You look like you tripped and fell into a brick wall."

Frank pressed his hand to his split lip. Talking was difficult, and he should have been home in bed—correct that: he *would* have been home in bed if Christine hadn't nagged him right out of the house. "It was more like aggravated assault. I had a disagreement with Fegan."

"Your brother did that?" Bernie whistled. "He must throw one hell of a punch. Guess he caught you off guard, huh? Looks like he chipped your front tooth, too. Maybe you should see your dentist."

"I don't need a dentist," Frank insisted. "I need an attorney—my attorney."

Bernie put down the pen he'd been turning end over end, and straightened in his chair. "What am I? Pureed goose liver? I'm right here, Frank, but you have to talk to me. Do you want to sue for damages? Because I'm thinking that Judge Rawlings might be sympathetic. She's got this sister that's manic depressive—way out on a limb, if you get my meaning. In fact, I heard that she recently took out a restraining order."

Frank shook his head. "I can handle Fegan," he insisted. "It's my grandfather I'm worried about. I've given this a lot of thought, Bernie. I want to have Amos Lee declared incompetent."

Claire had been trying for half an hour to get a phone call through to Angola. When Warden Cryer took the call, the news wasn't good. "I'm sorry to bother you with this, Warden, but I'm very concerned about my father. My last two letters were returned this morning.

I thought perhaps he would call, but we haven't heard from him."

"I don't want to appear unsympathetic, Miss Sumner, but if your father doesn't wish to have contact with the outside, he does have that right."

Claire cradled the receiver in both hands. She sat in a chair by the French windows in her second-floor bedroom, her legs drawn close to her chest. Outside the windows, the rain had stopped, and a low-lying fog crept over the cane fields that bordered the lawn to the north. "He's my father—" She paused and cleared her throat, then tried again. "You're right, of course. I'm sorry to have bothered you."

"I know this must be difficult for you." There was a second's hesitation, as if he hated what he was about to do. Hated saying it as much as she hated hearing it. "The chaplain spoke with him. He tried to convince him to make good use of the time he has left, to make his peace with his loved ones . . . but I'm afraid Jimmy wasn't receptive."

"I see," Claire said, struggling to hold it together, and barely succeeding.

"Miss Sumner," Warden Cryer said, "if I may be so bold? Try not to take it personally. I have worked in Corrections for twenty-five years, and I've learned a thing or two during that time. Men in your father's situation have different methods of coping with their situations, and sometimes it is easier for them to cut all ties with the outside world. It isn't common, I admit. But it does happen. If you like, I can put you in touch with Dr. Hayes, our prison psychiatrist. I am sure he would be more than happy to talk to you, and help you sort things through."

"No," Claire said in a rush. "Thank you, but that won't be necessary." She replaced the receiver in its cradle, let go, and stood, turning to the window, unable to stop the tears that streaked down her face. Everything was such a dreadful mess . . . an unmanageable tangle that couldn't be straightened out, or sorted through, and she had the awful, panicked feeling that her return to Angelique had only made things worse.

The air kicked on, and she hugged her arms at the sudden cloying chill in the room. Dampness did that, made it feel hot and cold and sticky all at once. The heat had been unbearable before the rain came, and when the barometric pressure dropped and the heavens opened, everything felt wet, indoors and out. *Hey . . . you okay?*

She knew the voice had no place in reality, that it existed only in her imagination, but she answered aloud anyway. "Yeah, sure. I'm fine."

Well, you sure don' look fine. What're you cryin' for, anyhow? Your daddy yell at you?

"At this point yelling would be an improvement," Claire said with a watery laugh. It ended on a weepy gurgle as she swiped a hand first under one eye, then the other. "He doesn't want me."

My daddy din' want us, neither. But I've got Fegan, Frank, and Amos Lee . . . and you got your Aunt Eule . . . and me. I ain't goin' nowhere, not so long as you need me. We'll be friends forever, just you wait and see.

The soft, wavering vow made the lump in Claire's throat more painful than she ever thought it could be. *Friends forever, just you wait and see.* It was a vow they'd made often. But it hadn't worked out that way. "They are going to put him to death soon," she said softly, miserably. "We're running out of time, and I'm not at all sure that I can do this."

Jean Louise was silent, but Claire thought she saw

her, hovering around the edge of her vision. *You asked Fegan, huh?*

"He made himself very clear. I wouldn't be at all surprised if he celebrates the execution."

Jean Louise moved a little closer, so that she was looking out of the window at the rain-drenched landscape, too. Claire imagined she caught a glimpse of the ghostly girl alongside her own reflection. *I still can't believe you did it with my brother.*

Claire groaned. "We are *not* going to talk about this."

Jean Louise smiled, coyly. *But you liked it, didn't you?*

Claire sighed, her thoughts dragged from the grim hell of Angola to the bliss she'd found in Fegan's bed. "Yes. I liked it," she admitted, tempted to laugh at the understatement. "I liked it very much."

You goin' over to the house again tonight?

Claire shook her head. "Not tonight. Not any night. It was a one-time thing."

The girl snorted, and a look of pure skepticism that only Jean Louise could give transformed her face. *You said you liked it! I know you like him—don' lie!*

"Fegan is—difficult. And it's unbearably complicated." She watched the brown flow of the bayou and thought of the shadows of the houseboat, of his sultry kisses, the expertise of his seduction. "He misses you."

But I'm here, she said. *Besides, he's got you. You're gonna ask him again, right? 'Bout your daddy?*

Claire sighed. What was it he had said? *Twice burned means that you might not get another chance.* "Twice is my limit. I'm not going to go begging. I'll just have to go it alone."

Jean Louise's bravado faded, and a look of stark fear entered her dark eyes. For the first time, Claire noticed the blue shadows under her lower lashes, the faint bruise on her right cheek. *Don' say that, Clairée. Please! Maybe it would be better just to leave things alone.*

"You know I can't do that," Claire said. "And you of all people know why."

There are things you don't know!

"Then tell me!"

"Miss Claire!" Jane's call sounded, followed by urgent rapping. Claire opened the door. The housekeeper wrung her slim hands until her knuckles showed pale beneath her toffee-colored skin. "Miss Claire, it's Miss Eulanie. She's collapsed. You got to come quick!"

"Oh, dear God. Where is she?"

"At the tractor shed. Ned called on the phone, just after he sent for the ambulance."

Mary Pershing sat at her desk, a cup of coffee at her elbow, her nose buried in a copy of the *National Enquirer,* and the phone pressed to her ear. "I know. I know. It's just so hard to believe that the divorce is final, but there it is in black and white. Tom and Nicole are definitely done for. I just hope they can remain amicable for the sake of the children. Divorce is so hard on the little ones."

"Hey, sugar, what you reading that trash for?" Fegan said, pushing the paper down so that she couldn't ignore him. "You know that some unscrupulous reporter made up all that shit, now, don' you?" He tugged the tabloid from her grasp and dropped it in the wastepaper basket beside the desk. *"Bat Boy Has Twins . . . Superstar Divorce Details . . .* get a life, darlin'—this ain't fit to line a hamster's cage with."

"Fegan Broussard, are you here because you want somethin'? Or did you stop by to ruin what's left of my crap-ass afternoon?"

"You had a bad day? Well, it's about to get worse. Tell your daddy I'm here, and I need to speak with him."

"He won't see you," Mary said. "He's workin', and he specifically said he doesn't want any interruptions."

Fegan took the toothpick from his mouth and pitched it into the trash. "Maybe, maybe not. But he either talks to me, or I talk to the *Picayune*. I may be out of the business, but I still know a few people who'd love to get a fresh angle on this latest murder."

Mary couldn't come out of her chair fast enough. She rapped on the door to her old man's office, opening the wooden panel far enough to speak through the crack, then turned to give him an arch, disapproving look. "You can get off my desk now. He'll see you. And while we're at it, you owe me a dollar eighty-five." She held out her hand as he passed by her.

"I'll do you one better," Fegan said, putting a ten-dollar bill in her palm. "You want horror, read Anne Rice."

The door clicked shut, and simultaneously Vance Pershing took off his reading glasses, folding them precisely, placing them on the stack of papers neatly piled on his desk. He didn't bother to get up, and he didn't offer his hand. "Mr. Broussard. I trust you have a good reason for threatening to ruin a perfectly good afternoon."

"Hey, Sheriff. I happened to be in the neighborhood, and thought a courtesy call might be in order—one investigator to another." He ignored Pershing's derisive snort, sinking into a chair in front of the desk. "You boys get an ID on that girl my granddad found in the swamp yet?"

"As a matter of fact, we did—not that it's any of your business. This came in over the internet a little while ago, and since it's going to be in the morning edition, I don't see any reason to keep it from you. Her name is Sherry Ellen Davis—she's a fourteen-year-old runaway from up near Shreveport. I've been in touch with the authorities, and she'll be goin' home this afternoon."

"I've been in touch with some people, too, and I hear she died of asphyxiation—plastic bag was still over her face when Amos Lee pulled her out of the bayou. I'm curious, Sheriff. What other similarities are there between this case and my sister's murder, besides the obvious?"

Pershing planted a hand on the edge of his desk and leaned slightly forward. "Exactly what are you driving at?"

"Nothin', Sheriff. Nothin' at all. Just seems kind of funny that two murders with glaring similarities in a town the size of Angelique haven't raised more eyebrows. But we're all goin' on, business as usual. Why is that, I wonder? What is there about this that you don't want anyone to know? Was it the method of asphyxiation? Or the red silk cord tied around her wrists and ankles?"

Pershing came halfway out of his chair, his face draining of all color, then going scarlet as his blood pressure soared. "How the hell did you come by that information?" His voice sounded choked, strangled.

"Just a shot in the dark," Fegan said. "Funny, how that kind of thing can pay off. Is there anything else I should know about this?"

"Get out of my office."

Fegan stood. *"Mais,* yeah, man. I'll go, but I'll be back. You can count on that much." He barely noticed Mary's glare as he passed by her desk and into the hallway. He didn't wait until he was outside to light the cigarette. Nicotine had a calming effect, but it didn't even touch the tension that gripped him.

Red silk cord.

Red silk cord. He'd had a front-row seat in the courtroom every day. He'd seen the photos introduced as evidence. His sister's swollen hands, bent at an odd angle. Red silk cord tied and knotted so tightly that she hadn't stood a prayer of breaking free.

Fegan got behind the wheel of the Pontiac, but he didn't reach for the keys. Clairée's arguments that Jimmy was innocent kept running through his head. Her stubborn insistence that there was a connection between the two killings went far beyond mere conviction, and bordered on zealotry. Judging from what he'd just learned, it was easy enough to understand her frustration at no one being willing to listen, not even him. . . .

Two girls, with similar looks, close to the same age. Both asphyxiated in a similar manner after being raped and tortured, with red silk cord binding wrists and ankles.

Stubbing the cigarette out in the ashtray, Fegan turned the key in the ignition. Was Clairée right? Could Jimmy be innocent of Jean Louise's murder?

Fegan resisted the thought. He needed proof, and there were still too many unanswered questions for him to change the beliefs he'd held fast to for a decade.

And then there was Jimmy, himself. One week into the trial, he'd shocked his counsel, the town, and the press by changing his plea to guilty and confessing. Not long after, he'd been sentenced to death. And the ordeal had ended, at least as far as outsiders were concerned.

For Fegan, it had never really gone away, and he only had to speculate to bring it all rushing back. Jean

Louise's loss, Clairée's bewilderment and devastation, Amos Lee's confusion, and the feelings of fury and lust for justice that had somehow taken the place of his sorrow. He'd felt his sister's loss keenly, but he'd never grieved—not really. Instead, he'd lived with her loss every day since . . . like Clairée lived with the loss of a friend, the loss of a father. . . .

"He had to have done the murder," Fegan said aloud. "Nothing else makes any sense. Why would a man confess to something that horrendous if he had no part in it? Knowin' what it would do to his family?"

There were too damn many questions all of a sudden, and not enough answers, and the doubts that hadn't been there an hour ago sat on his stomach like hot lead. If he couldn't reason them away, then he'd do his best to drown them. He shoved the floor shift into first and eased off the clutch just as Remy tapped on the passenger window. "Hey, cuz. You lookin' kinda thirsty. You headed to de Cadillac? How 'bout a ride?"

"Matter of fact, I am," Fegan said. "Get in."

A hoarse-sounding scream echoed down the corridor, blending with the noise of a dozen radios. Jimmy did his best to ignore it, focusing instead on the difficult passage in the book open on the steel table in front of him. He made it a point to mind his own business. It wasn't just a strict rule with him. It had become a way of life, and it was the only way to maintain the smallest shred of privacy in a place where privacy didn't exist. Each cell had a toilet and sink, an open-barred front on the cage, and a clear view of the corridor's walk and the windows beyond. Everything a man did, he did with witnesses. The only thing that remained his own were his thoughts, and he was as jealous of those as an old maid was of her fantasies.

"Hey, Jewell! That you, screamin' like a woman down there?" Adesco held the jigger through the bars of his cell, turning it until he got the vantage point he wanted. Every inmate on the row had one, a scrap of mirror glued onto a strip of cardboard that allowed them a different vantage point than the one they were permitted for twenty-three hours a day . . . every inmate but Jimmy. His view of his world was narrow, and he liked it that way.

"Shut up, Adesco, or I'll catch you in the yard an' whup your ass! Damn rat just about bit my balls off! Oh, mercy! I'm bleedin'. Somebody call the guard. I need to get to the doctor."

"Quit your cryin', Jewell, you chickenshit, you. Sumner's tryin' to get through this article on how rats carry rabies—ain't that right, Sumner?"

"Rabies? Aw, Jesus!" Jewell went into a frenzy of cursing and flailing at something unseen, something that squealed hideously while Trick Adesco howled in amusement.

Jimmy put aside his book and turned to the bars. "For Christ's sake, Jewell, just flush the damn thing! Send it back where it came from."

"Hey, Jewell!" Trick said. "Let that poor mother go. You know we got a strict no-pets-allowed rule here on de row, and rats gotta eat, too."

The rats came into the cells through the sewer system every time the hard rains came. Jimmy had learned to watch for them, but he didn't have the heart to kill the poor bastards. Rats, cockroaches, mosquitoes, and gnats. During the summer months, Angola was hell on earth, and there was no escape from any of it.

The tier door opened with a metallic clang, and the

noise immediately died as a host of jiggers appeared through the bars. "It's Warden Cryer," was passed along down the line. When the visitor's identity reached Jimmy, he marked his page and closed the book.

Flanked by a pair of guards, Warden Cryer stopped in front of Jimmy's cell. Jimmy got up and walked to the bars. The warden only came to death row for one reason, and he'd been expecting him. "James Buford Sumner, the Governor of Louisiana has decreed that on the thirtieth day of July in the year of our Lord two thousand and—"

His voice droned on, spelling out in bureaucratic terms the date and time and manner of the execution. When he finished reading, he turned and left as silently as he entered. And he never once looked Jimmy in the eye.

The row remained silent for a long while. Each man had been sentenced to die, and when one of their community was taken, it brought home their own grim realities. "Hey, Sumner?"

"What do you want, Adesco?"

"Rats? Do they carry rabies?"

Jimmy sprawled on his bunk with his arm pillowing his head, staring at the ceiling, seeing instead the solid red brick and sweeping green cane fields of The Willows. "Sumner? You there?"

"No," Jimmy replied. "They don't."

"Well, do me a favor and don' tell Jewell." Adesco was quiet for a minute, then his voice came again, his tone serious. "Listen, man, I been thinkin'."

"You're always thinkin', Trick. You got too much idle time on your hands. Why don't you try learnin' something? Put your brain to use."

"This is serious, man," Adesco said. "Dead serious. I got me a plan to get the hell outta here. You're a smart man. You know as well as I do the gov'nor ain't gonna grant us no stay. Don' know 'bout you, but I ain' goin' outta this pest house in no pine box. I got me a plan.''

Jimmy said nothing, unwilling to break his concentration by playing into Adesco's pipe dream. It was Clairée's thirteenth birthday, and Eulanie had insisted upon a surprise party. She and Melba had spent all afternoon decorating, and the courtyard was a fairyland of pink-and-white balloons and crepe paper streamers. He'd come home early from the garage, showered, and changed into his best summer suit, natural linen that Melba always said made him look like he belonged at a country club instead of Tyson's garage.

Doggedly, Jimmy followed the memory through the festivities to the dance he'd shared with his daughter under the crescent moon. She'd been radiant, a sweet Southern flower on the verge of womanhood, and he'd never been more proud of her than he was in that moment. She favored him, only she was pretty, so pretty, so grown up that looking at her made his heart hurt.

Charlotte Clairée. His baby girl.

It was something he relived in his mind over and over, every detail so meticulously examined that he could see the glossy, dark-green-and-white of the oleander, smell the light, powdery scent of her perfume, hear the sweet sound of her mother's laughter floating out behind them. Jimmy tried, as always, to slip into the memory, to physically remove himself from this place and its misery, but he couldn't quite make it real. Then, as he desperately tried to hold on to the image, it started to fade, the beauty of the garden dissolving into the gray-and-white of his concrete hell.

"Sorry, baby," Jimmy whispered to no one in particular. "I am so sorry. For everything."

* * *

Cash had been to Briar Rose more times than he cared to count, and the first glimpse of the Greek Revival mansion crowning the slight rise in a sea of deep, lush green never failed to stir a wave of jealousy and bitterness. "There, but for the insane whim of a crazy woman and a dying old man, go I," he murmured, pulling around to the service entrance. The self-conscious bastard insisted upon it, probably because somewhere deep down inside his black heart he knew how much it rankled for Cash to be denied the front entrance. It was the sort of petty vengeance Ashton got off on, and though Cash hated him for it, he didn't quite have the nerve to rebel.

He parked at the rear of the mansion and sat for a few seconds, surveying the grounds and garden. His great-great-grandfather, Joshua T. Morlay, had bought this land before the War of Northern Aggression, and built an empire on the blood and bones of a thousand slaves. Forced black labor had built the twelve-room palace, and the sweet yield of the cane fields had filled the Morlay family coffers. Joshua's fortune, greatly depleted by the war, had passed to his eldest son, John, Cash's maternal great-grandfather. John tripled the fortune in the years after the first World War, and made improvements to the mansion, which he planned to bequeath to his son Albert and daughter Helloise, until she decided to run off with a black-eyed gambler named Ellis Edmunds, and the old man cut her out of his will, leaving everything to Albert and his descendants.

Helloise Morlay Edmunds was Cash's grandmother, much to his eternal regret.

"From this to a bayou shack and no indoor plumbing," Cash grumbled. "And all for the love of a card shark's dick. I sure as hell hope it was worth it.'' He slammed the door on his Chevy truck and made his way across the carport to the side door. The cook was in the kitchen, scraping carrots for the evening meal. She glanced up, but didn't acknowledge him with anything but her eyes, her opaque stare following his progress across the length of the kitchen.

He found his cousin in the downstairs study—"the conference room," Ashton liked to call it. Cash caught his eye, and Ashton motioned him in. A small, slight gentleman with a perfectly round bald spot on the back of his curly, dark head plied a tape measure while the candidate paced the room. "This party is important, Ashton. I can't stress enough *how* important. A lot of influential folks have doubts about your abilities to perform in Baton Rouge, never mind Washington.''

"I know that, Percy, and I'm on top of it. Have I not been out pressing the flesh at every opportunity?''

"This time that's not enough," the voice on the speaker phone argued. "You need the backing of the parish, and that means the Committee for Democratic Leadership. Have you heard from their spokesperson yet?''

Ashton turned so quickly that he nearly trampled the man with the tape measure, who'd been doggedly trying for an inseam measurement. He offered no apology, riffling through a stack of papers on his desk. "Miz Eulanie Sumner. No RSVP as yet, though I can't say I'm surprised. She's no fan. Been turning down my offers for that scrap of land she owns for years. Stubborn as the day is long. Hell, Percy, she's almost as mule-headed as you.''

Percy apparently didn't find that funny. "This is serious, Ashton. If you want the seat in the senate, you'll make an effort to change the lady's opinion of you. I've researched it, and she holds a lot of sway in this parish. People respect her."

"I'll see to it," Ashton assured him. "Now, will you stop your frettin'? You sound more like an old woman than my campaign manager. Listen, somethin's come up. We'll talk later."

Ashton switched off the phone, glancing down in annoyance at the sweating tailor's assistant who reached out with the tape measure. "Oh, for heaven's sake, Henry! If you delay in my crotch any longer, people are goin' to start gossiping about us. That'll do for now."

Henry muttered an apology, turning a dull shade of red as he gathered his notes and tape and got to his feet. He barely glanced at Cash as he hurried from the room.

Cash snorted. "You always did have a way with the unwashed masses."

Ashton's silvery blue gaze flitted to Cash's, and Cash felt a sudden chill, like he'd been touched by ice. It was the same unflinching gaze that had stared down from the bench for eight years. Ashton's rise had been nothing short of phenomenal . . . from the prosecutor's office to a judgeship, and from a seat on the bench to a bid for the Louisiana State Senate. Cash had lost track of how many poor bastards Ashton had screwed over to get where he was, but he would be willing to wager the number was staggering. "Henry's a tailor's assistant, Cash, and a sweaty tailor's assistant, at that. Do you have any idea how many times he's measured my inseam for this particular suit? I'm beginning to think he's got some sort of unhealthy fixation."

"And you don't?" Cash said, then immediately regretted his sarcasm when that chilly gaze flicked over him again.

"I'm in a generous mood, so I do believe I'll let that

remark slide." Circling his desk, Ashton sank into the huge leather executive's chair, leaning forward to lift the lid on the teakwood humidor. "Smoke? No? Oh, that's right. Star athlete. Your body's a temple, and all that."

"That was a long time ago," Cash said. "I just don't like cigars."

"You have no idea what you're missing," Ashton said, trimming the end of the hand-rolled Cuban with a small pair of gold scissors, then passing the tobacco appreciatively under his nose. "Vice is the spice of life, Cash. Now, what brings you here? Have you found it?"

"No, but I do have news. Clairée Sumner's back in town."

"And staying with her aunt, I imagine?"

"You knew about it?"

He struck a match and held it to the trimmed end of the cigar, puffing the air blue. He shook out the match before he answered. "I do have other resources, cousin."

"Did your resources tell you that she's been asking a lot of questions?"

"Is she really? What sorts of questions?"

"Questions about the runaway they found in the swamp."

Ashton clucked his tongue. "Shame about that poor child. And so young. How is the investigation progressing? Does the sheriff have any suspects yet?"

Cash snorted. "Pershing? He's just tryin' to hang in there long enough to collect those retirement checks, incompetent old bastard. He'll never solve this thing. Not in a million years."

"You shouldn't discount Vance so easily, Cash. He was a good man in his day. In fact, there was a time when there was none better. Did you know that as a young officer in Atlanta, he cracked the Simons homicide singlehandedly? They say he had a nose like a bloodhound, and even if he is a little past his prime, he still deserves your respect. If you aren't respectful, he'll never trust you, and if he doesn't trust you, you can't keep me informed about this investigation, now can you?" He puffed out a perfect smoke ring, flicking a smile Cash's way. "You know how I feel about being kept in the dark, Cash. Now, get on out of here and see what you can find out before you outlive your usefulness and I'm forced to end our association. It would be such a shame if that happened."

"You po' child. Who did this to you?" Martha Felix bathed the girl's forehead with a wet washcloth, then folded it over her brow. "You ought to be in the hospital, that's what. Don't know that John did right, bringin' you here, but he was scared outta his mind. John don't like the po-leece, an' with good reason. They lynched his daddy back in Mississippi when he was just two years old. Trust comes hard after somethin' like that."

There wasn't much use talking to the girl, and Martha knew it. She was so deep in delirium that there was no way to determine if she even heard her voice, but it soothed Martha's nerves. It made her on edge to have a white child in her home, a sick white child who was so battered and bruised it was shocking to look upon her.

What if she died?

What then?

The authorities could break down her door, tear her home apart, lock her nephew away in some jail cell for the rest of his days. And even if they let him tell his story, there wasn't a police officer in all of Louisiana who would be willing to believe that this poor child had darted out of the woods and into the road in front of John's car, looking like she'd just outrun Satan and his legion of imps.

John might be blamed. He might even be accused of killing her . . . it had happened to countless black men all over the South. It had happened to Martha's brother, Abram, John's daddy . . . It could happen again, and John was the only family Martha had left.

Tucked away in a small closet of a room in the upstairs, with the doors locked and the blinds drawn and only a seven-watt bulb to keep the darkness at bay, Martha spooned broth between the girl's cracked lips, the worried frown on her face a permanent fixture. "Lord, look down on this child, an' have mercy. Don't let her die, Lord. Please, Jesus . . . don't let her die."

CHAPTER
NINE

The Pink Cadillac was full to overflowing with the dinner crowd. Deni Zane, a local girl who waited tables part-time to supplement her husband's income, plopped a plate of steaming boiled crawfish and two sweating mugs of draft in the center of the table, giving Remy a dark look. "I hope you brought your wallet, Fegan. If he tol' you it was his treat, you're about to get taken."

"Who, Remy?" Fegan said with a wink. "Stiff his own blood? Nah, *chère*. Remy likes his neck too much to try and pull that shit on me. Ain't that right, Remy?"

"Go on," Remy said, "talk trash 'bout me. *J'm'en fout pas mal.*"

"And a good thing you don't give a damn, Remy," Deni shot back, her dark eyes glittering with animosity. "Ever'body in this parish knows what a waste o' time you are. Won' be long till you gotta go clean to Plaquemines just to get yo'self a date!" When she turned to Fegan, she was as sweet as honey. "Anything else for you, Fegan, just give a yell."

Fegan turned back to his cousin, whose dark gaze followed the provocative sway of Deni's blue-jean-covered hips. "What'd you do to piss her off?"

Remy shrugged. "Nothin' much. Told her old man dat she was in the back seat o' my Camaro when she said she was visiting her sister. What?" Remy said at Fegan's doubtful look. "He asked, and he happens to be a friend o' mine ... He wanted the skinny, and I gave it to him."

Fegan shook his head. "Man, you're lucky you're still breathin'."

"Al's not the type to hold a grudge." He shook his head. "Chicks, man. Dey all crazy." He sucked the head of a crawfish, then pinched the tail, munching the tender meat. "So, you gonna tell Remy what you was doin' talkin' to the cops? Last time I checked, Vance Pershing wasn't no friend to the Broussards."

"That much ain't changed," Fegan said easily. "I went there for information. Thought I'd start at the top and work my way down. As the sheriff, Pershing's supposed to be aware of what's going on in the parish."

"You get what you went dere for?"

"Old Vance was his usual uncooperative self. In fact, I get the distinct feelin' the man don' like me."

Remy laughed. "Shit, man, don' sell yourself short. Dere's a lot of folks 'round dis parish don' like you. Fact is, I'm not too keen on you myself right now. You dis me, and you don' even know it. If it's information you want, how come you don' come to Remy?"

Fegan sipped his beer. "I'm here, ain't I? Nobody gets around like Remy Broussard, ever'body knows ... so give it over, cuz. What do you know about the kid *Pépère* found in the swamp?"

"I know it's the one thing everybody's talkin' about," Remy said. "Clairée was askin' me the same thing not long ago. I s'pose you want to know what she knows?"

Fegan fixed Remy with an unwavering stare. "Not that easy, cuz. You always hold a little somethin' back. What do you know that you ain't sayin'?

Remy sat back, ready to bargain. "You buyin' information from Remy? Now, dere's a first."

"Did I say anything about buyin'?" Fegan asked quietly.

Remy shook his head in disgust. "Shit! Might know you'd want somethin' for nothin'! I got expenses, man. I can't afford to give it away."

"You can't afford not to," Fegan told him, serious now. "You got two little sisters, and you don' want either of them to end up like Jean Louise any more than I do."

Remy glanced around, and his manner changed completely. "You sure know how to hurt a man," he said. "But you're right, too. Somebody's gotta stop this dude, Fegan. This latest kid was in sad shape. I opened the drawer one night while I was cleaning the office, and saw for myself. Somebody tortured her, man . . . electrical burns . . . like a stun gun, and dat ain't all. There was something weird I saw dat I ain't told nobody. She had punctures and contusions on the back of her right ankle consistent with bite marks."

Fegan frowned. "A human bite?"

"No, man," Remy said, shooting another wary glance around the bar. "Dog bites, and I ain't talkin' no terrier. From the way it bruised, and the tears to the flesh, I'd say she was on the run and it caught her and dragged her to ground. There was another bite on her calf, but the holes were punctures, like once she was down, it bit her again." Remy looked worried. "Jean Louise have a dog bite, Fegan?"

"No," Fegan replied. "She didn't." He didn't feel the inclination to share his recent discovery about the link between the murders with his cousin. Remy could be bought, and Clairée had deep pockets. It was a full-time job just keeping her out of trouble. The last thing he needed was for her to find out that her suspicions concerning Jimmy's innocence were well-founded.

Remy seemed to read his thoughts. "Dere's some heavy-duty nasty goin' on out dere. Too big maybe for Vance Pershing to handle. You figured out yet how you're gonna keep dis from Clairée?"

"It sure would help if you'd keep your mouth shut."

"Um, um, um. She turned out fine, dat one," Remy said slyly. "Me, I'd treat her right, or some dude wid more style and panache might just steal her right out from under your nose."

"You can't steal what I don' have," Fegan insisted. "Char and I are—hell, I don' know what we are. But it ain't like that."

Remy laughed, tipping his hat down on his brow. "Den you won' mind if I impress de chick wid my style and wit."

"I didn't say I was ready to throw her to the wolves," Fegan said sharply. "And if you know what's good for you, you'll keep your distance. Char's in a vulnerable position. The last thing she needs is you sniffin' around." He tossed a bill on the table and got up. Remy's talk about Clairée irritated him, despite his insistence that his own interest in her was purely casual. In reality, his feelings for her were anything but casual. When they were together, there was no escaping their sexual compatibility. Theirs was a perfect fit. She excited him, she teased his libido and played havoc with his senses. She drove him crazy, and he liked it that way. Clairée was hot: the way she looked, the sensuous way she moved, the way she pressed that luscious body of hers to his when he kissed her . . . and he was just as hot for her. Just thinking about it made him hard for her, and as he left the bar, there was no room in his mind for Remy, and no doubt where he was headed.

Claire stood by the window of the hospital room, hugging her arms as she watched rain sluice off the panes, and listened to the steady beep, beep, beep of the heart monitor. Dr. Trelawney insisted that keeping Eulanie overnight for observation was just a precaution. Eulanie was just as insistent that it was purely manipulative. "He is going to run those tests of his one way or another," she'd said. And the only way to keep Ned, and Jane, and Claire from nagging her into a nervous fit would be to have the damn things, and prove to them all that she was stronger and more fit than the three of them put together. Claire had been relieved that her aunt had finally given in.

"It's getting late," Eulanie said. "You've been here all day and you haven't even eaten. I want you to go home."

Claire resisted the idea of leaving. Eulanie was the only connection to Jimmy she had left, and she was afraid of losing her—she stopped the thought, cut it off. She wasn't losing either of them. Not yet, anyway. "I thought I'd stay until they bring your supper tray."

"What for? Do you get some perverse pleasure out of watching me eating their prefab potatoes and that dreadful brown mess they call gravy?" Eulanie put away her sarcasm, her look softening. "Claire, please. It's bad enough that fool Trelawney has tricked me into having

his way with me—you shouldn't be wastin' your time
in this place. Go home. Get something to eat. Give that
nice Mr. Broussard a call, and then get some rest. I insist.
I'll leave the order in which you do it all completely to
your own discretion."

"I'm going to pretend I didn't hear that." But Claire
couldn't quite suppress her answering smile.

"He's a real looker, that one," Eulanie said slyly.
"And a fine choice. Why, if I were thirty years younger,
I'd give you a run for your money." She was quiet for
a moment, watching Claire closely, as if for some sign
that her teasing had an effect. "He did say his answer
was still no. But he never said what the question had
been. Perhaps you'd care to satisfy a mature woman's
curiosity?"

Claire walked to the bed and, leaning down over the
metal railing, kissed her aunt's cheek. "I think I'll take
your advice after all, and go home to The Willows. The
idea of a late supper and a nice, warm bath is suddenly
extremely appealing. Listen to the doctor, please?"

"As if I have a choice," Eulanie grumbled.

It was nearly ten o'clock when Claire rounded the
bend and the lights of the BMW shone on the dark-
colored Trans Am waiting in their drive. A light, misting
rain fell, beading on the gleaming hood and fenders.
The hood was cold. He'd been waiting a while. As she
went slowly up the walk, his cigarette glowed orange in
the shadows of the first-floor gallery. After the stress-
and-worry-filled day, the last thing Claire needed was
company . . . but Fegan wasn't an ordinary visitor, and
she was astounded at how glad she was to see him. "Is
there a reason you're sitting out here in the dark?"

"Wouldn't have done me much good to knock.
Nobody's home. I heard about Miz Eule. How is she?"

"Horribly stubborn," Claire replied, "determined to

deny her own mortality, and I'm worried about her. She takes on far too much, more than she can possibly handle, and she refuses to listen to reason."

"Sounds like somebody else I know," he said softly. "You gonna invite me in?"

"It's late, and I wasn't expecting guests."

"Is that what I am?" he replied lazily. "A guest?"

"Maybe," Claire hedged, "maybe not. I don't know. I guess I haven't figured it out yet."

He drew smoke deep into his lungs and blew it to the misty night. "Worried that I'll take advantage of you?"

"In order for you to take advantage of me, I'd have to have feelings for you, and though I hate to break it to you, I'm not quite that naive."

"Oh, ouch!" he said, placing a hand over his heart, laughing softly. "Maybe I ought to go on home, after all. Don't know if I'm safe with you."

It was a game they played that went back to their youth, each dancing around the other, each wary of giving up too much for fear of betraying a vulnerability, of admitting the potential seriousness of their involvement, the potential for deep, abiding hurt.

"How 'bout if we both agree to be sweet to one another, just for tonight," he said, stubbing the cigarette out in the tall standing ashtray Eulanie provided for guests. "C'mon, Char, what'dya say? Not everything has to be at crisis point all the time, now does it? We can have a little fun. How long's it been since you had fun?"

"Too long," she admitted. She thought of their night at the bungalow, of his hands on her flesh, and shivered. It hadn't been fun, she insisted silently. It had been necessary, so driven that it had almost been involuntary . . . and it wouldn't be wise to let it happen again. Yet even as the thought faded, she felt herself weakening.

He wasn't just any man. He was Fegan, and where was the harm as long as she kept her heart detached, protected?

He watched her, calmly, coolly, while she struggled for a reply. "You hungry?"

"What?"

He came out of his chair, stopping before her, tall, strong, incredibly attractive. With him standing so near, Claire found it hard to concentrate. "You've been at the hospital most of the day," he said. "When was the last time you had somethin' nutritious?"

As if on cue, her stomach growled. "I wolfed down a bagel for breakfast."

"A bagel, she says." He took the keys from her hand. "Not much nutritional value in a bagel. In fact, I'm not so sure that even qualifies as food south of the Mason-Dixon. C'mon, darlin'," he drawled, taking her by the hand. "Ol' Fegan's gonna whip you up a midnight omelet."

Claire let him lead her through the house to the kitchen, then watched as he raided the fridge and found what he needed. Sitting at the table, with the radio on the windowsill playing softly, and her foot tucked under her, she avoided all thoughts of how perfectly natural it felt to be here with Fegan like this, how destined, how right. Thoughts like that were dangerous, and no matter how much she wanted to, she couldn't allow herself to depend on him.

This wasn't real, she reminded herself.

It was temporary.

His culinary talents were real enough. Cold diced shrimp, mushrooms and onion, cheese and red pepper, fresh basil and a splash of white wine. The omelet was fluffy and filling and wonderful. He watched her as she savored every bite, listened to her appreciative groan, and smiled. "Oh, God, this is good. Where did you learn to cook like this?"

"There was a woman I knew in Chicago. She liked to eat before sex, after, during ... We spent a lot of time in the kitchen."

"Chicago. Aunt Eulanie said you were at the top of your field there, a rising star. Why did you leave, Fegan? You had a career. Why come back here to Angelique?"

"Lot a water under that bridge, baby."

"Don't," Claire said, reaching out to touch his hand. "Don't hide behind the cool, smooth talk and smart-ass attitude. There's so much more to you than that."

He was half-smiling, but there was a tension building inside him. Claire could feel it. The muscles of his forearm felt tight, like a compressed spring, and she knew that something had to give. "What would you know about it?"

"You grew up poor. It's one thing we have in common, and people like us don't turn their backs on opportunity without a damn good reason." She didn't give him time to cool off, or even to catch his breath. If she gave him time to think, he would only find more evasions, more cunning camouflage to hide behind, to throw her off the scent. "Why'd you quit, Fegan? It's so unlike you."

"Yeah? Talk to Frank, why don' you?" he said with a harsh laugh. "You'll get a whole other take on the trouble with Fegan."

"To hell with Frank," Claire said. "I don't care about him." *I care about you.*

Fegan sighed, taking her hand, bringing her knuckles to his lips. "Look, sugar, I don' want to talk about Chicago. I don' want to think about what's past."

Jolie Blon came on the radio, a traditional Cajun ballad, heavy on the accordion and slow enough to dance to.

Fegan got up, pulling her out of her chair and into his arms. "Dance with me. You know you want to."

"Wanting to isn't the problem," Claire said with a laugh. "It's the resisting part that I can't seem to get the hang of."

He held her close. "Resist what? Me? And here I was, thinkin' you liked me."

He spun her around, and Claire caught her breath. It felt good to be in his arms, Vin Bruce crooning poignantly in the background. By slow degrees, she relaxed, letting the song and the moment and Fegan seduce her, so that her problems felt far away. "I *do* like you," she said.

"Uh-oh. I feel a 'but' comin' on."

Claire sighed. "I'm just not sure I trust you—and I know I don't trust myself. I'm not very good at relationships, Fegan, and I seem to constantly pick the wrong kind of guy."

He was watching her intently, his blue eyes dark and riveting. "And what kind is that?"

"Men who want a mother more than a relationship, men who run from commitment, men who are exciting, alluring, impossible to understand, dangerous."

"Yeah, but you like danger, don' you, Char? Danger gets your heart pumpin'. Ain't no thrill, no charm, givin' in to some choir boy." He lowered his dark head and kissed her, and she could feel his hunger. The dance hadn't ended, but their movements slowed to a hypnotic, sensuous sway that clearly indicated what was on both their minds.

Fegan had accused her before of thinking too much, but he was every bit as guilty. He couldn't seem to smother his thoughts, to just accept what was happening between them as a natural progression of events. Some small voice deep inside him whispered that this had been coming for years.

It felt so good to be with her like this, to hold her body close to his and just be . . . locked outside of time and place. Two souls seeking fulfillment, completion . . . and no matter how much he tried to reason that it was just sex, his heart knew the lie and silently acknowledged it for what it was.

It wasn't love.

Love was a cliché; it came, and it went.

This was different—more seductive, more complex, and he couldn't quite squelch the thought that no matter where their lives had taken them, eventually they would have still found themselves right here in a warm kitchen in Angelique, holding onto one another while they waltzed to some old Cajun melody.

One kiss sealed the evening's outcome. One kiss was never enough for either of them, and she was as eager for him as he was hungry for her. "Would you like to see the second floor?"

Fegan pulled back far enough to stare down into her eyes. "I thought you'd never ask."

In the shadowy intimacy of her bedroom she seemed to abandon all thought of the most token resistance, leading him to the bed. Nibbling, fleeting kisses told him what a tease she could be, but the small, quick hands that stripped his shirt open, then settled on his shoulders, pushing him down onto the mattress, stated her intent clearly enough. She followed him down, pressing him back into the pillows, kissing him so thoroughly that he couldn't seem to catch his breath.

There was an urgency in her tonight that he hadn't seen before, an aggression that was new and unbearably sexy. Straddling his hips, she unbuttoned her blouse, letting her short skirt ride up around her hips. Fegan slipped his hands under the fabric and into the back of her black lace panties. Her bottom was smooth as silk, kissable. Christ, he wanted to test its softness with his teeth, he wanted to feel her yield to him, then conquer and close around him like a hot glove . . . But she had control and she was loving it.

Rising slightly above him, she found his hands, forcing them down, threading her fingers through his, holding him a willing captive as she teased him with her body, taunted him with the sensation of sex without true penetration. It went beyond merely sexy into the realm of erotic, and the look in her brown eyes said that she knew exactly what she was doing to him.

Claire did know. She was as aware of his body, his breath, as she was her own. More so, because she was the catalyst that made it quicken, she was the cause of his ragged breathing, and God help her, she drank his reaction in. It wasn't right, maybe it wasn't rational, but she wanted him to feel the torment she felt, knowing that she'd been waiting all her life for him, knowing that it would never work out.

Too much had happened for them to ever achieve a lasting peace, the kind of ease of being together that allowed one to figure out if forever was an option, and the events that had brought them together would doom them to separate lives. The outcome was beyond her control . . . beyond his.

They should have been allowed to explore the possibilities without the specter of a murdered young girl between them, or a man hanging onto his life by a thin, weblike thread. The desperation she felt over her situation crept into her lovemaking. She kissed him as if it would be the last kiss they ever shared, and when he easily turned her onto her back and wrapped her in his loving warmth, she held on for dear life.

To start your membership, simply complete and return the Free Book Certificate. You'll receive your Introductory Shipment of FREE Zebra Contemporary Romances. Then, each month as long as your account is in good standing, you will receive the 3 newest Zebra Contemporary Romances. Each shipment will be yours to examine for 10 days. If you decide to keep the books, you'll pay the preferred book club member price of $15.95 – a savings of up to 20% off the cover price! (plus $1.99 to offset the cost of shipping and handling.) If you want us to stop sending books, just say the word… it's that simple.

BOOK CERTIFICATE

Yes! Please send me FREE Zebra Contemporary romance novels. I only pay for shipping and handling. I understand I am under no obligation to purchase any books, as explained on this card.

Name _____

Address _____ Apt. _____

City _____ State _____ Zip _____

Telephone (_____) _____

Signature _____

(If under 18, parent or guardian must sign)

Offer limited to one per household and not valid to current subscribers.
All orders subject to approval. Terms, offer, and price subject to change. Offer valid only in the U.S.

CN013A

Thank You!

THE BENEFITS OF BOOK CLUB MEMBERSHIP

- You'll get your books hot off the press, usually before they appear in bookstores.
- You'll ALWAYS save up to 20% off the cover price.
- You'll get our FREE monthly newsletter filled with author interviews, book previews, special offers, and MORE!
- There's no obligation – you can cancel at any time and you have no minimum number of books to buy.
- And – if you decide you don't like the books you receive, you can return them. (You always have ten days to decide.)

Zebra Contemporary Romance Book Club
Zebra Home Subscription Service, Inc.
P.O. Box 5214
Clifton , NJ 07015-5214

Claire was experienced, but she had never made love to any man and felt the need to meld into him, to have him meld into her, counting their collective heartbeats and dreading the moment he would leave her. She'd never known a passion that burned so hot and intense that it left nothing but cold, gray ash in the wake of the fiery conflagration. Until Fegan.

When she woke at dawn, there was a note on the pillow next to her.

I would've stayed to make you breakfast . . . but then, payback's a bitch, ain't it? By the way, Amos Lee wanted you to have this. You can come by and thank him for it, if you like. You may even learn something, though the conversations around the bungalow these days are pretty one-sided.

F.

Claire lifted the delicate gold chain and crucifix, pressing her other hand to her mouth as her eyes filled with tears. "Oh, God. Jean Louise."

She wasn't even surprised to hear the girl's reply. She was either getting used to the ghostly presence, or sinking deeper into her delusions.

You gonna marry him, Clairée?

"What?" Claire glanced at the shimmering presence at the foot of the bed.

Jean Louise hooked her thumbs into the front pockets of her faded jeans and swung her body from side to side, her expression one of childish glee. *I'd sit down, but it might be messy. All that huggin' and kissin' going on.*

Claire smiled and shook her head. "How old are you?"

I'm eleven. Don' you 'member?

"But you were fourteen when you—went away,"

Claire said, keenly aware of the strangeness of this conversation. "How can you be eleven, if you were fourteen?"

I liked eleven better. It was before.

Claire frowned. "Before what?"

Before I knew what boys did—before he came around, and things got scary.

Claire felt the chill overtake her, and the hairs on her forearms stood on end. "He? The man who hurt you?"

Jean Louise shimmered, then started to fade. Her voice got smaller, fainter. *You never did say—you gonna marry Fegan, or what?*

Claire realized the moment the presence departed. The atmosphere of the bedroom seemed less charged, less chilly. "I have no plans whatsoever to marry Fegan. In fact, at this point, I am more likely to win the Power Ball Lottery and give away my millions to join a Tibetan monastery."

A derisive snort. *They don' take girls, Clairée.* The rejoinder was tiny-sounding, far away.

Claire sighed. "My point exactly."

She showered and dressed in a coffee-colored vest and matching slacks. The rain had hiked the humidity, but brought the temperature down to a relatively cool eighty-six degrees. Claire took her bag and her keys, stopping just long enough before the mirror in the foyer to slip the crucifix around her neck and place it protectively against her skin. Then, she opened the door and nearly ran into a man in a blue uniform and fashionably expensive sunglasses.

Claire gasped, stumbling back, and might have fallen if he hadn't reached out and grabbed her arm. "Clairée, you remember me, don't you? Cash Edmunds. We bumped into one another the other night at the Pink Cadillac.''

Claire tugged her arm from his grasp. She hadn't known Cash well in the days before she left Angelique, and what she had known, she hadn't liked.

He smiled at her instinctive recoil. "Sorry. I didn't mean to startle you. Sheriff Pershing asked me to stop by and inquire after your aunt. He heard that she's ailin'.''

"You're exceedingly lucky you didn't get a knee to your groin just now," Claire told him. "I don't always deal well with surprises, and sometimes I react first and ask questions later." Claire glanced around. There was no car, no vehicle in sight. "How did you get here?"

His grin was sheepish. "On foot. I'm afraid my truck broke down just north of here, and my cell phone's dead. Yours is the nearest house, so I thought I'd kill two birds, so to speak." He mopped his forehead with the back of one hand. "It was quite a hike in the heat."

Claire's pulse had slowed enough to allow detail to creep into her awareness. The sweat rings darkening the fabric of his shirt and the hair at his temples, and the flush on his face told the truth of his statement . . . so why did his presence make her so uneasy?

"Would you rather I just left? I can probably catch a ride on the main road."

Claire softened, setting aside her reservations, her wariness. It was broad daylight, and he was not exactly a stranger. In fact, he was part of the same system of justice she worked so hard to uphold. The least she could do was allow him to make a phone call. "I'm the one who should be apologizing, Deputy. The fact that you startled me is no excuse for my being rude." She moved past him, unlocking the door, turning on the lights. "The phone's on the table in the hallway."

Cash Edmunds's fair hair and ruddy complexion only served to accentuate the illusion of youth, of good-natured, boy-next-door innocence he exuded. Claire couldn't help thinking that he had looked this way when he was eighteen, and would appear precisely the same when he turned forty. Yet looks could be deceiving, and though she had known Cash Edmunds, the high school football star, she didn't know Cash, the sheriff's deputy.

He made his call, and carefully placed the receiver back on its cradle, turning to Claire. "About Miz Sumner? I hope her illness isn't serious."

"The doctor wants to run some tests," Claire replied, unwilling to make it worse than it was.

"You'll tell her the sheriff asked after her?"

"Of course."

"She must be glad you came home to visit," he said. "Family's important. The only thing you can count on, really. Will you be stayin' long?"

He smiled, all clear-faced innocence, but there was something in his pale blue eyes that stirred Claire's hackles. "Are you asking out of simple curiosity, or in a professional capacity?"

"I suppose you could say, a little of both. It's unfortunate, but not a lot of folks around here remember your daddy with fondness. In fact, there are quite a few who'll be makin' the drive to Angola prior to the execution, and it won't be to hold a candlelight vigil."

"No need to beat around the bush, Deputy. Exactly what are you driving at?"

He shrugged. "Only that it might be wise if you keep your visit short, and don't outstay your welcome. Askin' questions'll only bring up the past, and cause trouble for everyone involved." He turned to go, then, at the door, turned back. "Nice seein' you again, Clairée. Oh. You want me to have a look around the place while

I'm waitin' for my ride? A woman alone can't be too careful."

"Thank you, no. I'll be fine. Good day, Deputy."

"Bye, bye, now." Cash Edmunds stepped into the blinding light. Claire waited a second, and then turned the lock, uncaring if he heard, or not. Shaken, she leaned against the oak panel, wondering precisely what had just happened.

"Daddy, where have you been? Mama's worried sick about you."

Nancy's voice, sounding much like her mother's when she was at full rant, was an unwelcome distraction. It had that same whining quality, as persistent and annoying as a hungry mosquito. Vance loved his daughter, but there were times when he couldn't seem to escape her proclivity to be totally and utterly frivolous. He'd hired her out of spite after the town council foisted Edmunds upon him.

Edmunds's connections had landed him the position despite the fact that Ray Simms, the man Pershing had handpicked for the job, had more experience and, ultimately, was better qualified. Simms, a friend of Vance's, took a job in Baton Rouge, and three weeks later was fatally shot in a drug bust gone bad.

Vance Pershing never forgot a slight, and he hadn't warmed to his deputy. "Pumpkin," Pershing said in a tightly controlled voice, "your mother knows where I am, and there is no reason for either of you to take me to task for tryin' to wade my way through this mess."

"Well, you could have called," she said.

Pershing took his glasses off and laid them with exaggerated care on the papers and notes scattered over the desk blotter. "Sweetheart, I will be goin' on home in twenty minutes or so. Now, isn't there somethin' in the outer office for you to do?''

"I suppose," Nancy said. "But are you sure you're all right?"

"I'm fine," Pershing said. It was the kind of lie a father told his daughter to prevent her from worrying unduly about things that had absolutely nothing to do with her, the sorts of things that should never touch a policeman's daughter. "I just need a few minutes, sweetheart. Now, be a good girl and close the door on your way out."

She didn't like it, but she honored his request and went out, leaving him alone with the paperwork that summed up the final hours of a young life. Vance shuffled the top of the untidy pile to one side, uncovering the photos taken at Broussard's Landing, and later at Pontier's Point in the heart of the swamp. Amos Lee Broussard finding the girl had been the first unlucky break, as far as Vance was concerned. The old Frenchman had broken every rule of crime scene procedure, and the only thing that had kept Vance from coming down hard on him was his addled state. Broussard had acted instinctively. He'd found a lost child, and he'd brought her back to civilization, exactly as he'd done with the body of his granddaughter, Jean Louise.

It had pissed Vance off from an official standpoint, but a part of him understood. Katy, his oldest daughter, had two children, and though she and her husband Mark lived in Iberia and he didn't see the girls often, he couldn't help empathizing with the old man. God help anyone who even considered doing harm to his grandbabies.

Empathy aside, Broussard's unthinking actions hadn't helped matters. Moving the body had compromised the location where it had been found, but it hadn't affected the crime scene because it hadn't been located yet. Just like the Broussard girl, Sherry Ellen Davis's body had been dumped at Pontier's Point, a location so isolated that only dedicated swamp-crawlers were aware of its existence . . . but both girls had been murdered elsewhere.

Though the very idea of agreeing with a reporter, even an ex-reporter, rubbed him like a hair shirt on sunburned skin, Vance had to admit that Fegan Broussard's theory that the same actor had done both girls carried the unnerving taint of an emerging validity. Broussard had no evidence, however, to prove his theory correct, and Pershing resisted the urge to embrace the idea that the murders were connected.

Things were bad enough in Angelique without making a low-life like Jimmy Sumner into a martyr to a miscarriage of justice. Folks already doubted the ability of the sheriff's department to provide adequate protection for the parish. Why, just yesterday, Mrs. Arley King had put in the ludicrous request for a permit to carry on the job; Vance had denied the request. Mrs. King was a crossing guard at St. Barnabas Elementary School. When confronted with the unusual request, Pershing had suffered a momentary thrill.

Had Broussard been shooting off his mouth?

A man with his background could make things damned uncomfortable for the sheriff's department, and that kind of trouble would only serve to complicate an investigation that had already stalled.

He gathered the papers into some semblance of order and deposited them in the file, pausing just long enough to select one of the photos, holding it out and tilting his head back to examine the swollen and battered face through his bifocals. Time had become a luxury he didn't have. He needed answers, and he needed them now. He could lock his files and deny Fegan Broussard access to his office, but he couldn't prevent him from asking uncomfortable questions, the sorts of questions a man like him excelled at asking. And unless he cracked the case himself very soon, he couldn't keep Broussard from blowing the investigation wide open.

"Speak to me, child," Vance murmured. "Where were you before you took that last boat ride? Who wanted you dead, and why?"

That same evening, the beam of a flashlight shone again on the small graveyard at the edge of the bayou. He wasn't sure why, but coming here brought him a sense of peace, and peace wasn't something he experienced often. Then, he thought about the Sumner family, and he knew that he wasn't alone in his restlessness.

Clairée was asking questions. Not that it would do her any good. Rumor linked her name with Fegan Broussard, information that had given him a momentary chill. An ex-reporter with an ax to grind could be a dangerous thing. The man would know how to dig to get what he wanted. Then he calmed, remembering who he was . . . all that he was. Protected, untouchable, beyond suspicion or reproach.

CHAPTER TEN

Remy's information about the dog bite on the back of the girl's leg had grabbed Fegan by the throat and wouldn't let go. He couldn't seem to get the kid out of his mind, the ordeal she had suffered, the terror she must have felt, or his cousin's reaction to what he'd seen. Remy was always cool, not the kind who shook up easily, and Fegan couldn't help wondering if there wasn't something his cousin knew that he continued to hold back, despite his insistence that he had told Fegan everything.

Remy always had an angle, and he knew exactly how to work every situation to his best advantage, but would he hold out on his own blood?

He would, and in a heartbeat if it worked to his benefit. The knowledge didn't help a great deal to ease Fegan's mind, but he wasn't quite sure what to do about it. He'd leaned on him as heavily as he dared for the moment. There was always the chance that if he was holding back information, and Fegan pressed him too hard, that he'd get scared and split. Weighing on the side of caution, Fegan decided to let things cool down for a day or two, then talk to him again. Fegan shook a cigarette out of the pack, sinking into the hickory rocker on the back porch. He could hear the muted noise from his granddad's TV through the screen door of the cottage, but his mind was on the woman he'd left at five o'clock that morning. Their night together had left its mark on him, and he couldn't seem to shake the feeling that intense and confusing was normal where Clairée was concerned. It was hard to even think about her quiet aggression without wanting her all over again. She was everything he'd ever imagined her to be and more: sexy, and exciting . . . even a little wild . . . the kind of woman every man dreamed about and damn few ever held for more than a night.

He'd picked up the phone more than once since he got back, intending to invite her over. He knew he should tell her about the sheriff's admission, as well as the facts gleaned from Remy, but was unsure if his true motive for bringing her to the house was so he could share his insignificant facts, or because he wanted something else from her, something he'd already enjoyed twice, and seemingly couldn't get enough of. Acutely aware of how serious she was about uncovering the truth about this latest killing, how desperate she was to save Jimmy, he'd put the phone down again.

The information he had didn't amount to much. It would be callous and cruel to get her hopes up for nothing. It was also a violation of the first rule of any investigation: don't set a client up for an emotional fall. Facts first. Answers came when all the facts were in.

"Red silk cord, and a dog bite." Fegan took a long

swallow and leaned back, propping his feet on an over-turned crate. "That's some strange stuff, all right."

Dogs sometimes attacked and killed, but this dog hadn't. The kid had died of asphyxiation . . . a plastic bag over the head, secured with duct tape, her wrists and ankles tied with red silk cord . . . like some macabre Christmas present . . . just like Jean Louise. He knew the cord had significance, but he didn't understand it. And there was only one man who did.

If Remy was right, then the dog had caught her by the ankle and dragged her down, which meant she'd been on the fly—running for her life at the time.

Had she trespassed on someone's property and been attacked? If so, why wouldn't the owner have found her, saved her?

And why weren't the wounds noted in the coroner's report? Fegan knew Homer Folley. He was conscientious, and it wasn't like him to miss something that obvious. There had to be a reason behind the omission, but he'd be damned if he knew what it was. He'd stopped by the funeral parlor to ask Homer and found William Keyes, instead. Homer, it seemed, was out of town on business.

Too many questions and not enough answers, and he couldn't seem to get the kid out of his mind. Or Jean Louise, for that matter. She would have been twenty-five years old last April, a year younger than Clairée, a grown woman by now with a life of her own, a boyfriend or maybe even a husband and kids.

Unfortunately, she hadn't made it that far. She hadn't been allowed to grow up, to make mistakes, to live and to love. Someone had robbed her of that chance, stolen her future, depriving their *pépère* of his will to connect to the world, and Fegan of the one person who'd truly loved him. Jean Louise had believed that he'd hung the moon, that he'd set the stars in place, and she'd never had the opportunity to discover just how wrong she'd been about him.

Missing her just never seemed to go away. Her absence was like a wound in his heart that refused to heal, and on nights like this one, he found no ease from the deep, abiding ache. No ease at all.

A few weeks ago, he'd been certain that the man responsible for taking her away would pay for that crime with his life. It had always been a pitifully small consolation, a hollow victory, and Jimmy's death couldn't replace what they'd lost.

Now, he didn't even have that much.

Fegan threw down his cigarette in disgust, grinding it under the toe of his sneaker.

Making his way into the house, he picked up his car keys and Panama hat. He'd always hated unanswered questions. John Albert Akins, a friend and mentor from Chicago, had often praised him on his talent for getting to the core of a story, for asking the tough questions. "Once a journalist, always a journalist," he'd proclaimed.

Fegan fought the notion. He'd left his past behind when he'd thrown the contents of his closet into a suitcase and caught the first plane from O'Hare headed to Lafayette. Fegan Broussard, journalist, was as dead as Jean Louise, as dead as Jimmy would be in a few short weeks, and he had no plans to revive him. "I'll ask a few questions, that's all, for Clairée's sake. A few questions can't hurt. But ain't no way I'm gettin' sucked back in."

And he meant it.

* * *

"I still don't understand why this is necessary. The last thing I need is a wheelchair. They allowed me to pace the halls while Trelawney stalled on the release forms. I must have walked five miles this morning—up and down, up and down, and they won't let me walk to the car? For heaven's sake! Whoever makes these rules could do with a little common sense."

Claire exchanged glances with Jane, who was nearly hidden behind a huge vase of red carnations and white lilies. "You know, Miz Eule, it's the *in*-surance companies that make the rules. They just don' want folks who insist on goin' home before they're supposed to havin' a heart attack in the lobby and dyin' on the property."

Eulanie glared at Jane. "No one is having a heart attack, though all of this fuss *may* give me an ulcer. Hospital stays and unnecessary tests—it's just Trelawney's way of plumping up his stock portfolio."

Claire sighed. "Dr. Trelawney is concerned about you, Aunt Eulanie. We all are. I wish you'd listen to him."

Eulanie set her jaw, and Claire saw shades of Jimmy. They were equally stubborn, each hellbent on following their own path, and neither of them would listen to reason. "I'm fine," Eulanie insisted. "Or, at least I would be, if everyone would just take one step back and give me room to breathe."

They wheeled her through the automatic doors, but the moment they reached the sidewalk, Eulanie waved Claire to a stop, got out of the chair, and set off for the BMW at her normally brisk pace. "Watch your step, Jane. At your age, you can't afford to fall and break a hip."

"My age?" Jane said, outraged. "Don' you mean *our* age?"

As the housekeeper huffed, Eulanie threw Claire a wink.

Once they arrived at The Willows, nothing short of a hurricane could stop Eulanie from assuming her normal workload. She spent the morning in her office and the afternoon with Ned discussing the aging farm tractor's newest ailment. Claire made several attempts to convince her aunt to rest, but finally gave the effort up as a lost cause and drove to Angelique and the small, white house with green trim on Mayfly Street.

Amos Lee was plying the garden hose, spraying a patch of grass beside the garden liberally with water. His bait bucket sat on the grass near his feet, along with a flashlight. When the sun went down the nightcrawlers would rise to the earth's surface to escape their wet burrows. When they did, they would be seized and dropped into the old man's bucket, bait for the catfish Amos Lee was so fond of. *You gonna help me and Pépère catch nightcrawlers?* The voice, sounding faint and far away, brought tears to her eyes. Claire saw the old man glance around, and for one crazy second she imagined that he'd heard it, too. Then, he caught sight of her, and raised a hand in a silent greeting.

"Mr. Prideau," Claire said. "Do you remember me?"

He turned off the hose, laying it on the grass. His dark eyes were still bright, shining with the unmistakable light of a keen intellect. There was not a trace of the vagueness at this moment that she had expected. Wordlessly, he held his hand out, chest high.

Claire understood. "Yes. As a child, I spent a great deal of time here."

Retrieving the bucket, he held it out to her, a spare, dark silhouette against the backdrop of a hazy, red sunset. In a few moments it would be dark. "If you don't mind, I think I'd rather hold the light."

Claire took the light. "Mr. Prideau, I know this won't be easy for you, but we need to talk about the murders . . . Jean Louise and the girl you found recently."

He didn't appear to hear, just caught a worm, pulled its thick, red-brown body from the ground, and dropped it in the bucket. Claire had never been good at finding bait. Jean Louise had been the brave one; the mere sight of the worms in the bucket made Claire cringe. "Mr. Prideau, you found both Jean Louise and this last girl. Did you notice anything unusual about the area in which you found them?" She heard her own voice in the stillness of the twilight, and grimaced. *Dumb question, Claire. If you found a body, what would you be focused on— the body? Or the crime scene?*

Only a professional would be alert to the kinds of clues she was hoping to find. Amos Lee would have been too distraught at finding Jean Louise to pick up on details, and with this last victim, perhaps too addled.

She gathered her resolve and pushed ahead. "Was anyone there? Did you see anyone? On shore, or in a pirogue? Did you see anything that seemed strange or out of place?" But Amos Lee just kept doing what he'd been doing, gathering fat worms to catch fat catfish for the parish supper tables, and his own. "Mr. Prideau, please. My father's life depends upon this." This last was wrung from her, and sounded as if it had been dragged from the depths of her soul. Claire heard it and wished to God she could take it back. She'd promised herself that she would maintain a firm grip on her emotions. She'd sworn to herself that she would not expect more than the old gentleman could give. Instead she was reduced to begging him to give what he hadn't given his own blood kin in a decade. "I'm sorry. Oh, God, I'm sorry. This isn't your worry, and I shouldn't be asking, but you're my only hope. I'm so sorry," she said, backing away, then turning to go. "I'm truly sorry."

"*C'est alright.*"

Said softly, almost muttered, it was enough to stop Claire dead in her tracks. Flashlight in hand, she turned and watched, stunned, as Amos Lee put the bait can on the porch and closed the door to his cottage, shutting her out, blocking out the night.

It wasn't exactly inspired thinking. Sheriff Vance Pershing had the paperwork on the girl Amos Lee found, and a lot more information than he was telling. From a legal standpoint, by not being forthcoming with a civilian asking questions about an official, ongoing investigation, Pershing was doing his job by the book, and all that went with it. But to Fegan's way of thinking, Clairée wasn't an ordinary citizen, and whether she knew it or not, he'd appointed himself her representative, at least for the moment.

He sat in his car with his hat tilted low over his eyes, pretending to nap until the sheriff emerged from the low brick building. His daughter Nancy was with him. Fegan watched as Pershing accepted the girl's kiss on the cheek, then got in his car. Nancy quickly followed suit, taking a left from the parking lot while Pershing took a right. As soon as the sheriff was out of sight, Fegan tilted his hat back and, retrieving the folders from the passenger seat, got out of the Pontiac.

Deputy Fred Rally, fortyish and sporting a seriously outdated comb-over, was eating a shrimp po'boy at his desk. Rally normally worked graveyard shift, but he also filled in for Cash Edmunds on his days off. "Oh, hey, Fegan," Rally said around a mouthful of sandwich, "what can I do for you?"

Fegan leaned a hip on the corner of the deputy's desk. "Hey, Fred. Sheriff Pershing around? I didn't see his car in the parking lot."

Rally wiped his mouth on the back of his hand. "Bad timing. You just missed him."

"That's strange. He specifically asked me to drop off these surveillance files for him."

"Must be important if he requested 'em," Rally said. "You want me to put 'em on his desk?"

"Nah," Fegan said with a grin. "I'll do it. Don' want to spoil your supper."

Fegan grasped the sheriff's doorknob and the phone rang. "Acadia Parish Sheriff's Department. Officer Rally speaking—how may I help you? Hey, Miz Reed. Oh, I'm fine. How are you? And James? Aw, that's good to hear. My wife? Fine, just fine. Kids, too. Yep. My rheumatism's kickin' up a bit, but other than that— you know how it is. Some things just seem to get worse in damp weather. Uh-huh. Uh-huh."

Rally was a windbag, and if he hadn't been manning the phones in the sheriff's office, he would have been hanging over a backyard fence somewhere shooting the breeze with the neighbors, a fact that worked to Fegan's advantage. He entered the office and went directly to the filing cabinet. The file marked "Sherry Ellen Davis" was an inch thick. Fegan scanned the coroner's report, but Remy was right. Cause of death: suffocation brought on by a plastic bag slipped over the head and bound with duct tape. "Jesus Christ," Fegan muttered, then read softly on, "Judging from the defense wounds, cuts and bruises on her wrists and ankles, and given the fact that there was no obvious head trauma, it is likely that the victim was conscious when asphyxiation took place."

Images swam blearily in the dark depths of Fegan's subconscious, but he wouldn't allow them to surface . . .

images of his baby sister in those last terrible moments. He riffled through the rest of the files, examining the crime scene photos as closely as he could in the short amount of time allowed him. The girl's half-naked body had sprawled on its back, but her right side showed mottled bruising.

Cancel that, Fegan thought, flipping through the photographs. It was lividity, not bruising. He'd seen it before, on the photos of Jean Louise, and later, on the corpses of several victims of the Chicago killer. Lividity happened when the heart stopped pumping and the blood ceased circulating, pooling in the lowest points of the body, turning them a livid purple.

The kid lay on her back in the photographs, but the lividity had occurred on her right side, which indicated that she'd died curled on her right side, most likely in a fetal position. And there was something else stuck to the shoulder of her white blouse . . . pine needles.

Fegan put the photos back in the file, and the file in the drawer. She'd been dumped in the swamp, but she hadn't been killed there. Pines grew on higher ground, ground with adequate drainage.

Rally hung up the phone as Fegan was leaving. "Fegan? The files? For the sheriff? You forget?"

"Could be somethin' he needs right away," Fegan replied. "I think I'll just take 'em by his house." He brushed past Cash on his way out of the building.

"Broussard. You here to swear out a PFA?"

"Protection from Abuse?" Fegan tipped his hat down on his brow. "What for? You ain't done nothin' to me lately."

"We released Manny Poutou this mornin'. His wife Terri dropped the charges. Said she needed him workin' so she could continue to collect child support."

"That's good news, Cash. Terri Poutou owes me money."

Edmunds grinned. "Well, I wouldn't worry too much. Ever'body says her old man pays his debts. Although you were the one holdin' a pistol to his head last time you saw him, and Manny's got a long memory." Cash chuckled. "See you 'round, Broussard."

Claire watched the screen door close on the cottage in stunned silence. The sky had gone from red to a deep maroon, and then to charcoal. Too cloudy to allow more than a handful of stars to shine through the rents in the darkening sky, with a moon that was on the wane, daylight fled before the swift advance of an inky night. Shadows overtook the yard, challenged only by the flickering light of Amos Lee's television set. Fifty yards beyond the cottage stretched the black expanse of the bayou, silent and mysterious one moment, then alive with the *boing, boing* of the bullfrogs, the cry of night birds, the throaty bellow of an alligator.

For a moment, Claire stood, mesmerized by the change in the landscape. She'd been away so long. She'd forgotten how eerie the swamp seemed at night, a watery world steeped in dark legend, rich with monsters, ghosts, and buried treasure. She felt the past pull relentlessly at her, and she resisted. She'd left its allure behind her when she'd left Angelique for college, and over the years she'd built up an immunity. It was beautiful, and it was deadly.

"You lookin' for somethin' in particular, sugar? Or just lookin'?"

The sound of his voice sent a wave of delicious shivers up Claire's spine. She spun, hit him with the flashlight's beam. "Fegan. Thank God it's you!"

He reached out, turning the flashlight's glare toward the ground. "It's me, all right. What's with the flashlight? You lose an earring or somethin'?"

"I was helping Amos Lee catch nightcrawlers, but none of that matters now," she said impatiently. "He spoke to me, Fegan."

He was watching her, his expression more doubtful than it would have been had she professed that she was Queen of England. *"Pépère* spoke to you—as in *talked?* Darlin', he hasn't said a word in ten years—not to me, not to Frank. Baby, that's not possible."

Claire grasped his forearm with her free hand. "Fegan, he spoke to me. I heard him. I asked him about the bodies, and if he saw anyone around out there— anything suspicious. Just when I'd given up, he answered me. I know it sounds crazy and improbable, but it's true."

Without a word, he headed for the cottage. Amos Lee was a mere shadow in the dimly lit living room, dwarfed by the huge, old-fashioned armchair threatening to swallow him. He was watching reruns of *Gilligan's Island,* chuckling silently at the small screen on the old black-and-white TV. When they entered, he didn't even look up.

Fegan dropped into a squat by the arm of the chair. *"Pépère,* it's Fegan. Look who I got with me."

Amos Lee didn't glance at Fegan, didn't even acknowledge that he was there. *"Pépère,* you know Clairée, don' you? She was Jean Louise's friend. Won't you say hello? Won't you say somethin'? Just say somethin', damn it! Say somethin'."

His voice, soft and liquid when he'd greeted her out in the yard, seethed with quiet sorrow. Claire could sense the ache in his chest, and she hated herself in that moment for what she had done to him. He stayed in a squat by the chair a moment longer while his hope dwindled and died; then he got up and slammed from the cottage into the night.

Claire lingered for a few seconds, long enough to place a hand on Amos Lee's arm, to bend down and pray her voice would somehow cut through his mental haze, that somehow he would hear and respond. "Mr. Prideau, Fegan needs you. I know you can reach out. I know you can. For his sake, I'm asking, please."

The television flickered from a commercial into the show, and Amos Lee silently laughed, but there was no sign, no indication that she'd broken through, that he'd heard. After a moment, she straightened, and followed Fegan into the dark.

She found him in the bungalow's kitchen, a bottle of beer in front of him, as yet unopened. From the look on his dark face she could tell that the incident had affected him deeply. "I'm sorry," she said, knowing how ineffectual, how lame it sounded.

"Nothin' to be sorry for," he replied. "You want a beer?"

"I thought you'd never ask." It was the same thing he'd said last night when she invited him upstairs at The Willows, and they'd made love all night long, a small inside joke to break the tension, but it fell flat. She went to the refrigerator and helped herself, then took a seat across from him. The beer was ice cold, and it burned her throat. But it was nothing compared to the pain she saw in his face.

"Somewhere deep down inside, he blames me for Jean Louise, just like Frank. Hell, maybe they're right. Maybe if I'd been here—"

"I *was* here," Claire said quietly, "and I couldn't help her. I was supposed to be with her that night, but I caught cold, and canceled at the last minute. Don't you think I've relived that night a million times since? Don't you think I've blamed myself for what happened? Maybe it would have made a difference if I *had* been there, and maybe it wouldn't have. I don't know. What I do know is that you can't blame yourself for things that were completely beyond your control. Neither of us can."

"Yeah, but maybe—"

Claire reached across the table, taking his hand. "Your grandfather's a good man, and he loves you. If he blames anyone, he blames himself."

He said nothing, unwilling just yet to let go of the guilt he felt over Jean Louise's death and Amos Lee's condition. Quietly, he reached out, lifting the gold crucifix away from her skin. "I need to know, Char. What did he say?"

His knuckles were so warm against her skin, his touch a comfort and yet such a temptation that she had to resist the urge to lean in and offer him her kiss. "I was asking him about the bodies, and I asked if he saw anyone, or anything unusual—out of place. When he didn't answer, I apologized, and started to turn away. That's when I heard it: *'C'est alright.'* "

Fegan frowned. "It's all right." He shook his head. "But you were askin' about the swamp, about Jean Louise."

"Fegan, I've seen this sort of thing before. Autistic kids in the system, elders who have been abused or neglected, or so traumatized that they retreat into themselves. The important thing in this situation is that he was able to breach the barrier he's created, even if it didn't last. It happened. And that's good news, because it means that it can happen again."

"Lightning strikes twice," he murmured, and Claire

knew that the topic of conversation had changed. "It happened with us. You think it'll happen again?"

It was amazing, Claire thought, how the slight change in his voice could jumpstart her pulse, how the lowering of his lashes over those incredible sapphire eyes made her think about how delicious it felt when he pressed her down onto the bed and covered her yearning body with his. Somehow, she managed to keep her voice steady. "Are you referring to last night, or to Amos Lee?"

"What do you think?" he asked, leaning across the small table to graze her mouth with his. Coming out of her chair, Claire met him halfway.

What did she think? That this was out of control, confusing, exciting, and it scared the living hell out of her. That she wanted him more than she ever had. That she needed his gentle touch, his passionate kiss, his secure embrace . . . needed the safety from the insanity that was her life, found only in his arms. Aloud, she said, "I can't stay. Aunt Eule came home from the hospital today, and I don't want to leave her alone."

"Call her and give her the number. Tell her you'll be back before midnight, that I've got a desperate need of a lady lawyer, but she can reach you here."

Claire answered his kiss with another and her heart quivered with wanting and fear. It was too soon, and their affair burned too hot to last. Sooner or later, he'd become bored with it, with her, and end it. Crazily, perhaps, it occurred that sooner was better than later, that by backing off she would not only salvage her pride, but some of the warmth she felt for him, a warmth that had always been there, and which she was loath to lose. "You shouldn't try to tempt me, and I shouldn't even consider it."

"We're good together, baby. Ain't nothin' wrong with that."

Too good, Claire thought, to have it end badly. "Fegan, I really have to—"

"Yeah, I got that part." He kissed her, then pulled back. "If you change your mind, the front door's always open." Fegan ambled out onto the screened porch and watched as she drove away. He didn't sleep well that night, torn between half-waking thoughts of his grand-dad and dreaming that Clairée had come back to him.

He was up early and trying to chase his lousy mood with a second cup of coffee when a strange car pulled into the drive. The man got out and, walking briskly up the walk, rapped lightly. Fegan opened the door. "Somethin' I can do for you?"

"Are you Fegan Broussard?"

"That's right," Fegan said, taking the envelope the suit thrust at him. "What the hell is this?"

"It's a summons, Mr. Broussard. You've just been served. Have a nice day, now."

Fegan opened the envelope and scanned the sheets. ". . . a hearing for the competency of Mr. Amos Lee Prideau, and request for guardianship by pursuant, Mr. Frank Eli Broussard." Fegan crumpled the paper into a ball and gave it a toss. "Over my fuckin' dead body."

CHAPTER
ELEVEN

Frank had a small office in downtown Angelique. It wasn't terribly impressive as offices went, especially given that he shared it with Simon's Travel Agency. Christine had been strongly suggesting for a while that he lease something bigger, something more impressive, but his ingrained conservatism wouldn't allow him to make such a big leap just yet. Leasing an office was a huge commitment, and though business was good at the moment, there was no guarantee that it would stay that way. Aside from his business concerns, there was the new house. They were due to close on the deal in a few days. A nice house in a nice neighborhood didn't exactly come cheap these days, and Christine had expensive taste.

Christine had been a Hosteddler, a northerner from Connecticut. A man couldn't marry a woman more thoroughly Yankee than that. Frank had never quite gotten over a woman like Christine falling in love with and agreeing to marry a Broussard from the banks of Bayou des Cannes. What Frank hadn't known was bound to change him, however, and Christine had spent the next twelve years grooming him to rise above his humble hardscrabble roots, encouraging him—sometimes not so sweetly—to be worthy of a close, intimate connection to the Connecticut Hosteddlers.

Power and money and connections made Christine's world go 'round. If you don't have it, make the world believe you have it, because you are what you aspire to, was the credo she lived by, and the standard to which she held Frank.

Though he couldn't admit it to anyone, ninety percent of the time Frank was cold-sweat terrified. Christine had them so overextended that if the market saw another Black Friday, he might well be headed for bankruptcy, and his pretty little Yankee-bred wife turned up her pretty little bobbed nose at grits and cornbread. If she had the slightest inkling that he stopped at the Cajun market downtown and bought a spicy *Boudin* sausage on his way to work each morning, she might well have had a coronary. As far as Frank was concerned, what his wife didn't know wasn't an issue.

Glancing at his watch, he settled back with his sausage. He had fifteen minutes till Alfred Grimling arrived to discuss some adjustments to his life insurance policy, but he'd just taken the first bite and enjoyed that involuntary little squirt of saliva as the flavor of the meat rolled over his tongue when the door opened and Fegan walked in.

Frank nearly choked on his bite of *Boudin*. He swallowed hastily, buzzing Cherie, who doubled as receptionist for the travel agency as well as playing the part of Frank's secretary. "Cherie, honey, call the sheriff's department. I need a deputy out here immediately."

* * *

Claire stopped by the bungalow, armed with a peace offering: two pounds of the best Arabica beans money could buy, and a small package of chicken gizzards for Amos Lee's turtle lines. Fegan's car wasn't in the drive, but the bungalow door was wide open.

Claire frowned. Rapping lightly on the door, she waited, then rapped again, thinking he might have parked in back.

No answer.

More curious than ever, she opened the door, stepping into the shadows of the screened porch. "Fegan?" she called, bending to retrieve a crumpled paper lying two inches from her left little toe.

Watermark paper.

She was familiar with the texture and the weight of it . . . the same type and grade of letterhead she used in the Lafayette office. Fegan was a bit of a neat freak. It wasn't like him to leave something like this just lying around. With an inexplicably ominous sense of dread, she pulled the paper flat and read.

"Don' bother, Frank," Fegan said. "I sent Cherie out for a cappuccino. What you want with a deputy, anyhow? You do somethin' wrong?"

"W-What are you doin' here so early?" Frank stammered. "I didn't think you rolled out of bed before noon."

"I don', but this mornin' I made an exception, just so I could come down here and see you. What's the matter, Frank?" Fegan asked, planting his palms on Frank's desk blotter and leaning down into his brother's face. "You're lookin' kinda shaky. Too much coffee?

Or maybe you're not happy to see me? Now, I wonder why that is? Could it be that you've done somethin' sneaky and underhanded? Like tryin' to railroad an old man into some Geritol Warehouse where he can sit around in a rocker and wait to die?''

Small beads of sweat appeared on Frank's forehead and upper lip, but whether from the heat of the sausage or his own nervousness, Fegan couldn't tell. "You have no right to come here—to my place of business—and threaten me, Fegan!''

"Threaten?'' Fegan laughed. "I ain't threatened nobody yet, but since you brought it up—if you go through with this, I'm gonna make you wish the hell you hadn't.''

"Sorry I'm late.'' Claire shot Fegan a warning look. "There was traffic at the light, the parking meter wouldn't take my quarter, and I almost had a heart attack on those stairs.'' She fanned the open neckline of her blouse, which was plastered to her chest, and fixed Frank Broussard with her coolest, most aloof look, usually reserved for uncooperative caseworkers or judges who got off on intimidating any female under the age of thirty-five who dared to undermine the stodginess of their oh-so-dignified courtrooms. "Mr. Broussard, are you aware that there is no air conditioning in that stairway? That's a dangerous circumstance in this heat. I'd see to that, if I were you, before someone becomes ill out there and decides to sue.'' She caught her breath, glancing from one brother to the other. "Now, where were we?''

"Nice o' you to stop by, Char, but this is a private conversation between me and Frank,'' Fegan told her. "Why don' you go on home. I'm not quite through here. Frank and me got to get some things straight. I'll stop by and see you later.''

"If you don't mind, I'd like to stay," Claire said, not liking the dangerous look on Fegan's face, not caring if he objected. "Everything that needs saying should be said in the judge's chambers tomorrow." She turned to smile blandly at Frank. "Tell me, Mr. Broussard, just for the sake of my own edification. How large a campaign contribution is required to encourage due process along to warp speed? A proceeding like this usually takes at least a week or two, in the most critical of circumstances. You managed it in what—three days?"

Frank turned bright pink. "Are you accusing me of an impropriety?"

"At this point, I can't accuse you of anything, but I will warn you of one thing—if I discover that you're guilty of anything more serious than ass-kissing, your brother's wrath will be the least of your problems. Oh, and by the way, you might be interested to know that I'll be representing your grandfather in his upcoming hearing, and you'd better be prepared for the fight of your life. Elder abuse is one of my specialties, and I intend to prove that Mr. Prideau's civil rights are being threatened by the action you have undertaken."

While Frank sputtered, Claire did her utmost to drag Fegan from the room before he had the chance to throttle Frank. "Maybe you'd like to explain yourself," she said once she got him back out on the street. "What do you think you were doing in there?"

"It's called dealing with Frank. My fist seems to be the only language he understands these days."

"Did you really think for a nanosecond that violence was going to improve this situation?" she demanded.

"It sure as hell would make me feel better."

"Mometarily, maybe. And when you're incarcerated for simple assault, what happens to Amos Lee? Coming here was a dumb move, Fegan, and you're damn lucky I got here when I did."

It wasn't what he wanted to hear. "You know, somehow I don' recall asking for your advice!" he shot back. "Or your help, for that matter."

"This isn't just about you, Fegan! And if you could stop being a self-centered jerk for two seconds you'd realize that!" She caught the ragged edges of her temper and pulled her composure together, bit by bit, embarrassed for losing it and knowing that she was no better, no different, from him. "I love that old man too, damn you. He was the granddad I never had growing up, and if you blow this hearing out of some insane sibling rivalry, I'll be seriously pissed!" She took a breath while he watched her, his expression completely inscrutable. "Let me handle this, please. I know what I'm doing, and it's the least I can do for Amos Lee."

It took a moment for him to let go of the tension that had gripped him since receiving the summons, but deep down he knew Clairée was right. Frank knew how to push his buttons. He'd been doing it for years, but this was bigger than his anger, bigger than the hatred Frank harbored toward a younger sibling he considered irresponsible at best. If she could keep a mixed-up old man from having to live out his days in a gilded prison, then the least he could do was step back and allow it. "All right. All right. But I'm gonna take *Pépère* to the houseboat. He likes it there, and I want him as far away from Frank as possible."

It was nine in the morning, and Martha Felix hadn't had a wink of sleep all night. Her house guest had lain caught in the throes of a terrible fever for almost a week. Through the early hours, between midnight and cock's crow, it had worsened to the point that Martha greatly feared the child might be dying. Jesus never deserted His children, though, and many a fervent prayer when Martha called upon Him saw the child through. An hour ago, she began to sweat. Cold and clammy, moisture seeped from every pore to soak the blankets, her dirty blond hair, her nightgown. And Martha sent thanks to the ceiling and her merciful Savior above.

The fever had broken.

In a few minutes, she went from thrashing so violently that she nearly threw off the covers to a sound, deep sleep.

In fact, she slept like the dead.

Martha feared to leave the bedside, but had no other choice. She had to walk Sparky and fetch the mail from the mailbox. Not that Sparky couldn't wait. He didn't drink a great deal, was in his middling dog years, and he had a bladder like a camel. But it was crucial that everything appear normal. Mrs. Reed, a white woman with more nose than any woman had a right to, kept a hawk's eye on the neighborhood, and on Martha's place in particular. Mrs. Reed was Louisiana old school. She didn't trust blacks in general, and black men in particular. And Martha surely didn't trust Mrs. Reed, who seemed to have a hotline to the sheriff's department.

Leaving the girl's bedside, Martha carefully closed the door and went downstairs. Sparky sat down at her feet, waiting for his leash to be attached to his harness. A stroke of his small, sharp terrier head, and they went out onto the porch and along the path to the mailbox, stopping to water the fence posts and selected blades of grass.

"Junk mail," Martha muttered, retrieving a stack of envelopes and fliers from the mailbox. As she reached the gate, a car appeared on the road to the rear. Sparky, hell on anything that had wheels, jerked the lead from her grasp and gave noisy chase. "Sparky! Sparky, you bad dog, you come on back here!"

Martha was still standing by the front gate, shading her eyes and peering into the dust, when John showed up in his little white Volkswagen. For a moment, Martha's attention was diverted from her runaway dog to the marvel of six feet, six inches of lanky young man unfolding out of the tiny vehicle. "That old dog run off again, Aunt Marti?" John asked, balancing two shopping bags from the grocery store.

"Yes, he did. Rascal hound, don't know what's good for him."

"He doesn't know I've got dog food in this here bag," John said, laughing. "He'll come back once his belly starts to growl." They headed for the porch, Martha catching sight of the kitchen curtains in Mrs. Reed's window being moved aside the smallest bit. "Old biddy's watchin'. Ain't she got nothin' better to do?" Then, in normal conversational tone, "How you feelin' today? Your arthritis botherin' you? You takin' your medicine like the doctor says?"

Martha closed and locked the door. "You get the herbs, like I told you? And the soup bones?"

"Yes, ma'am. Everything's in the bags. How she doin'?"

"Better, I think."

"She ain't gonna die, is she?"

John's concern was genuine, Martha knew. A black man and a dead white girl was not a good combination, no matter how innocent the circumstances that brought them to that point. "Lord willin', no. She ain't gonna die. Fever broke this mornin'. She's sleepin' peaceful, now."

John let go a sigh. "Whew! That's good news, Aunt Marti. That's real good news. I ain't had a good night's sleep since this happened."

Martha's brow creased with genuine worry. "What we gonna do with her, John? What if she wakes up screamin' that we done this to her? It's happened, you know. It could happen, still. I don' like to think about calling the sheriff. I ain't sayin' Sheriff Pershing ain't fair, but he ain't no black man, either."

"Aunt Marti, sooner or later we got to tell someone. She's gonna get better and she'll need to say what happened. Ain't there somebody we can trust?"

Martha shook her head. "Don't know, but I'll think on it," she promised. "Think on it, and pray."

"The burden of proof falls upon Frank. He has to convince the judge that Amos Lee is a danger to himself, or a danger to others. As long as he's living his life, able to conduct his business, and his environment does not present a problem, you have nothing to worry about. No judge in his right mind these days is anxious to tamper with a man's civil rights." Claire caught Fegan's look, the skepticism and doubt, and shrugged. "Okay, so I would rather we were coming up before anyone but Ashton Morlay. I don't like him any better than you do, but you can't deny that he's gained a lot of prestige in this county."

Fegan gave a soft snort. "What you mean to say is that he's got a lot of very influential people in his pocket."

"That, too."

"You want some coffee? I put some on to brew."

"Coffee!" Claire said, fingertips to her brow. "I completely forgot." She dug in her Gucci bag and held out the offering. "I was bringing it by this morning when I saw the summons. The vendor said they're good-quality beans. They're a peace offering, for my running out on you the other night."

Fegan put the bag to his nose, closed his eyes, and inhaled. "The way to an insomniac's heart?"

"Actually, they're decaffeinated," she said, then laughed at his expression. He couldn't have been more appalled if she'd handed him a head in a bag.

Claire shrugged. "I didn't want to keep you up nights."

"It's a little late for that, sugar," he said, leaning in so close that his breath teased her face. "You already keepin' me up nights, in more ways than one."

He would have kissed her, but the galley door opened and Amos Lee wandered in, walked to the refrigerator, and took out a white paper carton marked "Live Bait," then wandered back out onto the deck without ever acknowledging either of them.

Claire's gaze followed him, and the moment was broken. "Has he seen a doctor, Fegan?"

Fegan moved away. "A couple of times, after. They wanted to hospitalize him. At least, that's what they called it. The psychiatric ward. Not much better than what Frank wants—in fact, it's a hell of a lot worse. I couldn't do that to him—not after everything he did for us. It just didn't seem right."

He stood by the windows that looked out over the deck. Beyond the glass, Amos Lee sat, silently watching out over the bayou, his line in the water. Claire went to Fegan. "Yes, but is it right to leave him like this? There might be something they can do to help."

Fegan's gaze never left his granddad. His brow furrowed, and his voice softened to a raspy whisper. "Ever get tired, Char? So tired of livin' that you'd like to just chuck it all and disappear? Just wink away. Doctors with their degrees and their mind-altering chemicals can say what they want, but I think that's what he's done. He just got tired of livin' in a world where a half-grown, innocent girl can be raped and tortured, her life and her future snuffed out like a candle's flame for no more reason than because some sick bastard got off on hurtin' her." When he turned his gaze on Claire, his blue eyes were dry, but there was an ache in his voice that made her swallow hard and blink back her own welling moisture. "I can't blame him for that, Char. I can't lock him away."

"Like they locked Jimmy away," she said.

"I hate to admit it, but I'm beginnin' to see the similarities," Fegan said, shaking a smoke out of a crumpled pack. "You want one?" Then, when Claire shook her head, he bent slightly and struck a match.

She was focused on his admission, totally focused. She felt a kick in her pulse, like her heart leaped forward and quickened its beat. "Give me a minute—I think I may be hearing things. Did you just admit that you think my father had nothing to do with Jean Louise's death?"

"I wouldn't go quite that far. I'm willing to admit there are similarities between the two murders, but I'm still stuck on the fact that Jimmy confessed. What could possibly prompt an innocent man into confessing to a murder this reprehensible? In my mind, it makes no sense. What's he said to you about this?"

"He refuses to talk about it," Claire replied. "No apologies for his actions hurting the family, no voiced regrets. I've tried to talk with him about it, and he says the same thing—'Get on with your life, Clairée. Forget about me'. This last time, when I showed him the sketch of the girl Amos Lee found, he turned the color of ashes, and I could feel the emotion ripple off him in waves."

"What sort of emotion?"

"Fear," Claire said. "Cold, stark fear. Something about it frightened him, and I've never known my father to be afraid of anything."

"I went to Pershing's office and looked at the files. The kid was dumped in the swamp, but she wasn't killed there. The body had been moved—and there was somethin' else. Pine needles. There were pine needles on her shirt. Ain't no pine trees at the dump site. Pines like higher, dryer ground."

Claire frowned. "There were pine needles on Jean Louise's clothing, too."

"Pine needles, and red silk cord." Fegan dragged on the cigarette and then shot out a stream of soft, gray smoke to the ceiling. "Could be a copycat killin'. By now, the public would have access to the court documents from Jimmy's trial."

"But you don't think so, and neither do I." Claire knew what he was thinking. The same thoughts she'd had, over and over, since first seeing the sketch in the *Times-Picayune*. It was just too chilling to be a coincidence. The murders were connected more closely than anyone imagined.

"There's one other thing," he said, dragging her from her thoughts. "The kid Amos Lee found had dog bites on the back of her leg. Remy saw them, and I double-checked. They were clearly visible in the pictures Vance has. But there was no mention of them in the coroner's report. Now, why do you suppose that is?"

"You don't think Homer Folley's in on this, do you?"

"I don' know." It was an honest answer. The only answer he could give at the moment. "Right now, I don' know enough to speculate on anythin'." He took the last drag on the cigarette and stubbed it out in the ashtray on the table. "Don't sugarcoat it, Char. How bad is this thing with Amos Lee?"

"If there was more time, I'd try to delay the proceedings. Rumor has it the judge is going to resign next week in order to make a bid for the senate. It's all happening so fast. It doesn't give us much time to prepare."

Fegan paced to the table and back. "That goddamned Frank. I ought to knock his fucking teeth down his throat."

"I want you to stay away from him," Claire warned. "I'm serious, Fegan. Amos Lee is conducting his life in a reasonable manner, and poses no threat to himself or to anyone else. It also helps that he has you to look after him, but all that changes if you're arrested." She glanced at her watch. "I have to go. I told Aunt Eule I'd be home in time for brunch, and I've missed it completely. Is there anything you need?"

"Only one thing I can think of. Am I gonna see you later?"

Claire hedged, fighting the urge to say yes, to take whatever he offered for as long as it lasted. But her instincts for self-preservation were strong. "That might not be such a good idea. I have to prepare an argument for tomorrow, and there are some personal matters that I need to take care of."

He reached out, touching her cheek, brushing the corner of her mouth with his thumb. "Hey, it's me, Fegan—remember? What's goin' on? First you bring me coffee, now you got to stay in so you can shampoo your hair? You always send your lovers mixed signals? Or are you just savin' that for me?"

"Is that what we are?" Claire said with a nervous laugh. "Lovers?"

He frowned down at her, clearly not liking where the

conversation was going. "You can't do that, darlin'. You can't pigeonhole what we have into some neat little slot. We just are."

She opened her mouth to hand him a glib response, but the truth came pouring out. "There's nothing casual about us, Fegan. And I don't know if I can do this."

"Char, what do you want from me?"

More than she had a right to ask. More, certainly, than he would be willing to give. She wanted their history to matter. She wanted the past week to count for something more than just sex, to lead somewhere other than disappointment, bitterness, and heartbreak. More than anything, she wanted to be able to discard her wariness, lay down her defenses, and not be afraid to let him touch her heart. Her reply squeezed out in a voice that was small and seething with fear and vulnerability. Hearing how she sounded galvanized Claire into acting. "I really have to go, before I say something I don't want to say and you don't want to hear. I'll meet you at Judge Morlay's office at nine a.m. And don't be late."

She fled the houseboat, walking as fast as she could without betraying her panic. Fegan followed her, down the ramp and onto the bank. "Damn it, Char! You can't keep runnin' from this!"

But she did run, and she kept on running. She got into her expensive car, covered her pretty dark eyes with sunglasses, and never looked back. As the BMW spun out and headed north along Bayou Road, a brown-and-white blur darted out of the bushes and ran barking after her for a few yards, then came trotting back to Fegan. "Sparky, what the hell are you doin' here? Miz Felix must be outta her mind, wonderin' where you are. Come on, I'll take you home."

* * *

A quarter-mile separated the houseboat from Martha Felix's little white house. Fegan could have taken the Trans Am, but preferred the walk, hoping the physical activity would clear his head, but all it did was help him work up a sweat. "Don' know about you, Sparky, but I sure don' understand women. Most of them want a commitment. This one, she runs like hell to avoid any mention of it."

Fegan wasn't sure why Clairée's tendency to run hot and cold should bother him so much, but it did. It should have made the chase more exciting, kept him off balance, kept him interested.

Instead, it confused him just like she confused him, and he wasn't sure from one hour to the next exactly where he stood with her. As for being interested, that much was a given. She was beautiful, and sexy, and intriguing, and he couldn't seem to get enough of her. She walked into his world, and he kicked into readiness. Yet on days like today, he was revving his engine with no place to go, and that was aggravating. "If I could just get her to hang around long enough, I'd ask the lady for a date, take her out somewhere real nice."

But that wasn't likely to happen, because Claire's focus was her father . . . the father who was about to be executed for killing his baby sister. Even worse, they both knew he was innocent. "Sparky, how'd everythin' get so screwed up? I didn't ask for any of this to happen, and neither did she. But we sure as hell got to deal with it."

Sparky proved one of those silent, thoughtful types that kept his own counsel and refrained from making judgments. Fegan liked that about him, and as they approached the gate, he reached down to stroke the terrier's small head. At that moment, John Delano, Miz Felix's nephew, came around the corner of the house with a lawn rake.

"Hey there, Sparky. Who you got there? Why, it's Fegan Broussard!" John said with a grin. "Hey, Fegan, how you been?"

"Can't complain, John. How 'bout you?" John took the hand Fegan offered and pumped it hard.

"Not so good. Sold that shrimp boat o' mine. Aunt Marti, she needs somebody to come by now and then, and business wasn't exactly boomin'. I'm workin' at a car dealership over in Lafayette till I find somethin' better."

Miz Felix chose that moment to open the door. John laughed. "Aunt Marti, look who Sparky found. It's Fegan Broussard, Mr. Amos Lee's grandson."

The suspicion on Martha Felix's face faded as she closed the door and came onto the porch. "Why, it is! And you found my Sparky." She took the leash from Fegan. "That was a bad dog. A very bad dog." She glanced at Fegan, her brow furrowed. "Now, how come you quit writing for the *Times-Picayune*? I enjoyed your work. Used to read your column every week. Then, you went off to Yankee Land, and somebody told me last week that you retired. I told them it must be a lie. Once a reporter, always a reporter—that's what they say, and you're too young to retire. Look at that Mike Wallace. He's still a reporter, and he's almost my age."

"I think it's *journalist*, Aunt Marti," John gently corrected.

"Same thing," Martha insisted. "Bein' a reporter's like bein' a policeman. It ain't just a job. It's a state o' mind," she said sagely. "You ought to go back to the *Times-Picayune*. Bet they'd be glad to have you back."

"It's kind of you to say so, Miz Felix, and I'll keep it

in mind. Just now, I'd better be gettin' back. Amos Lee's alone at the houseboat. John," he said, "stop by some time. We'll pop a couple of cold ones and drop some lines in the water."

"I'll do that," John said. "I surely will. Take care, now." John watched Fegan walk away. When he was beyond hearing, he turned to his aunt. "How's she doin', Aunt Marti?"

"Fast asleep. I doubt she'll wake until she gathers some strength. I got her to take a little beef broth, and she's keepin' it down. That's a good sign." She shaded her eyes, staring off after their visitor. "I'm thinkin' that ain't the only good sign. I'm gonna pray on it, John, but I think I finally know what to do."

CHAPTER
TWELVE

"Your Honor, I assure you that my client, Mr. Francis Broussard, has filed this petition only after the most careful consideration, not to mention many a sleepless night. He finds this adversarial situation with his brother difficult to bear, but the welfare of his grandfather, Mr. Prideau, must take precedence in this instance."

Ashton Morlay, looking like a golden-haired Solomon in his dour judge's robes, tented his fingers and waited patiently for Bernie Freeman, Frank's attorney, to finish. "Are we here to weigh Mr. Broussard's motives, counselor? Because I was under the impression that this hearing was directly related to Mr. Prideau's ability to function in the world, and not the purity of his grandson's heart."

The judge's chambers were air-conditioned, but after ten minutes in Morlay's presence, Frank's attorney began to perspire heavily. Morlay's temperament was as unconventional as it was unpredictable, and he tended to have that effect upon people. Claire wasn't exactly easy in his presence, either, and the thought that this cold-eyed, black-robed officiate was directly responsible for robbing her of her father proved impossible to set aside. Not only had Ashton Morlay convicted Jimmy, he'd ruthlessly built a career upon that conviction, and Claire hated him for it. Her own difficulties had no place in these judicial proceedings, however, and she kept her calm by staunchly reminding herself that another man's future was at stake. Gaining Morlay's sympathy—if, indeed, he possessed such a thing— wasn't just necessary, it was paramount.

If Frank succeeded and Amos Lee was confined to a facility, away from Fegan, away from the land that he loved, it would probably kill him, and it would wound his youngest grandson and only advocate beyond repair. She glanced at Fegan. He'd dressed in a dark blue suit and open-collared white shirt for the occasion, his only concession to his disdain for conservatism his small, gold hoop earrings. Seated beside Amos Lee, his dark face reflecting the seriousness of the situation, he barely resembled easygoing, smooth-talking Fegan, who knew how to take her body from zero to hot-for-him in less than a heartbeat.

She wished she could have spared him this. In lieu of that, she would make his brother Frank look like the arrogant fool that he was.

Claire watched as her opponent mopped his brow with a folded white handkerchief. "I was working my way up to that point, precisely," he said. "If Your Honor will please bear with me?"

"I am bearing with you, Mr. Freeman. But please get to the point in the most expedient method possible. I am privileged to have witnessed your courtroom technique before, and I suspect that Moses parted the Red Sea in less time than it takes you to draw a foregone conclusion."

Claire feared Freeman would choke on his fury. His dull red coloring flared brightly, and a thin rivulet of sweat trickled into his starched collar. "I apologize, Your Honor. We are asking for guardianship, a reasonable request considering the temperament of Mr. Broussard's brother, not to mention the hazardous nature of his occupation."

Claire came out of her chair. "Your Honor, that remark is prejudicial! Fegan Broussard's occupation in not in question here, and has no bearing on my client's competency. In no way does it affect his grandfather's well-being, and it is a ridiculous manipulation of the facts to suggest otherwise. I assure you that Mr. Prideau is quite capable of managing independently. He may be aged, but he is far from infirm, and he does not require constant supervision."

"Objection," Freeman said. "Mr. Prideau recently suffered an accident on Bayou Road in which he received a blow to the head. Surely Miss Sumner doesn't deny that fact?"

"It's Ms. Sumner, and we do not deny it, Your Honor. Mr. Prideau did have an accident, in which he put his pickup truck into a ditch. Accidents happen. In fact, my colleague, Mr. Freeman, also had an accident last week on Maple Avenue, and no one is questioning his competency because of it. You can read the account in the newspaper, if you like. I believe he rear-ended someone."

"She does have a point, Bernie," Ashton allowed while Frank's lawyer seethed. "You are supposed to have complete control of your vehicle at all times. What happened? Weren't you paying attention?"

"I dropped a cigarette and my trousers were smoldering, Your Honor," Freeman replied, his voice quivering with anger. "None of which has anything to do with the petition, or the fact that Mr. Prideau would be far more comfortable if he is remanded into Mr. Broussard's custody. Mr. Broussard has chosen a facility nearby so that Mr. Prideau can receive visitors. There is a nurse on staff twenty-four hours a day, seven days a week. He would receive the best of care—"

"Amos Lee don' need a nurse," Fegan interrupted. "He likes livin' where he is, and doin' what he does, and that shouldn't have to change just because Frank has the need to control somebody. Maybe Frank needs to look to his own life, and leave Amos Lee alone."

"Your Honor, I apologize for Mr. Broussard's outburst," Claire said. "I assure you it won't happen again." She threw a glare at Fegan, but Judge Morlay had latched on to the idea and seemed intent on pursuing it. The man was unorthodox—eccentric, even—and in his courtroom and out of it, he did as he pleased.

"Fegan Broussard? The reporter?"

"Not anymore, Your Honor," Fegan replied.

Morlay narrowed his pale eyes, stroking his chin with his fingers and thumb. "Well, I should say that I'm relieved to hear it. You said some unkind things about me when you wrote for the *Times-Picayune*. I'd just been elevated to the bench, as I recall, and you seemed to hold the opinion that my sudden rise had given me a 'permanent pucker'."

Fegan didn't blink. "Opinions are like assholes, Your Honor. Everybody has one."

Ashton chuckled. "I see that maturity hasn't taken the edge off your unique charm, nor dulled your wit. I am sure that the world of journalism mourns your loss, Mr. Broussard. Are you willing to assume responsibility for Mr. Prideau?"

"Amos Lee is self-sufficient, Your Honor, and he prides himself on his independence. He has a cottage in my backyard. I look in on him from time to time to make sure he's doin' all right."

Frank's lawyer shot out of his chair. "Your Honor! If you will permit, we have medical records and can provide expert testimony to the contrary."

Claire stood, bracing her fingertips on the table. "That medical examination was performed shortly after Mr. Prideau found his murdered granddaughter floating in the swamp. Of course he was traumatized! He would be less than human if he hadn't been profoundly affected by such horrific circumstances."

"Ms. Sumner has a point," Morley allowed. "It has also been brought to my attention that Mr. Prideau stumbled upon another unfortunate girl, not ten days ago. Is that true?"

"It is, Your Honor," Claire said. "Mr. Prideau once depended upon the swamp for his livelihood, and he still spends a great deal of his time there. If we may approach the bench, Your Honor?"

The judge waved his assent, and Fegan spoke in low-voiced French to his grandfather, who got out of his chair, then bent to retrieve an aluminum pail from beside the table. His gait slow but steady, he took the pail and held it out to Ashton, who looked dubious as he bent forward to peer at the contents. "Ms. Sumner! What on earth?"

"Crawfish, Your Honor, caught early this morning by my client."

Freeman was almost apoplectic. "Your Honor, I object! This is highly unusual!"

"Well, you're right about that, Mr. Freeman. This whole situation is highly unusual, but I am inclined to give Mr. Prideau the benefit of the doubt—temporarily, at least. Unless he expresses interest in giving up his hobby to become a resident of a retirement community, I am not inclined to force him to do so at this time. However, should Mr. Prideau's circumstance change, in that he becomes a danger to himself or others, I shall certainly reconsider. Until that time, this hearing is dismissed.''

"You were dynamite in there, you know that?'' Fegan was leaning against her front fender, his sunglasses a mirror that gave back her reflection in duplicate.

Claire was close enough to smell the light, crisp scent of his cologne. His nearness, as always, affected her, and she felt that queer but familiar flutter in her pulse as she reached out to smooth his lapel. "I was nervous,'' she admitted. "And if it hadn't been for the fact that Morlay turned Bernie into a bumbling fool, there might have been a far different outcome.''

"It didn't happen. You charmed them all . . . even Morlay, and I swear that man has his laundress put extra starch in his boxers. Thanks to you, Amos Lee gets to go home where he belongs, and I'm grateful for that. So grateful, in fact, that I'd like to take you out to dinner. What'dya say, Char? You want to go out on a real date? Someplace nice, with real linen tablecloths, vintage wine, and candlelight.''

Claire drew a slow breath. Her nerve endings tingled, and suddenly she didn't know quite what to do with her hands. They wanted so badly to reach for him, but this was bigger than her wants, her needs . . . so much bigger than both of them. Time was running out for another man, the most important man in her life. And though he refused to admit or accept it, he needed her help. "It sounds wonderful,'' she said, stalling, realizing that he would never know just how hard this was for her. "But I can't, Fegan."

"Can't? Or won't?"

Claire shrugged. "I feel like I'm caught in a whirlwind. This all happened so fast, and I have Jimmy to think about. He has to be my first priority."

"What about Char, and what she wants? What she needs?"

"That's a little presumptuous, isn't it?" Claire said with a short laugh. "What I want can't afford to take precedence right now, and you have to understand that." He didn't. She could see it in his face. There was no way he would ever understand the crushing sensation with which she existed every moment of every day, the violent conflict of being in this place that she loved, and she hated, feeling the tick of the moments in a life melting away . . . irretrievably trickling out. "I need to get home."

Without a word, he opened the driver's door for her, then closed it after she got in. To allay the heat, her windows were down. He braced a hand on the ledge, and for a minute Claire feared he would lean down and kiss her. Instead, he paused, as if he would say something more, make one last attempt to change her mind; then he abruptly turned away. "See you 'round, Char."

Claire flicked the switch for the power windows, and as the glass shield whirred closed, she cranked the air up full force. It cooled quickly, and within thirty seconds she turned it down again. Then, as she glanced in her rearview mirror and caught a shimmery outline in the back seat, she understood. *You always do that, Clairée,* Jean Louise accused.

"I don't know what you're talking about," Claire insisted, but the untruth didn't convince even her.

You run away from the stuff that scares you, the stuff you don' understand.

"I'm not running away. I'm trying to keep a level head, to remember what's important, and I can't do that when I'm with him. He makes me crazy, and I want things I shouldn't want. Things that just can't be."

The girl folded her forearms on the back of the passenger seat, propping her head on them. *Maybe they can be,* she said with the infuriating logic of an eleven-year-old child. *How do you know if you won' let it happen?*

"Damn it, Jean Louise, Fegan didn't bring me here. He's not the reason I came. You are! I have to find out who's responsible for taking you away, and I have to do it soon. I don't have the luxury of time, and I can't afford to fall in love—not with Fegan. Not with anyone."

Don' you get it, Clairée? It ain't up to you.

But Claire wouldn't hear it. "Why do you keep coming to me like this? And every time it has something to do with Fegan, or with the past. If you're going to hang around, then do something useful, and tell me about the murders. Help me, Jean Louise. Tell me who's responsible. Who is doing these terrible things?"

Jean Louise wavered, and then disappeared. *He's my brother,* her voice came, a faint echo barely audible above the soft whir of the climate control. *If you hurt him, we won' be friends no more.*

"Come on, Jean Louise! Don't go, please." Claire glanced sharply into the mirror, and as she looked back at the road, a uniformed man stepped off the curb and into her path. She slammed on the brakes, and skidded to a stop inches from turning Cash Edmunds into a highway statistic. Claire powered down the window. "Deputy, are you all right?"

"Daydreamin', Clairée? You're supposed to stop for pedestrians in this crosswalk."

"I apologize. I didn't see you."

Cash braced a hand on her window ledge, much like Fegan had a few moments ago, but Claire felt nothing but a mild annoyance. "You coming from the old geezer's hearing?"

"I suppose that would depend on who you're referring to."

"You know—Fegan's granddad."

"How did you know about that?"

"It's a small town," Cash replied, vigorously working his wad of chewing gum. "Not a lot goes on that I don't know about, one way or the other. You're getting kinda friendly with the Broussards. You and Fegan got somethin' goin'?"

"Aside from it being none of your damned business, that's a strange thing for a police officer to ask. I believe you are sworn to serve and protect the citizens of Angelique, not to meddle in their private lives. Now, unless you intend to issue me a citation, this conversation is over."

"Hell, there's no cause to get bent. It helps to know the players, that's all, and what they're up to." He scrawled something on a pad and handed it to her. "You're a good-lookin' chick, Clairée. You get tired of fuckin' that Frenchie, give me a call."

Claire glanced at his phone number, then threw the paper down in disgust.

When she arrived at The Willows, a black Mercedes was parked in her spot, beside Eulanie's beat-up red Chevy S-10 pickup. The heat index was soaring. Temperatures hovered in the high nineties with the humidity at a miserable eighty-eight percent. Claire felt wilted from the stress of the hearing, her exchange with Fegan, and her confrontation with her own private little haunt, Jean Louise. She'd ceased to speculate whether the girl's sporadic appearance stemmed from the depths of her overly active imagination. It hardly mattered whether she was conjuring her up out of some unknown subconscious need. Whether she was losing it from the pressure of her predicament, or not, the dissatisfaction resulting from their argument was very real, and it lingered.

Opening the front door to the sound of a rich, cultured male voice she had hoped not to hear again, ever, didn't help to elevate her dark mood; she had to steel herself against the impulse to back quietly out before she was noticed, and take the gallery stairs to her room. It took several seconds to squash the cowardly impulse. She loved her Aunt Eulanie too much to force her to deal with Ashton Morlay alone, so she took a deep breath and walked into the parlor.

Eulanie rarely entertained in the years following Jimmy's incarceration, so the parlor didn't see a great deal of use these days. It seemed strange to Claire to see Ashton Morlay's long-boned frame comfortably seated in the old armchair her mother had once occupied to read the evening newspaper. Elegant in his dove gray three-piece suit, not a fair hair out of place, he seemed very much at home there, and something about that impression rankled. "Aunt Eulanie," Claire said, pausing in the doorway. "I didn't know you were expecting company. Judge Morlay, is there some problem that we failed to clear up at this morning's hearing?"

Ashton got to his feet, the impulse to rise when a lady entered the room bred into his aristocratic bones. "Clairée," he replied easily. "You don't mind if I call you Clairée? It's how I remember you."

Claire bristled at the inference to the dark days of Jean Louise's death and Jimmy's arrest and trial. She felt a sudden chill wave and accompanying hiss as the air kicked on, both quickly gone. "Actually, Judge Morlay, given the unique circumstances, I would prefer that we keep things strictly formal.''

He smiled, and his pale eyes caught the white light of the table lamp, glinting strangely. "Very well, then, *Ms. Sumner.* I was just telling Ms. Eulanie that your performance this morning was impressive, to say the least.''

"My performance," Claire said with a tight little smile. "You make me sound like a trained seal instead of an attorney defending her client. Is that why you're here, Judge? If it is, I am not sure it's such a good idea. I wouldn't want to give Frank Broussard any ammunition by even the barest taint of impropriety.''

"Aren't you the consummate professional! If I didn't know better, I'd never have guessed that you're the daughter of a convicted felon. How is Jimmy, by the way?''

"Preparing for his death, thanks to you," Claire said flatly. Part of her bristling animosity stemmed from the fact that as prosecutor, he had pushed so hard for the death penalty in Jimmy's case. If not for him, Jimmy might have been serving a life sentence, the clock would not have been running out on the last phase of his life, and she wouldn't be under the pressing weight of an investigation that was clearly going nowhere.

Looking into his handsome face, Claire realized that she didn't just dislike Ashton Morlay. She hated him. He'd taken Jimmy away, robbing a young and vulnerable girl of the father she needed desperately at the most traumatic time in her life, destroying a family. It was as simple as that, and as complex, and even a threadbare veneer of the most strained civility seemed more than she could manage.

Eulanie seemed to pick up on it, because she was quick to enter and circumvent the taut exchange. "The judge stopped by to pay his respects—''

"And to issue a special invitation," Morlay put in. "We're having a gala next week at Briar Rose, and though I personally added your aunt's name to the guest list, my staff alerted me that we had received no RSVP. Mail being what it is these days, I thought I'd drop by on my way home to issue a personal invitation, and to express my sincere hope that you both will attend."

Claire saw the opportunity and seized it. "It's a distinct possibility. But, of course, that would depend upon a reversal on Aunt Eulanie's sugar contracts."

"Sugar contracts?" He pretended puzzlement, but Claire could see the cogs turning behind those unsettling, pale eyes.

"The Willows has had a long-standing handshake agreement with John Perry concerning the refinery, but all of that miraculously changed when his son Roy entered into partnership with Morlay Enterprises. And everyone in the parish understands that Morlay Enterprises is you."

Morlay's brows shot up in a feigned show of surprise. "My dear Ms. Sumner, precisely what are you suggesting?"

"Only that should you expect anything but rancor from the Sumner family, you will stop putting the squeeze on The Willows, and allow my aunt to run her business as she sees fit, without undue interference."

"You are almost as hardheaded as your father," Morlay allowed. "I can admire that in a man—*or* a woman. My, my, look at the time. I really must be on my way. Ms. Eulanie, I thank you for your hospitality, and I hope you will consider my invitation carefully."

Eulanie waited calmly until Morlay's door opened and closed, and his engine fired up, before turning a critical eye on Claire. "Perhaps you'd care to tell me what went on here just now?"

Claire shrugged, unable to put it into words. "I just don't like him, that's all."

"That was plainly obvious to all three of us," Eulanie said with a frown. "As for the chill in this room, I would be willing to bet Jane felt it all the way down the hall and into the kitchen."

"It hasn't been a great morning," Claire told her. "I just didn't expect to see him again today, after the hearing. And I especially did not expect to find him here, in this house."

"You won the judgment at Mr. Prideau's hearing, yet you're as prickly as a porcupine. Is there somethin' you want to talk about?"

Claire stared at her aunt for a moment, weighing her options, then sighed. "It's nothing that time won't cure. But thank you for the offer. Now, if you don't mind, I need some down time."

"Claire? You do know that you can tell me anything, don't you?"

"Yes, and I thank you for that." Claire bent to kiss Eulanie's cheek. "I'm just a little worn, that's all. And I'm worried about Dad."

"He's in God's hands," Eulanie said. "There's nothing we can do now but wait, and be accepting when the time comes."

Not *accepting*, Claire thought. She would never accept her father losing his life for something she was convinced he didn't do. "I think I'll lie down for an hour, and then I have some work to do," she said, and headed for the stairs.

"I've got a meeting this evening, and Jane's leaving early, but there are plenty of leftovers in the fridge. I should be home by eleven."

"I'll manage just fine," Claire reassured her aunt, refraining from questioning the wisdom of her going out so soon after being released from the hospital. Eulanie was a force of nature. Or at least she pretended to be, and any attempt to disrupt her normally hectic schedule would be met with quiet scorn and outright denials. Claire loved her; she worried about her; but she'd had her fill of confrontation for one day. All she wanted right now was a tepid, relaxing bath and a few hours of quiet contemplation in which to figure out what to do next.

Why he'd agreed to this unexpected visitor when he'd turned his own blood kin away was a mystery, even to Jimmy. He'd thought his curiosity had dried up, along with his connections on the outside, and then the corrections officer had informed him that there was a young man named Broussard to see him, and like the Biblical Lazarus who'd risen from the dead, it sprang to life.

Fegan Broussard had been a young man already at the time of the trial—dark hair, dark complexion, eyes full of the fire of a righteous hatred. He was still young by Jimmy's standards; there wasn't a strand of silver in his dark hair, but the hatred had been replaced by cold cynicism, and Jimmy couldn't decide which was worse. Maybe the hatred, because it was bound to go away from this place dissatisfied. It was damned hard to disappoint a cynic. With a rattle of chain, Jimmy sat down and waited.

"You know who I am?"

"I know who you are, all right. What I don't know, is what the hell you're doin' here."

"You know, Jimmy, it's strange, but I been wonderin' the same thing 'bout you." Careful of his words, Jimmy didn't answer, which prompted Fegan Broussard to share his speculation. "They tell you about that kid Amos Lee found in the swamp a couple of weeks back? Yeah, that's right. Clairée told you. She mentioned it."

"You been talkin' with my Clairée?" Jimmy snorted. "What sort of game you playin', Broussard?"

"No games," Fegan said. "I'm just here for some friendly conversation. You never would talk about why you killed my sister. Now, why is that, I wonder?"

"I confessed to the killin'." Jimmy's gaze hardened, turned brittle. "What more do you want from me?"

"Motive, for one thing. I need to know how a man who never speaks an improper word to a young girl, who always, to the best of my knowledge, treated that girl with a deferential, if distant, kindness, turns around and rapes and smothers her, and then refuses to comment on why he did it. No apologies, not a single word more than he has to say to blow his trial to hell and set himself up for a lethal shot in the arm."

The younger man paused, watching him with eyes the color of new denim, and Jimmy knew that nothing he could say was going to satisfy him. All he could do was stay cool and hope he gave up digging for information. "Red silk cord. What's that about, Jimmy? What's red silk cord signify to you?"

Jimmy drew a blank on the reference, but shrugged it off. "If you're thinkin' of draperies for my cell, don't bother. They ain't allowed."

Fegan eyed Jimmy critically, noting his guarded expression. The older man was no fool, but he *was* unaware that he'd just tipped his hand. "Who do you know in Angelique that's sadistic enough to want to rape and kill a pair of teenage girls?"

"Son, you're wastin' my time," Jimmy told him. He could have gotten up from the table, could have signaled the guard that the conversation was over, but he didn't make any move to end the exchange. He just sat there, watching Fegan as closely as Fegan watched him, silently speculating on how much he knew, on how large a threat he represented . . . but to whom?

"This second murder mirrored the first, except for one thing. The girl had dog bites on the back of her leg, almost like she'd been run to ground. Then, while she was still breathing and conscious, her wrists and ankles were bound with duct tape, tied up with red silk cord, and a plastic bag was put over her head and secured in place to cut off her oxygen supply. Hell of a way to die."

The pulse in the older man's neck jerked, then pounded harder, just above the collar of his faded chambray shirt, and his brown eyes, so like Clairée's, snapped with frustration and anger. "Well, I don't guess they can pin that one on me, now can they? I've got me one mean mother of an alibi."

Bracing his palms flat on the table, Jimmy started to rise.

"Is that what they did, Jimmy? Pin it on you?" He went very still for the space of a heartbeat, staring hard at Fegan. "More importantly—who are you protecting, and why?"

"If you know what's good for you and what's left of your family, you'll go back to Angelique and forget this conversation ever took place, and you'll stay the hell away from my Clairée. That girl's done well for herself, and it wasn't easy for her, her daddy bein' in this place. She's got no business havin' truck with some coon-ass from backwater Angelique. An' you sure got no business with her."

"I'll be sure and send her your love, Jimmy!" Fegan called after him. "You'd better believe, I ain't done with this yet."

CHAPTER THIRTEEN

Fegan didn't go straight to Clairée, despite his implied threat to Jimmy. He told himself that he needed to think things through without the delicious distraction she'd become, but the bald truth was that he couldn't stand the thought of another rejection. She was a living, breathing contradiction when it came to dealing with him, and he never quite knew what to expect from her because of it. One minute she wanted him, and her desire was so strong, so heady it sent his senses reeling . . . and the next she didn't seem to know what she wanted. To his way of thinking, it should have been simple and straightforward. They enjoyed one another, and where was the harm in that? Yet he was quickly coming to see that where Clairée was concerned, nothing was simple. He didn't understand her, and worse, he feared he never would. She was too damned complex, too contradictory, and she drove him crazy.

Relationships weren't supposed to give a man a migraine. Far from it. A man. A woman. Mutual attraction, respect, and maybe some steamy sex on the side. He and Clairée had the man-woman thing down pat, but he wasn't so sure she respected the fact that he wanted her, and the sex, though fantastic and unpredictable, left his head spinning and a gaping hole where his heart should have been. It was too casual—so casual, in fact, that he was beginning to think it hadn't meant anything more to Clairée than a convenient way to let off a fine head of steam.

She'd indicated she didn't want to get too close, but that could very well be some cleverly contrived way of letting him down easy. He didn't like that thought—he didn't like it a damned bit.

He was well into his third double-shot of Scotch and feeling a little defensive when she walked into the Pink Cadillac. A small knot of salivating men immediately circled, Remy with his hat tipped rakishly on his curly, dark head among them. Over the rim of his whiskey, Fegan watched her toss back her gleaming brown hair with a flick of one wrist, sending a cool remark Remy's way that Fegan couldn't make out, but that made Remy howl. The others backed off just a little, each turning to slink away. Remy, more difficult to discourage, followed the sway of her hips beneath her midnight blue China silk sheath with appreciative eyes, then fell into step behind her.

She caught Fegan's gaze and changed directions, heading straight for him, as deadly as a heat-seeking missile on a fixed target. Fegan tossed off his whiskey, and the bartender set him up again, but this one he didn't touch.

"Hey, sugar, don' I know you from somewhere?" Remy asked. *"Mais,* yeah, you dat lady lawyer who whooped ol' Frank's sorry ass this mornin' with a bucket

of crawfish. You got some fine moves, darlin'. Why don'
you walk on over here and show 'em to ol' Remy?"

Claire sent an annoyed glance Remy's way. "You
heard about that?"

"Heard about it? Ev'body heard 'bout it, sugar. It's
all over town by now."

She shrugged, seeming embarrassed. "I got a lucky
break, that's all. Don't make too much of it."

"Hey, cuz, you hear dat?"

"Remy, ain't you got some business to see to?" Fegan
said, fixing him with a pointed stare. "I'll catch up with
you later."

Remy looked from one to the other, then shook his
head. "Thought you two would be celebratin'! *Noncle*
Amos Lee done won his freedom. Dat's a good thing.
Dat's a fine thing! And you two lookin' like your mama
just tole you she's plannin' on claimin' a corner down
on Canal Street. You don' make no sense, man. I'm
outta here."

Remy sauntered off to find better company as Fegan
lit up a smoke. "Cigarette?"

"I never started. It's a lousy habit."

"Man's got to have some bad habits," he said, sucking
in a lungful of fragrant smoke, and shooting a blue
stream toward the ceiling. "Perfection's just too big a
cross to bear. How 'bout you, Char? What are your bad
habits . . . besides me, that is?"

She shrugged and he had a fine glimpse of her cleav-
age. Pale breasts, the sight of which made his mouth
water and his temper do a slow burn. "High expectations."

He laughed. "High expectations. I know that one.
What else?"

Claire frowned, unable to comprehend what had
gone wrong. After hours of stewing at the house, she'd

decided to surprise him and take him up on his offer. Fairly certain where the night would end, she dressed just for him—bare, sun-tanned legs and high stiletto heels, black thong panty and no slip . . . and through no fault of her own that she could determine, it was quickly headed down the tubes. He was angry. It showed in his face, his voice, his mannerisms. "Is that a trick question? Because I'm starting to feel like I've wandered onto a mine field."

"I don' know, baby. What you want it to be? You all dressed up and lookin' for somethin', that's for sure. Looks like somebody's about to get lucky." He glanced around, the smooth quality in his voice she found so attractive never wavering. "Anybody I know?"

Claire felt the simple question cut right through her, and it couldn't have hurt more if she'd been naked in an icy Alaskan wind. "Is this payback for this morning?" she asked, as calmly as she could. "Are you angry because I turned down your dinner invitation? Is that what this is?"

"Me, angry? Shit, honey, you did me a favor. Now, I don' gotta wear that tired old suit."

Flip. Always a joke, a comeback. But where was the honesty? Where was the truth? Claire stared at him for a full minute, but gradually her gaze was drawn upward, to their reflection in the mirror above the bar. The China silk that had seemed so provocative, so appropriate for what she'd been feeling, now seemed ridiculous in comparison to her surroundings. She was overdressed, and she suddenly felt like a fool, an imbecile. All along, she'd been holding back with Fegan, avoiding a messy entanglement to avoid being hurt, to avoid feeling exactly as she did right now. "It's becoming more obvious by the second that I made a terrible mistake in coming here. I wanted to apologize, and to take you up on your invitation. And I am sorry—sorry I've been such a stupid fool, sorry I came looking for you. Bad habits? Oh, yeah. I've got plenty of them. But you're right about one thing. Caring about you is at the top of the list.''

She slipped off the stool and stormed out. Fegan watched her until she cleared the door, then he turned back to his whiskey. But he didn't touch it, and in a moment he followed Clairée's lead, paid for his drinks, and went out, having lost his taste for oblivion.

''Oh, God, Claire! What were you thinking?'' Claire demanded. She'd just turned left onto Bayou Road, but she hadn't slowed the BMW, and she didn't even care that she left an enormous dust cloud in her wake. She was too busy castigating herself for her unreal expectations. ''That's what you get when you think with your hormones instead of your head. And you can't even plead ignorance on this one! You know Fegan, and you know what he's capable of, and what he isn't capable of, and this relationship, if you can call it that, has had some bad mojo from the start.'' Not exactly a wise choice for a lover . . . or for anything, for that matter.

''Hot off a string of failed relationships, and what do I do? Fall for the original no-commitment man. For a brainiac, you can be really dumb sometimes.''

The external-internal dialogue wasn't doing any good. It didn't make her feel any less foolish, or angry— at Fegan, at herself. In fact, she felt like she'd just been caught in a courtroom with her pantyhose around her ankles, and her thumb up her butt, and it wasn't a good feeling. It never even occurred to her that she might be overreacting, that she was being too hard on herself, until the gleam of headlights bounced into her rearview.

He was following her.

How dare he follow her when she was incensed with him? How dare he make her feel as if she'd done something wrong?

"For heaven's sake," she said to herself. "Get a grip. He's just a man."

She knew she was lying to herself. Fegan wasn't just any man, and like it or not, she cared deeply about him. In fact, she always had. He was part of her past, and a big part of her present. He was almost an extension of herself, who she was and who she had been. He was Jean Louise and he was this place, Angelique, the mystery of the bayou and the sun-baked earth on which her family had lived for generations, and nothing, nothing could make her stop caring about him. Nothing could make her stop wanting him, no matter how dangerous it was for her, no matter how much it hurt.

Yet Claire had a fine dose of Sumner bullheadedness, and seeing the truth for what it was didn't mean she was ready to admit that she was at fault for the evening's disastrous outcome, even partially, but it did burn the hard edge off her anger. She slowed the BMW, enough to let him catch her if he was inclined to.

The headlights shot off her mirror, filling the front seat with glaring white light. Claire shielded her eyes with her hand as the lights got closer, closer . . . Crushing disappointment. The double lights were too high to belong to Fegan's Trans Am. They were too bright, like halogen lights, positioned atop the roll bar of a pickup truck.

At first, she thought the driver would speed out around her, but as it became evident he had no such intentions, Claire stepped on the gas. The BMW was fast to respond, yet not quite fast enough, and the idiot behind the wheel of the truck easily caught her, touching her bumper lightly with his, clutching and revving the engine, blowing his horn.

Claire's heart was beating so fast, she feared it would seize-up and stop. Bayou Road was a narrow dirt path that shot through waist-high grass, standing water, and tangled vines on either side. Dark, deserted, and full of dangerous curves, it didn't stop Claire from pushing the accelerator to the floor and holding it there.

Whoever it was, was obviously out of his mind.

It was the only plausible explanation.

It couldn't be road rage. He hadn't been following her. He had come out of nowhere.

The truck seemed to slow. It dropped back a car length.

Adrenaline surged through her veins, a charge that electrified her senses, leaving her trembling as it began to recede.

He'd tired of the game. Or maybe he'd realized how lethal it was, and decided that terrorizing her wasn't worth the price he would pay if he got caught . . . Then, she realized her mistake. The truck hadn't fallen back completely, just enough to allow that frisson of hope to shoot through her before he stepped on the accelerator and raced forward again.

Claire's palms were damp with sweat, slick on the steering wheel, making it almost impossible to maintain control. She rounded a turn, taking it a little too wide, flinging gravel and dirt, then turf as the passenger wheels edged onto the shoulder. Laying on the horn, the truck gunned the engine and rammed the BMW from behind.

The impact jolted Claire, and her heart thumped harder. "Damn you!" she cried. "Are you crazy?" She glanced at the rearview mirror in time to see the dark, featureless face and glaring eyes of the ski mask . . . one fraction of a second that made her blood run cold, and the last thing she saw as the BMW careened through the next turn and into an uncontrollable spin.

Too startled, too stunned to scream, she felt the car slide round in a full circle, with the same sensation that she'd had as a kid riding the Tilt-A-Whirl at the carnival with Jean Louise, yet infinitely more terrifying. A full circle at lightning speed and a protesting metal screech as it slid onto uneven ground and pitched on its side in a shallow, water-filled ditch.

The light-colored truck sped on, not the least bit shocked by the accident he'd caused, uncaring if she'd been hurt or killed. Fighting down the airbag, Claire watched the malevolent glow of the truck taillights fade into the distance. Her heart was a deafening noise in her ears. She took several deep gulps of air, willing herself to calm as she quickly assessed the damage. She seemed to be in one piece, though the strain of the seat belt didn't allow for easy breathing. Reaching down, she unbuckled it, freeing herself from its tight constriction and struggling upright. With the BMW on its side at an awkward angle, it wasn't easy. She tried the door, but she couldn't get enough leverage to push it open. The engine had stalled, and the pungent, unmistakable smell of gasoline was getting stronger by the second.

Don't panic. Don't panic. Don't panic! Her heart had begun a wildly erratic beat, and she felt shaky from an overdose of adrenaline. *This is not good. Oh, God, this is so not good.*

The fumes were getting stronger. Filling her nostrils and throat, they made her nauseous. She had to get out! She had to get out, now! Fumbling with the glove box, she grabbed the first thing she could find, the only thing she could lay hands to, a medium-sized flashlight. Bracing herself, she pulled back, slamming it against

the window. The impact rippled up Claire's arm to her
elbow, punishing muscles and nerves, jarring her bones.
Gritting her teeth against the pain, Claire struck again,
this time shattering the glass.

"Char!"

At the sound of his voice, her heart nearly stopped.
"Fegan! Fegan, oh God, please be careful!"

He scrambled up onto the BMW; kneeling on the
back quarter panel, he pried the door open. "Jesus,
baby are you hurt?"

"No. No, I don't think so."

"Take my hand. C'mon. Let's get you out of there."

Calm. So calm, so strong, so damned capable. God,
she was glad to see him! Claire grasped his hand and
forced her way out, clawing for purchase and finding a
foothold wherever she could. Then, when she broke
free and into the hot night air, he eased the door back
into place and jumped down, reaching up to lift her
down and wrap her in a tight embrace. It lasted a few
seconds before he pulled back, but it was unbearably
sweet, and Claire felt her eyes prick with tears. Then he
was urging her away from the BMW and the thin thread
of gray smoke streaming up from the undercarriage.
"C'mon, I really don' think we should be this close."

By the time they reached the road and the Trans Am,
the first tongue of yellow flame had erupted. He opened
the passenger door, but Claire resisted. "I've got to call
the fire department, the sheriff—"

"You can use the car phone, but they won't be able
to save it," he said, all but forcing her into the passenger
seat. In a few seconds, he had taken the wheel and was
backing away from the scene. Then, at a safe distance,
they sat in silence and watched it burn.

An hour later, Claire sat on the steps at The Willows,
talking quietly with Sheriff Pershing. Fegan stood at a

little distance, his cigarette flaring orange in the soft darkness as he waited.

"A light-colored pickup truck, you say? But you didn't happen to catch the license number?"

"He was behind me, Sheriff. Besides, he was too close. I couldn't have seen it in any case."

Vance Pershing's calm, unlike Fegan's, was anything but reassuring. Claire found it infuriating. "Any other details you remember? White man? Black? Tall? Or short?"

"I don't know. He was wearing a ski mask, and he never stood up!" Claire snapped. "I don't know!"

"Well, you were the one at the scene, and if you don't know, then how we gonna catch this fella?"

"Excuse the hell out of me, Sheriff, but I was a little too busy trying to stay alive to notice details." She felt Fegan's hand brush her shoulder, then settle there— warm strength, stability, everything she lacked at this moment.

"She remembers anything else, she'll call," he said quietly.

"Make sure you do," Vance said, turning back to the squad car.

He was gone in a minute, leaving them alone in the velvety darkness. Seating himself on the chaise longue, Fegan pulled her down with him, cradling her close and kissing the top of her head. "You scared the livin' shit outta me back there. I thought for sure I'd lost you."

"I don't know what I would have done if you hadn't showed up when you did."

"Don' think about it. It's over now, and you're here with me. That's all that matters."

His voice was low and smooth, but there was an under-current running through it she sensed but didn't understand, something dark and unsaid. She meant to ask him about it, but his hand had slipped low on her thigh and was making a slow, sensuous slide up under her skirt. When he discovered the black thong panties, he growled low in his throat. "Those for me?" he asked, catching her gaze and holding it.

Claire smiled. It was starting, the delicious heaviness low in her belly, the sweet anticipation as their thoughts zeroed in on the same thing. "What do you think?"

"I think we'd better go inside, before this gets outta hand."

He would have risen, but she pushed him back, wanting to feel the soft night air on her body as they made love. "Not inside, Fegan. Here. I don't want to wait." She didn't want to risk anything else coming between them.

She kissed him, unbuttoning the rivet at the waistband of his jeans, making quick work of his zipper and letting him fill her hand. Fegan lay back on the chaise lounge, bringing her down on top of him as she slowly brought his arousal to the point of no return. He recognized the changes, the quickening of his breath, the rapidity of his pulse, the leaden quality of his lower body. She made him hot without even trying. That was physical, and physical, he understood. It was the rest that felt like sorcery, and he was definitely bewitched by her. Clairée and her problems. The fact that she was gonna be destroyed if the state had its day, and Jimmy died. He didn't want to see her hurt; in all honesty, he didn't want her touched by any of it, but it was way too late for that.

It was too late not to care. He did care for her, more than he wanted to, more than was healthy for either of them.

"You sure about this?" he asked as she poised above

him. "What's your aunt gonna say if she comes home to catch us makin' love on her front porch?"

"She won't be home till eleven."

Fegan resisted the urge to glance at his watch, opting for a wicked grin instead. "How you know we'll be done by then?"

"We will, if you'll just stop talking."

"You'll do me on the gallery, but you won' go out to dinner with me. What kind of woman are you, anyway?"

Claire stared down at him, noting his perplexed, perhaps troubled expression. What they had wasn't easy, but that didn't mean that it wasn't worth the effort. "I'm the woman who wants you," she said. "And I don't want to talk about how complicated things are. I don't want to think beyond this moment, beyond you and me together like this, sexy and wild and uninhibited."

That troubled look never wavered. "I'm too damned easy when it comes to you, Char. You crook your finger and I fall. You're all I think about, and I don' know if I like that."

"I like it," Claire admitted. "I like it very, very much, and I don't want it to stop."

"What about that whirlwind you mentioned?" he wanted to know.

"Whirlwind?" she said. "For the life of me, I can't recall." She guided his hand to her, tossing her head back as he slid his index finger into her warm wetness. Closely watching her expression, he caught his breath as her hand tightened over him. He didn't want her just to be ready for him. He wanted her aching, and moaning his name. Damned if a part of him, still sore from her recent rejections, didn't want her to beg.

The blue China silk was hiked up to her waist and the twin moons of her cheeks were too tempting for him to resist. He wanted her. He wanted all of her. All the things she had shared with lovers who came before him, and all of the things she hadn't. Everything, every part of her. Every secret place, every intimacy. Carefully, gently, he stroked the tender pucker of her anus, teasing her senses, weighing her reactions. She didn't recoil in shock, or pull back, just caught her breath, opening her eyes wide and staring down at him as he teased her with the tip of his smallest finger. Then, he leaned in and took her lips in a long and suggestive kiss.

The dual penetration was unexpected and unbearably erotic. Claire had never experienced a pleasure quite so intense, or a desire so deep and unfulfilled. She ached with the need to have him fill her completely, even as a low, thrumming throb began in the very center of her being, working its devastating way along her nerves to burst like tiny explosions upon her senses. Unable to withstand another second, Claire fought free of the mesmerizing spell of his hands, lying back on the chaise, urging him down on top of her. "Make love to me like you mean it, Fegan. I want to feel you inside me long after you've gone."

Fegan sighed as he settled into her hot depths. He wasn't quite sure it was real. The interlude had the surreal quality of a dream, him and Clairée joined in the midst of a hot summer night, her arms wrapped tightly around him as he drowned in her kisses. Had to be a dream, he thought crazily, and if it was, he didn't want to waken.

Claire didn't care to analyze it. She was lost in the moment, trapped by the rapture of their two bodies joining. His arms were around her, his forearms beneath her, one cradling her shoulders, one at her waist, so that he enveloped her completely, holding her as if she were something cherished. It made her feel good, so good, and for the moment she was able to forget that he didn't love her, didn't need her ... not like she needed him.

She hadn't allowed herself the luxury of facing it until now, but she'd been aware of it for days, aware that her feelings for him were deeper than they should be. It terrified her, and that was the reason she kept pulling away. Somehow, with his warmth wrapped all around her, and the steady, forceful thump, thump, thump of the chaise frame against the solid cypress of the gallery floor, it seemed okay to admit it, to lift the curtain she used to mask her feelings and peek tentatively in. Then, the climax overcame her, so strong that it stilled her breath in her lungs and forced her heart to falter ...

A little while later he was seated on the chaise, his long legs stretched out in front of him and Claire curled around him, her cheek resting against his collarbone. She liked this position. It was wonderful to lie with him in passion's wake, listening to the steady thud of his heart, the breath in his lungs, the deep timbre of his voice as it sang through him. Yet nothing could keep the troubling events of the evening at bay for very long. "What's going on here, Fegan?"

"Damn good question. And I wish the hell I had an answer. Whoever that was tonight meant business. You remember anything more about it?"

Claire shook her head. "It's all pretty much a blur. It was a light-colored pickup truck."

Fegan frowned into the shadows beyond the gallery where the croak of the tree frogs and strident hum of the cicada crowded close. "Light-colored, or white? Don't stop to think about it, just answer."

"White," Claire said automatically, a little stunned that she remembered.

"You said the glare of the lights blinded you. You happen to notice anything about those lights?"

"Yes, actually. They were double, one set higher than the other . . . above the cab . . . and they had a strange, bright quality . . . a greenish light. Brighter, clearer than a normal headlamp."

"Halogen running lights," Fegan said. "On a roll bar, maybe?"

"Maybe," Claire said, seeing the bright, blinding glare in her mind's eye. "They were above the grill. Above the windshield."

He was watching her closely. Despite the cloying warmth of the evening, Claire felt a chill sweep over her. "You've seen a truck like that before, haven't you?"

"Could be a coincidence. If it ain't, it sure as hell don' make sense."

"Why not?" Claire asked sharply. "Damn it, Fegan! Someone almost killed me tonight! I have a right to know."

"Don' make sense 'cause the guy that owns that truck's a cop."

"Cash Edmunds?"

"There some reason you can think of why he'd want you dead?"

"Not unless he was getting even for this morning, and got carried away."

"Say what?"

"I almost ran him down in the crosswalk in front of Julio's Market. I thought he'd write me up, but he asked about us."

That got Fegan's full attention. "What'd you tell him?"

"That it was none of his business. Then he did something really strange. He gave me his phone number, and said that if I got tired of you, I could give him a call."

"Good to have options," he said, laughing when she swatted him. "You gonna follow up on that?"

Claire snorted. "After his visit here a few days ago, I hardly think so."

Fegan's head came up. "Cash was here? What'd he want?"

"He said his truck broke down, and his cell phone was dead. He wanted to use the phone." Claire shivered, remembering how uncomfortable she'd been with him in the house. "He pretended to ask after Aunt Eulanie, but I got the distinct impression that he was on a fishing expedition. He asked how long I planned on staying, and warned me away from a lengthy visit. He said that folks around here didn't like Jimmy, and that asking questions would only cause trouble. I didn't like him being here. Cash always did creep me out. I can't even say why. But it's been that way since high school."

"Listen, how 'bout you layin' low for a while? Go on up to see Jimmy. Or spend a few days in the French Quarter, soakin' up the atmosphere. Anywhere but here."

Claire stared at him. "I can't do that, and what's more, you *know* that I can't do that! I've got to call my insurance broker in the morning and break the bad news, and I've got to find a rental until the check comes through . . . and then there's Aunt Eule. Besides, I'm not a coward, and I'm not going anywhere until I find out what the hell is going on. I've got an uneasy feeling that this is all connected—the murders, and what happened tonight. Someone wants to shut me up. If I leave Angelique, that person wins."

Headlights bobbed along the rutted drive. In a moment, Eulanie's pickup truck came into view. Claire pulled herself together and stood, and their pleasant interlude was officially over. "Well, if it isn't Mr. Broussard," Eulanie said brightly.

"These days it's just Fegan, Miz Sumner."

Eulanie fixed Claire with a frowning look. "Am I missing something? Where's the BMW?"

"I really should be goin'," Fegan put in.

Claire searched for an appropriate end to the evening. It was strange how they could have gone from intimate to awkward in so short a time, but they had. He was anxious to leave. She could see it. "If there's a problem with Amos Lee, you'll let me know?"

"If there's a problem, I'll call."

Fegan got in the TransAm and rolled down the windows. The radio was on, the volume soft and low. "Here's one for y'all. De timeless classic *Jolie Blon*. All you lovers out dere, have a slow dance for me."

With a flick of his wrist, Fegan turned down the volume. He wasn't in the mood for mellow, not given the day he'd had. The hearing had gone well enough, thanks in no small part to Clairée, but his conversation with Jimmy had left him feeling edgy and paranoid. He didn't like feeling paranoid. If it had been up to him, everything in life would be clear-cut, simplistic, easy to comprehend, and judiciously, scrupulously fair.

But life was anything but straightforward, and things weren't black and white in Angelique. Or anywhere, for that matter. There were so many facets to everything, so many shades of gray that just when a man thought he had things figured out, he found out he'd been looking at the wrong set of problems.

When Clairée first showed up on his doorstep, he'd been convinced she was out of her mind for trying to prove her father's innocence. Two murders, ten years apart. What possible connection could there be between the two?

Then he'd started asking questions, and the whole thing began to unravel. It hadn't taken much, and if he hadn't been so eager to believe that Jimmy killed Jean Louise, he might have seen that something was very wrong years ago. If only he'd opened his eyes, it would have saved them all a hell of a lot of grief.

It would have saved a man's life.

An innocent man. That truth ate at him, and every time it took a bite, the well of anger in him grew, got wider and deeper, blacker, more lethal.

"If Jimmy didn't kill Jean Louise, then who did?"

Someone who was here then; who's here now.

Someone who knew Jimmy.

Who knew Jean Louise. Who'd known where she was that night.

Someone who covered up his crimes by railroading Jimmy, and somehow convincing him to take the rap for him. Someone who was either lazy, or didn't really fear getting caught.

It didn't make sense. Why would a man commit a murder, and find the perfect scapegoat . . . then, on the eve of the completion of the execution sentence, commit another murder, a murder so similar that it aroused suspicion? Why now? He'd been home free. It didn't make sense.

Unless, like Chicago, it was a taunt.

Christ, he didn't want to think about it. He didn't want to admit that there was more than one mind warped enough to take young lives and brag about it. "Catch me if you can. Mr. Broussard? Are you listening? If you hang up now, you'll never find her in time. . . ."

But he had to think about it. Had to figure out what the hell was going on.

He'd dig deeper. Something was happening here, something unsavory, something frightening, and he was beginning to feel like a black cloud was hanging directly over him, a cloud that had followed him all the way from Chicago. But where the hell should he start?

"A white truck with a roll bar and halogen lights," Fegan murmured. He'd start with the one name he already had. The man Clairée said tried to warn her away from asking too many questions.

He had a lot of questions about what the deputy had been up to in his off duty time, and he'd better like the answers he got, or he was gonna mess up his pretty face.

CHAPTER
FOURTEEN

Local ordinance prevented places like Lightning from existing within town limits, but nothing prevented the owners from operating what was politely referred to as a "gentleman's club" on rural Highway 95. The low block building, glaringly white and lit with showy spotlights, didn't need to scream the title "strip club." In reality, there was no need to advertise. Everybody knew what went on behind closed doors at Lightning, and the place did a bustin'-at-the-seams business, especially on the weekends.

It also came as no surprise to Fegan to see the cruiser from the Acadia Parish's Sheriff's Department sitting conspicuously in the parking lot. Cash Edmunds's proclivity to the seamier side of things was common knowledge to anyone with half a mind to pay attention to such things.

Fegan paid attention.

You never could tell when information like that might be of use.

Like now, for instance.

Feeling on edge, on the other side of a burning anger, he didn't wait for Cash to come out. He paid the cover charge to the goon at the door, and took a seat by his man at the bar. Edmunds flicked him a glance, then pulled on his cigarette. "Hey, Broussard. You find yourself a new vice, or you here on business? I don't recall seein' you in here before."

"Just helpin' out a friend," Fegan said, signaling the bartender to bring him a beer.

"Anyone I know?"

"From what I hear, she's someone you'd like to know."

Cash laughed low, his eyes narrowed against the cigarette's smoke. "Ah. Sweet Clairée."

"That's right," Fegan said, shaking a smoke out of his battered pack. "She tells me she ran into you this mornin', and she said you made a pass at her."

Cash chuckled. "Funny. I've known you for a lot of years, Fegan, and I never once took you for the jealous type."

Fegan lit his cigarette and took a drag. "What about you, Cash? You the type that gets a bruised ego 'cause a lady turns you down? You get so pissed that you want to see her hurt—maybe even hurt bad?"

"I don't know what the fuck you're talkin' about."

"I came past the station house on my way here, and your truck wasn't parked in your usual spot. You have an accident I don't know about?"

Cash turned a sidelong glance on Fegan, and all the humor fled his face. "You got somethin' to say, Fegan? Then why don't you just come out and say it?"

"Somebody ran Clairée off the road tonight, totaled

her car, damn near killed her. Somebody drivin' a white pickup truck with a roll bar and high halogen runnin' lights. Only one truck that I know of like that around here, and it belongs to you. What time did you start your shift, Cash?"

"I came in late. Not that it's any of your damned business. Had some personal matters to take care of."

"Those personal matters wouldn't have anything to do with Clairée Sumner, now would they?"

"If it did, what makes you think I'd tell you?"

"You got a point there."

"For your information, I sold that truck last week," Cash said. "Damn thing gave me nothin' but trouble."

"Who'd you sell it to?"

Cash frowned, tilting back his head and blowing smoke rings into the air. "You know, memory's a funny thing. The name was right here on the tip of my tongue," he snapped his fingers, "and just like that, it's gone."

Fegan dragged on his cigarette, then, meeting the other man's gaze, flicked the smoldering butt into Cash's beer. "Vance Pershing don' like you any better than I do, does he, Cash? Matter of fact, he'd love a reason to get rid of your ass, ain't that right? Maybe it's time him and me have a little talk about this business arrangement you got with Remy."

Cash's expression never changed, but there was something in his eyes Fegan didn't like. "Remy Broussard's a two-bit hustler, and everybody in this parish knows it. Sheriff won't believe a word that comes outta his mouth, no matter how much you wish it was otherwise." He shoved the beer away without looking at Fegan. "Ain't you got a crazy old man needs lookin' after? Man can't be too careful these days. It's a big, bad world out there. Anything can happen—fires, accidental falls, pedestrian accidents. Why, he could overturn his pirogue and get eaten by an alligator.''

"That a threat?''

"Just an observation,'' Cash said. "Take that girl your granddad found out there. Who would've thought that a kid wouldn't be safe in a place like this? Just like your sister, Jean Louise. Just like Clairée gettin' run off the road.''

"Funny you should mention all three in the same breath . . . Clairée, Jean Louise, and the kid Amos Lee found. Not a lot of folks around here think they're connected, but some of us, we know better.''

"You buckin' to get your old job back?'' Cash wondered. " 'Cause you're sounding suspiciously like a reporter. You miss that life, Broussard? You miss the notoriety? Maybe you got bored with life in this backwater town . . . maybe you figured it's a little too tame for a big shot like you, and you decided to spice it up. A little mayhem, a little murder, make Clairée a target so you get to play the hero? Just how old were you when your sister died?''

In the time it takes to light a match and hold it to a short fuse, Fegan was off the bar stool. Grabbing Cash by the throat, he dragged him from his seat and shoved him facedown on the bar. "I sure as hell don' like your implication,'' Fegan growled low. "You so much as breathe my sister's name, you look Amos Lee's or Clairée's way again, and Pershing's gonna be lookin' for a new deputy. I'll see to it personally.''

He let him go and stood back, waiting for the arrest that he felt sure would come. But Edmunds just shook himself, like a dog shaking off water, and threw Fegan a dark look. "You're out of your depth, Broussard! You don't have a goddamn clue about anything!''

"Not yet," Fegan said, slamming out of Lightning. "But I'm catchin' on quick."

The door had barely closed on Fegan when Remy slipped from the back. He looked edgy and was covered with sweat. "I tol' you, man. I tol' you this was bad business!"

"Calm down, and shut your mouth," Cash told him. "Fegan doesn't know shit, and he won't find out if you keep your cool and keep your big mouth shut."

Remy was beyond being controlled, and beyond caution. "I don' like dis, Cash. I ain't no killer. I'm done, you hear me? You call de man, now, tonight, and you tell him I'm done wid this. Clairée could've been killed. She could've been killed, man!"

"Yeah, but she wasn't. She lost her car, that's all. It's not that big a deal, nothin' her insurance company won't take care of, and as long as she takes the hint, it'll end right here. No harm, no foul, and no reason for you to get bent out of shape."

Cash's reasoning didn't have much impact, and Remy's upset didn't seem to level off. "I want out, you hear me? I don't give a damn what de man does for laughs, long as you leave me out of it! No more favors, you hear me? Call me again, and dere's gonna be trouble." He threw a set of keys on the bar, and stormed out.

After a minute's hesitation, Cash took out his cell phone and punched in a number. Several rings later he picked up. "It went okay, but somethin's come up. I don't think I'll be able to make it."

"It must be serious for you to disappoint me again so soon. Speaking of which—is there news on that end?"

Cash's collar felt tight. He eased a finger into it and tugged it away from his throat. "Gator bait by now. Ain't nobody, or nothin', that could go into that swamp on foot and come out alive. If the snakes didn't get her, something else did."

"You'd better hope so, cousin. You can't afford another screw-up and I can't afford for you to become a liability. If there's nothing else, there are matters that require my attention."

"What matters?" Cash couldn't quite help asking.

"God is in the details, Cash," Ashton told him. "That's all you need to know." Then, he hung up the phone.

"Collect call from Louisiana State Penitentiary at Angola—will you accept the charges?"

"Yes, Operator." Claire's heart took a tiny leap. "Dad?"

"Clairée, why the hell are you still in Angelique?"

"I'm glad you called. It's good to hear your voice." It wasn't an exaggeration. The sound of his tobacco-roughened voice brought tears to Claire's eyes.

"I would have thought you'd gone back home to Lafayette by now. You quit your job?"

"No," Claire hastened to reassure him. "No, I took a leave of absence. I thought I'd stay on for a little while. Aunt Eulanie's been having some problems with the sugar contracts. It's something I can help with."

"That the only reason you're hangin' 'round there?"

"Dad?"

"I want you to stay away from the Broussards, you hear? That boy's got trouble written all over him, and you don't need him messin' up your life."

Claire frowned. "Fegan? I don't understand. How did you know?" Oh, God. He'd gone to see Jimmy, a choice bit of information he'd decided not to share with her, and for a split second, she wondered what else he was withholding. "When? When did he come to see you?"

"Yesterday."

Yesterday . . . before he'd gone to the Pink Cadillac . . . before they'd made love.

"Clairée, you listen to me, and you listen good. You forget about Broussard—forget about all of it. Pack your things and go home. You're meant for better things, and I won't have you throwin' away your future on some backwater swamp trash."

Claire sucked in a breath and let it go in a controlled effort to hold on to her temper. "Fegan isn't trash, and it isn't like that." She squeezed her eyes shut and gave the lie. "I'm not—it isn't like that. We're not involved. Not like you mean, anyway, and if it wasn't for him—" She stopped herself, but she was aware the moment the words left her mouth that she'd said too much.

"If it wasn't for him, what? Clairée, what the hell's goin' on down there?"

"I don't know," she said honestly. "I totaled my car last night. Someone forced me off the road, and I was trapped inside. The car burned, but Fegan got me out."

"Jesus." Jimmy's voice sounded choked, as if someone had their hands around his throat. "Jesus Christ. Are you all right? Don't you lie to your daddy. I want the truth."

"I'm fine, Dad. I was a little shaken up, that's all."

"This wasn't supposed to happen." It was barely breathed, a mere rasp of a denial so strong, so adamant that it chilled her.

"I don't understand, Dad. What wasn't supposed to happen?"

The operator interrupted. "Sir, your fifteen minutes are up."

"Dad? Dad? What wasn't supposed to happen?"

"Go home, Clairée! Now, tonight! Get the hell out of Angeli—"

"Dad?" Claire clicked the plunger, and the dial tone sounded. "Damn it!" She replaced the receiver on its cradle and stood for a moment, hand resting on it, praying it would ring again.

Eulanie chose that moment to come into the kitchen. She'd been to Angelique that morning, and her cheeks were flushed pink from the heat. She seemed slightly out of breath. "Claire? I thought I heard the phone."

Claire pulled herself together, offering her a half-hearted smile. "It was Dad. He had a surprise visitor yesterday, and he wasn't too happy—quite frankly, neither am I."

"Oh?"

"Fegan," Claire said. "He never mentioned it."

"Well, if he's hoping to get permission to court you properly, then he's wasting his time with Jimmy. No man is ever going to be good enough for his little girl."

"Oh, God, not you, too. Aunt Eule, it's nothing like that. We're not dating, and have no plans to. I don't have time for that sort of thing right now, and if I did— well, let's just say that Fegan isn't the kind of man you count on." But she'd counted on him last night, and he'd been there when she needed him.

"Not now, maybe," Eulanie said, pouring herself a glass of lemonade from the refrigerator.

"Not at all," Claire insisted.

Eulanie shrugged, smoothing the wrinkles from her periwinkle sanded silk before taking a seat at the table. "Well, you certainly know him better than I do, and I make it a practice not to meddle in my niece's affairs."

Her use of the word *affair* made Claire flinch. Was that what it was? A love affair? She'd thought she'd known what she was about. She'd been especially careful not to involve her heart; she'd been wise not to harbor any expectations where he was concerned, but it was becoming more blatantly obvious by the moment that it hadn't done her a damn bit of good. He'd still managed to find his way into her heart, to disappoint her, infuriate her with his highhanded, asinine male logic that insisted it was the natural order of things to keep secrets from her. "I thought I knew him," Claire said quietly. "Suddenly, I'm not so sure."

"Have some lemonade, dear," Eulanie suggested.

"Thank you, no. I need to go out for a little while."

"Would you mind lending a hand in the office first? I have some paperwork to catch up on, and I can't seem to find my glasses. I sure could use a younger pair of eyes."

"It wasn't supposed to happen. He swore to me that she'd be safe!"

"Who, man?" Adesco demanded, his voice hollow and disembodied.

Jimmy grabbed his radio, lifting it, ready to hurl it at the wall. Then, abruptly, he put it down again. Any commotion would bring the guards, and bring hell down on his head. They'd haul his ass to solitary confinement, away from the row, away from Trick Adesco.

"Hey, Sumner!" Trick said. "Hey, Sumner, you lost your mind over dere, or what?"

"No. No. In fact, I just found it." He'd sworn to Jimmy that Clairée would be protected, untouched. A life for a life. Jimmy's for his baby girl's. The threat had been mind-numbingly real at the time. He'd gotten to Jean Louise. He managed to plant the evidence in Jimmy's car, and set up a flawless frame. There was nothing stopping him from getting to Clairée.

He was powerful. He could do it easily, and no one would ever suspect.

Nobody *had* suspected. Hadn't he killed Jean Louise Broussard?

Jimmy's choice might have been more difficult for another man, but there had never been any question that any accusation he made would be discounted. The word of a no-account drifter who drank too much, and moved from job to job and place to place, didn't mean squat. And neither did his life, for that matter.

A life for a life.

His life for Clairée's. She was just a kid. A beautiful young girl on the verge of becoming a woman, a bright being with unlimited promise, and her whole future stretching out in front of her. She could do anything, be anything.

Jimmy had burned out at thirty-five.

His life for his daughter's.

It hadn't been a good choice, or an easy choice. It had been his only choice, and he'd been sure it had been the right one, until she'd shown up in the visitors' room, brandishing the picture of the kid found in the swamp.

"It was supposed to end with me, damn it," Jimmy muttered. "He said it was a fluke. A one-time thing." But it hadn't been, and he felt a deep sense of panic at everything he didn't know. What the hell had he done by going along with the deal? How many young girls' lives had ended because he'd opted to keep his mouth shut, and do what he was told? It made him burn to think about it, an anger so deep and so potent that it felt like he'd swallowed live coals.

Clairée was in trouble, and she wasn't even aware of it.

There was no way she could know the extent of the

evil reaching out to embrace her. Even Jimmy didn't know all of it, and he'd been a silent partner to it for ten long years.

The sacrificial lamb.

Cold sweat beading on his forehead, Jimmy went to the bars on the front of the cell, as close to Adesco as he could get. "Hey, Trick? You still got that plan you were mouthin' about a few days ago?"

"Who wants to know?"

"I do."

"You in?"

"Damn straight. I'm gonna get the hell outta here, or die tryin'. There's somebody on the outside I gotta see."

It didn't matter that he'd won the decision in the hearing, and that Amos Lee was free to do what he did best. Fegan didn't trust Frank, so he threw a few things in the back seat of the Trans Am, and headed back to the cottage. He found Amos Lee sitting in the rocker in the shade of the front porch. "Are you ready, *Pépère*? We'll stop and get us some bait on our way out there. Got our fishin' poles in the trunk of the Trans Am."

Amos Lee didn't seem to have heard. He was looking into the yard to Fegan's left, smiling slightly, as if amused. It wasn't the vacant stare of a man lost in reverie; he seemed to be watching something, something that only he could see. Every now and again, he would nod, but whether the movement was an affirmation or merely due to the motion of the rocker, Fegan couldn't tell. "*Pépère*? We're goin' to the houseboat for a few days, don' you remember?"

The old man's rocker never ceased its quiet, steady rhythm. Back and forth, back and forth. Fegan felt his frustration rise. The residue from his confrontation with Cash mingled with the strain of the past two weeks and combined with his seemingly unsolvable problems with Clairée, eroding his patience and further fraying an already worn temper. Cash, he could deal with. Clairée was another matter altogether. He wasn't sure what he wanted from her; he only knew that no matter how small the exchange between them, or how great, he always came away feeling like a rat was gnawing at his insides.

Hungry.

Dissatisfied.

Restless and confused.

That restlessness was transferred into a burning need to get as far away from the house as he could manage. Oblivious, Amos Lee smiled into the streaming sunlight in front of the porch, and kept on rocking.

"C'mon, *Pépère,* I got things to do, and I can't be here if Frank comes. It's better for you at the houseboat— least for a little while." Fegan tried to reason with him, but it was like arguing with a child. "Why you doin' this? You talk to Clairée, but you won' even *hear* me!"

"I hear you, man. Matter of fact, most o' de neighbors hangin' their heads out de windows, dey heard you, too." Remy came around the side of the bungalow, glancing twice over his shoulder, scanning the yard. He sat down on Amos Lee's porch, leaning back against one of the supports and propping a booted foot on the cypress planks, while the other one remained planted firmly on the ground. "Hey, Fegan, how 'bout a smoke?"

Fegan dug in his shirt pocket and handed the pack to his cousin. "Hey, *Noncle,* how you doin'? You feel like a cigarette?" With a wave of his hand, the old man declined, and Remy struck a match. "Wasn't sure I'd find you home," he said to Fegan. "Thought maybe you'd be with sweet Clairée."

"You want somethin'?" Fegan asked. "Or did you just come by to practice bein' a pain in my ass?"

"We blood, ain't we? We family, an' family sticks together. Dat's de natural order of things."

"What do you want, Remy? You want money? 'Cause I'm all tapped out."

"Shit, man. Gimme some credit. I just came by to pay my respects to *Noncle* Amos Lee, dat's all, and to ask if you could maybe put me up for a day or two? Thing's are gettin' kinda hot 'round Angelique, and I need a place to lay low—just for a little while."

"Your old lady throw you out again?"

"Nah, man. Ain't nothin' like dat." Remy finished the cigarette and crushed it into the grass with the toe of his boot, running his hand up and down the length of his denim-covered thigh. He seemed more high-strung than usual, but Fegan let it pass. He had enough on his mind without getting involved in Remy's business.

"I heard about Clairée, man. Dat's some heavy shit." He lit another smoke from Fegan's pack, shaking out the match after it burned down to his fingertips. "She okay?"

"Yeah," Fegan said. "Yeah, she's all right."

"Dat's good to hear. Real good. I like Clairée, you know. She's a real class act. You ought to treat her right, man. She deserves it. Nothin' bad should happen to her. It ain't right, man. It ain't right."

Fegan frowned at him. "You feelin' okay? You ain't strung out on anything?"

"Nah, man. Remy, he's right as rain. Just needed to touch base, you know? *Noncle* Amos Lee . . . he makes for good solid company. He's gonna let Remy do all the talkin', him! Ain't dat right, *Noncle?*"

Amos Lee smiled into the shifting sunlight, but whether he was amused by his grandnephew's antics, or by whatever he saw there in the yard, remained a mystery.

"Mais yeah, dat's right," Remy said. Sobering, he met Fegan's glance. "Thanks, man. I owe you."

"Yeah, you do," Fegan agreed. "And look out, 'cause one of these days, I'm gonna collect."

Remy smoked his cigarette, quiet for the moment. He seemed a little calmer. "Listen, man. You got a few minutes?"

But Fegan was already headed out. "Later. You'll stay with *Pépère?* I don' want Frank to pull a fast one when I'm not lookin'!"

"Yeah, sure," Remy said, "no problem." Fegan got the strange impression that he was somehow relieved.

Pontier's Point was a triangular island, dividing the bayou channel and jutting out into a deep pocket in the streambed, not unlike a sinkhole. The biggest catfish sought out the resulting deep water, preferring to lie motionless on the soft bed of silt, so deep, so dark that the sunlight couldn't reach. In turn, anglers sought the catfish, which made it a hot spot for local sportsmen.

Fegan had fished the spot himself while in high school, always hoping to catch a record "cat," and usually catching hell for being late to supper, instead. Quite a number of the local guys had fished that spot, Cash Edmunds among others. Fegan hadn't been out here since the summer he graduated from high school. He'd spent a lot of time here that summer; then, in September, he went away to college, and he put all of that behind him. He'd had to work for his tuition, and there hadn't been time for the luxury of lazy days on the sun-dappled green water, or visits home for that matter. In the summer months he worked on an oil rig, saving every dime to fund his education and his driving ambition to make something of himself so that he didn't end up like his old man. Winter nights, he pumped gas at a local service station. He wrote to Amos Lee and Jean Louise when he found the time, and called once in a while, but he never seemed to find the time to visit . . . and when he did, the natural inclinations of a nineteen-year-old pushed all thoughts of home and kid sisters aside.

It didn't solve a damn thing, feeling guilty over actions a man couldn't change, but it didn't stop him from knowing that he'd failed them, either . . . Jean Louise, Amos Lee . . . maybe even Frank. It was at the heart of Frank's resentment—the fact that Fegan had walked away and he'd been left behind, saddled with a wife and two little kids while Amos Lee looked after Jean Louise and made excuses for why Fegan wasn't around.

Oh, yeah, he'd failed them . . . just like he'd come up short in Chicago. It had become a life pattern with him. When things got tough, he turned his back and walked away.

"Only not this time." He killed the motor, and let the boat drift to the small island. Yellow crime scene tape had been strung from sapling to sapling like bizarre Christmas garlands. Meant to ward away the curious, it didn't stop Fegan from stepping over the ribbon and onto muddy ground. He needed to have a good look at the area. It didn't matter that he knew every tree, every plant and vine native to the bayou. He needed to get a good look at the place where Amos Lee had found the murdered girl, the place he'd found Jean Louise.

There wasn't a great deal to see: a mud spit jutting out several feet into the water, covered in raccoon tracks,

the weeds flanking it trampled by the investigating offi-
cers and perhaps by interlopers like himself. People got
off on the weirdest things.

And someone in this parish, maybe in Angelique
itself, got off on killing teenage girls.

But why?

Sex? Power? Some warped need to control, to play
God, and the Devil.

Jean Louise had been raped before she'd been killed;
Sherry Ellen Davis had been, too. Rape was a crime of
violence. It was about the control and the manipulation
of the victim . . . yet the attacker of both girls had possessed the forethought to wear a condom, so that there
was no DNA evidence left behind to process. That suggested to Fegan the crimes hadn't been random; they'd
been planned.

But what about the choice of victims?

Had he been stalking them, watching them? Awaiting
an opportunity to grab them? Or had he been trawling
for victims, and Jean Louise and Sherry Ellen just happened to be in the wrong place at the perfect time?

Fegan walked through shin-high weeds to the muddy
tongue of land thrusting out into the water where he
then crouched. Images, like shots from a slide show,
flashed behind his eyes. Jean Louise and Clairée running across the backyard, squealing as Jean Louise's
dog, Crawfish, gave chase. The image died as quickly
as it had materialized, replaced by that of a faceless
girl screaming in terror as a much larger, more vicious
canine caught her ankle and dragged her to the ground;
and then, by Jean Louise as she must have looked when
Amos Lee found her, lying lifeless on this small patch
of earth, her bound legs submerged in the murky water.

Fegan shook his head, but the image was slow to
fade. "Talk to me, baby," Fegan murmured, but she

remained as mute and as uncommunicative as Amos Lee. Then, the throaty hum of a boat motor caught his attention, and in less time than it took for him to get to his feet, a small aluminum craft glided into view.

Sheriff Vance Pershing didn't look very sheriff-like this afternoon. He had on a short-sleeved, plaid shirt in shades of blue and tan, a pair of worn khakis, and navy blue deck shoes.

"Afternoon, Sheriff. Nice day, ain't it?"

"Broussard, what the hell you doin' out here? I know you're not stupid, so I can only assume that you intentionally trespassed upon a known crime scene."

"This? A crime scene? I thought the bodies were discarded here—you tellin' me they were killed here, too? 'Cause that ain't what the evidence says."

Pershing turned his head and spat a stream of tobacco juice into the water. "I ain't tellin' you nothin', except that you'd better keep your nose out of this investigation."

"I would, except for one thing—the wrong man's about to be executed for killing my little sister. Jimmy Sumner didn't kill Jean Louise. You may be able to swallow that without it stickin' in your craw, but I can't."

"The evidence clearly indicates—"

"Evidence can be manufactured," Fegan insisted harshly. "As I see it, someone needed a scapegoat, and Jimmy happened to be a likely choice. He didn't have a lot of friends, did he? Never held a job for long, and he drank too much. Kind of quiet, kept to himself . . . not exactly the kind of man anyone would vouch for."

Pershing's face was tight, but there was something in his eyes that told Fegan he wasn't far from the truth, but he was too hardheaded, or too frightened, to admit it. "His confession is on record."

"And it doesn't mean much. Confessions can be

coerced. Not exactly a new concept, is it? All anyone needs is a little leverage."

"Throwing those kinds of accusations around may do it for you, son, but they won't help Sumner, now will they? You can run at the mouth all you want, Broussard, make so much noise that they hear you all the way to Baton Rouge . . . but in two weeks' time, Jimmy Sumner will be every bit as dead."

"And you don't like that any better than I do, do you, Sheriff?"

Pershing's face changed, anger and frustration settling in on his tight features, deepening the lines around his mouth and eyes. "I *don't* like it any better than you do, and just like you, there isn't a damn thing I can do about it."

"Maybe there is," Fegan said. "What do you know about your deputy's off-duty activities?"

"Edmunds?" He snorted. "I don't pry into a man's private affairs without good reason. I will tell you this much, though—he's about as close to a certain senatorial candidate as a man can get without committing a sin against nature."

That got Fegan's attention. "Ashton Morlay?"

Pershing gave a grim laugh. "It's no secret that Edmunds wasn't my first pick for the job. Hell, he wasn't my last choice, either. He was shoved down my throat because of an accident of birth."

"What did you just say?"

"Cash Edmunds and Ashton Morlay are kin, son, not that Morlay brags about it. If it wasn't for Ashton Morlay's influence, Cash Edmunds would be collecting unemployment compensation right now, or pushing pencils in some other parish police department. Now, why don't you get out of here before I cite you for interfering with an ongoing investigation."

* * *

Eulanie's "bookwork" consisted of the newly reworded contract from the sugar mill. The contract couldn't be glossed over, and there was some contradictory language that Claire didn't like. The hours ticked off while she worked on revising it; Eulanie reviewed and approved the revised version, and the changes were faxed to the Perry offices. By the time Claire glanced at her watch, it was seven-thirty and getting dark.

The rental company had delivered her temporary transportation: a black Chevy Malibu with white sidewall tires; it lacked the luxury to which she was accustomed, but it was more than sufficient to get her to the bungalow on Mayfly Street. Time hadn't cooled her anger with Fegan. She didn't know what he meant by going to see Jimmy at the prison, but she was going to find out. It infuriated her that he had met with her father before she'd found him at the Pink Cadillac, before he'd made love to her on the gallery at The Willows, and he'd intentionally, maliciously kept it from her . . . as if she didn't have a right to know, as if he totally discounted how important Jimmy was to her.

If she found out, as she suspected, that he was looking into the murders and withholding information from her because of some Neanderthal notion of protecting her, she'd, she'd—she didn't know what she would do, but he sure as hell wasn't going to like it.

When Claire arrived at the bungalow, a single light was burning in the kitchen. The mental image of Fegan in the kitchen at The Willows teased her thoughts, and she hardened herself against the warmth threatening to wash over her. Fegan was a fine way to pass the time; he knew how to titillate the senses, how to satisfy, but thinking beyond that point was foolish.

He'd told her more than once that he wasn't hero material, and he'd been right. He'd made the point so she wouldn't expect things from him that he wasn't capable of giving.

What he didn't seem to realize was that she hadn't come to Angelique looking for Superman. Hell, she didn't even need Clark Kent.

What she wanted was answers, and those she could get on her own. Forgetting all of her past insecurities and doubt, she stalked into the bungalow, fully prepared for a confrontation.

She walked swiftly through the darkened living room, the light of the kitchen the beacon that drew her, her anger the impetus that pushed her onward.

The kitchen was empty, but the house wasn't. It was a feeling, nothing more, a sense that someone was there, lurking, unseen in the shadows of the pantry.

Claire's nape prickled, as if an icy finger had traced a fragile line on her warm skin. In response, her pulse kicked up a notch, and her breath quickened. "Fegan?" Her voice quavered slightly and her impatience with her reactions increased. "Damn it, Fegan, I know you went to Angola, and I have a right to know what's going on."

The sound of a watery sigh came from the pantry. Growing angrier by the second, Claire fumbled for the light switch, and one hundred glaring watts of power flicked on. For the space of a heartbeat, she stared in stunned horror, fragments of a scene too terrible to take in registering independently when her mind refused to accept the whole . . . the bloody hands that clutched the side of the pantry cupboard and held him upright long after he should have fallen . . . the brilliant red of the arterial blood soaking the front of his white T-shirt

. . . the trademark Broussard good looks marred by the ghastly, grin-like slash across his throat. . . .

For one stunning split second Claire's heart stopped beating; then she realized her mistake, and her breath left her in a rush.

Remy staggered toward her, trying to speak. His lips moved, but he couldn't manage more than a whisper of sound as he grabbed her and started to fall, and Claire screamed, and screamed again.

CHAPTER
FIFTEEN

"You sure you didn't see anything? A strange car parked on the street? Someone hanging around that looked out of place?"

Fegan knew Pershing was just doing his job, but he resented it anyway. Clairée had been through a nightmare, and he hated for her to be forced to relive it so soon. "Look, Sheriff, can't this wait? She's been through enough already."

"You want the man who did this to your cousin walkin' free?" Pershing said sharply. "I thought you Acadian families were tight."

"That kind of remark is uncalled-for!" Clairée's protest hung in the air between them, but it was the darkening of Fegan's expression that caused Pershing to soften his tone. "Look, son. I'm not trying to be unsympathetic, but you, of all people, should know how this works. I need to get the basic information on what happened down, before she's had time to think about it. If you'd like, we can go someplace else—someplace away from here.''

The photographer had finished, and the EMT's were loading the gurney and its long, black bag into the back of the ambulance for transport to Homer Folley's Funeral Home. The sheriff, in his own gruff way, was trying to spare Clairée any more upset—to remove the distraction of being at the scene of her recent horror. Strangely, Fegan couldn't summon the smallest shred of gratitude. He couldn't help thinking that if the sheriff's department hadn't botched the investigation into Jean Louise's death, that none of this would have happened. Jimmy wouldn't be in prison, awaiting execution, and Remy would still be alive. He was about to tell him all of that and more, but Clairée spoke first. "No, it's all right, really. We can stay. Besides, we can't leave Amos Lee, but Fegan is right. I would like to get this over with.''

"I won't keep you a moment longer than necessary, Miz Sumner,'' Pershing assured her. He flipped the page on his small notebook. "You said that when you entered, the house was dark except for the kitchen light?''

"That's correct.''

"And you heard a noise coming from the pantry?''

Claire nodded. "I thought it was Fegan, but when I flipped on the light—''

She stopped, unwilling or unable to speak the words again. She'd told the story twice, the first time to Fegan when he'd arrived to find her sitting dazed and smeared with Remy's blood on Amos Lee's porch, holding on to his portable phone as if it were the barrier that separated her from hysteria. Then, she'd somehow managed to call the dispatcher and report the incident.

Incident.

Fegan closed his eyes.

Remy was dead, and it wasn't an incident. It was murder.

He'd arrived before the ambulance, before the sheriff, in time to kneel by the body and absorb the shock. It had numbed him for a little while, lending the whole thing a nightmarish, surreal quality . . . like it wasn't really happening . . . like he would wake up to the sound of the back door opening, and his cousin's good-natured jive as he helped himself to a cup of hot coffee.

But it was real.

Remy was gone, and Fegan hadn't seen anything that horrific in almost a year. Somewhere in his mind, the cold voice echoed, *"Do you run, Mr. Broussard? I think I caught a glimpse of you running along the pier last week. Would you run for this little girl's life?"*

"And the victim stumbled toward you."

"He grabbed me by the arms, and tried to speak."

"He tried to speak, you say? Was he trying to communicate the identity of his attacker?"

"I don't know—I suppose it's possible, but because of his injuries, there was—no sound." The last was quietly added. "I can't be sure."

"What happened after?" Pershing was undaunted by her inability to answer. His persistence might be justified; it might even be expected under the circumstances, but it pushed Fegan's buttons, and the anger that replaced his earlier shock boiled over.

"She told you what happened! What the hell do you want from her? You want her to name Remy's killer so you don't have to look for him?"

"I'm trying to conduct this investigation, and the more information I have, the more I have to go on."

Fegan snorted. "Investigation, now that's a laugh! You're gonna do just like you did with Jean Louise, like you did with the last kid Amos Lee found. You gonna go through the motions to make it look good—then you'll go back to your office, file this away, then sit on your ass till time to draw your pension check.''

Pershing's lean face turned a dark, dull shade of red, and his pale eyes seemed to glow. ''You think I enjoy bein' fucked over? You think I want the son of a bitch that killed those kids to get away with it? Then you don't know shit, boy.''

''I know incompetence when I see it,'' Fegan said. ''And I sure as hell ain't your 'boy'.''

Clairée put her hands on Fegan's arms. It registered in his brain that her flesh felt cold, despite the cloying heat of the evening. Still, he didn't attempt to break away from Pershing's hard-eyed stare until her compelling presence forced him to. ''I can manage. Why don't you check on your granddad?''

''He's watchin' TV. *Mr. Magoo.* I don't think he knows anything happened.''

The brief exchange broke the fierce tension, but it didn't fade completely. ''Miz Sumner?'' the sheriff prompted.

''I couldn't hold him, and we fell. When I got away, I found the phone—then I came here, to check on Mr. Prideau. I was afraid that he might have been harmed also. A few minutes after, Fegan came, and found something for me to wear. The clothing I was wearing was ruined.'' She smoothed her hands down over the black T-shirt and faded Levi's Fegan had torn from the dresser drawer and helped her into. She filled them out completely. He'd been thinking of getting into her pants on his way home; oddly enough, she'd gotten into his, only not in the way he'd intended.

''And you didn't see or hear anything out of the ordinary?''

She shook her head.

Vance Pershing closed his notebook and put the pen back in his shirt pocket. "I guess that's it, then. If you recall anything else—"

"Of course." Claire hugged her arms, watching Pershing get in the dark-colored car and drive away. "Where were you?" She didn't mean it to come out that way, but it sounded like an accusation. "Earlier, I mean."

He'd glanced up when she first spoke, and he looked at her long and hard before answering, as if trying to weigh his response against her anticipated reaction. Claire knew that look. He was wary of her emotional state and trying to shield her, protect her, by keeping her in the dark. She thought about Jimmy, and Fegan's trip to Angola, and wondered what else he wasn't telling her. "I was on a stakeout," he said quietly. "Remy said he'd stay with Amos Lee, and I didn't know you planned on droppin' by."

"A stakeout. Was it business? Or did it have to do with the murders?" She shouldn't be questioning him as to his whereabouts. She had no right to ask. Yet it didn't stop her. Maybe it was the fallout from finding Remy, or the fact that for one split second when she'd flicked on the light, she'd thought it was he staggering toward her. Same height, same dark, curly hair, same raffish good looks.

"*Mais,* yeah. You could say that." He shifted his weight to his right hip. "What's this about, Char? You trying to punish me for not bein' here when they came for Remy?"

"No," she said. "I'm not—or maybe I am. I don't know."

"Ain't no need, baby," he said softly. "I'm already kickin' myself."

"I'm sorry," Claire said, and she meant it. "About Remy. About everything." He reached for her, bringing her in, holding her close.

Claire succumbed to his embrace. She needed to be in his arms. Everything out there, beyond the perimeter of the small, intimate space they occupied, had gone crazy. Nothing made sense anymore, and she desperately needed someone to hold on to. Not just anyone. She needed Fegan. Yet, even the strength and security she found in his arms couldn't still the questions. "What did you mean just now? You say that you wished you'd been here when 'they' came for Remy. Who is 'they', Fegan?"

For a moment he didn't say anything. Claire pulled back just far enough to stare up into his face. "Do you know who did this?"

"I don' know. Remy had a foot in both worlds, you know? Could be he held out on the wrong guy. One thing for sure—he knew he was in some sort of trouble. Must've been the reason he asked me if he could hang around. He said he needed a place to lay low, and he seemed to want to talk to me about somethin'. I was in a hurry to leave, and I put him off. Jesus, why did I put him off?"

"You can't blame yourself for this. There's no way anyone could have known something so horrible would happen. Especially here."

"Of all people, I *should've* known," Fegan said. He seemed to retreat into himself, and his look was as troubled as his statement was cryptic. "After Jean Louise— after—I should have seen this comin'."

"'After Jean Louise, after' what?" Claire asked, frowning up at him. He was holding something back. Something big. She could feel it, like a huge, dark wall separating her from him, keeping her at a distance, permanently in the dark. It was a feeling, a perception, that she didn't like. "You don't think this has something to do with Jean Louise?" she asked suddenly. "With the second murder?"

"Her name was Sherry Ellen Davis. She was a runaway from near Shreveport, and I don't know. I can't imagine any of that being connected to Remy. He did a lot of things that weren't exactly legal, but murder?" He shook his head. "Not an innocent kid. Remy's got family, and he loved Jean Louise. No way could he have been directly involved in any of that."

Claire agreed with him. She couldn't imagine good-natured, slick-talking Remy being involved with something as heartless as the exploitation and death of a child. "What about indirectly?"

"Information," he said. "There wasn't much that got past Remy, and he always held a little somethin' back. Maybe he knew more about what was goin' on here than he was sayin'. One thing's for sure—somebody didn't want him talkin'. Killing with a knife—it's messy, but quiet. Cuttin' the throat's a good way to keep somebody quiet. Victim can't scream, and they can't get far."

"You said something before—that you should have seen this coming, but you never quite finished the thought, and I got the impression you were talking about something other than Jean Louise."

"Why don' I call you a cab? I don' want you goin' home alone, and I can't leave Amos Lee. I'll bring your car by in the mornin'."

He was closing off, shutting down, and this time, Claire wouldn't accept that. "I'm not going home, Fegan. Not yet, anyway. Not until you stop holding out on me."

"Who says I'm holdin' out on you?"

"I do," Claire said softly, refusing to back down. "You

can't protect me, Fegan. I'm in this as deeply as you are. Deeper, maybe. And I have every bit as much to lose as you do. More, maybe."

Fegan glanced up. "This about Jimmy?"

"Why didn't you tell me you went to see him?"

Sighing, he pushed a hand through his dark hair. "Not an easy subject to bring up. What could I say? 'Oh, by the way, I talked to your old man and you're right, he's innocent?' I felt like I needed time to figure out what's goin' on and what the hell to do about it."

"Time is the one thing we don't have, Fegan."

"I'm aware of that."

"There's something else, isn't there? Something's bothering you that you aren't mentioning."

"There are some things you don't need to know." Silently. *Things I can't forget, and don't want to face.*

Claire looked into his face, a searching look. She was a fool for saying the words, but she couldn't seem to help herself, and they'd been so long in coming. "You always did try to go it alone. Maybe it's time you realized you've got someone on your side." Framing his face with her hands, reveling in the scrape of his beard, she touched her mouth tenderly to his.

He watched her for a little while, as if he wasn't quite sure how to answer. Then, he drew a halting breath. "This ain't the first time I've been in the middle of somethin' like this. There was a string of murders in Chicago a while back. Not long after I started covering the story, the phone calls started comin'. At work, at home, day, night. He fed me clues about where to find the victims, and he taunted me about Jean Louise. There had been some coverage in Chicago about what happened down here to a certain crusading young journalist, and I guess he picked up on it."

"He knew about Jean Louise?"

"Jean Louise was my Achilles' heel, and it wasn't exactly a secret. The more notoriety I gained as a journalist, the greater the public interest. It was the personal angle to an up-and-comer. Tabloids love that sort of thing."

"It must have been dreadful for you."

Fegan shrugged. "Yeah, somethin' like that. Cops did their best to solve the case, but they just couldn't seem to outsmart him, and neither could I."

"What happened?" she said softly.

"The last victim was just a kid. A fourteen-year-old from the Projects. She was alive when he called me. He even gave me clues about where he was. I called the cops. They got there five minutes after I did, but he was already gone, and the kid was dead. They theorized that he killed her as soon as he hung up the phone. I quit the *Tribune* that next morning, packed my stuff, and caught the next flight to Louisiana."

"Did they ever find him?"

"As far as I know, he's still out there." Fegan shook his head. "I don' know, Char. Maybe I'm some kinda wacko magnet. Maybe you should stay as far away from me as you can get." It was a halfhearted attempt at lightening the mood, but neither of them so much as smiled. "It's weird, you know. But even after Jean Louise, I didn't think that somethin' like that could happen in Angelique. I guess lightning really does strike twice."

"Chicago doesn't have a monopoly on evil." Claire touched his face, shifting his focus away from the past back to her.

"You were right about one thing—it's all connected. The conversation I had with Jimmy underscored it. I mentioned the red silk cord that was tied around both victims, and he didn't have any idea what I was talkin' about."

Claire frowned, remembering that last day she'd gone to Angola, and the look on his face when she mentioned the second victim. "But why would he throw his life away, his family, knowing he didn't do it? It doesn't make sense."

"Maybe he didn't look at it that way. Maybe he's protectin' somebody, and maybe that someone is you." She would have shaken it off, but he wouldn't allow it. "Think about it. It's the one thing that makes sense. You and Jean Louise were always tight. If the killer could get to her, maybe Jimmy thought that he could get to you, too. It's somethin' I can understand. I don't know what I'd do if somethin' happened to you. No more hot sex on the gallery, that's for sure."

"Be serious."

"I am serious." He traced the curve of one cheekbone with his fingertips. "You're gorgeous, you know that?"

"In your shirt and jeans."

"In anything, or nothing at all," he insisted. "I like havin' you here in my life, Char, but you worry me."

"Laid-back Fegan? Worried?" It was a joke, but she could tell he was dead serious.

"I'm laid-back, all right, but I've still got a heart and I've got this sick little feeling right here that won't go away 'cause I know that you're gonna break it. *Je t'aime*, Char. I love you. I guess I always have—I don't know, maybe I always will."

"When I first saw Remy, I thought—"

"You thought it was me."

"I thought I'd die in that moment. I wanted to die." Claire took a shuddering breath. "If that's love, I'm not sure I want to feel it."

He looked away from her, but he didn't release her yet. "Somethin' tells me I don't want to hear what's comin'."

"No, Fegan. You have to hear. You have to listen. I've suffered through too much loss already. I can't go through that again—not when it comes to you. Forever isn't out there—don't you see? It just doesn't happen to people like us. If you don't believe me, just ask Jean Louise. Ask my mama, Jimmy, or Remy." She pushed from his embrace, turning away, skirting the house as she nearly ran to her car.

"Damn it, Clairée, don't do this!"

"I have to go," she said emphatically. "I have to tell Aunt Eule about tonight before she hears it from someone else."

"At least let me call you a cab," he offered.

"There's no need. I've got my pistol in my bag. After last night, I thought it would be a good idea to carry it."

Catching up with her, he took her arm. Claire felt a thrill of pure terror that he would try to convince her to stay, at what she would say. It had taken every ounce of will she possessed to resist giving him the response he wanted, the response he deserved, yet there was profound truth in her argument. Their relationship was risky, and she was terrified of losing him, of having her heart irreparably broken. "I'll see you out, then. No argument. You owe me that much, and I need to know you're safe."

They proceeded in tense silence, avoiding the bungalow, though neither of them could forget what had happened inside two hours ago. Fegan waited until she got in her car, then leaned in the open window and kissed her. There was a strange, unwelcome tenderness in the gesture. Unwelcome because it brought tears to Claire's eyes, and a lump to her throat.

"I don' want to lose you, Char," he said.

She sniffed, wiping a trickle of moisture from her

cheek. Then, before she could make matters worse, she pulled away.

Fegan kicked the crushed shell drive, scattering debris and sending a jolt of pain through his toes. "Damn it, Char!" He turned in disgust, but before he'd reached the front door, the sheriff's department's patrol car pulled into the drive, followed by Frank's Lexus.

Fred Rally got out of the patrol car and hitched up his uniform trousers. "Hey, Fegan."

"Sheriff forget somethin'?" Fegan said. "Or did you come to help me clean up the pantry, Frank? No, I guess not. You never had much time for Remy, and you wouldn't want to get his blood on your best suit."

"This is your fault, Fegan! Your fault! You brought it all on yourself, but I ain't gonna stand by and let you expose *Pépère* to any more of your nonsense!"

"Nonsense? Is that what you call this, Frank? Remy's gone, man! You're right about one thing, though— *Pépère* ain't gonna be exposed to nothin'. I'm takin' him to the houseboat tonight."

"That's where you're wrong, Fegan!" Frank said, his face red and shining with sweat. "You ain't takin' him anywhere!" He pulled out a fistful of papers and waved them in the air. "*Pépère's* comin' with me. I got me a court order, fresh from Judge Morlay. Officer, if he makes a move to stop me, you arrest him."

"Damn it, Frank, you can't do this! Amos Lee don' belong in no home! You might as well put him in prison."

"I *can* do it, Fegan! I *am* doin' it!" He marched through the side yard, more determined than Fegan had ever seen him.

Fegan made to follow, but Deputy Rally stepped into his path. "I'm sorry, Fegan. But he's got a court order, like he said. It's legitimate. I looked it over myself before we came over here. If you interfere, I'll have to take you into custody, and I *really* don't want that." Rally looked intensely uncomfortable. "Look, I'm sorry about this. I heard about Remy. Sorry about that, too."

"Not half as sorry as I am, Fred." Fegan watched in frustrated silence as Frank returned, hustling the bewildered old man along. "I'll come get you, Amos Lee," Fegan promised. "I won't leave you in that place. I promise!"

Frank opened the front passenger door, put Amos Lee in, then closed it. Then, without a word, he scurried around the front of the Lexus, jumped in, and sped off, as if he feared Fegan might try to stop him.

Rally hung around as the taillights of the Lexus disappeared. "Listen, Fegan. Is there anything I can do? Can I help you clean up, or anything?"

"No. But thanks, Fred," Fegan said. I'll take care of it. "You better believe, I'm gonna take care of everything."

Claire anticipated the unnatural chill that always accompanied her small, spectral friend. She waited for it to materialize, to raise the gooseflesh on her arms and at her nape, but she arrived at The Willows without so much as a ghostly whisper, and only the air conditioning to cool the teeming heat of the night. As she got out of the car and climbed the steps to the gallery, she struggled with a strange sense of disappointment.

Eulanie met her in the foyer. She grasped Claire's hands, and for a few seconds, seemed to struggle to find words. "We heard what happened. Thank the Lord you're all right."

Jane had stayed late, and came from the kitchen, wiping her hands on her apron. Her face clouded with worry, she hugged Claire, sniffing back tears. "Child, you frightened us near to death." She released Claire, then moved to turn the lock on the front door. "This town, it's under siege. Some kinda evil out there. An' nobody seems to know where it'll strike next. We got bread puddin' in de kitchen. Come on, both of you."

Numb from the horror of Remy's death, and all that had passed between her and Fegan, Claire didn't protest. The kitchen at The Willows had always brought her a feeling of warmth, of comfort. Family was basic, the simplest and most complex relationships in anyone's life were tied into it. Sometimes troubled, like her relationship with Jimmy . . . or easy and laid-back, like Fegan and Remy.

Claire slid into a chair at the old red-and-gray Formica table. It had been here as long as she could remember. During the first year of her practice, she had tried to replace it with a sturdy oak pedestal table and elaborately carved farmhouse chairs. Something nicer, more elegant. Eulanie had thanked her for her thoughtfulness and quietly insisted the deliverymen load them back into the truck. She said the old Formica table had seen a lot of hardship and a lot of love, but because of the memories it held for her, she couldn't bear to part with it. Sitting at the table, listening to the quiet conversation of two women who had played such a large part in her life, Claire finally understood.

There was great value in the familiar. People who shared a lifetime of memories, good and bad . . . laughter and tragedy, passion and pain. Jimmy, Eulanie, Jane, and Fegan. The thought was unbearably poignant, excruciatingly sweet. She accepted a small piece of the sweet confection from Jane. It tasted of heaven, and for an insane moment, she wished that things were different between them, and that he was here to share it with her . . . the quiet comfort of good food and loving family.

Fegan's family was disintegrating—Jean Louise, and Amos Lee . . . Frank, and Remy . . . .

Where was he now?

How was he?

In her mind's eye, she saw his face as he leaned in the car window to kiss her one last time. His expression had been one of pure intensity, but there had been confusion and disappointment as well.

"How is Fegan, Claire?" Eulanie asked with genuine concern.

Claire shook her head. "I don't know, really. Concerned about what happened, about his grandfather, but okay, I guess, considering."

"You tell Mr. Broussard we axed about him," Jane put in. "That poor fam'ly—they sure have suffered a lot of tragedies."

"If I see him again, I'll tell him."

Eulanie's brows came together over her straight nose. "If you see him again? I thought the two of you were becoming an item?"

"We're friends, that's all," Claire managed to squeeze out. She could feel the tension mounting inside her, a delayed reaction to everything that had occurred. In a moment she would start to tremble, or worse, break down completely. "Jane, this is wonderful, but I'm afraid I'm not very hungry. Aunt Eulanie? If you don't mind, I need some time alone."

She bolted from the table like an adolescent, running down the hall and pounding up the stairs, and when she got to her bedroom, she closed the door and leaned against it. The tears she feared didn't come, just a dry, empty ache in the center of her chest, a hollowness she couldn't fathom, and couldn't seem to alleviate.

Leaning hard against the solid wood, she closed her eyes and thought of all the times as a gangling adolescent she'd suffered a disappointment, a bump in the road of life, and cried her heart out to Jean Louise. Whispers of a distant childhood seemed to crowd the corners, but the room remained silent and still, the air a steady, fixed, climate-controlled seventy-five degrees.

"Jean Louise! Where are you?" Claire said softly. "Why won't you come?"

But there was only a brooding, empty silence, and Claire's recollection ringing in her head. *He's my brother, Clairée!* the spirit-child had said. *If you hurt him we can't be friends no more.*

And she had hurt him. Remorse mingled with her own hurt, her own certainty that in all probability, she had just thrown away the only real chance at true happiness she'd ever had. "Damn it, Jean Louise!" she cried. "Don't you think I've been punished enough?" She shoved away from the door and walked to the French windows. "That's good, Claire. Now, you're talking to the walls. What's next? A little drool on your chin?"

Pushing open the windows, she wandered to the railing and stood looking out over the cane fields and the bayou beyond. From the vantage point of the second-floor gallery, a portion of Bayou Road was visible. A pair of headlights edged along the invisible ribbon, moving in the direction of the houseboat. Claire strained to see how far they progressed, then lost them in the trees.

No point in lookin'. He ain't there, Clairée. The voice was small and shivery, like bad radio reception, flickering on her name.

"I never thought I'd say this, but I'm so glad you came."

Where else would I go? I can't go home. It's too sad there.

Claire's eyes began to sting. She blinked back moisture, and when that was no longer sufficient, wiped at the wetness on her cheeks. "Jean Louise, I don't know what to do."

The girl hooked her thumbs in her belt loops and stared at Claire. *Sure you do. You're older than me. Shoot, you're all grown up.*

Claire shook her head. "Everything's a mess, and I don't know how to fix it. I don't know what to do." With the admission, the emotional dam broke, and Claire's breath came in halting sobs. "I need—someone—to tell me what to do!"

It's not a test, Clairée. Just live . . . live for both of us. You can do it if you try. I know you can.

The last word shivered on the warm night air. "Don't go, Jean Louise. Please." But she already had, and Claire was alone. *Just live,* she'd said. *You can do it if you try.* But her spirit was eleven and it was harder than she could ever imagine. Standing at the balcony, hugging Fegan's black T-shirt to her body, Claire watched the headlights she'd seen appear again, this time at the end of the drive. The car was too far away for her to determine the make, model, or color, but something whispered inside her heart that it was Fegan. Claire gripped the railing hard. It sat for a moment, then the driver revved the engine and pulled away. Letting go of the railing, Claire abruptly turned and went back inside.

It was well after dark when Cash arrived at Briar Rose, but this time he didn't bother to park in back, and he didn't give a damn if anyone saw. Patrick, the butler, would have announced him, but Cash pushed past the older gentleman. "Where is he?"

"Sir, it's late, and Judge Morlay has retired for the evening."

"The hell he has! He hasn't had an early night since

he was eight years old." Cash checked the study, then headed for the staircase. "Ashton? Ashton, where the hell are you?"

As Cash headed up the first flight, a door closed somewhere above, and a soft, even, unhurried tread, muffled by plush carpet, approached the stairwell. Ashton appeared on the landing. "Good heavens! Patrick, what's all this racket?" Then his gaze settled on Cash, red-faced and out of breath. "I might have known. For someone who is always insisting on keeping a low profile, you do like to make an entrance."

"We need to talk—right now!"

"Can't it wait until mornin'? I was just about to settle in with the newspaper. If I'm goin' to represent my constituents to the best of my abilities, I need to keep up on current events."

Cash's blood began to boil. The earth was about to fall out from under him, and his cousin wanted to put him off so he could catch up on the latest headlines. It was nearly too much for him, and his fingers itched to close around Ashton's unnaturally pale throat. A heavy thread of insanity ran through the Morlay lineage. There was a chance that he might just get away with it. "Either you come down here, or I'm comin' up. Either way, we're havin' this out right now."

Ashton's gaze shifted to the elderly man waiting discreetly in the foyer. "Patrick, I don't think I'll require anything more of you this evening."

"Very good, sir," Patrick said, and quietly disappeared into the bowels of the house.

"Come, then, if you must."

Cash went swiftly up the stairs, and was ushered into a dressing room off the master suite. "Well, now that you have your audience, perhaps you'll tell me what this is all about?"

Cash barely noticed his surroundings. Everything was a blur, except for the man standing by the open closet, thumbing through several patterned silk smoking jackets. "Mother always liked rich colors, jewel tones, garnet, ruby, sapphire blue . . . Thank God Father's tastes were more subdued." He selected a soft gray silk and slipped it on, covering his bare torso.

"I didn't come here to discuss your fucking wardrobe!" Cash shot back.

"Then, why *did* you come?"

Not a ruffle, not a crack in that unflappable facade. As always, Cash was astonished by Ashton's ability to do the unspeakable and not have a hair out of place. That ice-cold calm had saved his ass once, but his mistake of coming to Ashton had cost him, and lately he'd begun to wonder if he would ever pay off that debt. The thought made him slightly nauseous. "I'm here because of Remy Broussard. Do you have any idea what you've done?"

Ashton settled his tall frame onto a chaise. It was a delicate antique, covered in gold brocade, imported from France in the last century, and he looked like he belonged on it. "You *said* you had a problem, Cash. Don't tell me you were exaggerating?"

"You didn't have to kill him."

"No. I didn't have to kill him," Ashton agreed, taking a glass of sherry from the table. He held the crystal to the light. "You could have bullied him into keeping quiet, and maybe we could have bought him off. Of course, either of those choices wouldn't have ended the problem permanently, now would they? And Mr. Broussard might have popped back up just when it was least convenient. My way is so much better."

"You're sick, Ashton. You know that? There's somethin' inside most folks that you don't have." His initial anger had passed, and nerves had set in.

"It's called a heart," Ashton replied, completely untouched by the scene. "And aren't you glad I don't have one? Sure made it easier for you a decade ago."

"I made a mistake. I never should have come to you. I should have known you'd make it worse."

"A mistake, is that what you call it?"

"I was eighteen years old, and you're gonna hold it over me for the rest of my life."

"I kept you from serving a prison term. I would think you could summon a little gratitude."

"You helped me out of a jam, but I had no idea what would come from it. And there's been no end to it. I thought there would be *some* end to it. It just keeps gettin' deeper, Ashton, and it has to stop. I need to know that it's gonna stop."

Ashton reached out and fingered the heavy silk cord that tied back the draperies. "Mother had ones just like these in her bedroom, did you know that? Only they were scarlet . . . like virgin's blood."

"Jesus Christ." Cash's stomach churned.

"Will you walk out with me?" Ashton asked, off on a different train of thought. "No, I suppose not. You're a bit squeamish about these things."

"What about Fegan Broussard?" Cash forced himself to ask, watching Ashton with a sick sense of fascination. He was on his feet at the closet again.

"The ex-reporter? What about him?"

"You killed his cousin. He's not gonna let that go."

"Remy was killed because of his involvement in the drug scene. Small-town dealer buys the big one. What's so strange about that? And as long as you keep your mouth shut, no one will be the wiser." Ashton took black trousers and a black T-shirt out of the closet and placed them on the bed. Then, almost as an after-thought, he turned, grasping Cash's shoulder. "Don't get the wrong idea, Cash. It's too bad about Remy. He was useful, at least for a while. He's got family, so I suppose that someone will miss him. But what about you? Would anyone mourn your loss? Then again, would anyone even notice?"

Cash's gaze locked with Ashton's and a thin trickle of sweat snaked a path between his shoulder blades. "I'll do what I can to discourage Fegan."

Ashton smiled, clapping the shoulder he'd painfully gripped a heartbeat before. "I knew I could count on you. They do say that blood's thicker—"

CHAPTER
SIXTEEN

Fegan had just finished pouring the dregs of his third pot of coffee into the sink when he caught a glimpse of movement out of the corner of his eye. Someone was on deck, just outside the galley windows. He could see the deep charcoal outline of a tall, male form silhouetted against the darker predawn sky. The prowler bent slightly, as if to peer in the windows. Fegan didn't look directly at him. Instead, he pretended not to notice, taking his coffee cup and moving into the living room, then down the hall. Between the bath and the bedroom was a side door. Careful not to make a sound, he opened the door and slipped out onto the catwalk, retrieving his .38 from the waistband of his jeans and noiselessly making his way to the forward section of the houseboat.

"You want to stand off real easy. I'm working off a caffeine buzz big enough to keep half of Lafayette awake for a week, and if I twitch, you'll be one poor dead son of a bitch."

In a half-crouch, the figure froze. "I'm standing as off as I can, Fegan. It's me, John Delano, Miz Martha Felix's nephew."

"Jesus, John. You mind tellin' me why you're lookin' in my windows at half-past six in the morning?" Fegan asked, but he didn't lower the pistol just yet, a fact that the bigger man seemed keenly aware of.

"I was on my way to Aunt Marti's when I saw your lights. I was tryin' to figure out if you was here, or if it was just a light to keep prowlers away. Some folks do that, you know. Leave on a light when nobody's home." John lowered his hands, but he was careful not to move otherwise. "Heard about Remy, Fegan. Remy was all right. He always treated me good, and I'm real sorry about everything. It sure is a shame that so many bad things happen around this place."

Fegan slipped the safety on and lowered the pistol. "I appreciate that," he said, but the response was automatic. He didn't feel appreciative. In fact, he didn't feel much of anything, and he wasn't sure why that was. Maybe it was due to the shock over Remy's murder, or Frank using circumstances spinning out of control to take Amos Lee . . . or maybe it was simpler, even more basic than that. Maybe when Clairée left, she took that part of him that could feel, grieve, empathize, and desire with her. It came to him, perhaps illogically, that he might never feel anything ever again.

He motioned with the pistol to the galley windows, spilling bright yellow light onto the decking. "You wanna come in, or somethin'? I was just about to make some coffee."

"You sure that's a good idea?" John asked skeptically, but he followed Fegan inside anyway. "Maybe you ought to eat something. Try to take the edge off."

"I'm fine," Fegan insisted.

It was only half a lie. He would be fine, just as soon as he figured out who was behind the evil in Angelique.

Evil. That felt a little strange. It was a word he rarely found a use for, but in this case nothing else seemed to fit. There was an evil in this place, something dark and malevolent that found comfort and anonymity in the shadows. Something, someone, who moved along the bayou's dim green channels as if born to them. And maybe he had been, Fegan thought.

John waited until Fegan made the rich, dark brew and filled a pair of mugs, then slid into a chair at the table. "Ain't nothin' like a hot cup of coffee," Fegan said. He stared into the cup, inhaling the fragrant steam, but he didn't drink.

John took a sip from his mug. That's good, Fegan," he said. "Real good." For a moment, all was quiet. "You know, I ain't never been any farther away than Lafayette. Not like you. You're an educated man. You've been places, and you know a good bit 'bout the way things are. You know a little about the law too, I guess."

Fegan snorted. "Enough to make me dislike most law enforcement officials." He watched John for a little while, noting how nervous he seemed, how anxious . . . like there was something he wanted to say, but feared to. "What's this about, John? I get the feelin' this is more than just a condolence call."

"You've known me a long while, ain't that so?" John asked.

"Since I was too small to pole a skiff on the water. Long before my old man left my mama, before we came to Angelique to live with Amos Lee."

"And you know how my daddy died."

"Everybody knows, John."

"They say it ain't like the old days. They say it's the New South, that things are different, but I have a real hard time believin' it. Things happen, you know. Redneck boys still take it into their heads every now and again to do bad things to a black man, and nothin' prevents it, least of all the law. They say that we got equal rights, but Angola's full of black men put there on the testimony of white men, and women, and the old feelin's of mistrust, they're still there."

"You'll get no argument from me there," Fegan replied. "Listen, are you in some kind of trouble? 'Cause if you are, I can give you the name of a good lawyer. As a matter of fact, she's here in Angelique."

"Who, me?" John said with a laugh. "You know I steer clear of that sort of thing. It's somethin' Aunt Marti and I been talkin' about, and I just thought I'd ask your opinion."

It was Fegan's turn to laugh. "You comin' to me for advice. That's rich. There was a time, I thought I had all the answers. But just when I thought I had things figured out, everything changed." Fegan glanced up from the steady contemplation of his coffee cup, and something in his gaze made the other man flinch. "You ever want to kill somebody, John? You ever want to wrap your hands 'round somebody's throat and just squeeze the life from them?"

"No, sir. Can't say that I have."

Fegan took a determined sip of the black brew, as much to drown the fire in his belly as anything. "I've been in situations since I came home where I could have dropped someone to save my own skin, but I never really wanted somebody dead . . . till now. Worst part about it is, the man ain't got no face."

"This about Remy, ain't it?" John asked quietly.

"It's about Remy . . . and my sister, Jean Louise, and Clairée's old man. Somebody's gotta pay for what's goin' on in Angelique."

John finished his coffee and rose. "I better get goin'. Aunt Marti's got some chores need doin', and I mean to get started before the heat sets in. Been right steamy, ain't it?"

Fegan didn't answer. He just returned to staring into his cup as John quietly went out, and it was a long while before Fegan realized that John had forgotten to ask his question. He was too concerned about where Cash Edmunds had been when he'd been watching Cash's place last night, when Clairée was at the bungalow and Remy had been dying.

He'd told Clairée when she questioned him that he'd been on a stakeout, and it was the truth. What he'd failed to mention was that he'd been watching Cash's place, waiting for him to come home. He'd parked on the little-used dirt road across from Cash's mobile home for several hours, but the deputy had never shown. And he hadn't been on duty, either. It was common knowledge that Cash had a broader source of income than his deputy's pay—not that he spent it on improving his accommodations. He'd been known to shake down dealers, and Fegan had noticed Remy with bruises on his face a time or two.

But were the two things related?

Had Cash pressed Remy for money he didn't have?

Or wouldn't give?

And was it motive enough for Cash to kill him?

Somehow, Fegan didn't think so. But that didn't rule out Edmunds as Fegan's number one choice in all of this.

Logic told him that Cash would have murdered Remy in a heartbeat in order to protect himself . . . but protect himself from what? Where was the threat?

Remy had cultivated some home-grown weed, and sold a little dope. But it was small-time stuff, too insignificant for even the big boys in Lafayette to notice, or demand a cut of. Remy's business was nothing to get worked up about. And a shakedown, even if word of it got back to Pershing, would not be sufficient grounds to cost Cash his job. Not in southern Louisiana, and not with someone as rich and powerful as Ashton Morlay pulling the strings in Cash's law enforcement career.

The method by which Remy had died also seemed significant. The killer had employed stealth, and a vicious cunning that was downright chilling to contemplate. Remy had been attacked in Fegan's backyard, Pershing had determined, a few feet from Amos Lee's porch. But how had the killer managed to pull off such a grisly crime without being noticed?

Fegan had spoken with the neighbors last night, and no one had seen or heard anything out of the ordinary. There had been no strange vehicles on the street or in the drive, which seemed to indicate that the murderer had been on foot . . . or on the water.

If he was on foot, there would have been almost no chance for him to avoid notice. Remy's attack would have left a spray of arterial blood over the attacker. Unless he'd stopped to change his clothing, an escape like that wasn't feasible, but the bayou . . . now that was another matter altogether. The channels that made up the waterway were numerous and winding, and a man could easily lose himself in the watery green maze.

The explanation made sense, but it definitely threw another light on his suspicions. Cash Edmunds didn't own a boat, and even though he knew the bayou as well as Fegan did, he wouldn't go near it after the sun set. The waterway became a different world after dark, even more eerie, filled with haunting cries that weren't easily identifiable at night. There were always stories circulating about the ghost of Jean Laffitte, the Gentleman

Pirate, being spotted out there, and tales similar to the Honey Island swamp monster, some Bigfoot-like beast supposedly seen in the watery wilderness from time to time. Amos Lee used to tell the stories to Fegan when he was a boy, and even as a teen, he and his friends had found the tales highly entertaining . . . except Cash, who had hung around the Broussard house sometimes, and who had an unnatural fear of the swamp after dark that he'd never been able to shed.

Fegan's train of thought was leading precisely nowhere. Cash, Remy, Jean Louise . . . where was the connection?

He felt sure that Cash had been the one to threaten Clairée, to destroy her car, and almost burn her alive . . . but while the incidents seemed to have a direct correlation to Clairée's questions about the murders, and Jimmy's conviction, it had nothing to do with his cousin, unless . . . unless Cash was somehow involved in the most recent killing, and Remy had found out about it. . . .

But what about Jean Louise?

Jean Louise's murder had sent an innocent man to prison—Jimmy, who had taken the rap to protect someone.

Fegan glanced up from his brimming coffee cup. He'd barely touched it, and it was already stone cold. "If Cash was somehow involved in Sherry Ellen's death, then that means that he killed Jean Louise, and when Remy found out about it somehow, he killed him, too," he muttered.

The pieces fit neatly together, and Fegan wondered why he hadn't seen it before . . . and the only thing left unexplained was Jimmy.

Cash was two years younger than Fegan; ten years ago, he would have been eighteen. Old enough to rape and murder a teenage girl, but not to orchestrate the kind of setup that had put James Buford Sumner on death row. He wouldn't have had that kind of knowledge, wouldn't have possessed the leverage, the power to coerce a confession from an innocent family man with a loving wife, a young daughter, and everything to live for—but Ashton Morlay had.

"Jesus Christ," Fegan muttered. "Ashton Morlay, Cash's kin . . . Jimmy's prosecutor. Cash killed Jean Louise, and Morlay railroaded Jimmy to save him."

"Guard! Hey, you, Peterson! C'mon, man, we need somebody up here on de row!"

Sherman Peterson put down the newspaper he'd been reading and waddled from his post to within shouting distance of the disturbance. "You got any idea what time it is, Adesco? It's two minutes of three in the a.m. Time for you to shut your mouth and go to sleep."

"How's a man supposed to sleep wid all dat moaning goin' on?"

Peterson scratched his balding head. "What moanin'?"

"It's Sumner. He's sick, man. He needs to see the doctor real bad."

"Probably that shit they fed you guys for breakfast this mornin'," Peterson said with a noiseless chuckle. It emerged like a wheeze, a small ratchet of air escaping his windpipe, and not loud enough to be heard above the noise of the sick man's shuddering moans, or the uneasy whispers of the cons down the row.

"This ain't no joke, Peterson, and you can't let him go on like dat. It ain't humane, man, and we ain't animals."

Murmured protests boiled out of the cells, most an uneasy ripple of sound, an angry underscore, a few louder, more audible. "If Sumner dies 'cause he's denied medical attention, you'd better believe there'll be trouble."

"Yeah, man. He ain't no dog, to be treated like that!"

"Shut up down there, or I'll call for a lockdown! No showers, no exercise . . . y'all want that?" They quieted, but the tension didn't lessen until Peterson moved toward Jimmy's cell. "Jimmy? Hey, Jimmy! It's Sherman Peterson. You all right?"

Jimmy didn't answer. He just kept on moaning, the shiver that wracked his wiry, five-foot-eight-inch frame rattling the metal bunk where he lay. Peterson bent forward and peered through the metal cage. His eyesight wasn't as good as it once was, and it was hard to tell what was wrong with the man from outside the cell. "Sumner?" he bawled again, louder this time. "Jimmy Sumner? Can you hear me?"

A long moan escaped the man on the bunk, followed by a strangling sound as he stiffened, then started to jerk violently. "Jesus, what's dat? He takin' a fit? Peterson, you better get somebody up here now to take him to the infirmary! He could die, man!"

Peterson grabbed his radio, requested a gurney, then stood back to watch the man seize while he waited.

Adesco was agitated, and Peterson's actions didn't satisfy him. "Jesus, God, you got to do somethin'! He'll swallow his tongue b'fore they can get here! You got first aid trainin', man! Do somethin'!"

"All right! All right! I don't suppose I can just stand here and let him die." Peterson opened the cell door and stepped cautiously inside. "Sumner? Jimmy Sumner, you hearin' me?"

Jimmy continued to jerk and twitch, his head thrown back and the veins popping in his neck. His eyes were slitted, and nothing showed but the whites. "Mother

Mary, this don' look good,'' Peterson said, bending over the bunk. He loosened Jimmy's collar, then spoke into his radio. "Look, will y'all hurry up? This man's in the middle of a grand mal seizure, and he's gonna need medical supervision.''

"Almost there,'' a woman's voice answered, preceded and followed by static.

Peterson didn't have a tongue depressor, so he took the pen from his pocket and held it out; at the same time, Jimmy's arm snaked out, catching Peterson by the collar, the shiv in his other hand pressed tightly to the larger man's belly. "Not a word, you hear me? I got no reason to hurt you unless you try to stop me.''

"I hear,'' Peterson said. "What do you want me to do?''

"Unlock Trick Adesco's cell—then you and me are gonna sit on that bunk until those attendants get here. Be careful what you say. You try to keep me from leavin' here, and I'll shove this shiv right through your rib-cage.''

"Don't worry. I ain't about to give you no trouble. I never did like this damn job, anyway.''

Claire watched the sun rise from the second-floor gallery. Shielded from the dampness by a thick terry robe, she curled in a large wicker chair with her feet tucked under her, nursing a lukewarm mug and trying not to think about the numbness that had settled over her. She'd gone to bed, dutifully, but sleep remained elusive and she'd lain there for hours, trying to think of anything but the tangled mess her life had become. Her efforts unsuccessful, she finally gave up all pretense of resting just before daylight to creep down the stairs and microwave a cup of tea.

The birds woke first in the swamp, their noisy tittering echoing over the water and fields, filling the soft air with cheerful noise that seemed to increase in volume in direct proportion to the deepening pink of the sky. The sun came quickly, a large fuchsia fireball, a brilliant backdrop for the ghostly black of the cypress, the limbs of which were shrouded in tattered streamers of Spanish moss.

Another day dawning, and one day closer to Jimmy's execution.

A day of pain and sorrow for the Broussards.

Claire's fingers tightened over the ceramic mug as flashes of Remy stumbling toward her rose behind her eyes and were stubbornly pushed back. She felt the warm welcome of Fegan's embrace, heard his dear, sweet voice. *"Je t'aime, Char. I love you. I always have. Maybe I always will."*

Claire squeezed her eyes shut.

What a fool she'd been. After all they'd been through—the sexual dance, the attraction and denial, the line she'd so meticulously tried to draw between love and lust—he'd still fallen for her. And when he'd admitted his feelings for her, she'd panicked.

She'd made a wreck of everything—her life, his heart. She'd been worried that he would hurt her, and in the end, she had been the one to cut and run. Even worse, she wasn't sure the situation could be remedied. She didn't know if what they had could be salvaged, or if she should even try.

Some things hadn't changed. She still desired him, still felt a little dizzy when she heard his lazy drawl, still couldn't imagine her life without him in it . . . but in what capacity? Friend? Lover? Adversary? Someone who wanted more than she could give, whom she hurt and rejected at every opportunity?

She ached when she thought of him. Should she try to see him, or would it only make things worse? She sure wouldn't blame him if he didn't want to see her again.

Thinking about it gave her a headache, added to her confusion. Opening her eyes again, she forced her thoughts away from Fegan. As soon as this was over, she would leave Angelique behind and return to her life in Lafayette. Putting distance between them would help her to put it all into perspective.

In time, she would go on with her life, make strides in her career, but she knew in her heart that she would never forget Fegan or the way he made her feel. Without him in her life, a piece of her soul would always be missing. *"Je t'aime, Char. Je t'aime. . . ."*

Claire sighed. Her plans were already going forward, but she couldn't help wishing things were different. Wishing everything were different.

The cypress limbs in the distance teemed with dots of living black. The birdsong rose and fell with the flock as certain restless individuals flapped their wings and rose, then settled down again. At the edge of the cane field, near the dock's pilings, a snowy egret waded in the pink mirror of the shallows.

She'd returned to help Jimmy, her heart full of resentment for this place, never suspecting that she would be so susceptible to the allure of Angelique. Without her even realizing it, the wild beauty of the swamp had seeped into her soul, just as surely as the people who lived their lives on its lush fringes had. She could go back to her life in Lafayette, but she would never be able to turn her back on Acadia Parish completely.

This place, like its people, was in her blood. Home. How long had it been since she had thought of it in that way? Fegan had given her that, with his easy ways, his earthy sensuality, his loyalty to family. He'd brought half-remembered feelings stirring to life in her that otherwise would have remained dormant, unexplored, a part of her heart that would have always been empty.

Even with the heartbreak resulting from their broken relationship, she owed him a debt for awakening that side of her buried by past pain, bitterness, and regret.

Taking a sip of the tepid liquid, she stared at the ripening sunrise and thought about Remy. His activities had been slightly shady, and the possibility existed that his death had been drug-related. Yet something told Claire that wasn't the case. While she considered herself a thoroughly modern, fairly enlightened, well-educated woman, she was also a native of southern Louisiana, and as such she couldn't fully discount the existence of things she couldn't see. Like intuition . . . and the rare gift of the eleven-year-old Jean Louise.

Intuition, that sense of just knowing, nagged at Claire's conscious mind, insisting that Remy's death had its roots in the dark cloud that seemed to hover over Angelique. Remy had been a sly one, ferreting out and collecting information like a prized and valuable resource . . . a resource he'd grudgingly imparted, for a price.

Claire frowned. Was that it? Had Remy known too much about the murders? Had someone felt threatened by that knowledge? Someone with a great deal to lose?

But who?

Surely even Remy would have drawn the line at protecting Jean Louise's killer. But then, maybe he *had* come forward with information . . . or threatened to . . . and was betrayed by someone he trusted. Someone with an unknown stake in keeping the real truth about what happened to Jean Louise buried deep.

For a fraction of a second, Claire's thoughts flashed on Cash Edmunds and his cryptic warnings about Claire's presence in Angelique the day he'd appeared at The Willows. She'd gotten the very real impression that day, and afterward, that he was threatening her, and he'd left no doubt in her mind that it had everything to do with Jimmy, and the questions she'd been asking.

Why?

What did Deputy Edmunds have to do with Jimmy? Why should he care that she was asking questions, unless he was involved?

Or taking orders from someone else who had played a part in sending Jimmy to death row?

Like Sheriff Pershing?

Pershing hadn't exactly welcomed her questions, either. In fact, he had done everything in his power to discourage her.

Yet no matter how badly she wanted answers, she could not imagine the sheriff in the role of a child-killer. Vance Pershing was rigid and lacking in personal charm, but he wasn't conscienceless, or cruel, and she had gotten the distinct impression that his reluctance to delve into Jean Louise's murder, a matter he already considered settled, had more to do with not wishing to have a blight upon his record than any secret desire to thwart justice.

Dismissing Pershing brought her back to his deputy. If Cash Edmunds wasn't taking orders from Sheriff Pershing to pressure Claire into leaving town, then what was his motive? What reason could he possibly have for his veiled threats?

The sun shone above the swamp and steam rose in wispy, gray threads off the bayou. There seemed to be no clear answers, and Claire, unsure where else to turn, decided to pay the deputy a visit. Returning to her room, she showered and changed, and blew her hair dry. She pulled out the clothes Fegan had given her the night before, then settled on a pair of jeans and a neat-fitting Ralph Lauren T-shirt. It wasn't her normal business-casual, but the cool white cotton would keep her from melting in the damp heat of the morning. Pulling her sleek brown hair into a low-slung tail at her nape, and grabbing her shoulder bag, she went downstairs.

She found Eulanie at the kitchen table, lingering over coffee and a newspaper. She looked up as Claire entered. "Well, I'll be damned. I didn't think it was possible, but I do think I see shades of Charlotte Clairée in you this morning." Eulanie folded her newspaper, removing her reading glasses and laying them beside her cup. "Silly of me, I know, but Lord, how I wish your father could see you now." Her dark eyes welled, and she blinked back the tears, neutralizing the tension with a quick laugh. "Welcome home, darlin'."

A few weeks ago, Claire would have argued, strenuously. Instead, she smiled, sliding into a chair and grasping Eulanie's hand. "Yeah. Me, too." She hadn't realized until now that her aunt was aging. Or maybe she had made a real effort to ignore it. This morning, with the clear morning light pouring through the windows, there was no ignoring the signs. The fine lines at the corners of Eulanie's eyes and mouth seemed a little more noticeable, the smattering of age spots on her sun-browned hands impossible to ignore. More than anything, she looked tired. "Aunt Eulanie, are you feeling okay? You're not having any more chest pain that you're not telling me about?"

Jane rattled the pots and pans, but said nothing.

Ignoring the wordless statement, Eulanie sighed. "Heart's okay, I think. But *I'm* not. I've got to get into my truck this morning and drive to Marie Theresa

Broussard's. It's kept me awake most of the night, wondering just what I'm going to say to her. Truth is, I don't know. I hardly know what to say about any of this.''

"I know. I'll be going by later today, myself.'' They were quiet for a moment, Claire accepting a glass of juice from Jane and wondering if going by the Broussards' was wise. The last thing she wanted right now was to run into Fegan, and there was a good chance that he would be there.

"Things are bound to be mighty tense 'round that place. Heard from Emma Mordeau this morning, and she says the police came last night and took old Mister Amos Lee away. That Frank Broussard was with them! Marie Theresa, she didn't just lose a son—her uncle's been dragged off to some old folks' home like a mindless thing! Marie Theresa, she's awful fond of that old man.''

Claire pushed the juice away. "Aunt Eule, I have to go. I have some things to take care of.''

"Claire, can't it wait? I thought perhaps it would be easier if we went by the Broussards' together.''

"I can't,'' Claire said hurriedly. "Not right now, anyway.''

"This is about Fegan, isn't it?'' Eulanie asked. "For heaven's sake, Claire, when are you two gonna stop dancin' around the fact that you belong together?''

"I have to go,'' Claire said, grabbing her bag off the back of the chair and rushing from the room. She pounded down the gallery stairs, not stopping until she'd closed the car door. Safely inside, away from her aunt's scrutiny, she covered her face with her hands. Frank had heard about Remy, and had used his death to punish Fegan in the most hurtful way possible . . . by taking his grandfather away.

In her thoughts, the old Frenchman held out the flashlight to her, smiling in his own distracted way . . .

"C'est alright." It's all right. But it wasn't all right. And Claire could only wonder if it would ever be all right again.

The Louisiana State Trooper flagged down the white Fiat, peering briefly into the driver's face. "Is there a problem, officer?" the priest asked, his slight Irish accent sounding strangely foreign, even to his own ears.

"License and registration, please."

The driver, hard-faced and middle-aged, with close-cut brown hair, black suit, and inverted white collar, handed the requested cards out the window and patiently waited. Two minutes later, the trooper handed him back his license and registration and, bracing a hand on the window ledge, leaned down. "You might want to take another route, Father. There's been an escape from Angola, and a couple of cons are on the loose. Got roadblocks on most of the major roads between here and New Orleans."

"Dear me. I should get to a phone and call my sister. It looks like I'll be late for her son's christening."

"You performin' the ceremony?" the officer asked.

The priest nodded. "I drove down from Boston."

"Louisiana's a long way from home, Father."

"Indeed it is. Uh, can you perhaps suggest some way around this mess?"

The trooper gave the priest directions, and the Fiat drove on. A few minutes later, the back seat of the small car folded down. "Damn, Sumner. How'd you do that? I figured he'd have us the minute you opened your mouth."

"I worked with an Irishman on the Gulf rigs. A guy named Timmy O'Malley. He was a decent sort. Never did find out what became of him."

"Man, if I'd known how easy this was gonna be, I would have gotten clear of The Farm years ago."

"Don't get too relaxed yet. It's a long way from over," Jimmy warned, but he knew exactly how Adesco felt. Despite the fact that Trick's plan was well thought-out and simple enough to work, he wouldn't have given betting odds that it would succeed. But it had, thanks to Polly Ammerman, the corrections officer involved with Adesco. Polly had accompanied the gurney to the row and gotten Trick an EMT uniform. They'd ridden out of the prison in the ambulance, Jimmy zipped into a body bag and Trick driving. Polly had taken care of everything, including the Fiat, the black clothing, and the inverted collar Jimmy wore.

"You s'pose they found old Peterson and let him outta dat broom closet yet?" Adesco wondered, then answered his own question. "Yeah, I s'pose so. Hey, Jimmy. What's de first thing you planning to do, man?"

It was a common thread among convicts—dreaming, fantasizing about freedom and all of the privileges denied to them on the inside, and it was a game Jimmy never allowed himself to play. Living on the inside was difficult enough. Damned if he'd torment himself by thinking about the things he'd never have. Never . . . It was the one thing that separated him from men like Trick, men who actually believed there was a chance for them to start over.

Jimmy's ride out of the prison in a body bag strapped to the gurney had said it all. If nothing else, he was a realist, and he was keenly aware that he'd be going back to Angola one more time. The last thing he was likely to see in this world was that little room with its soft-gray concrete walls and large viewing window, the IV that would drip the drugs into his arm.

Somehow, none of that mattered now. By the time

they caught him, Acadia Parish would be mourning the loss of its favorite son, and he would have the satisfaction of knowing that Clairée was safe.

"Jimmy? What you gonna do first, man? I'm gonna get me a cheeseburger. Not that shit they feed us inside, man. Something with relish and a big slice of sweet Vidalia onions. I ain't had a sweet Vidalia onion in five years. Makes my mouth water just thinkin' about it. How 'bout you, man?"

Jimmy glanced at the rearview mirror, meeting Adesco's gaze while seeing the hardness in his own. "I'm gonna take care of one small detail I should have taken care of years ago. I'm gonna kill Ashton Morlay."

CHAPTER SEVENTEEN

Fegan checked all of Edmunds's usual haunts and came up empty. He tipped Freddie at the Lightning Strip Club and Alberta at the Pink Cadillac and slipped them both his cell phone number and a request that they call him the moment Cash showed up; then he drove to his Aunt Marie Theresa's house at Lemon Terrace. It hadn't been an easy visit, or a brief one, and he'd stayed longer than he'd anticipated. Marie Theresa, sedated, had barely recognized him. Clutching Remy's picture, she rocked slowly back and forth, not uttering a sound as tears rolled down her cheeks. Fegan found himself at a loss as to what to say.

She missed Remy, needed Remy, grieved for Remy, and there wasn't a damn thing he could do to ease her loss. Hugging his cousins Mary and Regina, he promised to stop back later; then he went quietly out. He couldn't bring Remy back, but he could find the bastard who killed him and see that he was punished for it.

Fegan stopped at the houseboat for a thermos of coffee and to check the answering machine. There hadn't been any calls from Clairée, and nothing from Frank concerning Amos Lee. He tried not to be disappointed by that.

Clairée would do her best to avoid him. That didn't stop him from wanting her, dreaming about her. He'd barely looked at another woman since the day she showed up on his front porch, and he wasn't quite sure what to do about their situation.

If only she weren't so damned unpredictable!

He snorted at that. "Give it up, man. You know that's what you like best about her. The intrigue. The way she keeps you guessing."

Someone rapped on the galley door. Fegan glanced up sharply at the neatly dressed older woman. "Miz Sumner," he said.

"Eulanie, please. There really is no need for formalities, and I prefer a first-name basis. It promotes honesty in an exchange. Given your background, my guess is that you can appreciate that as well."

"Yes, ma'am."

"If you can spare a few minutes, I'd like to come in."

Fegan held the door for her.

"Nice place you've got here. You keep a tidy kitchen. I like that. It says a great deal about a man."

"Is there something I can do for you? It's been a difficult mornin', and I was just about to leave."

"I understand. My condolences on your family's loss," she said politely. "And I promise not to take up a great deal of your time." She turned to face him, and Fegan was surprised at her resemblance to Jimmy. There was that same sharpness about the eyes, their no-nonsense air. "You're anything but slow, so I gather you already surmised that this is about Claire."

Fegan indicated the living room and his most comfortable chair. "Can I get you some coffee, or somethin'?"

"No, thank you, but I will take you up on your offer to sit. It's gonna be a scorcher out there today, and I'm already worn, despite the early hour." She sank into the armchair with a sigh.

"You said this was about Clairée," Fegan prompted. "She all right?"

"Well, I suppose that depends on who you're askin'. She, I am sure, would insist that she's fine. If you ask me, however, you'll get a far different answer." She pinned him with that sharp gaze. "Fegan, I'm going to be frank with you. I don't know that in this circumstance, anything less than complete candor will get through to either of you."

"I'm not gonna like this, am I?"

"I suppose that depends."

"On what?"

"On what kind of man you are, and how you really feel about my niece. It seems that Claire's father doesn't exactly approve of your *association* but he doesn't know you or your family very well. Jimmy and I—well, I love my brother, but he can be uncompromising, and we don't always see eye to eye. I've noticed the changes in Claire since she came home to Angelique, and I know that you've played a part in that."

"I'm not sure where any of this is goin'," Fegan said. "But I'm a little pressed for time right now." It was a mild assessment of his situation. His impatience rode him relentlessly. He needed to get going. He needed to find Cash before something else happened, and as much as he respected Eulanie Sumner, Clairée had made her decision, and her aunt's argument in favor of their relationship, if that's what it was, was a bit moot at the moment. "Clairée knows how I feel. Not a whole lot more I can say."

"So, that's it, then? You're really going to let her walk away?"

Fegan let out a slow breath, striving for a grip on his emotions. "No disrespect intended, ma'am, but I don't seem to have a choice. Clairée's got a mind of her own, and once it's made up, she ain't likely to change it. Besides, I'm not so sure she made the wrong decision." He had already taken a risk, letting her know how he felt. Maybe it was time to pull back, while he still had his heart.

"You're the one who's losing out, Fegan. The kind of love you and Claire have doesn't come along every day."

Fegan said nothing. A car pulled up on the bank outside; the driver got out, but he didn't approach the houseboat.

Partially hidden by a tangle of honeysuckle, the man was not completely visible. Fegan eased the .38 from the waistband of his jeans and took two steps in the direction of the galley. He had blond hair and a blue shirt and trousers, but the man was presented in partial profile. Fegan thought he saw him reach in his pocket and take out a cigarette lighter. Starting to turn, he flicked it to life, holding the slim orange tongue to the tip of the rag protruding from a bottle in his hand . . . a bottle filled with pinkish-orange liquid. Cash Edmunds and Fegan spun simultaneously, Cash hurling the home-made firebomb through the air, Fegan launching himself at Eulanie, who had started to stand, knocking her to the floor as the glass missile smashed through the window and the galley exploded in smoke and flame.

In an instant, the houseboat was transformed into an inferno. A thin line of orange raced across the carpet.

The galley exit was blocked by a wall of flame, the heat so intense it seared the skin on Fegan's forearms. Billowing clouds of sooty black swirled near the ceiling, and just taking a breath was almost impossible. "We'll have to go out the back. C'mon."

"My—chest," Eulanie wheezed. "I—can't—breathe."

Pulling her up to her knees, Fegan half-dragged Eulanie across the living room and away from the intense heat and suffocating smoke. The hallway acted like a chimney, quickly filling with thick, black smoke, offering little relief. Each inch of ground they gained was hard-won, and Fegan's lungs ached from the effort.

"Leave me—here," Eulanie said. "I'll follow—in a minute."

Fegan didn't loosen his grip on her. "It's only a few more feet. We'll get you out in the air, and I'll call an ambulance."

She moaned and fell flat. Struggling to his feet, he hauled her up, lurching the last few inches to the door, then over the threshold into the relatively clean air of the catwalk. Away from the heat and smoke, Fegan bent, putting the older woman over his shoulder and staggering down the gangplank to the grassy bank of the bayou where he laid her down. "Miz Sumner? Miz Sumner?"

Her lids fluttered. "Nitro. My shirt pocket. Guess—Trelawney—was right, damn him."

"It's gonna be all right." Fegan found the medication and slipped a pill under her tongue. The smoke, visible from a distance, brought the neighbors running. A crowd was forming a few feet away. "Somebody call an ambulance!"

Nellie Vreen broke from the crowd. "Mr. Broussard, I'm a registered nurse." She glanced once at Fegan. "Are you okay?"

"I'm fine. Can you stay with her? There's something I got to do, and it can't wait." At her nod, Fegan got to his feet and started to move toward the Pontiac. Halfway to the car, John Delano intercepted him.

"Fegan, you got to come with me."

"Not now, John. I need to find Cash Edmunds."

"You lookin' for the deputy?"

"He threw a cocktail through the houseboat window."

John looked uncomfortable. "And that ain't all. This is some big trouble. Fegan, I need you to come to Aunt Martha's real bad. There's something there you need to see. It has to do with the deputy, and that little girl your granddaddy found in the swamp."

Martha Felix showed Fegan to a small upstairs bedroom. The curtains were drawn and the room dimly lit, yet even the lack of light couldn't completely conceal the condition of the girl propped against thick pillows. She was covered in bruises and scrapes on her face, neck, and arms; her lower lip was split and scabbed darkly over. One blue eye shone from the midst of a deep purple bruise, swollen nearly shut, the other regarded him with suspicion. Fegan couldn't be sure, but he doubted that she was more than fifteen. Close to the age Jean Louise had been when she was murdered.

"This here's Mr. Fegan Broussard," Martha told the girl. "He's a reporter for the *Times-Picayune*. You can trust him, child."

Ignoring Miz Felix's slightly altered description, Fegan nodded. "What's your name?"

The child looked at Martha, and at her nod, replied. "Evangeline King."

"Evangeline, like Longfellow's poem. That's real

pretty," Fegan said gently, quietly. "John says you were lost in the swamp, and that he found you when you ran onto the road in front of his car."

The girl was hesitant. Fegan could see she was upset, but she contained it beneath a steely will. She wasn't about to let him know how profoundly the mention of her ordeal affected her. "Are you really a reporter?"

"I was. Now, I'm just somebody who's here to help you, but you have to talk to me. I need to know what happened, all of it. Do you think you can do that?"

She looked at him—a level look, as if she were judging him, attempting to determine if he spoke the truth or if he was a threat, instead. "There was another girl at that house. Her name was Sherry Ellen."

Fegan's stomach knotted, but he kept his voice low. "You and Sherry Ellen were together?"

She nodded. "We were hitching, headed to New Orleans, and this guy picked us up. But instead of taking us to the city, he took us to that place."

"What place?"

She shrugged. "A little house, away from the swamp. Back in the woods. It was surrounded by trees. The branches brushed the window—a soft, scratchy noise."

"Pine trees?"

"How'd you know?"

"Lucky guess," Fegan said softly, remembering the debris on his sister's clothing. "This man—can you tell me what he looked like?"

Evangeline stared at him. "He looked fine. Like an angel. Even Sherry Ellen thought so. She said the way he talked gave her shivers."

"The way he talked? How do you mean?"

"Not like you," she said. "Fancy—like someone in a limousine should."

"What did you say?" Fegan asked.

"He had a limo, with a driver. We thought it was cool. I didn't know what he was like, and when we found out, it was too late."

Fegan listened to the details of the girls' two-day ordeal as they came trickling out. It had been Morlay, not Cash, behind the killings. The judge, the former prosecutor, the soon-to-be senatorial candidate was just a mask, and behind that mask was a ruthless, cold-blooded predator. . . .

Cash was in on it. Edmunds had been there the night the girls had escaped and fled the house of horrors where they were being held, and he'd pursued them with a pair of large and vicious dogs. Evangeline King had made it into the swamp, and somehow managed to get away . . . her companion, the girl Amos Lee found, Sherry Ellen Davis, hadn't been quite as lucky.

Terrified of being caught and dragged back to the place where they'd been held, Evangeline had remained hidden for days until fear of starvation and the onset of delirium had driven her from the bayou and onto the road in front of John Delano's car.

The conversation sapped the girl's small store of energy, and before Fegan had a chance to ask anything else, she drifted off to sleep. Miz Martha hustled Fegan and John from the room.

"Can I use your phone, Miz Martha? I'll give Lyson Reid a call. He still writes for the *Times-Picayune*. He'll interview her and blow this whole thing wide open."

"What about the sheriff?" John asked. "Should we notify him?"

"I want Lyson here first, just in case Pershing decides to bury this thing. And John? You're gonna need that lawyer I mentioned." Fegan made the call, then headed for the door. "I have to go, but for God's sake, don't mention this to anyone until you hear from Lyson Reid. He'll know what to do.''

Cash Edmunds lived in an antiquated mobile home on Silver Echo Road, six and three-tenths of a mile to the east of Angelique. A bullet-shaped residence made dull by too many years in the punishing heat and humidity so inherent to southern Louisiana, it squatted like an aging metallic egg a few dozen yards from a tar paper shack. Claire didn't know a great deal about Cash Edmunds or his family. They had moved to Angelique in the last quarter of his sophomore year of high school, but he'd been older than her. She'd seen him a time or two at the Broussards', but then Jean Louise was killed, and her focus turned elsewhere as her world did a lightning-fast crash and burn. She had passed Silver Echo Road a number of times, but she'd never seen the Edmunds place, and she hadn't known that the deputy's roots were quite so colorful.

Claire got out of her car and climbed the cinder block steps, rapping hard on the front door. She could hear the rattle and whir of a portable air conditioner and the barking of dogs somewhere in back, but she couldn't detect any sign of movement inside the small dwelling. She knocked again. "Cash? It's Claire Sumner! We need to talk.''

Claire waited while perspiration beaded in a fine mist on her forehead and upper lip, but no one came and no one answered. "Well, just because he's not home doesn't mean I can't have a quick look around." It was exactly what Fegan would have done if he'd been in her position, and the only way she was going to learn anything.

She came down from the steps, surveying the small,

ratty house as she skirted the trailer, but she could detect no sign of life there, either. The wind shifted, and she caught it again—the barking of dogs in the distance. Shielding her eyes with her hand, Claire scanned the property and that was when she saw it: a building constructed of rough-cut lumber at the edge of the open field, nearly concealed by the trees.

The quarrelsome noise issuing from the shed drew her. Many parish families owned dogs, but she'd never known anyone to keep them so far away from the house. Just caring for them at such a distance would present challenges. She reached the shed, stopping to peer in the window, but the panes were thick with dust, smeared from the inside, and she could just make out the dim silhouette of a vehicle in the gloom. It appeared to be light in color, but details eluded her. She rubbed at the pane of glass with the heel of one hand and bent close again.

Not light. White.

A white truck with a roll bar and high halogen lights atop it.

Claire's stomach knotted. "Oh, God. It was him. It was him all along." The words left her mouth and simultaneously something large, hideous, and black lunged at the window, inches from her face. Lips skinned back and fangs bared, it growled and barked, saliva flying from its mouth as it leapt at the window again and again, trying to get through the glass.

Claire cried out, stumbling back, turning to run, bumping into Cash Edmunds. "Like dogs, do you, Clairée?" he said menacingly. "I can tell that they like you."

"Where were you?" Claire asked, gathering her composure by slow degrees. "I stopped by the trailer and knocked, but no one answered."

"I stepped out to get my mother some cigarettes. She has emphysema and a two-pack-a-day habit. Won't quit for anything, even if it kills her. Not that anyone would miss the crazy old hag. Too bad I didn't get back a little sooner. I sure could have saved you a lot of trouble. 'Course, I expect it would have come to this anyway, sooner or later."

Claire stepped to the left, and he moved to block her, and when she broke and ran, he cruelly caught her wrist and dragged her back, twisting her hand up until she feared her bones would snap.

"Leavin' so soon, Clairée?" he asked, grinning into her face. "I thought you wanted to see the dogs."

"What I want is to get the hell away from here, away from you."

"Now, is that nice?"

"It was you that night on the road. You tried to run me down."

"It's called discouragement," he said simply, "and it was my truck, all right, but it wasn't me. You can thank old Remy for that little thrill ride." He tilted his head and smiled. "On second thought, I guess thankin' Remy won't work, now will it?"

"You killed him," Claire accused. She had precious little to lose. Unless she could get away, he would kill her too. Just like he killed Remy. She could see it in his cold blue eyes.

"Me, kill Remy?" He snorted. "You've got me all wrong, Clairée. I'm no killer. I'm what they call a glorified gopher, but in the worst sense of the word."

"Pershing's behind this?" Claire demanded, flashing back on her earlier misgivings.

"Iron ass? Hell, no. Old Vance is just waiting out his time till retirement, and hopin' none of this shit sticks to his fine, unblemished reputation."

"If you don't work for Pershing, then who do you work for?"

"The word *work* would indicate that I have some stake in all of this. Somethin' to gain, and that's not quite the case. In fact, your daddy and I have a lot more in common than you can imagine. We've both been used by a master. Only, I get to walk away. Jimmy . . . well, he isn't quite so lucky, now is he?"

"What does this have to do with my father?" Claire asked. "And if you didn't kill Remy Broussard, then who did?"

"Jimmy was the scapegoat. Somebody had to pay for Jean Louise's death, and Jimmy was handpicked by William Keyes. He delivered the car to Tyson's garage and waited while your daddy worked on it. William Keyes made the suggestion to Ashton, and at Ashton's direction, he planted the evidence in Jimmy's car that linked him to Jean Louise's murder. Keyes and Ashton go way back. Keyes omitted the dog bites from the coroner's report. That little piece of news kept old Vance from bein' quite so persistent, and kept him away from here."

"Ashton Morlay?" Claire felt sick. Ashton Morlay, the man who had prosecuted Jimmy's case, the favorite son of Acadia Parish, handsome, powerful, and well-respected. The one man who was absolutely above suspicion. "Ashton Morlay killed Jean Louise?"

"Among others," he said cryptically. The quiet reply raised the hairs on Claire's arms. She felt suddenly chilled, despite the blistering heat of the late morning, and she thought she heard a sibilant hiss coming from behind his left shoulder. "Jean Louise wasn't the first, or the last. Ashton took his first life at fourteen. He killed his younger sister—strangled her with the red silk drapery cords from his mother's bedroom. Instead of dealing with Ashton's peculiarities in a punitive fashion, they sent him off to boarding school."

"You said that Ashton Morlay had used you, like he used my father," Claire prompted. He'd eased his grip on her arm, though her wrist still throbbed alarmingly. She had to try to get away, yet the hideous quarrel of the huge canines inside the shed was enough reason to delay. She must have glanced at the structure, because Edmunds chuckled.

"If I were you, I'd put any thought you might have of runnin' right out of my head."

"You used them to run that poor girl to ground," Claire said.

"I cherish my freedom, Clairée. Ashton's got me by the short hairs. He has had since I was eighteen. Given the circumstances, I couldn't very well let her get away, now could I?"

"I don't understand. What sort of leverage could he have over you that would be so powerful that it would make you an accomplice to murder?"

He snorted, and a look of self-loathing came over his face. "You still don't get it, do you? My part in this started because of Jean Louise. If not for her, I wouldn't be tied to this fucking parish, taking orders from a hard-ass, small-town sheriff and a lunatic I despise." He shook his head, glancing at her, weighing her reaction. "Well, I don't suppose it'll hurt for you to know. He'll kill you, anyway, just like he killed Remy. Jean Louise was a pretty little thing. I could see the way she looked at me when I was around—real sly, like she wanted it, but didn't want me to know. That last night, I found her at the football field and I offered her a ride, only I didn't take her home. I didn't pick her up with anything in mind— it just happened, and afterward—"

"Oh, God," Claire said. "You raped her."

"I tried to reason with her, but she kept cryin', sayin' she was gonna tell Fegan. I panicked! I didn't know what else to do, so I took her to Ashton. At the time, I didn't know about his peculiarities with women, and after it was over, it was too late. I had to go along with whatever he wanted, or he would have hung me out to dry. He said he would pin the whole thing on me, and I believed him. There was no reason not to. Look what he did to Jean Louise."

"And Ashton killed Remy because he knew about all of this?"

A bark of laughter. "Remy didn't know about Jean Louise, or anything else. I hired him to scare you off, and he turned on me. Said he wanted out. I should have put pressure on him myself, but I called Ashton."

"And Ashton Morlay tracked him down at Fegan's and slit his throat. I'm surprised he'd soil his hands with something so grisly."

A derisive snort. "He used to hang out with this old caretaker at the estate. The old guy taught him everything he knows about the swamp . . . and Ashton paid him back by making his daughter disappear. He's a heartless bastard, but I expect you'll know everything there is to know about him—probably a lot more than you ever hoped to find out."

Claire let him propel her toward his car. When they were a few feet away and removed from the immediate threat of the dogs, she broke away and ran for the rental. Clawing at the door handle, she flung it open and threw herself into the driver's seat, grappling for her handbag. Her fingers closed over the cold metal of the pistol's grip, but he was already grabbing for her. His head and shoulders were halfway in the car. His fingers dragged at her sleeve. Claire threw herself back, kicking him;

then, bringing the pistol up hastily, she squeezed off a shot.

A blotch of red blossomed on his sleeve. With an enraged curse, he grabbed her ankle, pulling her out as she fired again. At the last second, he seized her wrist, forcing it up, and the shot went wild . . . piercing the roof above his head. Panting, sweat trickling over his temple, he tore the pistol from her fingers, angrily tossing it into the weeds, then hauled her roughly from the car. "Don't you get it?" he demanded, jerking her to the trunk of his car and fumbling for his keys. "You aren't going anywhere without me!"

"Someone will find out about this," Claire insisted, wishing she could believe it. "Someone will figure it out."

"Nobody's figured it out in ten years," he said with unshakable logic, seizing a roll of duct tape from the trunk. "What makes you think that's gonna change?"

Claire winced as he forced her wrists behind her back and bound them tightly together. "What about Fegan?"

He tore off another piece of tape, whirling her around, placing it securely over her mouth. Then, he leaned down into her face. "Oh, didn't I tell you? Fegan's dead. Can't you smell the gasoline?" he said, shoving a hand in her face. "I mixed him a cocktail twenty minutes ago and delivered it myself. I expect that Cajun palace of his is burned to the waterline by now. Too bad he didn't have a chance to get out."

Then, Claire was pushed into the trunk, the lid came down, and there was nothing but the grind of the ignition, the suffocating blackness, and a crushing sense of unconsolable loss.

CHAPTER
EIGHTEEN

At ten a.m., the temperature reached a sweaty eighty-nine degrees and kept climbing, but the heat index made it feel more like ninety-eight. Inside the trunk of Cash Edmunds's car, Claire struggled to fight back a rising panic. The instant he'd closed the lid, she'd felt the heat pressing in on her. Breathing was difficult, and the space was so close, so saturated with the odors of oil and gasoline that it was a supreme effort to hold down her nausea.

If she got sick with the duct tape over her mouth, she would choke on her own vomit, aspirate, and die within minutes.

She had to concentrate, put her mind, her conscious self anywhere but in the sweltering darkness where she was trapped, sick and feeling as if her heart had been ripped from her chest. She tried to concentrate on The Willows, and the buffeting breeze that cooled the gallery on the hottest days, but the ache in her chest refused to allow it.

Fegan ... dead ...

Oh, God, Claire. Don't go there!

But she couldn't seem to help it. The pungent smell of gasoline was thick in her nostrils, the look on Edmunds's flushed face indelibly burned on her mind's eye. An unwelcome sob welled up from the depths of her being, forlorn-sounding, brimming with hurt. Claire struggled for breath, tears leaking from her eyes as she thought about giving up. What was the point in fighting? Where was the logic in going on? Everyone she loved would soon be gone, with the single exception of Eulanie. The battle for her father's freedom was almost over. She'd fought hard for Jimmy when he wouldn't fight for himself, and she'd lost to overwhelming odds. There was nothing more she could do for him now. Nothing anyone could do. His was a lost cause, a fight that would end in shame, misery, and death without the smallest scrap of dignity. Jean Louise was gone—Fegan, too, and she was tired and sick and frightened.

The car turned off the blacktop and onto a dirt road. Claire could tell by the increased vibration and the choking smell of the dust that filtered into the trunk from a pin-sized hole in the side of the trunk's wheel well.

Where was Cash taking her?

How long would he leave her to languish in the horrible heat and darkness?

Would she ever breathe freely again?

Or would he just take the easy way out, ditch the car, and leave her to suffocate?

And once she was gone, who would be left to mourn Fegan's loss? A grandfather far removed from reality?

A brother who despised him? An aunt and two cousins who'd already suffered too much?

Tears flowed more freely now, and Claire didn't attempt to stop them. They traced a scalding path across one hot cheek, welling in the shallow dip near the bridge of her nose. Unexpectedly, the sensation of coolness washed over Claire, and for a crazy moment she wondered if she were dying? Then she heard it . . . a plaintive whisper inside her head, and the temperature in the trunk dropped markedly. Claire shivered in reaction to it. *Don' cry, Clairée! You're not alone. I'm here—don' cry.*

She could see her so clearly, more clearly than she ever had. In fact, she seemed dense in form, almost human. Love and gratitude filled Claire's chest, crowding her lungs. She was so glad to see her! So glad! She couldn't respond verbally, but inside her head was a continuous wail. *He's gone, Jean Louise! Fegan's gone!*

Ain't so! the little ghost insisted. *Don' you think I'd know? Don' you give up on Fegan, Clairée. Don' you give up on me!*

Jean Louise remained, a gawky adolescent with her dark head bent and her pale cheek resting on her updrawn knees . . . Claire's one hope—strangely, her salvation.

The car made a sharp turn, slowing, onto pavement. For a moment it stopped, and she heard the murmur of distant muted conversation and a whirring sound, like a small motor . . . or an electronic gate being opened. Claire felt a chill that had little to do with her spectral companion.

He was taking her to Ashton Morlay.

Edmunds was a large enough threat, volatile and panicked, but he might be reasoned with. Judge Morlay was another matter altogether.

It was impossible to reason with a madman. If everything Cash had told her was true, Morlay had no conscience, no soul.

Cash didn't stop the car immediately, and after a moment, the smoothness of the pavement ended. A few more moments and the vehicle halted and the motor quieted. The door opened and closed, and she heard his footsteps approaching the rear of the vehicle. A key scraped in the lock, and a shaft of blinding sunlight pierced Claire's eyes. For a few seconds, she couldn't see anything; then, gradually, her eyes adjusted to the light.

Cash's left sleeve was soaked with blood and he appeared flushed, his skin damp with perspiration. "C'mon out of there, Clairée," he said, dragging her to her knees with his right hand.

Claire glanced around. A small house sat a few yards away. It had a forlorn look about it. She wasn't sure why that particular description leaped to mind, but it did. Constructed of clapboards, it had been painted a garish yellow at some distant time, but age and humidity had taken their toll and the paint was peeling. Situated on a shallow knoll, and shaded on three sides by pine trees, its windows gaped blackly at her, like lifeless, empty eyes. The structure seemed to emanate a sense of loss, of desolation, and the last thing she wanted was to go inside.

Cash reached out with his uninjured hand and tore the tape from her mouth. Claire gasped at the stinging pain. "Thank you for that, at least," she said. "I nearly suffocated in there."

"Might have been better in the long run if you had," he said. "You can go on and scream, if you want to. I expect you'll be doin' a lot of that later on. Ain't nobody near enough to hear you, and the trees help to cushion the sound."

"What is this place?" she asked.

"It was the overseer's cabin, back in the old days," he answered. "Now, it's Ashton's fun house. The swamp's a half-mile that way," he said, indicating the rear of the house. "And then, there's the estate."

"Why are you telling me this?" Claire wondered. With everything he'd confessed, and all that she had guessed, she still didn't fully understand his part in all of this.

"Because it won't matter what you know. In a few hours, you won't be any livelier than that last little girl I dumped in the swamp."

"You put her there?"

"It's part of my penance for Jean Louise. I get to clean up after my cousin. The kid died on the anniversary of Jean Louise's death, and he thought it a fine way to commemorate it. So, I put her in a boat and took her there myself. The others are in the crypt out back. Clever, don't you think? No one will ever find them— or you, for that matter."

"You really don't like any of this, do you?"

"Like it?" he shot back. "I'm as much a prisoner as those kids were . . . only difference is, my hell's lasted ten long years."

"Then, why go along with it?"

"Don't even say it," he said, cutting her off. "As bad as this is, it's better than life at Angola. Do you have any idea what they do to cops on the inside?" He grasped her elbow and dragged her along, up the brick walkway to the crumbling steps. Claire risked a glance back once. Jean Louise was standing beside the car, her sorrowful gaze locked on the structure, and in that instant, Claire knew that Jean Louise Broussard had spent her last horror-filled hours here. Strangely—irrationally perhaps—she wanted to go back and comfort the child.

But as she was propelled roughly across the porch and shoved inside the house, there was no time.

Their footsteps echoed eerily through the interior. The hallway was clean, but barren. Cash urged her up the stairs. With her hands still bound behind her back, Claire had little choice except to cooperate, and pray for a miracle.

Sherry Ellen Davis hadn't been alone in her nightmare. *There had been two victims, not one* . . . but it seemed so incredible that if Fegan hadn't sat on the edge of the bed in the dim bedroom at Martha Felix's house and listened to Evangeline King recount the events leading up to her escape, if he hadn't witnessed her battered condition for himself, he might not have believed it.

It was a miracle that she'd escaped when her friend had been caught and killed, and a testimony to the strength and tenacity of the human spirit that she'd made it out of the swamp alive. The rest, she owed to John and Martha.

He'd do everything he could to make sure nothing bad came out of this for them. But first, he had to locate Clairée, and tell her about Eulanie. He called The Willows from his car phone.

Jane, the housekeeper, answered. "Sumner residence."

"Jane, it's Fegan Broussard. I need to talk to Clairée. It's urgent."

"Miz Claire ain't home. She left early this mornin', just before Miz Eule."

"Did she say where she was goin'?"

"No, sir. She didn't say. Just that she had somethin' to do. It sounded important, though."

Fegan swore softly, debating whether to tell the housekeeper about Eulanie's collapse, or to wait. Finally, he

decided that it might be better if Clairée heard it from
him. "If she comes home, can you have her call me?"
He gave her the number of the car phone. "Tell her
it's important. And Jane—"

"Sir?"

"If she shows up, keep her there. I don't care what
she says. Don't let her leave." Clairée had gone out,
and no one seemed to know where she was, or what she
was doing, a circumstance that didn't set well with
Fegan. Where the hell had she gone? Jane said it had
sounded important, yet the only business Clairée had
in Angelique had to do with Jimmy.

Uneasiness settled over him like a chill, creeping fog.
He hadn't told her about his suspicions, and she didn't
know about Evangeline King . . . but that didn't mean
she hadn't jumped to conclusions on her own. Clairée
was as bright as she was stubborn, and just because he'd
tried to convince her to steer clear of all of this didn't
mean she had listened. In fact, she was notorious for
not listening, and no doubt believing that she was on
her own in this, there was no telling what she would
do. She wasn't at the bungalow, or at The Willows, so
he drove to Cash Edmunds's place.

The black Chevy Malibu Clairée was driving was
parked in the drive. Fegan felt sick. The driver's door
was hanging open, and the keys were in the ignition.
He started to reach for them, but the rusty stain on the
tan leather seat stopped him cold.

Blood.

"Clairée!" He grabbed the keys and, barely able to
breathe, opened the trunk. Empty. The air left his lungs
in a rush. "Clairée!" As he returned to the open driver's
door, something caught his attention—the flash of sunlight on polished metal. He bent to retrieve it. A small-

caliber, chrome-plated pistol, the kind that a woman might carry.

The pistol, discarded in the weeds near her abandoned car, and the blood on the front seat had ominous implications. Twin troughs, the width of a tire, had been dug into the shell at the edge of the drive . . . someone had left here in a hurry, and that someone must have been Cash.

With a sinking feeling in his solar plexus, Fegan surmised the events that had played out here. Clairée had come looking for information, and when Cash had showed up, he'd felt threatened by her. He tried not to think about the blood in her car, tried not to dwell on the possibility that he could lose her.

"It can't happen," he told himself. "I'm not gonna let that happen."

He had to find her.

But where had Cash taken her?

If Evangeline King's story was true—and he had no reason to doubt her—then Morlay gave the orders and Cash carried them out. "He'll take her directly to Morlay," Fegan said. "To that damned cabin in the woods."

It was five to eleven, and the additional staff hired to set up the tables in the tree-shaded garden were sweating their asses off. Ashton, his back to the speaker phone, observed the activity through the French doors of his study. The new maid passed by the paned panels with a tray and several pitchers of ice water, which she placed on the table. She was a pretty little dark-haired thing who reminded him a great deal of the Broussard girl, Jean Louise. It was something in her eyes, he decided, a dark and sultry quality which intrigued him even while he despised it, and he wondered idly if she was from the parish.

"Damn it, Ashton! Have you heard a single word I've said?"

"I heard every syllable, Percy. What I'm not sure of is what you want me to do about it."

"Call the damn thing off!" Percy said, clearly upset.

"Now, Percy," Ashton said with a calm he didn't actually feel. "Anyone who's anyone in Louisiana is going to be here in a few hours, including my opponent. It's crucial that my guests see that I can handle any situation. Besides, the state police have beefed up their patrols, and they've blocked every road between here and Angola. James Sumner will be back inside in time for supper."

Percy was still sputtering when the door opened and Cash walked in. Ashton took in the heat in his cousin's cheeks and his blood-soaked shirtsleeve. "Percy, I'm afraid I'll have to cut this short. I'll see you later this afternoon." He put down the receiver and sat on the corner of his desk. "What in hell happened to you?"

"Clairée Sumner. That's what happened to me. I caught her at my place, puttin' her pretty little nose where it didn't belong. She found the dogs, and when I tried to get her into my car, she broke and ran. She had a gun in her purse. Who would have thought a classy bitch like that would carry?"

"Did you take care of it?"

Sweaty and pale, his cheeks flushed a dull red, Cash sneered. "Don't I always take care of everything, Ashton? Haven't I been cleaning up after you since the night I brought the Broussard girl to you?"

"I kept you out of prison. One might think that you'd be grateful. If not for me, you would be sitting where

Jimmy Sumner is right now. Forcible rape carries a long sentence in Louisiana.''

"So I've been told at least a thousand times," Cash said. "But what about abduction and murder, Ashton? I could always turn state's evidence. . . .''

"And you'd be an accessory," Ashton said. It was a conversation they'd had many times, too many times for him to be upset by it. "Come now, let's put our differences aside for the moment, shall we? Where is Clairée?''

"She's at the overseer's cabin. I locked her in and left her there.''

"How's your arm?" Ashton asked.

Cash glanced at his sleeve. It's just a flesh wound, but it hurts like hell.''

"Go upstairs and clean up. Take what you need from the medicine chest, then get back to Clairée. I've got to make a few calls, then I'll join you directly.''

The security officer at the gate to Morlay's estate wasn't local, but he was wilting from the heat. "Your invitation, suh?''

Fegan presented his Press pass from his days at the *Picayune*. "Broussard from the *Times-Picayune*. Judge Morlay's campaign manager arranged for an interview and photo op." He shot a look over his left shoulder. "Looks like my photographer got lost.''

"Nobody told me about an interview," the guard grumbled.

"That's funny. They arranged it last week. Played hell with my day off. Listen, why don' you call up the house and tell Morlay the reporter from the paper was here on time, as he specified, but was turned away because he didn't have an invitation, and I'll go on home and catch the Astros game on TV like I'd planned. That way, I don' have to do this interview, and you can take the heat for it instead of me." He shifted into reverse, but before he took his foot off the clutch, the man waved him on through the gates.

At the back of the mansion, the drive forked, and a dirt path barely wide enough for the Trans Am meandered through a maze of low azalea and white oleander. The rutted track looked fairly well-used for a road to nowhere and the dull brown cloud in the distance proclaimed that it had seen very recent use. Fegan hesitated, glancing back at the mansion. Cash had Clairée and he couldn't afford an error in judgment. The thought filled him with a sense of frustration he hadn't felt since Chicago . . . *Do you run, Mr. Broussard? Would you run for this little girl's life?*

Fegan's stomach clenched violently, and his fury burned like a low, continuous flame. "Ain't no way this is gonna happen again," he said, tamping down his emotions, allowing clear, rational thought to take over. "Pines. Evangeline said the house was surrounded by pines."

There was nothing remotely resembling a pine anywhere in his range of vision, but the road snaked over a shallow knoll before it dropped out of sight. The King girl had gone from the cabin across the cane fields and into the swamp, and the swamp, Fegan knew, lay to the east, to the rear of the mansion.

"You can't afford to be wrong, Broussard," he told himself, turning onto the rutted path. For a few hundred yards, he held his breath. The point where the grounds were meticulously kept ended at the top of the shallow knoll. The wild grass in the middle of the track rose up to brush against the Trans Am's undercarriage. The underbrush and low growth thickened, finally giving way to forest, but there was no sign of a dwelling.

Where was she?

For a moment, he felt sick. If he turned back now, there was a chance he could find Morlay and pressure him into taking him to her. But would it be too late?

"Damn it, Clairée. I can't lose you, too."

Then, he saw it . . . an opening in the forest just ahead, and beyond it, a darker, more jagged line above the trees . . . a pine grove. Seating his .38 more securely in his waistband, he parked the car and closed in on foot.

Claire sat on the bare floorboards of a small, closet-sized room, listening to the settlings of the old house and fighting down a rising sense of panic. She could barely feel her fingers, and what sensation she did have was painful, like needle-pricks along the skin of her palms, her knuckles, her fingertips. Movement was difficult. Escape would prove impossible . . . but that didn't stop her from thinking about it.

Four walls and a small, shuttered window. By bracing her back against the wall, she regained enough balance and stability to stand and walk slowly to the window, the shards of glass scattered over the floor crunching with each step. A warm blast of humid air filtered through the slats of the louvers. The windowpanes were missing, which explained the glass underfoot.

Someone had broken the glass.

But had they escaped?

Claire pressed close to the shutters, but she couldn't peer through the down-slanted slats. How far off the ground was the second-floor window? If she managed to push her way through the wooden barrier, would the fall take her life? Or worse, leave her broken and unable to get away, at the mercy of the man who had killed Jean Louise and so many others?

A flash of white moved outside the shutters. "Jean Louise?"

"I can't come in there, Clairée," the girl whispered, and Claire felt the terrible mixture of terror and regret, all combined with the stunning certainty that life was over, and knew that what she was feeling was what Jean Louise had felt while in this house, this room. The room shimmered with a resounding grief, the walls bled sorrow, and she knew that she could not begin to imagine the breadth and scope of the atrocities that had occurred in this place . . . this room.

Blond hair and a perfect face flickered behind Claire's eyes . . . the image and the embodiment of evil; then she heard someone's tread on the stair. But it was only Cash, wearing a fresh shirt and carrying a small plastic bag containing first-aid supplies. "Don't look so disappointed," he said. "He'll be here."

"I didn't expect to see you again," Claire admitted.

"I didn't expect to be here. But I follow orders. It's become a way of life, even though I detest it." He took a seat on the floor, slipping off his shirt. He managed to take the lid off the alcohol and dampen some cotton with the liquid, but when he tried to look at the wound, he turned ashen. "I can't do this," he said. "Never could abide the sight of my own blood."

Claire watched him for a moment. "If you untie my hands, I'll do it for you."

"Now, why would you want to do that?"

Claire shrugged. "You could have killed me back there, but you didn't. And if everything you say is true, then you're as much a victim in this as I am."

"Pardon my skepticism, but I raped Jean Louise. Do

you expect me to believe that you're willing to forgive and forget?"

"I haven't forgotten," Claire replied. "But I haven't forgotten who killed her, either, and the tape is cutting off my circulation. You're the one with the gun," she pointed out. "What are you afraid of?"

Cash nodded once. "All right. But if I get up, I'm gonna be sick. You'll have to come to me."

It sickened Claire to approach him, but Cash was less of a threat than Judge Morlay, and with her hands bound behind her, she wouldn't have a prayer of defending herself against either of them. She walked to where he sat, then slowly knelt in front of him. She felt the tug on the tape and heard it pull loose, punctuated by the excruciating pain of blood flowing into her fingertips.

She shook her hands, flexing her fingers. Then, she turned toward him.

"It's not as bad as it looks. The bullet passed through and the bleeding was actually a good thing. It'll wash out impurities and help prevent infection." He watched her clean and bandage the area, uncomplaining. When she was finished and she started to rise, he closed the fingers of his other hand over her wrist.

"If it wasn't for Fegan, this might have turned out differently," he said softly. "We could have walked away, started over somewhere, together, you and me."

"Knowing what I know about you, it would never happen, and Fegan doesn't even begin to enter into the equation." She looked down at the hand gripping her wrist. "Let go of me."

Cash opened his hand. "Doesn't matter anyhow," he said, getting to his feet. "Ashton'll be here any minute, and then I won't have to think about you again." He went to the door, stepped into the hallway, and turned the key in the lock.

He wasn't really disappointed that Clairée had turned him down. The offer had been impetuous in the extreme, and the truth was that she had done him a favor with her refusal. She knew too damn much, and he never could have trusted her anyway. Ashton would be doing him a service by putting an end to her. It would save him from doing her himself, and he didn't have the stomach for murder, unlike his cousin.

He stepped off the porch, thinking he heard the murmur of a gasoline engine in the distance, but car or boat, he couldn't tell. The pines tended to muffle noise, and there was always a chance that it was just wishful thinking on his part, wanting to see an end to it all. The threat of Clairée, his involvement with Ashton. As soon as this matter was concluded, he was leaving the parish, cutting all ties with this place and the dreadful happenings here. He'd change his name, and start clean. It was the only way, he thought, that he would ever be free.

Fegan watched in disbelief as Cash stepped off the last stair tread onto the soft, bare ground and walked to the large pine closest to the house. The tree was old, perhaps as old as the estate itself, its circumference large enough for a man to hide behind. Fegan held his breath as Cash paused, just inches away, turning his back, unzipping his fly . . . then Fegan stepped up behind him and brought the butt of his pistol down hard on Cash's head.

Cash sank without a whisper of sound, and lay unmoving. Fegan vaulted the steps and headed into the house. A quick check of the first-floor rooms revealed little. Dust cloths cloaked old furniture, and the air smelled of must, age, and disuse, but there was no sign of Clairée.

He glanced at the staircase and, palming his pistol, started to climb. He tried to brace himself mentally, but it was impossible. Her name was an endless, desperate litany inside his head. *Clairée, Clairée, Clairée . . .*

There was a trio of rooms at the top of the stairs, but only one was locked. He braced the heel of the hand gripping the .38 against the old wood and slowly tested the knob with the other. Someone inside the room gasped, and he heard the sound of footfalls. "Clairée?"

Claire heard his voice and ran to the door. "Fegan? Oh, God. Fegan, is that really you?"

"It's me, sugar. You all right in there?"

Tears welled in her eyes, emotion clogging her throat. She pressed close to the panel, everything she wanted to tell him crowding in on her, so that she could only nod and choke out, "Yes. Yes, I'm fine. Cash locked me in. He has the key, but he's armed. Oh, God, Fegan. Please be careful."

"Cash ain't a problem at the moment, but we need to get you out of there. Stand back, away from the door. I'm gonna try to break it in."

Fegan braced back and shouldered the door. The impact jarred his shoulder and arm. The lock was strong, but the wood was old and weak, and the blow had opened a crack in the bottom panel. Hitting it high hadn't succeeded, so he planted a well-aimed foot at the newly formed crack and saw the wood splinter. Another blow and the bottom panel gave way . . . a small space, but sufficient for Clairée to escape through.

Seconds later, her sweet warmth was filling his arms. "He said you were—that he'd killed you."

"Not quite," he assured her, stroking her hair with one hand, unendingly grateful that she was alive. "C'mon. Let's get the hell outta here."

Taking her hand, he started down the steps, Claire

following closely behind. But as he stepped through the door onto the porch, Ashton Morlay swooped, wrapping the length of red silk cord around Fegan's throat, pulling it tight as he dragged him back.

"No!" Claire screamed, lunging for Morlay, who twisted the ligature even tighter.

"If you want him to live a while longer, you'll stand where you are. If you run, or try to interfere in any way, I'll kill him now."

"All right! I'll do whatever you ask, only please, don't hurt him!" Claire shrank back, but he didn't loosen his hold.

"Easy does it, Mr. Broussard," Ashton said. Claire watched Fegan claw for the cord, but he couldn't pry it loose . . . couldn't break the other man's hold . . . his face turned dark, his eyes clouded, and then the light in them that begged Claire to run was extinguished. He went limp in Ashton's grasp, and Ashton eased his grip on the ligature. "Inside," he told Claire.

Claire obeyed him. He still held Fegan's life in his hands, and she could not jeopardize it, not even if it meant risking her own. She couldn't lose him, couldn't imagine a life without him. "The first room to your left. The door is closed. Open it, and step inside."

"Please don't separate us," Claire begged. "Please don't take him from me." She did exactly as he directed, stepping into the room, waiting while he dropped Fegan's body onto the bare boards of the cypress plank floor.

"Your concern for your lover is heartrending," Ashton said. "I almost felt a twinge of sympathy hearing you beg for his life. It's too bad that my own concerns conflict with your wishes, but I *would* like to live—you understand. I can kill you first, however, if that would help matters."

"What kind of monster are you?" Claire demanded as he stepped over Fegan's unconscious form and stepped toward her, the length of red in one hand . . . a small, sharp knife in the other.

Claire's gaze settled on the knife, which he held at an angle. "The cord," he said. "It's just for decoration."

He advanced while Claire backed away; then, all at once, he grabbed for her, his hand wrapping painfully in her shoulder-length brown hair. Jerking her to him, he pressed the knife to her throat. "I would have preferred something less messy this time, but matters being what they are, I don't have the luxury of attending to details. My guests are expecting me. You understand."

The tip of the knife pricked Claire's skin. He held her tightly, her head bent at an angle. She could barely see the tip of Fegan's shoe twitch beyond Morlay's right shoulder. Her eyes widened as she caught a blur of movement in her peripheral vision, then an arm snaked out and Morlay was seized from behind.

Jimmy's forearm was slowly, steadily crushing Ashton Morlay's windpipe. Veins popping, Morlay croaked for air like a fish on dry land; his eyes rolled up to meet those of the man squeezing the life from him.

Jimmy glared down at Ashton, his face inches away. "Did you think you could get away with hurtin' my daughter? You think I'd let you hurt my Clairée? Well, you think on this while your lungs collapse. The state can't kill a man twice, so it doesn't really matter if I take you with me, now does it? But we'll both know that you won't ever hurt another little girl."

"Dad, please! Don't kill him!"

"Go on, get out of here!" Jimmy snarled. On the floor behind him, Fegan groaned and sat up.

"Daddy, please!" Claire cried. "Please, I can't lose you again!"

Jimmy hesitated, but it was the quiet click of the pistol that convinced him. "Mr. Sumner," Fegan rasped, "I sure don't want to be the one to cause Clairée more grief. Do as she says. Ease off."

Jimmy met Fegan's gaze, then he let Morlay fall to the floor. "He'll worm his way out of this," Jimmy said.

"I swear to you on my sister's grave," Fegan promised, "I won't let that happen." He reached out a hand to Clairée, and she grasped it tightly, bringing it to her lips, then releasing it as she turned to Jimmy, and Jimmy opened his arms.

"How did you find me?"

"I rammed the security gate and followed the black Trans Am."

Jimmy stroked her hair, doing his best to soothe her. She was crying uncontrollably. "It's all right now," he said against her hair. "My baby girl. Daddy's here. It's all right."

There was a commotion in the front yard. Claire heard the siren, heard a voice bawling that he wasn't armed . . . Cash Edmunds's voice, and then Vance Pershing appeared in the doorway, his service revolver drawn. "Jimmy, drop your arms to your side and move away from her."

Jimmy met Fegan's gaze with eyes that swam. "Look after her, will you? She'll need someone strong to lean on."

Fred Rally handcuffed the judge and hauled him to his feet. As he marched him down the stairs, Claire heard the deputy reading him his rights.

"Jimmy," Pershing prompted.

Jimmy nodded, putting Claire from his arms; then he turned, offering his back to Vance Pershing, waiting for the handcuffs. But Vance put a hand on Jimmy's shoulder and led him out unfettered.

Claire looked at Fegan; then, without a word, she came into his arms. For a long time he held her, saying nothing. He felt her calm, felt the moment when her tears stopped, and relief settled in. When she raised her gaze to his, the look in them cut right to his heart. Her fingers trembled as they framed his face. "I thought I'd lost you," she said. "I thought I'd never get the chance to tell you."

"Tell me what, darlin'?" His voice was a thready whisper, and his head felt twice its normal size, and all that mattered, all he could think about, was Clairée.

She laughed, a watery bubble of mingled mirth and irony. "Something I should have said days ago. Something I intend to tell you every day from now on. *Je t'aime*, Fegan. *Je t'aime.*"

Fegan kissed her, a lingering kiss embued with a promise of many more to come. Then, together, they walked from the house.

Six Months Later

Life meant *life* at Angola, and few men who entered the institution condemned to serve out their days there ever left The Farm. A death sentence was nearly inescapable, yet miraculously, James Buford Sumner walked out of the gates on a clear midwinter day and didn't look back.

Back in the parish where Jimmy was born, the neighbors had gathered on the Broussards' lawn. Some had come because they knew Jimmy and to celerate his release, some for the chance to fill a Saturday night, and still others for the boiled crawfish and the ice cold beer on tap. A few couples had stepped out, and faces shining, danced to the frenetic zydeco music spilling from the radio on Fegan's back porch. The night was soft and cool, with a full moon rising over the black ribbon of the bayou. Fegan's mug was brimming, but he'd held it so long that the glass felt warm in his hands, and still he didn't drink. "Young Mr. Broussard, may I have this dance?"

"Why, Miz Eulanie, I'd be delighted." Fegan placed his mug on the porch and waltzed with Clairée's aunt.

"I'll have you know that you were not my first choice," Eulanie said slyly. "I asked your grandpa, but he just smiled and waved me over to you. He's a canny old bird, that one, and I get the feeling that the joke's on the rest of us, and he understands a great deal more than we know."

"He doesn't say much," Fegan admitted, "but I can tell that he's glad to be home."

In the weeks and months following the grisly discovery of the crypt on the Morlay estate and Ashton Morlay's subsequent arrest on multiple counts of murder, Claire had been kept very busy. With the help of the State Attorney General and new legal counsel, she had managed to overturn Jimmy's wrongful conviction. Morlay's incarceration had resulted in the petition granting custodial guardianship and power of attorney to Frank being given over for review to Judge Neal Houser. With the testimony of the second victim, Evangeline King, corroborated by Claire, and Cash Edmunds's full cooperation, Morlay's conviction was certain.

Amos Lee's release had been another matter altogether, and had hinged on Fegan abandoning his investigation business for something slightly less risky.

"I saw that article you wrote last week about the parish's favorite son," Eulanie said, "and I'm sure a lot of other people did, too. You're good at what you do, Fegan. Too good, maybe. Should I be worried that you'll outgrow this parish and look for greener pastures, taking my niece with you? I just got my family back together. I'd sure hate to think of her movin' away.''

"If I tried to lure her away, I doubt she'd go with me," Fegan said.

"Don't be too sure about that," Eulanie said with a wink. "You're a smooth talker. Why, I bet you could persuade her to marry you, if you had a mind to try."

"Me and Clairée?" he said doubtfully, but the idea took root, and as the music ended and Eulanie took her leave from him and the party, he found himself moving with determination toward Amos Lee's porch. Amos Lee sat on the swing with Jimmy, watching moonbeams play on the lawn, smiling his distracted smile. Clairée glanced up as Fegan approached. "Mr. Sumner. I was wonderin' if I might have a word with you in private?"

"Sounds serious," Jimmy said.

"Yes, sir," Fegan said formally. "You might say that."

They walked to the edge of the grassy bank, within sight of the water's edge. "This has to do with Clairée, I take it," Jimmy surmised.

"Yes, sir. I'd like to ask—that is—I'd like your permission—"

Jimmy laughed. "Hell, Fegan, if it's that hard to ask me, how the hell are you gonna ask her?"

Fegan was a little stunned. "Is that a yes?"

Jimmy was a hard man to know, and Fegan wasn't convinced that he would ever totally shed the scars a decade in prison had left on him. But he was fair in most things, and he seemed to be settling into life at Eulanie's farm. He'd lightened her load considerably, and had been a godsend to his sister following her heart attack. It had been a mild episode, but she would have to be more cautious in her approach to life in general.

"Clairée's pushin' thirty. If you expect to have any young'uns, you'd better get a move on."

Back on Amos Lee's porch, Claire saw Fegan approaching. As he neared the spot where she was sitting, *Jolie Blon* came on the radio. Without a word he took her hand, pulling her up onto her feet, leading her through the other couples slow-dancing on the lawn. At an isolated spot with a perfect view of a perfectly beautiful moon, he turned and pulled her into his arms. "Would you care to tell me what that was about?" she asked, curious about his conversation with Jimmy.

"I was thinkin' about the bungalow. Thought I might hire a contractor to rip out that wall, maybe have him put on an addition."

"You asked Jimmy his opinion on a remodeling project?" Claire said, frowning up at him. "What did he say?"

"He said you ain't gettin' any younger, and neither am I, and if we want to have babies, then we'd best start lookin' to the future. How 'bout it, Char? We gonna make this permanent, or is *forever* too scary a concept for you to think about?"

"Fegan, exactly what are you asking me?"

"I'm askin' you to stay with me always, baby. I can't even contemplate a life without you. What do you say?"

Claire smiled up at him. His face, one side silvered by the light of the moon, the other cast in shadow, had never been as dear to her as it was in this moment. *"Je t'aime, Fegan. Je t'aime."* She whispered her answer, and he wrapped her in a tight embrace, lifting her feet off the ground and swinging her around as she laughed.

The old man on the porch sat watching them in smiling silence, his gaze breaking away only after the silvery sprite finished her caper on the moonlit lawn and came to sit beside him. *She said yes, didn't she?* the childish voice demanded slyly. *I knew she would.* She sat back and gloated a little. He didn't mind. It was just her way. *You think they'll be happy?* she wondered.

Amos Lee nodded, then, taking out his tobacco, filled the bowl of his pipe, watching as his spritely grand-daughter skipped a joyous ring around the couple, her laughter bubbling up on the night breeze. Then, as Fegan and Claire turned toward the bungalow, the vision that was his Jean Louise winked away.